Garrison

Mr. Kevin C. Popp

Copyright

Print ISBN: 978-1-7323211-2-0
Kindle ISBN: 978-1-7323211-3-7

Written by Kevin C. Popp
www.TheGarrisonSeries Instagram www.instagram.com/popp.kevin or Facebook at www.facebook.com/TheGarrisonSeries

Interior Design by Nita Robinson, *Nita Helping Hand?*

Introduction

Is god concerned about man achieving perfection? Have you ever wondered what it would feel like to have full command or control of perfection at a moment's notice? We have all either witnessed or been a participant in rare, isolated bursts of exact precision during certain extraordinary moments in our lives, but these happenings are particularly fleeting and infrequent. For example, hitting the perfect golf shot, throwing a football with an unforeseen perfect tight spiral, or knowing all the answers to a difficult exam. Some people might experience a breathtaking moment during a sunset with the one they love or the way their child might glance at them. It is where any event forces the human mind to peer into a world of utopia, where everything is so perfectly coordinated it leaves one breathless. Now, envision having the ability to call upon that power of flawlessness on command. Oh, what it must feel like to be perfect on command, to never make a mistake or error because of bad judgment.

Imagine if a man who possessed this characteristic existed. Visualize a man capable of being faultless on more than a few occasions in his life. Imagine a man who could call upon all his senses to help him achieve exactness and demonstrate perfection naturally, with little thought or effort. He could control all five senses and force them to work together beautifully as one, as no one has witnessed since god graced us with his brief visit on Earth. Impossible, you say? Please think again. There are people out there who can achieve perfection—not all the time, mind you, but at certain moments throughout their lives. For some, it comes naturally, by instinct.

Instinct is god's little invention for allowing his subjects a small glimpse into the paradise that he has so teased us with since the beginning of time. This self-serving, sadistic deity only allows us to imagine, think, or dream about but never, *never*, to see, hear, smell, feel, or taste his self-made utopia—a utopia that he reportedly has talked about, but no one has seen. The ultimate paradox, is it not? Does this god exist, or is it the greatest hoax that man has played on himself to exert control over others?

What if 'God' truly does exist and is the one who controls our present and our future? Imagine what it must feel like to be a bottomless pit of knowledge and understanding of everything that exists or has existed in this world. Can you imagine creating something from nothing or watching your creation develop, learn, make decisions, and act out those decisions? Have you ever thought what it would feel like to have the ability to see both the good and the bad of what your creation did with its so-called freedom of choice? Have you ever wondered how god could allow his creations to have freedom of choice even as he knows what the future holds, because he knows all? Freedom of choice. Do you really believe that? Have you ever contemplated how someone could rule or control the knowledge of the ending before the beginning started, and then have the audacity to pass judgment on his creation?

Oh, what it must feel like to understand all and to never err. What it must feel like to be able to look at anything in this world and to possess the knowledge of how it was made, to know the very essence of what makes up that knowledge. Oh, what it must feel like to be the best at something, to reach a level of perfection such that no one person or animal could be your equal. To be the best is difficult and to be perfect is almost impossible, but maybe, for some certain moments in a person's life, perfection may not be impossible. One must wonder whether people like this exist or can exist in this world. If they did exist, what would they look like? How would they sound when they talk, and what personalities would they possess?

Now, imagine having the power to make an ordinary animal or human transform from an imperfect being into a perfect being. What would something like that be worth to a non-perfect human? All that would be required of them is to take a pill or drink a formula to obtain full command of any subject matter in a short time period. Imagine living forever, disease-free and able to enjoy all the little pleasures in life in ways you have never experienced before in your previously limited world. Tapping into a world that only god understands; a world of perfection, where all your senses work together as one to transpose that perfect world into reality. Imagine your sight, hearing, smell, and basic intuition all working as one to perform any act with extreme precision and accuracy. What would you give to possess such a power?

My name is Garrison Seawick. The events that I am about to tell you were told to me by my parents and other influential people in my life. What I will demonstrate through the spoken word and actions of others will have you question the purpose of your relationship with your God. It might cause you to question the role and purpose of that deity's existence in your lives. As the years pass, I find myself questioning its existence. I call into doubt the very concept of such a being. Through this journey, you will begin to understand that I am only at the threshold of discovering a dimension that is foreign to all humans. This strange and unexplained path will lead to the discovery of who or what I am.

CHAPTER 1

Adaptation

$\mathcal{M}$any years ago, there was a massive valley near a dense forest. The cool autumn air whistled through the trees, making some of their leaves float to the ground. The smell of dew in the air and the warm sun on a chilled morning brought a smile to even the most disinterested animal. The morning fog lifted slowly from the deep valley littered with trees. Overly large and daunting houses stood as guardians on the sides of huge, tree-lined hills. The leaves rustling through the air and along the ground made beautiful music.

I often whisper to myself, "Oh, what music the trees make on a windy day. The constant symphony of predictable sounds and sudden changes in tempo bestow upon the listener an opportunity for serenity if they would allow their senses a chance to give in to the beauty of what nature created." If one would allow nature to express itself to open ears, one would discover the peaceful but hurried movement of the multitude of sounds nature provides. Including the creatures of the forests, along with the smell of the interwoven vegetation around the trees, tends to highlight and move the senses to new levels of enjoyment.

Picture a being that could appreciate all these experiences with all five senses working together as one. All five senses would work in unison, developing and processing information previously heard, seen, smelled, felt, and even tasted. This is what separates animals from humans. Animals tend to rely on all five of their senses more than humans do. It is in their nature. Humans tend to rely on just one or several senses during a moment that would require the human to react.

It is extremely rare for humans to be aware of their environment and to understand all of what surrounds them. Most people are not interested or intellectual enough to notice. Maybe that was god's intention even before he started the utterly complicated process of life experiences on this planet.

I understand these attributes because I was born and abandoned in the forest by my parents. I survived against all odds. I possess the unique characteristics of being able to utilize all my senses as one, just like I have previously described. Have you ever felt like you just don't belong in your part of the world? That somehow you are different from the others that you know, but you just cannot comprehend why you are that way? For as long as I can remember, this is what I have experienced early on in my life. I was often confused and at times scared.

My story begins with my grandfather, Winthrop Douglas Seawick. In his younger days, he was a successful real estate developer in Louisville, Kentucky. He owned many large office buildings in downtown Louisville, as well as vast amounts of land on the outskirts of the city. He bought up as much vacant land as possible and created affordable neighborhoods throughout the suburbs. Winthrop was a tall, thin man with dark, wavy, short hair. He had extremely light brown eyes that glowed when the light hit them at a certain angle. Winthrop loved all forms of classical music. Though he had neither the time nor the interest to play a musical instrument, he constantly bought and played music and listened to it throughout the days and nights.

Winthrop was involved in many ventures that produced impressive financial results for his businesses. He developed a keen interest in precious metals due to the current economic conditions. During this time, there was great economic strife in America. The country went into a second Great Depression that some say was worse than the one in the 1930s. As Winthrop became more successful, he developed Seawick Holdings. The company's main responsibility was to invest in businesses that developed unique market niches. One of the companies Winthrop bought, Calpac, was a small and unknown gold-mining company that discovered and successfully mined different types of deposits. Winthrop found himself reinvesting more of his newfound fortune into this company's reach and development projects. In not too long a time, the additional money from these projects produced further positive results. The company grew as each gold find created more capital. This windfall allowed Winthrop to buy more real estate around town and in the areas surrounding the city. In turn, this created more opportunities to buy small businesses at competitive prices. He turned those businesses into profitable entities, some of which he sold to investors at inflated prices, while others he kept for himself and continued to make money from them.

Calpac was so successful in gold mining that Seawick Holdings expanded to mining for silver, platinum, and onyx. After several years of successful expeditions, the company's value increased exponentially. Winthrop then ventured into construction, mostly commercial real estate. He would buy the land, develop it, and then rent out the office space to other companies. This provided Winthrop with a nice, steady income through the years. His fortune advanced further when he sold some of these parcels of land to the local government.

Winthrop loved Louisville and wanted to make the city his permanent home. He particularly loved one exclusive area just outside the northeastern part of town. He had his eye on this part of the city for years. He had always dreamed of living in a place that had land separate from his neighbors but also had the convenience of a city or town lifestyle. Winthrop made some deals with the neighborhood people, buying adjoining land from two of them, and developed a beautiful home on top of a large hill that overlooked a valley of trees. The two plots of land were considerable, and the purchase ensured him as much exclusivity as he needed.

Winthrop lived in this upper-class neighborhood on the outskirts of the city and had a privileged lifestyle. He wanted his newly constructed home to have a specific look. He wanted the house to look old, like a relic from the past, yet have the modern conveniences of newly constructed housing. He wanted an enormous kitchen with a spacious eat-in area. He wanted an oversize great room with an open bar large enough to entertain over fifty guests comfortably, with an enormous dining room just off the kitchen. Winthrop built a massive house with high basement ceilings, a sidewalk, a four-car garage, and a separate one-and-a-half-car garage for lawn-care equipment. The open marble-floored foyer made for a magnificent first impression with its sheer size in width, length, and height. Winthrop loved big entrances into homes. He always wanted to wow his guests, and he certainly did with his house.

On the other side of the great room was a rarely used music room. Next to that was an oversized Florida room with many houseplants and flowers; a running fountain created the focal point of the room. Next to the Florida room was a billiards room with three pool tables and a walk-behind bar.

The house's wide and curving staircase led to four main suites on the second floor. Each suite had a supersized walk-in closet and an attached bathroom. The library was also located on the second floor. Winthrop broke trend and placed it there because he wanted to keep this area private from the rest of the house. He did most of his business dealings by phone from this room. The construction on the estate took almost two years.

The driveway was long and winding as it went up and around a few hills that led back to the estate from the iron-gated entrance. The numerous thick iron bars that formed the structure twisted into multiple designs. In the back of the estate was a deep and thick forest shared by many homes, but the bulk of the trees were on the Seawick property.

Every morning, especially during the fall months, Winthrop would take time from his busy schedule to walk out to his backyard that overlooked a small, very well-to-do neighborhood. Most of the homes were built years ago from old money, but as time passed, the people who inherited the land either moved to other places or lost what had been given to them. Many people lived peacefully in this vicinity and had little time to introduce their lives to others. Winthrop admired and adopted this attitude.

Winthrop enjoyed classical music and through his connections, he was introduced to a lady named Marlene, whom he later married. Marlene, an accomplished cellist in the Louisville Orchestra, was a tall woman with long limbs and long, flowing black hair. Her athletic build matched Winthrop's taste as well as his own physical makeup. Many would say it was love at first sight. They had a short courtship, and in less than a year, Winthrop and Marlene married on the grounds of the Seawick Estate.

The happy couple enjoyed their new life together. During the first couple of years, they took many vacations. Rome, Prague, London, Austria, Switzerland, and Germany were all on the list of their adventures. Both Winthrop and Marlene had visited many places around the world, Winthrop for business, Marlene on her tours as a cellist. About two years after their marriage, they decided to have a child. One year later, in the middle of winter, Winthrop and Marlene brought a young man into this world. His name was Trevor Winthrop Seawick.

Trevor was a handsome baby with deep, piercing dark-brown eyes and thick black hair. He was well put together physically and was always active. He was tall for his age and strong, especially in his arms and chest. The small family of three was happy together, and they lived a great life from the start.

Before the Seawicks brought Trevor home, Winthrop had hired a nanny. Her name was Loren, and she assisted in nurturing and caring for Trevor.

Through the early years, Trevor showed signs of being a highly intelligent little boy. He was vastly superior to all the children in his age bracket. He was not spoiled by his parent's wealth. Winthrop gave his son the necessary attention but did not have the time to spend playing with him as many fathers do during the early years of their children's lives. The Seawicks did not shower Trevor with expensive gifts, but Trevor was not impoverished in the toy department. Although he preferred books over toys or video games, he loved to build things with blocks or Legos. He also loved to play with his Army men and would set the little figures up around a room and have mock battles with them. As a young boy, Trevor was content with having just the basics in life and nothing more.

One very cold winter night in February, as Winthrop and Marlene were coming home from the theater, Winthrop hit a patch of ice and slid uncontrollably off the road. The car flipped over four times before hitting a tree and exploding. Winthrop and Marlene tragically died in that car accident. Trevor, who was seven, was at home with his nanny, Loren, when they got the news. He was old enough to understand the pain of losing the two people he loved the most in this world. They had nurtured and cared for him all his young life. Trevor didn't know what was going to happen to him. He was totally a broken little boy with nowhere to turn. He wondered who was going to take care of him and where he was going to live.

After the funeral, per the burial instructions of Winthrop's will, the bodies of Trevor's parents were interred on the Seawick grounds on the hill that overlooked the valley of trees. The grave markers were placed on the far side of the hill so they could not be seen from the house. About a month after the death of Trevor's parents, Trevor's grandfather, Edward Seawick, sold his house in Massachusetts and moved into the Seawick Estate to care for young Trevor. Edward, a successful business owner, had helped his son Winthrop get his business off the ground. Edward was a quiet man with many faults. His relationship with his son had deteriorated over the years, mostly because of the distance that kept them apart and Winthrop's business ventures; they did not have the time to stay close. Their personalities usually clashed, and they often ended up in heated exchanges. They were too much alike.

Loren, Trevor's nanny, was like a second mother to the boy. Loren kept the tradition of playing classical music all throughout the house. She played movements from various composers every day, and the music grew on Trevor until he eventually accepted the music as part of his life. Through the years, Trevor grew into a strong young man. His grandfather, Edward, held a special place in his heart. Edward was an older and fragile figure in the small family and was always willing to give advice at a moment's notice. He was a great storyteller, and Trevor loved to listen to his grandfather's tales of the adventures he had experienced. Edward had served many years in the United States Army. He was highly decorated during the later stages of his fifteen-year career. When he retired from Army life, he became a successful small-business owner, selling electrical supplies to large manufacturers. Trevor loved his grandfather very much, but because of Edward's age, Edward could not play with the boy as much as he would have liked. Edward grew weaker over the years. He was confined to a wheelchair for the later part of his stay at the Seawick Estate. One summer afternoon, just a month before Trevor went away to college, Edward died while taking a nap. He was buried in a graveyard near downtown Louisville.

CHAPTER 2

Restoration

Trevor was a smart, handsome, but quiet young man. He was very popular and had many female admirers. Some of his friends were jealous of his money, but most accepted him for who he was and treated him like other young adults who were not as privileged. Trevor was always well dressed in the latest fashion, wearing the best clothes and shoes that money could buy. Many of his follow students who were of the opposite sex knew that a date with Trevor would mean a chance at financial freedom for the rest of their lives. When Trevor did go out on dates, most found him to be quiet and studied. At times, he would fidget with his napkin at the dinner table or would zone out during a conversation.

Trevor was a busy young man who had monthly meetings with many of the estate's accountants, financial advisers, executive managers, and attorneys. The many trusts that had been set up for Trevor made his life financially worry-free, but he still experienced a great amount of stress with the decisions that he had to make.

Trevor had to grow up faster than other kids because of the awesome financial responsibility that Winthrop had thrust upon him at a very young age. Loren attempted to help with the financial decisions and was very conservative with the monthly checks allotted for the estate and Trevor's well-being. Edward helped in the beginning, but over time, his mind lost its sharpness and he began to leave the bulk of the decision making to Trevor and Loren. Both Trevor and Loren were bound by the terms of Winthrop's will, which limited what they could do with the money from the estate. One of the stipulations was that, after time, the numerous trusts put in place to manage the estate would expire and Trevor would gain full control, but that control was contingent on Trevor earning a four-year college degree.

Trevor never seemed to want the money for pleasure. In fact, he loved to see the money grow and the estate accumulate as much money as possible. He was wealthy from the start; however, over the years and through his financial team's smart planning, the estate grew to enormous proportions that well exceeded multiple billions in net worth.

Trevor played basketball in high school but never developed into a player of substance. He later gave up the sport, took up golf, and did quite well. He developed his golf game to the point where he could consistently break eighty on most of the courses throughout town during his early high-school years. He later got better and became a scratch golfer by his senior year in high school.

Trevor loved classical music. His first love was the violin, not only its sound but its form. He used to marvel at the majestic movements and the flawlessness of concert violinists, and envy their talents. He found the body, arm, and shoulder movements of violinists compelling, and he wanted to copy those actions. He had always wanted to play the violin, but he never took the time to pick up the instrument in his childhood. Later, after high school, he took some lessons, but he was not coordinated enough to master the finger placement and bow strokes necessary to make the proper sounds.

Because of Trevor's money and status, he always found himself around influential people. As time went on, he met the right people, and they learned of his love for not only the orchestra but the arts in general. After many decades of his family donating to the orchestra, he was voted an honorary member on the Board of Directors of the Louisville Orchestra at a young age. He was so proud of the honor that he made sure to never miss a meeting or a concert as long as he was a member of the board.

Trevor's physical appearance was striking. He stood six feet three inches tall and weighed a solid 220 pounds. He had nice muscle tone and a barrel chest, with long, strong arms. His hair was dark and wavy. His large, dark-brown eyes were his best feature per the girls in his life. Trevor was a soft-spoken, quiet young man with an array of interests that many of his friends did not share, which also made him attractive to girls his age. He was a teenager going on forty.

As Trevor's high-school days were fast ending, he applied to various educational institutions. Trevor was interested in law, and he applied to many colleges and universities that specialized in that interest. Because of his reputation, financial status, and intellectual capabilities, he was accepted to several Ivy League colleges. He had offers from Dartmouth, Yale, Harvard, and Colgate. Trevor only visited those Ivy League schools that offered enrollment. He spent many weekends with Loren at those institutions. After careful thought and many hours of discussion with Loren, he concluded that he felt most comfortable with Harvard and decided to enroll in their prelaw program.

Loren assisted him on his trip to Harvard and got him settled in before the fall classes started. It was an emotional good-bye, but they knew this was the best for Trevor. He wanted to board away from home to broaden his horizons. At first, he was a little intimidated by the thought of leaving his home and moving to a new and strange land, especially a place where money and intelligence were not only the norm but almost a requirement. But he handled the transition with ease and found out that being a small fish in a large pond created a sense of freedom for him, a feeling he had never felt at any time during his life in Louisville. He found school to be fun and relatively easy for him.

Trevor came home for holidays but spent his summer months at Harvard so he could graduate early. He studied with friends and did very well during his prelaw days, graduating in three years, a full year earlier than planned.

Throughout college, Trevor oversaw the financial decisions and always agreed with the decisions that Loren made on his behalf. He wanted Loren to continue to run the estate and the grounds. Since the estate was too large for one person, they needed to contract most of the care and maintenance that needed to be done on the estate. A small staff took care of the house but was never allowed to live on the premises. Trevor was not a trusting man, but Loren was special. Loren would do some housework herself, even though Trevor begged her to stop. He knew Loren well, and he loved her like a mother. Loren became so self-sufficient through the years that Trevor let her pay the bills, not only on the house itself but on groceries, utilities, pool maintenance, and lawn care. Trevor trusted Loren with his life.

When Trevor entered Harvard Law, it was a different story. He found law school challenging but rewarding. He loved the analytical process of the law, and he excelled in that area. He kept his same study routine from his undergraduate days. He loved the interaction with people, and it helped his concentration on his studies. Among his classmates, Trevor had a reputation for being a little dry-witted and overly serious. He did not like fantasy or comic relief; he preferred to analyze and gave great thought as to how to improve situations. He loved to plan and act on his processed thoughts.

In the back of his mind, Trevor thought he wanted to pursue a life in politics, but he did not want his many businesses to suffer in the process. One of the main reasons he wanted a law degree was that it would help him in running his businesses. Trevor also loved order and discipline. He believed that everything was either black or white. There were no gray areas in life, there were only different variables. If you change the variables, you change the situation. He was also analytical, and before he gave an opinion on any subject, he would study both sides of the situation. Trevor believed there was only one right answer to every problem, and that was why he took his time to mull over all the options and opinions before he took a side. This was an advantage for Trevor while going through law school because he was a passionate man about all matters in life. He had an opinion on every subject. He would fight to the end to have his opinion accepted by others who did not share his view.

Trevor loved the library at Harvard. It was one of his favorite places to go, not only to study material for his classes but to learn new subjects as well. In the library, he would let his mind wander over a range of topics. Trevor was a laborious college student, and because of his intellect, he had more time on his hands than the average law student. He would pick up books that did not pertain to his studies and would start reading. Something would always catch his interest. Trevor was drawn to animals, particularly different species of predators. He was interested in how they hunted and how they caught and ate their prey. He also loved space and the makeup of the different planets' atmospheres. He loved to read up on the different weather patterns of these planets. He also liked to read about the different composers that he had listened to during many of his childhood mornings and nights. Trevor was interested in only the facts, not opinions. He would read and study different forms of music during the centuries. Trevor had a vast knowledge of music through his connection with the Louisville Orchestra.

One day while Trevor was studying in the library, he noticed someone sitting down in front of him. Instead of smelling the musty old odor of yellow-stained pages from well-aged books, he inhaled a hint of rose petals. He looked up to find one of the most beautiful women he had ever seen. The sunlight came through the window behind her, so he could not fully see her face and hair. Her silhouette hinted at long, flowing, never-ending hair around a petite face. She was tall and thin, and she sat upright in her chair as if she were modeling for a camera. After a minute or so of his staring, she looked up from her notebook and smiled at Trevor with a somewhat bewildered look. Trevor maintained eye contact for a few seconds, smiled, and leaned over his book to introduce himself, extending his right hand toward the lovely vision who was still a blur because of the sunlight behind her.

"Hello, my name is Trevor Seawick."

The mystery lady looked down at the strong but well manicured hand before her. With a noticeable German accent, she said, "Hello. I am Adelle Vonsick."

"I love your accent. German, correct?"

"Yes, German. I am here to study law. Where are you from?"

Trevor smiled, "I am from here. I mean, I am from Kentucky. Louisville, to be exact. I am also a law student."

"Kentucky. Do you own a horse?"

Trevor laughed and said with a smile, "No, I don't own a horse, but I do own some bottles of bourbon back home. So, what is your opinion of America? Do you like it here?"

"I love it, especially Harvard. At first it was intimidating. Leaving home and coming here to a foreign land was not easy but once I settled down and fell into a routine, I was fine. Life here is different but that is what you expect, you know, moving to another country. Everyone is so friendly it made the transition less challenging." Adelle caught herself staring at Trevor, so she looked down sheepishly and opened the book before her.

Trevor thought the conversation was ending, which was unacceptable to him. He said spontaneously, "If I may be so forward, I must say that I find you very interesting and attractive. Would you like to go out sometime for coffee or drinks?"

Adelle looked up at him, smiled and looked up out of the corner of her eye. "I would like that."

From that moment on, Trevor and Adelle were inseparable. Adelle, whose name meant kind and noble, was born and raised in Germany. She was a tall woman, about five feet ten, and very thin. She had an athletic build, was always active in sports, and kept in shape by eating healthy and running every day. She had shoulder-length blonde hair and an oval face with a prominent V-shaped chin; large, light brown-and-green eyes; and a healthy smile. Adelle had a thick German accent but a high command of the English language. Like Trevor, Adelle was very intelligent. She had accepted an offer from Harvard while in Germany. She had wanted to study abroad, and when the Harvard opportunity arose, she could not turn it down.

The couple ended up falling in love almost instantly. They shared the kind of love that did not require much nurturing but that developed through time, building on little moments that brought their hearts closer and closer together with each passing experience. From the moment they met each other, they did not date anyone else. They fell hard for each other and spent all their time together.

Like Trevor, Adelle was a Harvard Law student, but while he was doing quite well in school, she had grown tired of the amount of studying required. They began to study together, but Trevor was more advanced than Adelle. Her grades faded as his improved. However, as much as their academic careers were diverging, their love life was growing closer. Adelle was a year further along than Trevor, but she decided that she did not want to continue law school. Instead, she took a job at the city's government accounting office near Harvard and rented a small apartment nearby. Adelle had her four-year degree from Harvard and she thought that was enough. Her family was outraged that she did not finish law school, but at the end of the day, it was not for her.

Adelle did not want to leave Trevor and go back to Germany, so she supported herself for over a year until her love graduated. Adelle's parents wanted to meet this Trevor, the love of their daughter's life. Trevor wanted to make sure Adelle's parents understood that he had not wanted her to drop out of law school at Harvard and that he was not the reason she gave up her schooling. He wanted to assure them of that in person, so one summer when he had some time away from his studies, they went to Germany to visit Adelle's parents.

Adelle's parents had wanted their daughter to fall in love with a German, but they had known when sending her away for school that she might find someone in the States. She did, and though that somewhat disappointed them, after meeting Trevor, they felt better about their daughter's decision. They were happy that Adelle had found the love of her life. They really liked Trevor and thought he would be good for their only child. They knew that marriage was in the couple's future even though Trevor and Adelle never actually spoke about it. They were taking their lives one day at a time.

As for Loren, only on two occasions did Adelle meet her, both times occurring when Loren visited Trevor for business purposes. Loren only came to Massachusetts to see how Trevor was doing and to fill him in personally on how the businesses were operating. Trevor did not want to scare Adelle away with his wealth, so he decided not to take her home with him while they were dating. Trevor ended up graduating from Harvard Law School with top honors. He had some opportunities to work in Boston and New York, but he missed his home in Louisville. He talked Adelle into moving to Kentucky with him. She did not even think twice about the offer; she gladly accepted the invitation to go back with her love to his home. This decision upset Adelle's family quite a bit, but they realized the couple would end up marrying and would probably stay in the United States. Adelle's love for Trevor was uncontrollable, and she could not separate herself from him. Adelle loved America and the American way of living and thinking. She was a free-spirited woman, and she knew that she would follow Trevor, the love of her young life, no matter where he went.

Trevor knew he had control of most of the estate after his graduation, so he wanted to meet with his financial people in Louisville. He wanted to settle the estate so he could put that part of his life behind him, to get all his finances in order, and to learn more about his future endeavors. Over time, additional trusts would expire. By the age of thirty, Trevor would have complete control and say over the estate.

Trevor wanted to live in the house he had grown up in. It was home to Trevor, and he had missed it while he was away at college. More importantly, the house and grounds had been special to his dad, and he wanted to keep the house in the family's name.

Adelle had an idea that Trevor had money, but she did not understand the extent of his worth. She knew Trevor's life history, including the tragic death of his parents, and she always had a soft spot in her heart for that part of him. Adelle was not poor by any stretch of the imagination either. Her father, Wilhelm Vonsick, owned a sewing company and leather shop in downtown Berlin. Her mother, Greta

Vonsick, was a successful interior designer who ended up going into business for herself. Both of her parents' businesses did quite well.

The day Trevor and Adelle flew into Louisville, Loren greeted them at the airport. Loren had stayed in the mansion and taken care of the estate and the grounds as well as some of the financial decisions for Trevor while he attended Harvard. She had contracted workers around the city to clean inside and to work the outside grounds as well. Trevor did not want anyone but Loren living on the grounds. She was trustworthy and had an outstanding financial mind. She was also, along with the family lawyers and financial advisers of his firm, an administrator of Seawick's numerous trusts.

Loren was like a second mother to Trevor. He loved her very much and did not want her to depart from his life. She had been planning to move out of the house after Trevor's arrival, but with a request from Trevor and encouragement from Adelle, she decided to stay at the house.

After the plane arrived at the airport, the couple collected their luggage, walked to Loren's car, and loaded up the trunk. Loren then drove the couple to Trevor's house. Along the way, Adelle told Trevor she was nervous about seeing where he lived because she did not know what to expect. Louisville was so different from the life she was used to in both Germany and Massachusetts. She was captivated by the beauty of the spring flowers and newly sprouted leaves on the massive trees along the expressway.

The conversation in the car was a bit choppy for Adelle, mostly because Trevor and Loren dominated the conversation. They had so much to talk about; so much had happened during the time they were apart. Loren told Trevor all that had happened recently in the city and with the house. She had sent numerous e-mails and text messages to Trevor through the years. As they drove along the expressway, some of the sights had obviously changed. Trevor tried hard to include Adelle in the conversation, making a point to keep her interest up during the car ride by pointing out landmarks.

Loren exited the expressway and turned onto the city's most prestigious roads where many affluent families resided. After a fifteen-minute drive, the car turned right onto a long narrow road. Adelle noticed the massive houses along the hilltops. She was starting to love her new place in the world, but her mind was racing as fast as the car was traveling on the country road. The closer the car got to their destination, the more Adelle felt at ease. As they approached the entrance to the mansion, Adelle wondered how her new home would look. Loren drove up to the gates and hit the remote button in the car. Adelle watched as the eleven-foot wrought-iron gates opened slowly, splitting the large S that was the centerpiece.

Trevor was talking about how the trees had grown and how everything had changed as the car drove through the closing gates and up the long winding road toward the estate. Adelle was deaf to the conversation. As they approached the house, she moved from side to side in the back seat, ducking her head up and down, left and right, to catch a glimpse of the house through the surrounding trees. The long road up to the mansion was covered with small twigs and leaves. Adelle kept looking until finally the house came into full view. The mansion was beautiful—large and long with a sense of newness about the structure. The house was not as old as the others in the area, but it still seemed to belong to the land. The house had five oversized gables and brick veneer, in a mixture of dark reds, rusty browns and grays, with a hint of cream, which covered all sides of the house. A large semicircle of cut glass above the ten-foot-high French-cut glass doors adorned the entrance to the house. The two large bay windows on each side of the front doors gave the appearance of eyes. The house sported three visible fireplaces, one to the side of each bay window.

As the car moved along the winding road and approached the circled driveway, the house seemed to grow in size. The car stopped, and Adelle got out with help from Trevor. They embraced, and Trevor said, "Welcome home, my love."

Loren smiled, laughed, and then winked at Adelle. Adelle felt at home already. The wind rustled through the trees, sending a beautiful and relaxing sound echoing around the house. Many steps led up to the house as the curved, semicircular steps spread over the front landscape like the flowing train of a bride's wedding dress in front of a church's altar. The shrubs were neatly cut and spaced properly from one another. Not one weed could have been found in the landscape.

As the couple entered the house, Trevor was eager to introduce Adelle to her new home. He seemed to float from room to room as he showed his soon-to-be bride the entire house. He was busy pointing out the locations of the Christmas trees during the holidays, his favorite hiding places from when he was a kid, and his other favorite parts of the house. He showed her the many bedrooms, the billiard room, the library, and the large kitchen with the massive attached dining room. Trevor showed her the basement, which Adelle did not feel particularly comfortable seeing. She had never liked basements because they were all so dark and dreary. She was amazed, however, by the total size of the basement.

After the personal house tour, Trevor showed Adelle the grounds. He loved the backyard of his house. The grass was always green during the spring, summer, and fall months, no matter the weather. The rich dirt was as dark as the newly painted wrought iron that surrounded a thirty-by-forty-foot patio. Inside the solid-black wrought-iron fortress was an Olympic-sized, heated swimming pool. Adelle thought that it must be wonderful to swim in view of such a beautiful scene. It was almost like something out of the Swiss Alps, but instead of snow-covered mountains, there were hills covered with a multitude of different sizes, colors, and shapes of trees. Poplars, maples, pines, oaks, and others made their home in the hills. Their only job was to fill the landscape with their beauty as they provided shade for the many animals that lived in the forest.

Trevor's father had loved the trees, and they had been the main reason he purchased the land and built his home where he did. As time passed, others built homes, but Winthrop waited for a few years before he broke ground on the mansion. He wanted the prefect look, and he achieved his goal. The lot was perfect for Winthrop's needs. He wanted a long, twisting driveway that went up a hill, but he didn't want it to be too steep. He wanted the house to sit on flat ground with a sidewalk out for the basement but the backyard to be on the same level as the first floor of the house. He wanted a long spacious backyard that wasn't too deep. He wanted trees surrounding the back of the property. From his backyard, Winthrop had wanted to be able to look over the deep, recessed, V-shaped valley filled with trees and a few homes.

As Trevor and Adelle continued with their tour of the backyard, they visited the gravesites of his parents, which were nestled on a hill that fell away from the main property. From that spot, the view was breathtaking. Adelle stopped to admire it. She felt a little uncomfortable with the view because of its spaciousness. She had never seen anything so beautiful. The massive homes looked as if god himself had placed the large structures perfectly in their resting positions on the sides of the hills, being oh so careful not to disturb the trees that had been there for many decades before the homes existed. Adelle wondered about the history of these places and the stories they could have told if they had been able to speak for themselves.

The smell in the air was fresh and clean, and the wind through the trees made constant noise. Adelle's senses were on overload from her new environment. She did not want to leave this earthly paradise, but she wanted to see the rest of the house's exterior.

Trevor walked around the house, showing Adelle all its architectural masterpieces and complicated structures. She was taken aback by the largest of the three fireplaces in the back of the house. She marveled at the size of the chimney that thrust out of the middle of the house. They circled the building, and Adelle was amazed by the landscape that hugged it. Of course, time had changed the view of the grounds, but the beauty was still in full force on the day of Trevor and Adelle's arrival. As the couple made their way into the house, Adelle looked back at the pool area and nodded in acceptance. She felt a peace that she had not felt in years. The views were nothing like what she had seen while growing up in Germany. Everything was on a sufficiently grander scale.

The couple did not waste any time in finding jobs. Trevor felt comfortable with Loren running the businesses, and he had always wanted to practice law. He felt this time in his life was the best opportunity for him to go into practice. Trevor wanted to gain experience in the law profession before he went on to pursue a potential political future. He was not sure he wanted to go into politics, but he kept an open mind to the idea. He also wanted to be on top of the decisions and the future of his companies' ventures. He thought that when he grew older and Loren decided to retire, he could take over the conglomerate as an experienced lawyer. That was Trevor's long-term plan. He had some contacts, and in less than a couple of months, he ended up accepting a job at Patterson, Brown, and Lee, a prestigious law firm in Louisville. He hired Adelle as one of his assistants.

A few months later, Trevor asked Adelle where she wanted the wedding to take place. Without hesitation, she said she wanted it to be at the estate. He agreed, and she immediately started planning the wedding. No marriage proposal had occurred between the two lovers. No offer had been needed. They had an understanding that marriage would come after they got their lives settled and in order.

Adelle and Loren made all the wedding decisions. The guest list was long, and they had trouble reducing it. Trevor invited a few of the members of the Louisville Orchestra to attend and perform background music during the ceremony and the following reception. Adelle got to meet many of Trevor's friends and a few of his distant cousins. The neighbors were not invited. Because Trevor had been gone for more than six years, many of those he'd known had moved on, and he did not feel comfortable inviting strangers to his wedding.

Adelle had her parents flown in from Germany. Trevor and Adelle picked them up at the airport. The Vonsicks stayed at the estate and were treated as part of the Seawick family. Wilhelm and Greta were fond of their future son-in-law, but mostly they were happy for their only daughter to have found the love of her life. They were elated that their daughter was marring into money. They had money back in Germany but not of Trevor's magnitude. In Germany, the Vonsick family was noted for their entrepreneurial skills, and they respected Trevor and his family for being in such good social and economic standings. As for Adelle, she did not care about money. It was nice, but she only cared about experiencing love, living life, and being happy.

The wedding was peaceful, and it was a great success. The ceremony took place outside in the back courtyard, overlooking the valley. The music from the orchestra members set a fairy-tale mood. Adelle and Trevor were at the happiest point in their lives. The couple embraced in a long kiss after they were declared husband and wife. At that moment, both knew they were going to have a wonderful life together. After the wedding ceremony, the Vonsicks went back to Germany, and Trevor and Adelle left on their honeymoon for a three-week tour of Europe. They were going to visit most of Italy and France, as well as parts of England, Ireland, Spain, and Germany.

CHAPTER 3

Ratification

During the first year of marriage, work was going well for the couple. Loren still lived at the estate and continued to take care of the grounds and the house. After many months of coming home together to a large and empty house, the couple wanted more out of life. They thought the next logical step was to have a child together. After a year of trying, they had produced no child. They consulted with a few doctors to see what the problem was, and the results indicated that problems existed on both sides. The doctors gave them no hope of having a baby together. Trevor and Adelle were shocked and greatly disappointed. Not only was this the first time in their lives that something did not go right for them, but they also had to answer questions from friends and family as to why there was no baby after so long a time.

When I contemplate on this event, I can only imagine how they must have felt. Most people don't stop to think about these things or the rudeness involved in asking someone about such private matters. It is ironic that so many couples have kids they cannot afford, and other couples have too many children to love, or have kids for the sake of having them and end up not taking care of them; no one really cares about those situations. Those situations are not criticized even by the many public judges who are ready to pass verdicts down before the presentation of a case. When couples have trouble bearing children, the unfortunate couples are sometimes treated poorly in their communities. Sometimes they are even isolated from certain parts of society. When couples have trouble conceiving children, their friends and adversaries treat them poorly. They are sometimes forced into isolation, kept away from certain parts of the world of parents. They are sometimes treated as though their access to some areas of life have been revoked.

Trevor and Adelle quickly found out about all of this. Most of the people whom Trevor and Adelle knew had kids, and it seemed as if they never really wanted kids or appreciated them from the start. In Adelle and Trevor's case, they wanted kids but could not have any. Trevor and Adelle were well liked and respected, but because of their extreme wealth, some of the people whom Trevor associated with would get their digs in about his and Adelle's failure to conceive a child. Most of this unnecessary hatred was a product of jealousy. An interesting but cruel, real-life paradox befell the couple.

Meanwhile, the Seawicks' financial estate was growing; Trevor and Adelle had amassed an even larger fortune. Money was not a problem in the young couple's life. As the years went on, they gave up on the idea of having a child. They thought about adopting, but they never followed through on the idea. Trevor wanted to have his own child and not someone else's. For Adelle, adoption was not out of the question, but she had always wanted to carry a baby inside her and go through what billions of other women had gone through since the beginning of time. Adelle, for the longest time, did not feel like a real woman because she could not carry or produce a child. She was depressed and felt inferior to many other women. This greatly upset Trevor, and, through the years, he lost all interest in having children. He came to a point where he no longer wanted or even liked children. The problems he and Adelle had faced in trying to conceive pushed him over the edge. He was happy with his life the way it was, and he did not want it to change. Adelle did not feel that way, and they often fought about this issue.

One morning, Adelle received a call from her native Germany, from one of her cousins, named Sonja. Sonja and Adelle were lifelong friends, and they had remained so after Adelle left Germany. Sonja was a tall blonde-haired woman, a slightly overweight bookworm with an old-maid look to her. She, like Adelle, was very intelligent. She had started her own printing business in Germany. Sonja loved books and did lots of research on early German cities and towns around the area where she lived. Her company printed some local authors and had a small biweekly newsletter, of which she was the editor.

Sonja had called to tell Adelle about a story she had recently covered. In a small village, about ten miles from the nearest town, a local hunter had found a newborn baby wrapped in a blanket near the edge of the forest, next to a small lake. The area was remote, visited only by a few hunters. The man who discovered the baby boy took the infant to the nearest hospital. The young boy had been lying in the woods for a while, long enough to suffer from exposure and dehydration. It was a miracle the little boy hadn't died in the forest. The baby recovered after receiving medical attention. So far, the identities of the parents had not been discovered. The baby was a week or so old, Sonja told Adelle. He was currently in the hospital, and if the parents were not located soon, the young boy would be sent off to the local orphanage.

After hearing the news, Adelle was horrified. Before they hung up, Sonja told Adelle that if anything new occurred, she would notify her cousin of the situation. Adelle was upset after the phone call, and she told Trevor the story. Trevor knew where this might end up, so he abruptly cut off any conversation on the issue. Adelle's heart was big and as good as gold. She hated to see anything happen to anyone, especially a little boy like the one whom she had always wanted but who had escaped her grasp. Trevor did not want to get involved–and certainly not with a child who was halfway across the world.

The small-town authorities never found the parents of the young child, and they ended up placing the baby in an orphanage. They had no leads, even though their investigation covered many towns around the area and beyond. No information came to the surface, and thus the case remained unsolved.

The situation quite moved Adelle. She had not been herself over the past few years. She wanted a baby in the worst sort of way, and her that maybe this might be an intervention from God—a sign, if you will.

Trevor knew that he had to see this through. If not, he thought
Adelle might hold it over his head for the rest of his life—or worst yet,
leave him. Therefore, when Adelle told Trevor that she wanted to see
the baby and she wanted Trevor to go with her to Germany, he
reluctantly agreed. He told Loren to make arrangements with the
airport and Adelle's friend Sonja. Trevor was totally against adoption,
but to save their marriage from a major knock-down, drag-out fight, he
knew he had to pursue this. Unbeknownst to Trevor, Adelle had already
asked Sonja to look into the possibility of adoption.

A couple of days went by, and Trevor and Adelle got on a plane
headed for Germany. When they arrived, they met up with Sonja and
Adelle's parents at the airport. Adelle was very excited to be back; it
had been a while since she was home. They had visited Adelle's parents
a few years prior but had not been back since. Adelle reintroduced
Trevor to Sonja. As they left the airport, Sonja drove them to her house
where they stayed the night. The next morning, they would visit the
baby and then spend the rest of the days with Adelle's parents.

Trevor always felt alone on these Germany trips; he felt left out
because of his inability to understand or speak the language. Most of the
people spoke English, but still he felt out of place. Adelle and Sonja
spoke in perfect High German, a language of which Trevor knew very
little. Many times, they would break from the German and flow into a
half-broken mix of English and German.

The morning after they arrived, the couple and Sonja got up
early. Sonja drove them to the orphanage, where they visited the little
baby boy. Adelle was moved to tears when she picked the child up from
his crib. He looked at her with his big, beautiful blue eyes and smiled at
her as if he had known her all his young life. The young baby had a few
scratches on his left cheek and more down his arms and on the top of his
head. Overall, he looked good considering what he had been through
recently.

To Trevor's surprise, Sonja told them that many people in the nearby villages were interested in adopting the young boy for their own. This did not sit well with Adelle. Trevor knew that if he did not at least make an attempt at adopting the newborn, their marriage might be severely wounded. Therefore, he spoke up and asked what they would have to do for an adoption to take place. Adelle's eyes were swimming with tears, and she was overcome with emotion. Then the young baby started to cry with hunger. Sonja took Trevor to the front desk to fill out some paperwork as Adelle sat down in a chair and prepared to feed the baby his bottled milk.

Trevor knew that he had to follow through with the adoption. They contacted the proper authorities, and he got his lawyers on the case. He told his lawyers that money was no obstacle and requested that they do what needed to be done for them to get full custody of the baby. After a few days, the Seawicks left Germany and returned to the States.

A month went by, and after lots of paperwork, Trevor and Adelle were awarded custody of the baby boy. It was not easy. Germany did not look upon overseas adoptions favorably, but after a few checks found their way into certain people's pockets, the adoption was final. The local government and the authorities from Germany approved the adoption, and it was finalized. Money has a way of changing people's minds and in some cases, it may alter certain laws that might have been difficult to circumvent in the past. Trevor was glad, and Adelle was ecstatic. They took the first flight to Germany they could get. While on the plane, they thought of names for their new baby.

When they arrived at the airport, Sonja met them again and took the couple to the adoption house where the little boy was located. Trevor and Adelle signed the necessary papers, and the woman behind the counter said they would get Garrison ready. The couple looked at each other, and at that moment they knew they wanted that name for their child. The workers at the adoption house had used the name Garrison because in the German language it means "to fortify or to protect," and so many people in the town had protected the young boy and helped support him through donations and offers of help.

Trevor and Adelle stayed with Sonja, and after the large congratulatory party that Adelle's family threw, the new family packed up and left for the States. The flight was long and hard, and the couple discovered that young Garrison did not like to fly. After many hours, the Seawick family came home, and Loren met them at the airport. Loren drove the same route that she had driven years ago when taking Adelle to the Seawick Estate for the first time. Adelle was in the back of the car with young Garrison, and she explained to him all the interesting highlights along the way.

Garrison was a beautiful baby; he had deep, piercing blue eyes and blond hair with a hint of red throughout. He was long and thin but very strong for his age. The first night with him was the toughest on the couple. Garrison cried hard throughout the night. He knew something was different in his young life, and he was scared. Trevor and Adelle both attempted to console the young one but with no luck. Eventually Garrison stopped crying through pure exhaustion, but even when he slept, Trevor and Adelle could hear cries of pain through his slumber.

Nights like that one continued for quite a while. Garrison was also not the type of baby who liked to lie still or be held. He would always move around and attempt to free himself from the holder's grasp. After a week or so in the house, Garrison released random cries of pain. The pain would come upon him as fast as it would go. What was interesting and almost disturbing was the fact that Garrison never developed a cold as all other babies did during their first couple of months. Another interesting fact was Garrison's rare blood type. The doctors in Germany had been puzzled by it; they could not really determine exactly what blood type Garrison had flowing through his body. The doctors at the time had thought the blood had been contaminated or that the hospital had messed up the test results. However, when Garrison visited the Seawicks' pediatrician, they discovered the same results as the doctors in Germany had. Trevor and Adelle were concerned, but Garrison was never sick and never displayed even the smallest symptoms of being ill, outside of the occasional crying. Unlike most kids, Garrison never had a cold, an ear infection, or a sore throat. In fact, he never had been sick, outside of the mysterious pains. Trevor did not want Garrison to go through more painful and uncomfortable tests, so the couple decided to let the issue with the blood type go for a while.

Garrison grew up in a very happy household during his first couple of years, but he grew at an alarming and unnatural rate. He grew twice as fast as a normal child his age but showed no signs of awkwardness. His rapid growth came so smooth and natural that he never felt physical pain during this period. For him, he did not understand why everyone was alarmed over his growth rate. He never crawled, but he walked at six months of age. For him it was normal and, in his mind, he did not understand why others were not growing like him. The doctors who saw Garrison were beside themselves. They could not offer any explanation as to why he was growing so fast. He learned to walk before his first year was completed. Adelle could not keep him in the same clothes or shoes for longer than a month. His hand and eye coordination were so superior to others his age that many of his classmates were frighten of him. Many of his classmate's parents thought he was strange and did not want their children around him.

He was an extremely intelligent baby, and Trevor and Adelle were amazed and encouraged by their son's zest for knowledge. They were also astonished by Garrison's extraordinary hand-eye coordination and motor skills. Their pediatrician was likewise amazed by the expediency of the skill set that Garrison had developed and, in some cases, mastered at such a young age. The Seawicks' pediatrician said that baby Garrison was the most gifted child he had ever seen in his more than twenty years of being a pediatrician. His mental advancement out paced his physical growth. He formed words before his first couple of months of life. Before his second year he could read, write, and articulate full sentences. He could speak on any subject matter before he was three. He constantly read, asked questions, and reached every avenue for knowledge. Adelle and Trevor were proud of his accomplishments inside the classroom, but they never truly appreciated just how intelligent the young body was for his age.

Garrison wanted for nothing in his young life. He was given and mastered the latest technology that was on the market. He had the best designer clothes that money could buy. He owned every new electrical gadget that was available.

Garrison loved his parents but grew very close to Loren. When Adelle was busy with household chores, Loren would be there playing with him, and vice versa. Garrison wanted to play intellectual games that challenged his mind whereas Adelle wanted to play mindless games that normal children his age wanted to play. Loren understood what Garrison needed and she fed his mind with material that he was interested in learning. She taught Garrison basic business models and accounting concepts. She showed him the entire business from a macro prospective. She encouraged him to study basic chemistry and biology subjects. She read to him constantly when she had free moments. She would push him to study subjects that interested him and never passed judgement on him which made him feel good about himself. Loren gave him relief from the pressures from others who viewed him as a weird prodigy.

Loren never married and never had any children, so this opportunity was a pleasant experience for her and a nice diversion from the stress of work. She loved nurturing the young boy and took great pride in teaching him how to read financial reports, prospectuses, and other complicated avenues of the many facets of the Seawick's businesses. Garrison was constantly busy and had full attention most of the time from the women in the house.

The only problem that Garrison had in his young life came from the sudden, sharp pains that seemed to strike him without warning day and night. Certain times throughout a week or a month, the pain would rear its ugly head without warning. The pain attacks would ease as fast as they had begun. His parents could not predict when the attacks would occur, but one could predict the effect on his parents. Trevor and Adelle were loving and caring parents, but the toll of the painful attacks on their little boy created stress for the young couple. Trevor and Adelle would attempt to comfort Garrison; sometimes the comforting worked, and sometimes it did not. Trevor's patience always wore thin, but Adelle, the more understanding parent, was always calm; she displayed the patience of a saint. To help relieve the pain, they turned to music. Trevor loved to listen to works by Vivaldi, Haydn, and Mozart. He had a vast collection, ranging from simple piano solos and wind or string divertimenti to complex works such as operas, symphonies, and string quintets. Adelle first discovered this while she attempted to calm Garrison one night during a particularly nasty attack. They attempted to experiment with a simple Mozart violin sonata. Moments when the movement started, young Garrison's cries subsided. Many times, he would stop immediately as if the music put him into a trance-like state. The pain seemed to ease with certain types of musical works, mostly with violin and piano compositions. They discovered that playing Mozart had the greatest effect on Garrison, more than the other composers.

Garrison's eyesight was beyond normal, better than twenty-fifteen. His sense of smell was also off the charts. He could smell things that others could not smell or distinguish. He knew exactly what was in almost every food that was prepared for him. Garrison's hearing was extraordinary as well, and it sometimes kept him up at nights because he could hear a deer walking about in the backyard or a small batch of leaves rustling from the wind outside his closed bedroom window. He could hear a car coming up the long curving driveway, or hear a car start up even if it was far away from the house. All of Garrison's senses were somehow elevated to extreme levels. Some doctors thought he was autistic, but they never diagnosed him with that condition.

The boy also had a wonderful gift of hand-eye coordination. He could throw a ball with uncanny accuracy and hit any object or spot that he was aiming for. Garrison was also a very fast learner, and he had a photographic memory. He picked up any task easily and completed it with great precision. Garrison developed more of an interest in classical music. He would sit for hours listening to different genres from many different composers but for some reason his interest was mostly with Mozart's music.

As Garrison grew older, Loren seemed to age twice as fast. The responsibility of keeping the house and managing the financial interests of the estate was taking its toll on her. Because of her responsibilities to the Seawick businesses and to Garrison, Loren never dated. She lived in the basement of the house, where she had every convenience available to anyone in an average single dwelling. Her residence covered over 1,200 square feet and included a small kitchen, laundry room, and everything else that a small house would have but with the added aura of stylish wealth that graced the Seawick Estate.

Loren was getting busier as time went on. Trevor thought they needed another person to take care of Garrison and some of the chores around the house. The idea displeased Loren. She loved her employer and his family with all her heart. She had given up her life in order to take care of them. Trevor knew this, and he would constantly comfort her, telling her that he needed her talents in other areas of his life, like his finances and the continued care and maintenance of the house.

Garrison's condition never changed, and after the monthly and yearly checkups, there were no new answers, only continued questions, and amazement at his blood work. One of the areas in Garrison's life that was developing rapidly was his interest in the violin. Trevor would always play violin music at Garrison's request. The variation of sounds the instrument made brought great pleasure to the little boy's ears. The numerous recordings of violin music pleased him greatly.

Trevor loved classical music, especially the violin, but he never could play the instrument to the level of his expectations. In fact, he had never possessed the talent or the patience to learn to play any musical instrument well. He was a perfectionist, and in the back of his mind he always thought it would create more stress than pleasure if he tried to perfect his talents. Trevor was the type of person who, if he started a venture, would end up being obsessed with trying to master it.

As the year passed, Adelle had become increasingly bored with and stressed from her job. Working so close to Trevor had put strain on their marriage. Therefore, Adelle and Trevor made the decision for her to quit her job as Trevor's assistant a short time after they brought Garrison home. Adelle wanted to focus on taking care of their son. Although she had no nursing skills and had never been a caretaker, she was a mother now and felt that Garrison needed his mom at home. Adelle felt that Loren had been more of a mother than she was to Garrison, and she wanted to stay home and spend more time with her son. Both Trevor and Adelle knew there was something special and even different about their son, and they thought it would be in the family's best interest for Adelle to be available to Garrison on a twenty-four-hour basis.

One night, Garrison was lying down in his bed while Trevor was downstairs watching television and Adelle was on the computer. Trevor heard his son crying out. Garrison was shaking, and every inch of his body was in a violent spasm. During the attack, he vomited. Adelle came rushing into the room with her robe half on, drooping around her shoulders. She picked Garrison up and held him. Garrison felt warm to the touch and was as stiff as a board. Trevor started to call 9-1-1 but stopped. Suddenly, Garrison's convulsions stopped. His crying went from a fever pitch to a soft moaning and half-crying state that normal kids Garrison's age might experience after a night terror or a bad dream. As Trevor and Adelle watched with expressions of great despair and worry, they noticed that young Garrison was beginning to relax. Trevor put the phone down, and after a long discussion with Adelle, he decided not to call a doctor that night.

The next day, Trevor and Adelle decided they needed some assistance with Garrison, as well as some help around the house. After interviewing many highly qualified nannies in less than two months, they decided on a young woman from East Lansing, Michigan. Her name was Carolyn. She had been a registered nurse years before but liked being a nanny more, and she was working toward a teaching degree at Michigan State. Carolyn was a plain-looking woman with extremely short hair, and she was slightly overweight. Her bottom teeth were displaced, causing her to speak with a distinct lisp. She had a pleasant personality and was quite witty and friendly. She had one of those faces that reminded one of a character out of a children's book. This trait was one of the main reasons Trevor and Adelle decided to hire her. Because of Carolyn's looks and calm but funny personality, they thought she would ease Garrison's pain when he had his attacks and provide a soothing yet playful retreat for Garrison in his times of trouble.

At first, Loren did not accepted Carolyn as part of her family, but when she saw how happy Garrison was with her, she began to warm up to her. Loren was aging fast, and she suffered from arthritis throughout her body. She knew that Carolyn would be good for Garrison and allowed her the freedom to work and play with the boy. All Loren wanted was for Garrison to be more at ease, and she would help him at all cost. If Carolyn was the answer, then so be it. Garrison instantly liked Carolyn and warmed up to her. Garrison still played and had fun with Loren, but Carolyn was more childlike and playful. After a few months, Loren began to realize this and felt some jealousy toward Carolyn.

When Garrison turned two, he was starting to read full sentences in adult books. Carolyn helped him daily with his reading and writing. Garrison's body was rapidly changing during this time. He was off the charts when compared to other children in his age group; he was taller and stronger. Garrison's pains were changing as well. The sudden attacks ended, replaced by a dull ache from time to time. According to the doctors, Garrison's pain was the direct result of his rapid growth rate. His muscles seemed to grow a bit day by day, more than those of his peers.

Garrison attended a small school for gifted children. At almost four, he was doing the classwork of children twice his age. This delighted Trevor and Adelle. Adelle wanted Carolyn to be more involved as a teacher in Garrison's life. She wanted her to homeschool Garrison until he reached the limits of her ability to teach. However, after many discussions and meetings with the teachers, they decided to transfer Garrison into a special school in town for only the most gifted children. Adelle was concerned because, even though Garrison was physically and intellectually superior to his peers, he was not emotionally ready. At the new school, Garrison was the youngest in his class. He was still a very young boy inside a middle-school body and intellect. He was so intelligent that he tested out of kindergarten, first, second, and third grade at the tender age of four and a half years old. His mentality changed as rapidly as his growth rate. He started to notice his classwork to the point where it was becoming difficult for his teachers to challenge him.

Adelle had other concerns about her son, but she kept them to herself. Garrison's joints ached, and over time, the pains never seemed to ease as they had before. No one could offer any logical advice as to why he was still suffering these short bursts of pain. Another issue was more concerning for Adelle. During Garrison's short life, they had visited the local zoo on more than one occasion. Adelle and Trevor noticed that when Garrison talked or walked near the animals, they reacted, some more than they would at other people. They would either growl or run away. Even when they took Garrison to some of the exhibits with snakes or frogs, the animals reacted the same. Either they moved away, or they assumed an attack position. At first, Adelle did not think much of it, but eventually she noticed that even the forest animals at the estate, like squirrels, birds, or deer, had strange reactions to his presence. Spiders, insects, and some fish did not react the same. Garrison, for his part, loved animals and always wanted to be around them. At first, their negative reactions went unnoticed by him, but after time he noticed them. It never seemed to upset him, but he did wonder why they reacted this way to him and not to other people.

Another problem was that whenever small dogs or cats made their way around Garrison, they tended to run, bark, and whimper. They seemed to be out of sorts whenever Garrison was in their company. Trevor dismissed this as some negative vibe that Garrison was giving off and said there was nothing to worry about. Adelle and Loren were more concerned. Countless times animals had come out of the woods around the house and, noticing Garrison right off, had run away. Now this is a common course of action for animals, but after repeated scenes, Adelle and Loren saw a pattern. The animals showed more fear of Garrison and ran more violently away than they did from other people.

CHAPTER 4

Imminent

*W*hen Garrison was five, Adelle had a friend and her little boy over to the house for a playdate with her son. Adelle didn't invite over many of Garrison's friends, but on this occasion, she allowed the visit. The woman's name was Terra, and she used to work alongside Adelle at Trevor's law firm years before. Terra and Adelle had kept in touch because they had a lot in common, especially with Terra being pregnant at the same time Adelle was trying to adopt Garrison. Terra had wanted to visit her friend for a while, but with work, her own baby, and life in general, her visitations were limited. Terra had been to the house before and admired the estate. Now, she really looked forward to another visit. Terra brought her son, Jason, and her dog, a little Pomeranian named Snowy, with her. Terra never left her dog at home. She took Snowy everywhere she went. As they entered the house, Garrison and Jason looked at each other, smiled, and ran off to play. Meanwhile, Snowy was barking furiously and squirming around in Terra's arms. Terra patted the dog's back and whispered to him to settle down. As the children left the room, the dog immediately stopped barking. Adelle loved dogs, but she never entertained the thought of buying a dog because Trevor did not like animals in the house, not to mention the odd way dogs and other animals acted toward Garrison. Terra asked if she could put Snowy down. Adelle said it was fine and he could run around the house freely. Adelle was apprehensive about the dog running around the house unguarded, but she did not want to be rude to her friend.

Garrison and Jason played with each other for a long time. Garrison had many toys, extremely nice toys other children his age did not possess and couldn't afford. Jason loved seeing all of them. Most were mechanical in nature and walked, talked, or made shooting sounds. Garrison had a fascination with soldiers in the Army, or soldiers of a spaceship, or any special, elite fighting-force type of action figure. The boys played in Garrison's room upstairs. It was one of the bedrooms made into a playroom. Trevor always thought Garrison had too many toys for one boy to play with and called the playroom a storage room.

Next to the playroom was an oversized guest bedroom, and next to this room was Trevor's study. There, Trevor had some old law books that he had picked up from a friend's father years ago because he thought they would make a nice addition to his study—a place where he did most of his business when he was in the house. On the bookcases were some of his favorite books and items, picked up from foreign countries that had personal meaning to him. The walls and ceiling were all made of mahogany. The ceiling was beamed with massive crossed wooden gables with impressive crown molding. The floors were a deep red hardwood that made for a daunting appearance. The study was similar but smaller than the downstairs library located off the main entrance to the house. Trevor loved this room. This area of the house was off limits to Garrison; he was not allowed in the study unless Trevor was at home and with him in the room.

As Adelle and Terra talked, Snowy went from room to room like an only kid in a large candy store who had been given permission to eat anything he wanted. The dog ran and barked, and the sound of his little paws on the hardwood floors could be heard all over the house. Terra was visiting Adelle downstairs while their children and Snowy were upstairs. Garrison was very happy and was having lots of fun. Garrison loved playing with kids his own age, but he didn't often get the chance.

Garrison didn't have much experience with dogs, cats, or any animals. Snowy made him a little nervous. As the boys were playing,

Garrison had a funny feeling come over him periodically. The feeling had started once the dog entered the house. As the dog passed the room the kids were playing in, Snowy would bark and then run away if the kids looked up to see him. Snowy would then run down the hall and a few minutes later return and repeat the same bark, sometimes growling a little. Garrison was getting increasingly nervous because this experience was all new to him.

When the dog made another pass by the room, barked and growled again, Jason asked, "What's wrong with that stupid dog?"

Garrison answered with a sight chuckle, "It keeps barking at us." Then his demeanor toward the dog started to change. He had been considering the dog a nuisance, but now he was becoming annoyed. At this point, Jason was beginning to ignore the barking dog and pay more attention to Garrison's robot, a toy that not only made shooting sounds but also shot out little bullets at the Army men the two boys had set up on the floor. Garrison's attention turned from the robot and Army men to the annoying animal that was running through his house.

As Jason was busy playing, Garrison was totally absorbed with the little dog. He kept hearing the dog barking down the hallway. The barks were not loud woofs but the constant short and sharp yips that Pomeranians made naturally. These noises were really getting on Garrison's nerves, and an unfamiliar feeling in the pit of his stomach was irritating him. Garrison got up, left Jason in the playroom, and started to follow the barking dog. As the dog ran out from one of the rooms, Garrison started to chase the animal. The boy chased the dog down the long winding stairs, across the foyer, and through the great room, where Adelle and Terra were sitting.

Adelle said, "Garrison, stop chasing the dog around the house."

Terra said, "Don't worry about it. Snowy is used to being chased by Jason."

Garrison was having difficulty keeping pace with the dog. He could sense where the dog was going to run but as the dog would make a sudden turn, it was just faster than Garrison. It was obvious the dog did not like the boy and was afraid of him. The chase started to anger

Garrison, and that funny feeling that at first came and went now became a constant sensation that almost overwhelmed him. The feeling confused Garrison because he had never experienced it before. He was so concentrated on his pursuit of the dog that he could not think about anything else. He knew that he had to capture the barking dog. He could not explain it or understand it, but this feeling was getting to the point of obsession.

Eventually, Garrison grew tired from all the chasing, and he had to rest. He sat down in the hallway to catch his breath. His mind raced with his plans to capture this barking, irritating animal. A part of him wondered why it was so important to him. Why did he feel so compelled to touch the animal? Why the anger? Why the passion? Why the desire to capture, touch, and hold this dog? Why did he feel so compelled to chase and catch a little, skinny, hairy, mop-looking animal? He could not explain why he was chasing it, but after a while he started to get angrier with himself and the animal.

Throughout Garrison's short life, he had become accustomed to getting his way. His view of the situation had now elevated from a desire to pet the dog to a burning quest to capture the thing because he believed the dog had been teasing him. He had never experienced such teasing from anyone, much less from a dog. This was his first time up close and personal with an animal, and Garrison could not understand why the animal would not come to him when he called for it. The dog seemed to fear him. It would run madly in any direction to avoid contact with him. Garrison was totally convinced the dog was now teasing him, and he did not like it one bit.

Jason was still busy playing with the electronic robot and Army men in the playroom. As Garrison sat in the spacious hallway, he heard the dog in the guest bedroom. Snowy then came out of the room while Garrison remained still. The dog turned his small head to his right and noticed Garrison looking at him. Garrison's heart stopped and his eyes widened. He called for the dog to come to him, but instead it ran down the hall and into the study. Garrison's anger reached a fever pitch. He could not control the sensation growing inside him. He leaped up, ran into the study, and slammed the door behind him.

He stopped and thought, *Did Mom hear the door slamming? Will she come up here?* He knew that he should not be in the study without permission.

Then the dog's barking interrupted his thoughts. In between barks, the creature growled at Garrison. It was clearly scared. Garrison sensed the fear as he looked into the animal's face. Garrison stared at the dog. That feeling that he'd had ever since the dog entered the house became so uncontrollable that he lunged forward, but the animal was too quick for him. It ran from one side of the study to the other, further heightening the boy's anger. Garrison, being smart for his age, knew that the only way he could capture the dog was either to jump toward it and potentially slide on the hardwood floor in hopes of tripping the dog or to capture the dog with his body instead of his hands.

Twelve feet lay between the entrance of the study and the handmade area rug that was under the desk. Garrison, who had been standing in front of the desk, raced toward the dog, fell, and slid forward. The dog jumped to the side. Garrison slid over and hit the closed door with his right foot. He then got up, lunged again, and slid toward the barking dog. This time Garrison's outstretched right hand grabbed the dog's rear leg. After he stopped sliding, he pulled the dog closer to him and placed his left hand on the dog's shoulder. The dog tried to bite him, further enraging him. He grabbed the dog by the throat and applied some pressure while still holding the dog's leg. The dog's body moved around like a fish out of water. Its free hind leg was kicking frantically to free itself while its front paws scratched at the hand that clasped its throat.

Garrison meanwhile admired the struggling dog and marveled at the makeup of such an animal. He watched the rib cage expand and then deflate rapidly. He smelled the fear in the dog, his nostrils filling with the musky odor of sweat mixed with fright. He began to salivate. His left hand applied more pressure to the animal's neck as the dog emitted a muffled bark that turned into a whimper. Garrison's mind raced. He heard a ringing inside his head and felt himself enter a trancelike state. The dog's legs continued to kick to free itself from its capture.

Garrison's eyes widened and his mouth opened slightly as he knelt before the helpless animal. He moved the dog a little farther in front of him as he held the throat and rear leg. Without warning, he dove toward the dog's side with his mouth wide open and attempted to bite it. The dog yipped and struggled. Garrison repositioned his mouth for another bite and attempted to dig deeper into the animal's side. He attempted the third time at another angle. Then he increased the pressure on its throat, choking the dog. Within moments, it was dead. Garrison had trouble biting into the hairy side of the deceased dog. He could not completely get through the hair to tear out a chunk of the meat he wanted, so he stopped and slowly released his grip until the dog lay lifeless on the floor.

Garrison looked around the room and went to the desk. He found a pair of scissors in the front drawer. He was trying to process everything in his head. He struggled with the idea of what was right and what was wrong. He knew he had done something that he should not have done. He understood that something was not right about the act that he had performed, but his rage and borderline hatred for the dead animal had propelled his actions. He cut the long hair close to the dead body and then laid the scissors down and bit into the animal's flesh again, this time making a major break in the skin. Garrison fixated on his enjoyment of the feast, but the flesh was tough. He decided to use the scissors. Without hesitation, he plunged the instrument into the cut he'd made with his mouth. The animal slid a few inches across the floor. Blood oozed from the wound. Suddenly, Jason screamed.

Jason had heard noises coming from the closed door to the study and opened the door to find his friend using a pair of scissors on Snowy. The blood gave away Garrison's deed. It covered his mouth, nose and chin. The blood oozed from the dog and created a pool of gore on the flooring. Jason shook violently and stumbled out of the study, needing to get away from the scene. He ran down the stairs. His body hit up against the wall while he ran. He tripped with three steps remaining, and before he knew it, his body hit the hard floor.

From the great room, Adelle and Terra heard Jason's screams and his fall. They raced to him. Jason got up and attempted to form words, but nothing that made any sense came out of his mouth. Adelle rushed up the stairs, looking around for Garrison and calling out his name. She thought something terrible had happened to her son, and she was a nervous wreck. She ran down the hallway and looked in the study. Her forward momentum carried her past the entrance. She quickly regained her balance and looked inside the room.

There she saw her son in front of a partially eaten dog, with a pair of scissors in one hand and a piece of flesh in the other. Garrison's face looked as if he were devouring a chocolate birthday cake. Shocked, Adelle walked slowly toward her son. She felt sick to her stomach and vomited in front of the scene. Before she could compose herself, a loud scream from Terra startled her. The other woman had run up the stairs, worried not only about her son but also about what had happened to make Jason scream. The boy stayed in the foyer at the bottom of the stairs, still shaking uncontrollably.

Terra shook as she gazed at the scene, yelling through her hands as they hid her mouth. "Why? How could you?"

Garrison stopped eating and stared as if he were awakening from a short nap. He placed the scissors and a small piece of meat on the floor and started to cry softly. Then the cry grew into a violent and uncontrollable sobbing. Terra ran out of the room and down the stairs, screaming at Jason to get out of the house. Adelle attempted to move Garrison away from the dead animal. Then Carolyn came to the study's entrance. She gasped in horror and told Adelle to take Garrison to the bathroom and clean him up. She would take care of the mess on the floor. Carolyn was in as much shock as Adelle and Terra. None of them had ever experienced anything like this in their lives.

Adelle cleaned Garrison up by giving him a shower. She was mad at Garrison for what he had done. She scrubbed him hard at times as she wondered what would possess a little boy to do such a thing. She felt complete disgust but also wanted to understand why her only son would act like that, especially to an animal that had been his friend's pet. Garrison could not explain his actions; he sobbed and said he was sorry.

Adelle decided to take Garrison to the doctor. She was worried he might be at risk for disease from his afternoon snack. The boy seemed to be remorseful. As they made their way to the doctor's office, Adelle attempted to contact Terra to issue an apology or say something that would begin to explain what had happened. At this point, she was prepared to say anything to her friend. Terra did not answer.

At the office, the doctor decided to run some psychological tests on Garrison. The psychologist asked Garrison why he had done such a monstrous thing. All Garrison could muster from his quivering lips were the words, "I don't know. I'm sorry. I am so sorry. I had this feeling that came over me."

Adelle said, "A feeling came over you? That kind of feeling is not normal Garrison."

Garrison's doctor at the time, Dr. Goodlure, said, "Do you have these kinds of feelings often?"

"Yes, sir, all the time," Garrison answered. Adelle and Dr. Goodlure looked at each other with grave concern.

Meanwhile, Loren informed Trevor about what had happened. He ended up meeting his wife and son at the doctor's office. Trevor entered the office and went back to the room where his wife and son were sitting.

When he opened the door, he immediately began yelling at Garrison, "Garrison, what in the hell did you do?"

"I don't know, Daddy. I did a bad thing."

"A bad thing? A bad thing? I cannot believe what you did. What in the world would possess you to do such a thing to that poor little dog? I don't understand what the hell is the matter with you."

Garrison began to cry uncontrollably. "I'm sorry, Daddy. It won't happen again. I'm sorry."

Trevor was appalled. He yelled at the boy for long stretches of time until the doctor had to escort Trevor outside to calm him down.

Later that night, Terra, who was still shaken by the incident, returned Adelle's phone call. When Adelle answered, Terra started in on her. "You bitch! What in the hell is wrong with you people? What is wrong with your son? Snowy was our pet for over seven years. I loved him. He was a part of the family." Her voice was shaken, confused and angry.

"I am so sorry. Is there anything I can do?"

"What can you do? How about institutionalizing that freak of a child you have? How about bringing back our little Snowy? I have never heard of anyone doing that to an animal. Where did he come from?"

Adelle attempted to say a few words, but Terra wouldn't allow her to speak. After Terra said her peace, she ended by saying, "I am so appalled over this, and I never ever want to see you or that monster of a son you have anywhere near us. You keep him away from my family. I hope the little monster rots in hell over what he did to my pet and my family. Your demented little creature has marked Jason for life. I hope you are proud of yourself. What did you raise? Is that how you rich people live your lives? I mean, I have never heard of such a thing. Leave us alone."

After Terra hung up, Adelle closed her eyes, pressed her lips together, hung her head in shame, and began to cry.

The results from Garrison's blood tests came back normal; Garrison had not caught any disease from eating the dog. However, his blood type was once again unidentifiable, renewing concern with the doctors and Adelle. Trevor didn't want the information out, so he talked to Garrison's doctor and told him that he was going to hire a private physician to handle his son's case.

Garrison was slowly getting back to his normal self after the incident with Snowy, but his parents were still concerned about his behavior. Since Jason didn't go to Garrison's school, news of the dog incident didn't spread. Trevor and Adelle worried that it would still get out, so Trevor offered to buy Terra another dog. After many phone calls, he convinced her not to press the matter further, either by filing a lawsuit or by involving the police. Terra was having some financial difficulties, and he helped her with some of those difficulties in return for keeping the entire matter private. The news did not spread, and the matter was put to rest.

CHAPTER 5

Specialization

arrison continued his accelerated growth. The dull aches and pains he'd experienced periodically were a daily occurrence now. Trevor and Adelle sought out a doctor in town who specialized in growth disorders and behavioral issues. Dr. Lewis Page was a handsome young family physician who specialized in difficult cases of behavioral and emotional difficulties. He was also a member of Trevor's fraternity at Harvard. Dr. Page had ended up in Louisville because of business ties and his marriage, though the marriage had ended in a nasty divorce.

Trevor was highly concerned about Garrison's discomfort, and even though many tests, both physical and mental, were performed on the young boy, no one could come up with an answer for his problems. Trevor offered Lewis a large sum of money to be Garrison's personal physician. Lewis agreed to work with the boy but told Trevor that he would still have other patients. Trevor agreed, so Garrison had another doctor in his life.

Lewis and Garrison got off on the right foot. Garrison seemed to like the doctor, more so than the many other doctors he had seen in the past. At first, Garrison's high intellect surprised Lewis. Garrison would carry on conversations about things an average six-year-old would or could not. Many of the conversations seemed to be geared toward music. Trevor would always listen to Mozart or Vivaldi while he was in his study, in the car, or around the house. Garrison had such an aptitude for music that he would sing along with the notes for fun. Trevor would turn down the sound and allow Garrison to hum the notes and then turn the volume up without Garrison missing a note. Garrison had a wonderful ear for music, and his memorization for musical notes seemed an unworldly gift from God. Trevor wanted Garrison to explore this side of himself. He thought he might have a young Mozart on his hands. Lewis agreed with that assessment but was more interested in Garrison's rapid growth, the lack of known illnesses in his life, the way animals reacted to him, and of course the behavioral incident with the dog.

The attack on the dog came up in many of the conversations the boy had with Lewis. Garrison finally revealed his reasons for it. He said he had had an overwhelming desire to feast on the dog, especially the tough part of it. Later, the doctor discovered that Garrison was referring to the muscles. This greatly disturbed Lewis. When he asked Garrison if he had desired this kind of meal just one time or wanted it all the time, Garrison answered that he had not wanted it until the incident, but ever since, the feeling would come and go. He said that he forced himself not to act out his desires. He ate what normal people ate, like his friends and his parents did. At first, it was hard for Garrison to stop thinking about the desire, but he had learned that he was not supposed to give into the craving. Garrison compared the desire to liking a dessert or a candy bar. Sometimes it would overwhelm him, and sometimes it was more manageable; it depended on his mood.

During the continued meetings with Lewis, Garrison opened up more. He admitted that he knew what he had done was wrong. He further explained what was going through his mind when the attack took place. He talked about how he could sense things around him more than others could. His hearing was exceptional, not only in his ability to pick up sounds that very few people could hear but in his ability to distinguish between many different types of sounds at the same time. Garrison also explained his elevated sense of smell.

He passed many tests administered to him by Lewis. In one test, Lewis would walk out of the room and lay some kind of fruit down on the floor out of Garrison's sight. Lewis would then walk back in the room and ask Garrison what he smelled. Almost without fail, Garrison would guess the fruit. However, Lewis noticed during these experiments that Garrison's heightened sensory gifts would come and go. Some days his senses were exceptionally strong, and other days they were closer to normal. Lewis had trouble figuring this out; he could not understand why or how it was happening.

Intellectually, Garrison had blossomed beyond his years. He was reading, writing, and working complicated math problems that many children twice his age could not understand. Trevor again pondered the idea of homeschooling Garrison, but he thought social interaction with kids the boy's own age was important. Both Trevor and Adelle had grown up highly educated, very intelligent, and were tops in their respective classes, so educating their son was important to them.

One day, the doctor suggested that Trevor encourage Garrison's violin playing. Trevor ordered a highly priced violin for Garrison to fiddle on to see if he had any interest in playing. At first, he was very clumsy with the instrument, but with some instruction, Garrison soon learned how to hold the violin, draw the bow, and read notes. Garrison's tremendous grasp of musical notes, timing, and rhythm needed to be explored. Garrison liked the sound of the violin and wanted to have his own personal violinist to practice with and teach him more about the instrument. Trevor consulted many of the violinists in the Louisville Orchestra who knew him or knew that he was a major financial contributor to the orchestra. Some of them actually came over to the Seawicks' house to listen to the young prodigy. They all walked away rather amazed. Garrison had outgrown his previous violin, and Trevor had to go out and buy another that was big enough for the young virtuoso.

Eventually, at the doctor's request and at the badgering of Garrison, Trevor found the boy a mentor who had been referred by one of Trevor's friends in the orchestra. The mentor, Jim Levertine, was a highly recommended music teacher and violinist. Jim taught Garrison at home, and after a full discussion on how to take care of the instrument properly, he let Garrison try his hand at the device. Garrison began to better himself day by day, and after a month he was playing the violin at the level of a two-year student. To the absolute amazement of Jim, Garrison's parents, and Lewis, Garrison was playing some very difficult works from a handful of the great masters. He would occasionally make a mistake, but after only a few repeated attempts, he would correct his errors. Garrison's incredible hand-eye coordination served him well in this area.

Over his years of involvement with the Louisville Orchestra, Trevor had befriended many of the orchestra's players. Jim asked Trevor if he knew of a gentleman named Alex Gingerson. Alex had been with the Louisville Orchestra for over eighteen years and was well respected in the music circles in many neighboring states. Trevor had obviously heard of Alex and they met on several occasions through the years. Trevor asked him to stop by to listen to his son play the violin. Alex went to the Seawick Estate and listened to young Garrison play some notes. Alex was very taken with what he heard. He could not understand how in just a couple of months a child of Garrison's age could pick up the instrument and play it as well as he did. Typically, it would take years for an average person to accomplish such a feat, even if the person was talented. After a week or so, Jim stepped out of the picture because Garrison had become more advanced than he was. Alex was Garrison's new mentor.

Garrison continued to play work after work, from Haydn to Mozart to Vivaldi. Most of the time he memorized the works first, and then he would improvise, much like what Mozart had done many centuries ago. After a couple of months of nonstop hours of playing, Alex decided that in his professional opinion, Garrison was ready for the next step: performances. Alex was excited and wanted to tell the world about the boy who was playing at a level that some of the current members of the Louisville Orchestra had taken years to reach, and Garrison had already passed some of them in ability and talent. There was something different about Garrison's playing. It was in the certain way that he would draw the bow, how he moved his fingers, how he adjusted the bow just so at precisely the right time. Alex marveled at the superior harmony of Garrison's hand-eye coordination, but also at his instinct for the emotions the composer wanted to express through the music.

Alex wanted to set up a recital for a gentleman, his music teacher from his Harvard days, so his former professor, Ed Montgomery, could hear the wonderful and extraordinary music that young Garrison was making. He set the recital for the next month. Garrison had few flaws in his playing, but one of them was the power with which he drew the bow across the strings. Garrison did not care about playing for everyone. In fact, he thought they were making fun of his playing and had to be reassured many times by Lewis, Alex, and even Trevor that this was not the case.

When the critiquing of the recital was over, Ed was absolutely amazed at the young boys' ability to play so well and flawlessly. Ed said to Garrison, "Young man, for a beginner, I have never heard anyone play so beautifully. You have a gift. If you would relax the tension on some of your draws, I believe you could play for any orchestra anywhere."

"Thank you, Mr. Montgomery. I play only for the enjoyment of playing and I draw my bow with just enough tension just like the great masters that wrote these pieces wanted."

Ed did not like the sharp retort from the boy's mouth. He left the estate with a heavy strain that filled the air. Only Garrison was comfortable after the recital.

During this time in his life, Garrison was lonely. After his schoolwork, he usually played his violin. He was getting so proficient at it that he started playing pieces that were more intricate, mostly by his two favorite composers, Vivaldi and Mozart. He also loved to play outside, especially on sunny, hot days. He would play near the tree line at the entrance to the woods on the property. The Seawicks' property went on for several acres. The land was smothered with trees and brush. Garrison loved the scenery and smells, and he loved to hear the voices of the forest. He admired the way the birds sang, the sound of the wind slithering through the leaves, and the sound of leaves being pushed or moved around by the animals that called this oasis their homeland.

Lewis and Garrison grew closer through the months. Garrison almost thought of Lewis as more of a father figure than his own dad. Trevor always seemed to be a little cautious with Garrison. Trevor also had so many appointments and deadlines relating to the family businesses that he rarely had time to spend with Garrison. Garrison somewhat understood this, but he never really accepted the fact. He could also sense that his father was a little jealous of his musical ability, and concerned about the incident with the dog. This upset him because all Garrison wanted was to please his father.

Trevor's concern over Garrison had been increasing. Ever since the dog-biting incident, his relationship with his son had changed for the worse. Garrison was very astute, and he noticed his father's displeasure with him. He knew he was different and that other kids did not like him or feared him. Then he began to realize that he was so different that even some adults might be jealous of him as well as afraid of him. This was quite an interesting observation from a six-year-old child prodigy, a prodigy not only in music but in life as well. Throughout the years, Garrison had developed his level of awareness of his surroundings. He had learned to read people's feelings and emotions.

At times, Lewis and Garrison talked for hours about everything that Garrison had experienced in his life, what he was thinking and sensing, and how he dealt with those emotions. Many of their conversations came back to the killing of Snowy. Garrison always demonstrated remorsefulness for his actions on that day. He knew what he had done to the little dog was wrong. He also understood and accepted Lewis and knew that he was there to help him through the trauma of the event both physically and emotionally.

As Lewis continued his research on Garrison, he remained amazed by Garrison's memory and his aptitude for music. He was also advanced not only in all phases of reading, writing, and arithmetic but even in social development. Garrison was ahead of any kid his age in terms of maturity level. Lewis came to believe that it would be in Garrison's best interest to be homeschooled for a while. Lewis consulted with Adelle and Carolyn about the possibility of Carolyn becoming Garrison's main teacher. Adelle agreed. The only worry was the social effect of holding Garrison out of school. Garrison enjoyed playing and interacting with other children, but many of Garrison's classmates did not want to play with him. They all had some uneasy feelings about him, even before the incident with the dog. The news had never really gotten out, but there had been some rumors, and those rumors affected the attitudes of his peers toward Garrison. Many older students who went to school with Garrison were extremely jealous of his abilities, and because of his young age, they picked on him. Garrison didn't like the idea of staying home to learn, but he had little choice in the matter. It was a way for him to get away from some of the bullies at school. Although Carolyn was highly intelligent herself, she worried whether she was smart enough for Garrison. Everyone ended up agreeing that, for now, this was the best option. Garrison could always go back to school later.

A few months went by, and Carolyn, like the others, was amazed by the rapid progression Garrison made in his schoolwork. Garrison was now six and a half years old, and most of the books that Carolyn was introducing him to were meant for children twice his age.

What really puzzled everyone was that Garrison still never got sick. His immune system was unworldly. Lewis took many blood samples and had them analyzed multiple times at numerous clinics, but no one could come up with a plausible theory regarding his unusual blood or other traits. Garrison's parents did not want the doctors to make a medical experiment of him and refused further study by anyone except Lewis. It became Lewis's primary job: find the underlying cause of the abnormalities with Garrison's immune system, his incredible intelligence and heightened senses, as well as his psychiatric and emotional issues.

Garrison knew in his heart that he would never want to hurt a human being on purpose. He had no interest in hurting anyone. He was bewildered by the fact that animals ran from him or got very nervous when he was in their presence. Other people didn't have this issue with animals. Garrison saw this in himself, and though it did not scare him, it angered him to such a degree that he began to dislike animals.

Lewis had been discussing this with Garrison for many months now. Lewis was becoming very worried about Garrison's attitude toward animals and their reactions to him. On numerous occasions, he would bring a cat or a dog to their sessions for Garrison to pet. The cat or the dog would immediately start to hiss or bark at Garrison and scramble to get away from him. Every animal that was introduced to Garrison reacted the same. The animals sensed something about Garrison, something that scared them so much they had a violent reaction when they were near him.

Garrison also could not understand why he was spending so much time with Lewis and hardly ever seeing his dad. Trevor buried himself not only in his work as a lawyer but in his investments, companies, estate planning, and other areas of the family business. Garrison moved from not understanding his situation and being almost afraid of himself to being an angry child. He wanted to be accepted and loved, but he felt that he was always on display for his talents with the violin or for his intelligence. He felt that he was being used. He still enjoyed Lewis's company, but he was saddened with the long-distance relationship he had with his father. Garrison wanted a closer and more normal relationship with his dad.

The doctor asked to speak with Trevor one day about his relationship with his son. Trevor throughout the years had gone from a very happy, loving person to a reclusive individual. Most of it had to do with work and stress. Trevor had become sharper in his responses to people, and it was starting to have an impact on his family. Lewis wanted to know what was going on inside Trevor's head. They ended up meeting one night at Trevor's to discuss the issue and seek a remedy for these problems. Of course, Trevor did not want to participate; he had better things to do than to talk about the subjects that Lewis wanted to cover. As far as he was concerned, Lewis was there to help Garrison and not to dig into Trevor's brain. As they sat down at the desk facing each other, Trevor leaned back in his chair and stared at the spot where

Garrison had attacked the dog. The doctor asked Trevor what he was thinking when he looked at the spot and how it made him feel when he was in the room.

Trevor looked as if his mind was a thousand miles away. After several moments passed, he said to Lewis, "How can a child of mine be so different? How can I love a child that is so strange, so bewildering? He ate a fucking dog, Lewis. Sometimes when I look at him, I think, what is he going to do next? Am I next? Is my wife next? No animal wants to be near him. I watch these movies about demonic possession and kids doing things to their pets or their parents or to their friends. I mean, he hasn't hurt anyone other than the dog, but it is the fear of what he might be capable of. I sometimes wish he was never born."

The response saddened Lewis, but he understood what Trevor meant. He said, "You don't mean that, Trevor. There is good in the boy."

Trevor moved his eyes away, lowered his head, and stared at the spot on the floor. The doctor returned to the office that had been built for him in the house.

Suddenly, Garrison walked in the door. He asked Lewis, "Does my daddy love me?"

Lewis responded, "Yes, of course he loves you. With all his being. He is worried about you, that is all."

Garrison didn't believe him. As any small child would, he tended to notice even the slightest lie.

Lewis knew that Trevor loved Garrison deep down in his heart but that he was partly afraid, jealous, and even angry with his son. Lewis wondered how someone could explain that to a child, even to a child as brilliant as Garrison.

Then he had an idea that might bring the father and son closer together. It might be somewhat risky, and it would require a lot of work on Trevor's part. Garrison and Trevor's relationship had grown distant, but it was not totally devoid of togetherness. The common denominator was music. Lewis thought that their shared love of music might be the key to bring the two closer. Lewis wanted Trevor and Garrison to sit down together with Adelle and listen to music or listen to Garrison play his violin for them. Lewis thought this might bring the family together and stop the growing divide between them.

Lewis presented the idea to Adelle and Trevor. He even suggested that Garrison play the violin and tell how he felt when he played. They agreed to try his suggestion, although Trevor would have preferred to either finish some work on the computer or make some phone calls on pressing business issues.

Garrison knew even at his young age that his father was disappointed and scared of him. He knew it was because of the dog issue that his father never wanted to spend time with him. Trevor rarely played with him, and he never spoke much to his son. He had sensed that Trevor only agreed to the adoption to calm the waters of his marriage. The lack of attention made Garrison sad, but at the same time it angered him. Garrison always had anger issues to some degree, although most of the time he kept them under control. Much like his aggression fluctuated, so did his anger. The older Garrison got, the more these feelings and urges increased. This confused Garrison and scared him.

Garrison practiced his music exercises with his family for a little over a week. It was a total bore to Trevor, and Garrison sensed it. Adelle loved the time they had together as a family. She loved to hear her son play and loved to listen to music with him.

One rainy night, Adelle, Trevor and Garrison were all together in the great room of the house. Garrison was playing the second movement of Mozart's third violin sonata, a soft and slow section of the piece. He was softly drawing the bow back and forth, playing a very simple section, even adding a few notes of his own as he played.

Garrison looked up from his violin and saw his dad working on his laptop. A sudden and overwhelming feeling of rage rose up within him in a matter of seconds. His dad was not paying attention to his playing. He was not supposed to be on his laptop. His father was supposed to be paying attention as his mother was, sitting on the couch enjoying every note. His dad was not following the rules of the game.

Garrison controlled the rage as he played, and the feeling went away as fast as it came upon him. Minutes later, he felt the same feeling of rage as before. He could not help but stare at his father while he played.

A few minutes of continued playing passed. Trevor looked up and noticed Garrison staring at him. As Garrison continued to play without missing a note of the music that he had memorized by heart, he smirked. The smirk ate at Trevor.

Garrison was on autopilot with his violin. The musical notes came to him so readily that even he knew he was doing something special with the instrument. While he played, Garrison continued to think about his father's dislike and disapproval of him. The anger kept building inside him, and with his father now staring back at him, he was becoming enraged. He knew that his dad was jealous of his ability not only to play the violin but also to play the instrument almost perfectly. He knew that his dad had always wanted to play the violin but did not have the ability. This pleased Garrison and made him feel good about himself as a person. It delighted him to know that he had an ability that his father did not. Garrison knew that this ability really bothered his father. He enjoyed upsetting his father because it was his only way to get back at him for hurting his feelings and making him feel bad about himself throughout this life. Garrison knew that his dad viewed him as the most difficult challenge in his life. His feelings of hurt turned into a feeling of joy. Through the violin, Garrison could hurt his father as he had hurt him.

Garrison continued to stare at his father, taunting him with his small wooden fiddle in the company of tightly wound strings. The longer he played, the more he felt a familiar feeling growing in the pit of his stomach. The faster he played, the more anger built up inside him. The angrier he felt, the harder he played.

It seemed that the harder and more forcefully Garrison drew the bow across the strings, the more it angered Trevor as well. Trevor liked silence, peace, and quiet, and Garrison was the opposite of what Trevor wanted, not only on this night but in his life.

The hard, loud, and fast playing made Adelle nervous as well. She asked Garrison, "Honey, please stop playing your violin so loud."

Garrison did not stop playing. He did not slow down. In fact, he increased his speed to the point that the music sounded as if it came from a CD on fast-forward. Garrison continued to look at Trevor with a deep, piercing stare while maintaining the slight crooked smile on his face. Then Garrison opened his drooling mouth and made a quiet groaning sound. He had a wild look in his eyes that greatly disturbed Trevor. Garrison's eyes watered as his right arm moved the bow riotously across the strings and the left hand moved rapidly up and down the neck of the violin, making an eerie, overly fast version of a Mozart serenade.

Trevor yelled at Garrison, "Stop. Stop the music."

Garrison ignored the order.

Trevor barked it out again. "Garrison! Stop the damn music!"

Adelle inched her way to the edge of the couch, bending her head and shoulders toward Garrison, encouraging him to stop. "Honey, please stop playing the violin! Garrison! Please stop!"

In a rage, Trevor yelled for the third time at Garrison. "If you don't stop, I am going to come over there and make you stop! You don't want me to do that, boy!"

Garrison seemed to be in a trance. He did not stop. He continued to play, groan and drool.

"Damn it, Garrison, you better stop," Trevor said as he jumped up. He walked hard and fast toward Garrison and reached for the violin. "Give that to me," he said. Garrison's natural instincts caused him to move away from his father's outreached hand.

Garrison, who had played without missing a single note the past few minutes, was now drawing out notes haphazardly. He was lost in a world of his own. Through the loud notes, which had now turned into noise, he heard his father's voice. But he also heard more than the voices of his parents. He heard the rustle of his parents' clothing as it slid across the leather furniture. He could distinguish between the voices of his parents, the sounds of their clothes as their bodies moved in them, and the scuff of their shoes on the floor; all the while, he listened to the notes from the violin. His senses were working overtime as never before in his life.

As his father got up from his chair, Garrison heard the leather spring back into its original shape. He heard his father's footsteps, short then quick, and he even heard the friction of his father's clothes as he walked toward him. Then he heard and saw his father's right-hand reach toward him. He stopped playing immediately as he awoke from the trance. Garrison let loose of the bow on the downward draw and allowed the tip to hit the floor. He left his hand on the neck of the violin as he lowered the instrument to his waist. He focused on his father's right hand and arm whipping through the air toward him. Garrison leaped toward his father, dropping his violin on the hardwood floor. He locked his father's arm under his armpit while his left hand took hold of his index finger. Garrison acted as if he was an animal in the woods. He opened his mouth and bit the inner side of his father's wrist. As he bit, he smelled the fear in his father. Trevor's scent went from massive rage to startling fear in a matter of seconds. Garrison could smell the different hormones that his father's body produced. It was the same experience as with the dog. Maybe he was attracted to the adrenaline of his victims, but something was driving Garrison to enjoy these attacks. They gave him a high.

Garrison bit harder into his father's wrist as Trevor attempted to pull away. The boy enjoyed the struggle; his teeth moved across the bone and muscle. Then he noticed the taste of blood in his mouth. Screaming in pain, Trevor fought to release himself as Adelle ran to his side, screaming at Garrison to stop. Garrison increased the pressure as he felt his dad's muscles slide in his mouth and heard the slight tear in the skin. Trevor used his left hand to pull Garrison's mouth off him and then punched Garrison on the side of his head. Garrison fell back, slightly stunned. He attempted to gather himself and wiped his hand across his mouth. As he did, he noticed this father's blood on his hand. He looked at the blood and began to tremble. Trevor fell on the couch while Garrison began to cry uncontrollably.

In shock and dismay, Trevor and Adelle looked at their son sobbing on the floor. Neither went to his aid. Adelle held Trevor's deeply bitten and bloody wrist. Garrison stood while still crying and held his hand up to his mouth again. He cried harder as he withdrew his hand from his mouth and tried to wipe the blood off.

Carolyn had heard the commotion. She suddenly appeared and was shocked by what she saw. She asked if Trevor was okay and told him to remain sitting. She told Adelle to call 9-1-1 while she took care of Garrison. Trevor spoke up immediately and told Adelle not to make the call but to call Lewis instead. Adelle agreed and made the call. Trevor knew he did not want the police involved or the issue made public. The family name and its status had always been of the utmost importance to him.

When Lewis came to the house, he quickly cleaned and wrapped Trevor's injury while listening to Trevor and Adelle's account of what had happened. No major damage was done to Trevor's wrist aside from a very deep bite. Trevor was furious at his son, and Lewis was beside himself in disbelief. Trevor described the entire scene as it had unfolded, leaving out only one small detail: he did not tell Lewis how he had felt toward Garrison prior to the attack. He did not tell him the feelings of fear and anger he had toward his son. He wanted to keep them a secret not only from Lewis but from Adelle. He was embarrassed to admit that Garrison scared him at times.

Lewis wanted to know what had caused Garrison to act in such a way toward his own father. He could understand the fear as well as the anger that Trevor felt toward Garrison in light of the incident. In fact, Lewis was now extremely concerned about the potential for future attacks. He was worried they might become more violent and more frequent.

Just before Lewis had been called, Loren had come up from the basement, where she'd heard the commotion. She quickly got a small bucket and soap to clean up the mess.

Adelle sat on the couch and watched Loren clean the bloodstained rug. She wiped away the tears that were pouring from her

Garrison

eyes. She had never cried this hard in her life. She could not understand how such a cute little boy could commit such a heinous act, not only once but twice in his very young life. Adelle loved Garrison but did not understand what was happening to her little one. She was afraid of him now more than ever. Loren continued to clean the blood from the floor and the rug without saying anything.

Meanwhile, Carolyn managed to calm Garrison down and get him under control. After having some time to process what had happened, Adelle was very stern with him, telling him that what he had done was wrong, that he could not continue to act in such a violent way. Carolyn and Adelle attempted to understand what possessed Garrison to attack his own father, but all Garrison could say was, "I had to do it. My mind told me to do it. I could not help myself."

These words bothered Carolyn to no end, but they bothered Adelle even more. She had dark thoughts of her son as being possessed. After cleaning Garrison up in the shower, Carolyn put him to bed. She could see that Garrison was sorry for what he had done and that something else was making him act that way. She closed the bedroom door and met up with Trevor and Lewis. She reported to them all that Garrison had told her.

Trevor listened to Carolyn, whose opinion he totally respected. His emotions went from a small bit of hatred and lots of anger toward his only child to a sense of bewilderment. He did not understand why his own son would attack him, but he had seen the almost animalistic look on Garrison's face before the attack. He thought Garrison had even enjoyed toying with him before the act. He also felt guilty because he knew he had been egging Garrison along for many minutes leading up to the attack. Trevor wanted to find the underlying cause of the situation and attempt to understand why it had happened, but he feared what he might find out. He used to watch horror movies when he was young, and he thought he might be living one of those movies. He was also struggling with his desire to avoid giving the impression that he might be losing control of the situation. Trevor was not the type of man to explain or dwell on his emotions or feelings. He kept those human traits in the deep recesses of his mind.

The next morning, Lewis came to the house and brought Trevor and Garrison together. Garrison was reluctant at first, but then he burst into tears and begged his father to forgive him. Garrison wanted to be held by his father, and as he ran toward him, Trevor held out his arms as if he wasn't in pain from the bite, and stopped Garrison by gripping his shoulders. He looked into Garrison's eyes and told him to never do that again. Trevor may not have been an emotional man, but many feelings went through his mind during the meeting.

Trevor explained, "With help from the doctor and everyone involved, I will get to the bottom of your behavioral issue." He then slightly shook Garrison by the shoulders and asked his son if he understood. "You need to tell the doctor why you did what you did."

Garrison nodded. "I will, Dad, because I love you." Trevor relaxed his grip, and Garrison wrapped his arms around his dad's legs. Trevor was very uneasy with the display; he pushed Garrison to the side with his good hand after just a few seconds. This broke Garrison's heart.

Over the next few days, Lewis and Trevor spoke to Garrison individually, sometimes for over an hour, to find the underlying cause of his actions. They found that there was no simple explanation for the situation. Even though Garrison's intellect was way beyond his years, he had trouble gathering and explaining his emotions. He said that when he was playing the violin he had been in some sort of deep meditation. These are the words that Garrison used to describe his feelings to Lewis.

Lewis seemed to think playing the violin somehow made Garrison feel that he was in another world. His concentration was so great that he forgot where he was. That emotional state might have triggered the attack or increased the desire for it. Lewis could not explain the dog attack, but the only information that he had from Garrison on that issue related to a feeling that he had to attack the dog, the same feeling he had experienced when attacking his father. Lewis believed that somewhere in Garrison's psyche, his imagination or his thoughts went to a place of anger and he felt compelled to act upon those feelings. It was like a soldier coming back from war and having a nightmare about something terrible that had happened in the field. His mind took him to a place of horror, and he acted on that horror by either waking up screaming or acting out the terror itself. Something was triggering this reaction in Garrison. It seemed that some form of stimulation of anger was the root of these attacks.

Lewis also found out that, before the dog attack, what bothered Garrison the most was the dog's barking, along with the fact that it ran away from him. He became obsessed with the irritation until it turned to anger. Lewis also believed the attack on Garrison's father was directly linked to Trevor's lack of acceptance of his son.

When Trevor heard the news from Lewis, he was disappointed in himself, but he knew down deep in his soul this was the truth. He had never really wanted a child of his own, but he had known that Adelle wanted one. Trevor didn't hate children, but he had never really wanted to be a father. He didn't want to be responsible for nurturing another's life. He was afraid that he might screw up the job. Trevor told Lewis his thoughts in the strictest of confidence.

During one of their sessions, Lewis and Trevor were in the study. After some small talk between the two men, Lewis said, "Trevor, allow me to ask you a very personal question. Are you jealous of Garrison's musical talents? You have shown some jealousy for Garrison's violin talents from day one. I know you don't play a musical instrument, but you love classical music. So, are you jealous of his ability? Garrison seems to think you are when I speak with him on this issue. That is why he might have been taunting you that night, to get your attention, and it was his way to get back at you. What do you think about this?"

Trevor was looking down at the floor where the dog-biting incident had happened. As Lewis waited for an answer, Trevor got up and looked out the window. He stood there for a moment, took a deep breath, and began to speak softly.

"You know, I grew up in this house. Alone. Oh, I had Loren. She took care of me, but I was always alone. I missed my mom and dad.

I will never forget that night when I heard about their accident. From that moment on, I was a different person. I was so young at the time, but even to this day, you could never imagine the pain I felt when I heard the news of their death. I felt so alone. As time went by, I knew that I would never get to know my parents. That was taken from me. It made me sad back then, and it makes me sad even today. I remember one day I was playing with a radio, as most kids do. I moved the dial to all the stations that I could find. I discovered this one channel. It was the classical-music station sponsored by the local university. They were playing this… this music. I couldn't describe it at the time, but the notes were flowing. Page after page of notes seemed to be falling on my ears, as if I was standing under a waterfall of sheet music that kept caressing my head and entertaining my ears. It was beautiful. My foot even kept time with the music. I had never heard such beautiful music before in my life. I finished listening to the music, and after it stopped, the audience on the radio clapped. The guy on the radio said it was a work by Mozart, his Symphony Number Thirty-Nine in E-flat Major. From that moment on, I was hooked. I would stay up late at night and listen to that station. I would listen for my music to come back on. When it did, I would lie down and admire the piece. I did some research on my own, you know. I read everything I could about Mozart. I found out that I loved the violin. I never really took it up because I never had the patience to learn the instrument. I knew that I could never achieve perfection. I guess I was never pushed into playing. I didn't have a mom or a dad to push me or encourage me." Trevor turned around and looked at Lewis sitting there hanging on his every word.

Then Trevor smiled and tears formed in his eyes. "I guess my son is a lot like me. Maybe I am jealous of him—jealous of his ability. I should be happy and proud, but, yes, I am jealous. I am jealous of my own son, and it doesn't stop with his musical talents. Everything comes so easily to him, easier than it did for me. I guess I am jealous of his intellect as well."

Lewis waited a few moments to make sure Trevor was done with his thoughts. Then he spoke, "Maybe it's about time you accept your son and his gifts for what they are: gifts from God."

Trevor gave Lewis an icy stare. "Gifts from God? How can you say that? Gifts from God. I have a son that attacked, killed, and partially ate a fucking dog. And then he tried to do the same with me, his own father for Christ's sake."

Lewis swallowed hard. "I understand what you are saying, but Garrison's problems can be corrected. We will get to the bottom of this issue. But for the time being, you must look at the positives. Garrison is a smart, beautiful, and very gifted child. You are gifted as well, so is your wife, and it is not a surprise that your child should end up being gifted as well. He is a prodigy, not only in music but also in math, reading, basic knowledge. He is a genius. There are worse problems than that to have in this world. We will be okay. You need to calm down and have more patience. We will get through this, Trevor."

Trevor quickly walked away from the conversation and out the door of the study. As he was leaving, he said, "I hope the problem gets fixed before he attacks or kills something else."

CHAPTER 6

Overture

A few weeks passed, and Trevor's injury healed, but he never felt quite right after the bite. He kept this information to himself. The joints in his arms and legs ached. His neck was always stiff, and he had numerous intense headaches that lasted for days on end. His stomach seemed to be constantly upset. After two weeks or so of feeling worse, Trevor finally consulted with Lewis about his symptoms. Lewis was quite curious as to what Trevor was experiencing because the symptoms were similar to what Garrison, Trevor, and Adelle had described when Garrison was younger. Sometimes the boy still experienced them, though without the same regularity of his baby years. This very much intrigued the doctor.

Lewis analyzed a sample of Trevor's blood and noticed that somehow the blood type and even the makeup of the blood had changed. After more tests, he discovered that Trevor's blood had changed in the same manner as Garrison's. This was captivating for the doctor, but it frightened Trevor. In the back of his mind, he thought that maybe Garrison was infected with a disease, possibly a virus that only he carried. Lewis and the many doctors before him could not understand why the makeup of Garrison's blood not only changed but also went through rapid mutations from test to test. This had always bothered and perplexed Lewis.

Trevor had always had concerns about the fact that Garrison had been found in the woods, and he thought about it even more in light of Garrison's blood condition and the fact that he had never been sick, unlike most children. This had been the underlying reason for Trevor hiring a private doctor. What was the reason for or the cause of these oddities? Even after all these years, many of Garrison's past doctors had attempted to contact the Seawick family to get permission to perform more tests on the young boy. Trevor never allowed or even entertained the thought of having more tests run because he did not want information about his son to get out in the public eye. It would hurt his profession and even his standing in local society. Trevor, throughout the years, had grown very fond of being part of the social elite. He did not want to be shunned by his friends or his social groups. Trevor liked his social life, and his social life was good for his business.

Lewis and Trevor had always been concerned about Garrison, but the fact that he never got sick or showed even the slightest signs of a cold mystified them. He was developing mentally at an astonishing pace. His mind was more advanced than most adults', and Carolyn was having problems keeping Garrison's interest alive and well. Garrison started to read more books in rapid progression until he was teaching himself more than Carolyn was teaching him. Garrison's educational interest was widening, and he started to get more interested in the fields of chemistry and biology.

Garrison's violin playing was now on par with that of most fifteen-to-twenty-year professionals. Numerous violinists from the Louisville Orchestra, most of them friends of Trevor's, had come to the house many times to watch and listen to the young marvel. Many of them, including his teacher, Alex, wanted Garrison to go on tour, but Trevor did not want his son paraded out like some freak at the circus. Many times, Garrison would play with as many as five or seven violinists at the house. Sometimes other members of the Louisville Orchestra would come to join in and play some of Mozart's serenades and divertimenti. Even Adelle would join in at times when they needed a cello player. Garrison loved playing for his mom, but he was more excited to have the opportunity to play along with her.

Trevor, down deep, was very proud of his son, but he remained jealous as well. This bothered him so much that at times he would leave the room when they started to play. Trevor even attempted to pick up the violin, but he was terrible. He didn't understand the notes, and his fingers would always land on the incorrect string. He also didn't have the time that it would take for him to learn to play the violin at a high level. If Trevor could not perfect something, he wouldn't attempt to tackle the task. He had been like that all his life. The two things he was good at were business and the law. Trevor admired people who could play sports or musical instruments, though. He was very proud of Garrison. He would brag about his son repeatedly to all his friends, and he wished that he had a tenth of his son's talents. Nevertheless, he did not. Many times, Trevor even blamed God for his misfortune.

Trevor despised the way he felt toward his adopted son, but deep down, he never really considered Garrison his son, precisely because the boy was adopted. He and Adelle had never told Garrison that he was adopted. They were waiting until he got older, hoping that he would accept it. Even with all the events that had taken place over the past year, along with his rapid development, the topic never came up in any of their conversations.

Lewis had developed a very good relationship with Garrison, so Garrison felt that he could trust the doctor. He felt that Lewis cared and somewhat understood what he was going through. He viewed Lewis as a friend, an adult who was there to help guide him through a difficult part of his life.

Lewis wanted to understand what had gone through Garrison's mind during the two attacks. He found his patient to be an interesting yet disturbing challenge. Why would a boy do such a thing, not only once but twice? To attack not only an animal but his father? That was what intrigued Lewis the most, even more than the metabolic makeup of Garrison's and now his father's blood. Quite often, Lewis took time out of his day to play with Garrison in an effort to discover what made him tick.

Garrison, who did not have many friends or kids to play with, enjoyed Lewis as a friend. He had Loren, but she was busy managing the grounds and the estate, as well as some of the finances, for Trevor.

Carolyn, on the other hand, was more of a teacher than a playmate to Garrison. Garrison loved her, but she could not entertain him mentally as she had in the beginning.

Lewis thought that if he could gain Garrison's trust, he would share more with him, and maybe something would trigger a solution to the underlying cause for the attacks. Lewis was becoming obsessed with the challenge. He couldn't get over the fact that throughout Garrison's six-plus years, he had never been sick. Garrison still had pain in his joints and sometimes he got sick to his stomach, but overall, he was better than he had ever been.

Meanwhile, Trevor's relationship with Garrison was improving. Trevor was growing more confident that the biting episode had been a one-time thing. He started to come to grips with the idea that Garrison was a child prodigy with the violin and as a student. Trevor learned to be proud, not jealous, of his adopted son and to thank God that he was the way he was. Trevor would hear from his business associates about how their kids struggled in school or with a musical instrument or with sports. Trevor never experienced these problems with Garrison. In fact, Trevor was quite excited about the prospect of Garrison someday trying out for sports, especially baseball. With the boy's hand-eye coordination, he could be a great hitter. That was down the road; for the here and now, Trevor attempted to appreciate his son more. Trevor was learning to have more patience with him, and Garrison recognized the efforts of his father. Garrison loved to play with his toy cars on the floor. He also liked to play Army men and have mock battles. Although this was not Trevor's favorite thing, he did find some pleasure in engaging with Garrison this way. As time passed, Garrison had numerous friends over to the house, and no problems occurred.

Trevor and Adelle's marriage was also improving. Trevor seemed to be more attentive and relaxed at times. This pleased Adelle on many levels. She knew that her husband was trying to change, attempting to be a better father and husband.

Trevor's eyesight had been getting worse through the years prior to the bite. He was becoming more farsighted. This normally happened to men and women when they approached the age of forty. Trevor had prescription bifocals that he wore when he was working on the computer or reading. Usually, they hung around his neck so he wouldn't lose them. After the bite, however, he started to have trouble seeing through his bifocals—so much so that he noticed himself taking the bifocals off his nose to read up close. His eyes were getting better. He kept this from Lewis because he didn't want another problem to worry about; he also didn't want Lewis to put more worries in his head with his medical jargon, which sometimes irritated Trevor to no end.

Trevor also noticed that he had more energy and a higher sex drive. Of course, this pleasantly surprised Adelle, and the two spent many nights in bed engaged in intense lovemaking. Trevor noticed another thing: he was getting stronger and a little bigger everywhere on his body. One day, he noticed a slight improvement in his hearing. By this point, he no longer wore his glasses and his taste buds seemed to be changing as well. He could taste all the different flavors or spices in anything that he put in his mouth.

Life was getting better for the Seawick family. Garrison had noticed the increased attention and care from his father. This pleased the boy, and for Trevor this was the first time in his life that he was enjoying being a father.

One early morning Adelle awoke, rushed out of bed, and ran to the bathroom. She vomited in the toilet and afterward felt terrible. She'd had an upset stomach the past few days and thought it was some sort of stomach flu. After a few more days of feeling poorly, she consulted with Lewis as to what might be the problem. Lewis asked her if there was a possibility of her being pregnant. Adelle told him the history, that she and Trevor could not bear children and that both had problems. Most of the problem arose from Trevor's low sperm count and other hereditary issues. With some hesitation, Adelle agreed to a simple blood test, but she wanted to keep this from Trevor for the time being. She didn't want to worry or bother him over a false alarm. Adelle and Trevor had tried to have kids for years and had consulted with numerous doctors on the issue, including the best fertility doctors in the

States. Adelle knew the possibility was very low that this issue would be pregnancy-related.

Lewis had the blood test run and analyzed. After a few hours, he paid Adelle a personal visit.

As soon as the doorbell rang, Adelle's heart rate increased significantly. She answered the door and let Lewis in. She quickly asked, "So, am I pregnant?"

Lewis smiled and reached out with both arms. He placed them on her shoulders and said, "The test came back positive. You are pregnant."

Adelle was shocked. At first, she wanted to cry because at this time in her life she didn't want to have a baby. In the beginning, she had wanted a child, but Garrison's issues had sucked the life out of both Adelle and Trevor. The problems with Garrison also had taken a toll on their marriage. In the beginning, when Garrison first became a part of their lives, even up to and through the biting incident, Trevor had been more withdrawn and angrier, whereas Adelle had been more worried and stressed out. Now the relationship between all three of them had improved to the point of being wonderful over the previous few months. Adelle did not want to upset the balance between them.

She was confused, but she listened to Lewis's thoughts on the issue. He thought that maybe a newborn child would help bring them even closer and might help Garrison and his emotional state. Adelle had other thoughts. She was concerned that Garrison, God forbid, might attack the baby some day or, perish the thought, even murder the baby. That was her immediate reaction to the news of a newborn coming into their lives. First, it had been her best friend's dog and then her husband. Who was next?

Later, that day, Adelle met Lewis for the second time to discuss her worries. Lewis laughed and said that was ridiculous thinking on her part.

"Garrison is a good boy. He is not evil. He was confused, Adelle. Look, most kids bite at some point in their lives, and Garrison has taken it to another level, but you cannot go through life worried about what might or might not happen."

Adelle started to cry. "You know I love Garrison with all of my heart and soul. I would do anything for him, but he scares me at times. He has done nothing to me. In fact, he has been a perfect little boy with me. But his anger with his father scares me."

Lewis attempted to console her. "Adelle, Garrison and Trevor have been getting along better now than ever before. A newborn will not affect Trevor's relationship with Garrison."

Adelle looked at him and said, "I'm not worried about their relationship as much as I am worried about my baby's well-being."

A few days passed, and Adelle got more anxious. She had been keeping her secret from Trevor for going on a week.

Trevor knew something was happening with Adelle. He knew something was wrong and wanted to confront her over dinner. Later that night when they were having dinner, Trevor asked what was bothering her and whether he could help in any way. Adelle was very tense. She finally broke down crying at the dinner table. Trevor got up and raced to her side, bent down, and held her. He asked her over and over what was wrong.

Adelle broke the news to him. "Honey, I'm pregnant."

Trevor didn't respond. He relaxed his hold on his wife. Adelle sat there with her eyes swimming in tears, waiting for a response.

She repeated, "I am pregnant, Trevor. We are going to have a baby." Trevor looked shocked. His shoulders slouched as he looked down and turned away. He placed his hands on the sides of his head with the most worried look on his face. He couldn't believe the news that was coming out of his wife's mouth. Adelle spoke again. "Trevor, we are going to have a baby." He finally seemed to grasp the news, and Adelle continued. "I had Lewis run a blood test, and the test came back positive. I was going to tell you sooner, but I didn't know how to break the news to you. I mean, you and Garrison really have been doing so well these past few months. I didn't know how you were going to handle the news. I have wanted a baby for so long. I gave up on the idea of bearing a child when we were trying to conceive. Never in a million years did I expect this to happen. A part of me is overjoyed, but another part is worried to death."

Trevor slowly stood up, took hold of his wife's hands, looked into her shaken eyes, and listened as Adelle continued her concerns. "I know you are going to think less of me, but I have this horrible fear, and I don't think Garrison would do this, but I fear that he might hurt the baby one day. I don't even want to think about it, but I cannot stop. I just keep thinking about what he might end up doing. Maybe nothing will happen. I don't know. I am so confused." Adelle got up fast and hugged her shocked husband.

Trevor's mind was racing. He quickly thought that this was not a good time for a pregnancy. They didn't need it at this point in their lives. Then he thought back on the years they had spent attempting to get pregnant. He thought of the long nights of sadness that they had felt while lying two feet apart from each other in bed, knowing they would never bear a child together. Trevor knew that Adelle wanted to have a child of her own, and he knew how important this was to her. For him it was not as important, but he loved his wife and wanted her to be happy. He then thought about Garrison, and he, like his wife, was afraid that the boy might end up hurting their newborn baby. But Garrison had been doing well, and Trevor was closer to his son now than ever before. He thought that maybe the two biting incidents had been just that: incidents.

A few moments passed before Trevor finally gathered his thoughts and looked his wife in her eyes. He said, "Okay, I don't know what is going to happen or even how this has happened, but what is done is done. We are going to be all right. We will work through this. In fact, maybe this is what we need. Garrison has been a perfect little boy since the biting incident. Like you said, we are closer today than ever before. I just hope Garrison takes the news well. I just don't understand how you got pregnant. We saw the best doctors around, and all of them said we could never have children, mostly because of me."

Trevor gently grasped Adelle's face with his hands and kissed her. He then slowly separated himself from his wife and was walking back to his chair to finish his supper when he noticed Garrison staring at him. Trevor stopped dead in his steps.

Garrison asked, "Daddy, are we getting a new baby?"

Trevor swallowed hard and looked right into Garrison's excited eyes. "Yes, Garrison, your mom is pregnant, and we are going to have a new baby join our family."

Garrison jumped around, ran past Trevor, and raced toward his mom. He hugged her legs, and as Adelle bent down to hug her son, he wrapped his arms around her neck and hugged her harder. "Don't worry, Mommy. I will not hurt my brother. I have always wanted a brother. Now I will have someone to play with."

Adelle started to cry, and as she stroked Garrison's smooth blond hair, she said, "Now, Garrison, I know you wouldn't hurt the baby, but you know the baby might be a little girl."

Garrison popped his head up and said, "Oh, I like little girls. I can protect her because I am strong, and I can teach her to be strong."

Trevor and Adelle laughed as if all the stress of the situation had been relieved. Both were still concerned, but seeing Garrison's immediate excitement made them feel better about the situation. They were leery and nervous, but they thought it was very sweet that Garrison was happy about the news.

Meanwhile, Trevor was still having issues, and his concern was growing. His pains were continuing and in fact had been more intense over the past few days. They came with more regularity, and he was experiencing additional pains in his joints, arms, legs, shoulders, and back. His neck was stiff and sore to the point where he could hardly move his neck from side to side. Day by day, the soreness had increased.

Trevor still had recurring pains in his joints, and his stomach had been very upset. He had lost nearly twenty pounds. All of this frightened him so much that he finally told Lewis his theory.

"You know, Lewis, I have not told you this before. I kept it from you but feel I must expose my secret. Ever since the bite, I've had these incredible pains all throughout my body. At first, they would come and go. When the pains left me, I felt great. Then over the past few weeks, my joints have been aching. So much so, I sometimes cannot stand the pain. When I think I cannot stand it any longer, it goes away, disappears in a matter of seconds. Now I have made my wife pregnant. What the hell is going on with me, Lewis? I mean, even my eyesight has improved. I don't need to wear my bifocals anymore, and I can see things at a distance that I could not have before the bite. I feel stronger, I feel better, and I can actually hear things that I could not hear before. What did Garrison do to me?"

Lewis just stood there and said, "I don't know, Trevor. I just don't know. I have never seen anything like this before in my life. I beg you to allow me to bring in more doctors on these cases because I don't know the answers."

"No! No more doctors. I have my business, my reputation, my social standing to think about, and I do not want people to know what happened here. I don't want my family to be looked upon as outcasts, and I certainly don't want to be part of some medical experiment." With that said, Trevor left the room.

Lewis continued to monitor Trevor's situation closely. After running a few tests, he could not come up with an answer as to the cause of the pains. Lewis even thought that it might be a mental problem, but Trevor quickly dismissed that theory. He still believed that the pains had something to do with the bite because he was now having the same pains that Garrison was. This scared Trevor. His pains, like Garrison's, would go as fast as they came.

Again, the doctor noticed that the blood count and type changed rapidly. The blood under the microscope changed almost by the minute. This was beyond Lewis's comprehension. He wanted to bring another doctor in on the case, but Trevor refused in a very violent manner. Trevor also brought up the pregnancy and questioned Lewis as to how he and Adelle had gotten pregnant. Lewis had Trevor's sperm tested and discovered that it was perfect. All the irregularities that Trevor had previously experienced with his sperm had cleared up. The sperm count, the motility, the movement, and the shape of the sperm had corrected. Trevor was now fully capable of fathering a child. Trevor's attitude and demeanor had changed gradually over the past couple of months, in both good and bad ways. He seemed to be annoyed by little things that did not bother him before. He started to notice sounds that he hadn't noticed in the past, and other sounds that were clearer to his ear than ever before. His taste buds began to come alive as he ate, and he noticed a massive change in how his normal, everyday food tasted.

Trevor knew that all of this was because of the bite from his son. He knew that Garrison was a very special little boy. Trevor's feelings and emotions toward Garrison had swung from love to almost fear or even dislike, and now to understanding. Trevor now believed that he could relate to his son. He found this new feeling to be a peaceful retreat of reflection. For some reason, Trevor knew this newly discovered knowledge was now something he had in common with his son.

Garrison was aware that something was different about his father, but he did not care, nor did he even worry about the issue. Finally, Garrison felt there was someone who understood what he was going through. Maybe this was why their relationship had been improving so rapidly over the past couple of months.

They were bonding at a spiritual level, but at the end of the day, Trevor had many worries.

CHAPTER 7

Neurotic

Adelle was having a hard time with her pregnancy. She was violently sick almost every day. She knew other women who had been sick during pregnancy, still, she thought she was having a harder time than they had. She also knew that something was wrong with her husband and that he was going through some kind of issue she could not help him solve. She repeatedly attempted to help him by getting him to open up to her. But Trevor loved his wife. He did not want to bother her during this time. Yet his problems made it impossible for Adelle to concentrate totally on her own condition.

With all the issues now surrounding the family, Trevor asked Lewis to be the Seawick family's full-time family doctor. Trevor paid him handsomely so he would accept his new job with the Seawicks. Lewis would administrate everything medical per Trevor's instructions, even the ultrasound tests. Trevor needed to have someone whom he could trust. He needed someone to help the family out.

He especially needed to be able to confide in a person he trusted regarding his own personal issues. Trevor's increasing sensory abilities made him more paranoid than ever before. He felt as if he was losing control of his body. He didn't understand the changes that were happening to him. Trevor had always loved to be in control of everything. It was in his nature. He had to be controlling when he lost his parents at such a young age. He was also a secretive person who valued his privacy. He didn't like to flaunt his wealth or his high-class acquaintances. Maybe that was a part of his heritage because his parents had never liked to flaunt their wealth or put their name out in the press when they were alive.

Trevor decided that he didn't want everyone to know about Adelle's pregnancy, at least for a while. This demand enraged Adelle. Part of the joy of being pregnant is telling all your friends so they could join in the excitement. Yet after repeated heartfelt attempts, Trevor ended up convincing Adelle that it was not a good idea. Trevor didn't want to tempt fate. With all the issues they had getting pregnant, there was no way to know what might happen, he argued.

Adelle reluctantly agreed that keeping the baby a secret for a little while longer was not a bad idea, but she was not happy with the deal, and the idea made her angry and disappointed. She wanted all her friends to know that what had seemed to be an impossible event a couple of years ago was now a reality. She had a feeling that Trevor was not enjoying the moment and that he was approaching the pregnancy as he did his business activities, with a cold and calculated heart. Adelle wanted Trevor to be warmer and more caring and to open up more not only to her but also to their situation.

While the baby was growing inside the womb, Lewis noticed something different about it. He was a little concerned and had another ultrasound administrated on Adelle. After seeing what was going on inside her, Lewis continued to use the ultrasound machine every few days for a couple of weeks. Adelle repeatedly asked why she was undergoing so many tests. She was starting to get very worried about her baby, wondering if something was wrong. Lewis had a difficult time keeping his concerns from Adelle and Trevor, but he stopped the early tests to ease her fears. He wanted to keep Adelle as calm as possible and believed that would be in everyone's best interest.

Adelle soon began complaining of sharp pains that were increasing in regularity and scope. When Adelle was almost a couple of months into her pregnancy, Lewis wanted to take her to the hospital, but Trevor vehemently denied his repeated requests. The baby was growing at an amazing rate. Lewis had seen nothing like it in his career

Garrison

as a doctor and had never read anything like it in any of the medical journals.

Adelle was getting very upset with Trevor, and she asked him why he didn't want to take her to the hospital. Trevor was becoming more paranoid about the situation at hand, and he told Lewis to find out what was causing Adelle's pain. For that reason, Lewis performed another ultrasound on Adelle. He was shocked by what he saw. The baby was horribly misshapen. It moved around in the womb rapidly, racing from side to side.

Adelle knew something was wrong as soon as she saw Lewis's face. She insisted that he tell her what was wrong with the ultrasound. She was horrified when he broke the news. Lewis showed her the ultrasound, and Adelle didn't know what to do or where to turn. When Lewis told Trevor about the discovery, Trevor was distressed and wondered if this had something to do with Garrison's bite. Maybe whatever had affected him had somehow affected the baby as well. Maybe the improved condition of his sperm had somehow affected the makeup of the baby. Trevor was deeply worried and remorseful. He knew that he was to blame for this. Trevor asked Lewis about his theory, but Lewis was at a loss for words. The situation was out of the ordinary, something that Lewis had never seen before. He was attempting to research the issue with Garrison, but nothing had turned up. He had no case study to follow or to draw any conclusion from.

Meanwhile, Trevor's own problems were only beginning. Intense pain continued throughout his joints. One day his joints would be so sore that he could not move them, and the next day he felt fine. The most noticeable problem for Trevor was accelerated hair growth on his body. He had gotten hairier, not only on the arms and legs but on the chest, back, and face. He ended up shaving more throughout the day, and he even started to trim the new growth with scissors or the electric trimmer. He was embarrassed of his looks and worried about what others thought, especially his wife.

Trevor was quite worried, not only about himself but also about his wife and unborn child. He didn't know what was happening to him, and he didn't want to give whatever he had to them. Adelle was aware of the increased hair growth, and she even confronted him over it. Trevor told her that he was concerned about his condition but that he didn't want her to worry about him. He also told her that Lewis knew about it but that he was dumbfounded as to the cause. Adelle and Trevor agreed that all of this was the product of Garrison's bite, which made them more worried over what it might have done to the unborn baby and what else it was doing to Trevor.

Neither held this against Garrison, however, because now they felt that it was not his fault. They believed that he was carrying some kind of disease or that something in his chemical makeup caused these issues.

Trevor and Adelle were both physically and mentally exhausted by everything they had gone through over the past months. They were not getting any answers to their problems. Lewis was working as hard as he could on the subjects, but he was dealing with something beyond his comprehension. Trevor and Adelle felt that maybe it was time for Lewis to make some calls to other doctors while remaining discreet about the situation.

Lewis called some trusted friends. He didn't go into vast detail, and he spoke in general terms of their condition. The doctors all told him that they needed to do some research on the issues and that they would get back with him. On the surface, none of his friends had a clue as to what was happening with the three main subjects.

A week went by. Adelle tried to calm herself not only about her baby but about her husband as well. She concluded that she wanted the baby. Lewis wanted to perform an abortion, but Adelle was totally opposed. When she informed him of the decision, he was beside himself. He reminded her that the unborn child was grossly disfigured and might not even live through the pregnancy. Nevertheless, Adelle wanted to carry the baby to full term. She was Catholic and believed that any form of life, no matter how disfigured, should be allowed to live. For Adelle, abortion was murder and thus not an option for her. Lewis believed having the baby would affect Adelle and the family in a negative way. In his mind, he was offering the best piece of advice that he could give.

Trevor was not in favor of his wife's decision whatsoever, although he understood and even appreciated her line of thinking. He wanted the abortion, but on the other hand, he felt the same way that Adelle did about killing an unborn child. They agreed that neither one of them could take part in killing a living human being. Lewis reluctantly agreed, but he made it known that he was against their decision.

Trevor wanted the birth of his son to take place at the estate. He didn't want this to be in the public eye, especially now that they knew the baby was extremely disfigured. Adelle was concerned about having the baby at the house, especially in the basement area where Trevor and Lewis talked about having the birth take place. Adelle had never liked basements to begin with, but she understood that all the equipment was down there. So, Lewis made the necessary preparations to have the delivery at the estate. Trevor said he would provide any materials that Lewis needed.

Trevor insisted Lewis live on the grounds of the estate. Lewis was happy with the home he already had, but when someone of Trevor's stature tells someone to do something, that person just does it. Lewis kept his home but moved his essentials into his new residence. Trevor offered Lewis to stay in one of the bedrooms upstairs. This was an act not to be looked upon lightly. Trevor valued his privacy. For him to offer this to anyone, it had to be an individual whom he trusted with his life. Lewis didn't want to move in, but he understood why Trevor wanted it and thought it was a good idea, at least in the beginning. Against his better judgement, he took one of the bedrooms upstairs as his sleeping quarters. Trevor let him have half of the basement to himself as his own personal living quarters. He had a kitchen, his lab, and a living room of sorts that he could relax in when he wanted.

Adelle was fine with Lewis living on the grounds, but it did concern her a little because she knew how Trevor had been in the past. For him to let Lewis live on the grounds and have full access to the house, she knew that something must be very wrong with Trevor. She feared that they were keeping something from her. Adelle confronted Trevor again and asked him if he was dying, if he was sick, or if he knew something and was not telling her. Trevor told Adelle that he thought it would be prudent to have Lewis in the house, especially with her being pregnant and with the baby being abnormal. He thought they would need him with so much going on with the family.

Lewis knew that Trevor was worried about his condition, and he thought Trevor needed someone to confide in more than anything. He knew Trevor was alone in his own personal battle with his body. It was a lot for one man to handle by himself. Therefore, in a matter of a few days, Lewis moved some of his belongings into the house and tried to make himself at home.

Lewis worked longer hours after he moved in. It was common for him to stay up into the middle of the night. He read anything he could find that would give him clues about how to help Trevor. Lewis was not only preparing for the arrival of the baby but also attempting to find out more about Garrison's birth parents. He began his search by contacting Sonja, Adelle's cousin in Germany. Sonja could provide only the basic facts about the baby's location and condition at the time they found him.

Lewis worked long hours with Sonja. They both made countless calls to many of the locals and the local authorities to see if anything new had ever come up in their investigation into Garrison's parents. It was so strange, as if Garrison had been placed in the woods magically, with no clues as to who had placed him there or why. Many of the locals had forgotten the story or some of the details about what had happened the day Garrison was found or the events that transpired afterward, up to and including the adoption proceedings.

What puzzled Lewis more than anything was the fact that Garrison had been found in the woods. *Why the woods?* he asked himself. *Why not at the doorstep of an adoption house? Why not on the front porch of some local farmer? Why in the woods near a small lake?* These questions were driving him mad.

Lewis was obsessed with the idea that Garrison's original parents were the key to finding some answers to questions not only about Garrison's strange biological makeup but also about Trevor's and the baby's problems. He hoped he could discover information that might provide insight into Garrison's behavior during the two attacks. He attempted to contact some of the local German people by phone, but the broken English through the thick German accents made communication very difficult. It was almost impossible for Lewis to gather any technical information from them.

In all this confusion, Garrison was very excited about the new arrival. His behavior and demeanor had been improving a great deal. He had been playing with Loren and Carolyn each day, and his schooling had been going according to schedule. Garrison had had no recent behavioral issues, and he had been very supportive of his mom and dad during this very difficult time by not being an issue for them. Garrison had also been growing physically at a fast rate, but with all the problems with the baby and Trevor, this fact had gone unnoticed to most in the house. Garrison had been a little unhappy because he had not played with someone his age in a while. He really missed going to school and socializing with kids either his own age or closer to it. Garrison did learn to overcome his loneliness by reading books and doing lots of research on subjects that he didn't understand very well. He was at a point where he was now teaching himself on a full-time basis.

During everything that was transpiring, Trevor started to notice more changes in his body. After every painful attack, his arms, legs, or torso would grow a little. Trevor was obviously very concerned, but he was beginning to get used to the idea that whatever was wrong with him was beyond his control. Trevor began to think that, whatever his son's illness was, it had not killed him yet and that maybe he would be spared. In fact, aside from the painful moments in his joints, he felt better than he had in years.

One person who was not feeling better about Trevor's situation was Adelle. Her nerves were almost shot with the pregnancy, and now to see her husband physically changing before her very eyes unnerved her. It was not something that she had bargained for when she first met him that sunny day at Harvard. Just the thought of watching his baby change in the ultrasounds and just imagining its development repulsed her to no end. She could not have imagined this would ever happen to her. She felt sick to her stomach every time Trevor touched her or looked at her. Adelle felt so alone in her newly found life. She felt as if she were a part of something unholy, and she was beginning to hate her life. The only rock in her life was Garrison, and even he was not a normal boy. She was surrounded by a man, a boy, and a baby who were all very unusual. This association with such an array of abnormality was driving her slowly insane. She never dreamt that she would be in this type of position in her life. Like any new mother or parent, the very thought of not having that perfect child was a difficult moment to accept.

Meanwhile, Trevor stopped showing up at the Louisville Orchestra, and he stopped showing up for work. Trevor had ended up quitting his job at the law firm at the start of his physical change, and, in fact, he had ended up purchasing the firm. He loved the law, and he wanted to be a silent partner in the firm. As for as his private companies, he quit seeing any of his managers in person. He decided to run his businesses from home by phone or electronic correspondence.

Over the months, Trevor's joint pain had been increasing, and in a span of about two weeks, he underwent the most pain he had encountered in his life. Adelle had noticed the behavior change as well as the obvious physical changes from the beginning, but now Trevor's body was changing more rapidly. None of his clothes fit him any longer. Adelle was frightened to death about what was happening to her husband. She thought of herself as being in some kind of horror movie, with her son grossly disfigured and now her husband's body changing physically day by day. It made any issues with Garrison seem mild in comparison. Lewis was working overtime, trying to figure out what was going on with the unborn monster, with Garrison, and now with Trevor. All three had different problems, and the research on Garrison had been put on hold.

Trevor's aches had changed his body to the point where he couldn't be seen in public. He had grown a solid four inches in height and now stood six feet six inches tall. He had added fifty pounds of weight, most of it muscle. He had never felt or been this strong before in his life. He was becoming quite good at controlling all his senses. His vision kept improving. He was at a point where images were so crystal clear that every detail of the objects were moving in slow motion. He began to see at night almost as well as he could during the day. His hand-eye coordination had reached a level that he had never experienced before. He would walk around the grounds and pick up a rock or an acorn and throw it at a tree, a weed, or a bush. He would hit what he was aiming at with almost 100 percent accuracy. His hands and fingers were growing as well. His fingers had grown at least an inch and a half in length, and his palms had grown an inch across in width. His head grew, and his legs and arms were sprouting out and becoming disproportionate to the rest of his body.

Trevor's relationship with Adelle was changing as well. Adelle saw the changes in Trevor before Trevor saw them in himself. They scared her. What scared her even more was the lack of care Trevor showed for his condition. For him, it was almost a game in some ways. This scared her to tears at night. She constantly questioned Trevor about his weight gain and his increased height. In fact, she moved out of their bedroom and took a room down the hall.

Trevor began to think of his condition as a hobby. He wanted to see how strong or how big he could get. He was feeling more alive than at any time in his life, and the pains in his joints were lessening by the day. He loved his new and improved hand-eye coordination. He loved the way he felt inside his body. His mind was clearer than ever before, and he seemed to be able to understand new information, new ideas, complicated concepts, as if he was uncapping his mental limitations. Mentally, he never had been as sharp as he was now. He could memorize anything and everything and recall it verbatim days or weeks later.

His relationship with Garrison was developing into a more typical father-and-son relationship. Adelle was happy about this, but she was feeling more left out by the bond they were establishing. She was the outsider now in what she saw as a very twisted relationship.

One day, Adelle confronted Lewis and Trevor. "I want to know what is going on with you. Your body, looks and attitude are all changing. What is happening to you?"

"I honestly don't know. I don't understand it myself. I must admit, I am scared of what is happening to me. My joints hurt from time to time and then suddenly they feel fine. When I am not in pain, I have never felt better in my life, Adelle. I have so much energy. I never get tired. I feel as if I can go all day without stopping. Then I started noticing the improvement of my eyesight. I can read labels on soup cans from across the room. My hand-eye coordination has been out of this world. I have never felt this strong. I am working out with weights that I have never been able to use before in my life."

"Stop it, Trevor. Just stop it."

"What's wrong?"

"You're scaring me."

"You know, this all started when he bit me."

Adelle didn't want to hear anymore. "That's enough. Don't go blaming Garrison for your messed up physiological problems."

"You don't understand. At first, yes, I blamed him and, in the beginning, I was very concerned, but since I have been getting used to these changes I am not as worried. I feel great most of the time. Better than I have felt in my life."

Adelle was very worried and wanted to seek out another doctor for more opinions. "You need to seek medical attention. See another medical doctor or at least see a psychiatrist."

"I don't need to advertise my condition to the public, to any other doctor or some nut job psychiatrist."

Lewis rushed into the conversation and said, "I agree with Trevor. We don't need this to go public.

Adelle left the two men, shaking her head in disbelief. She was worried not only for her husband but for herself. She began to wonder if she was safe in her own house with him.

Trevor didn't want this news to get out in the public or to have more people involved. He wanted to understand what he was dealing with first, but mostly he didn't want the issue in the public eye or ear. Trevor didn't want anything to affect the Seawicks' business interests. He didn't want any scandal to hit the press and thus potentially cause the business to lose money. He also didn't want a slew of doctors probing and sticking him with needles, asking questions, doing tests. Trevor made this very clear to both Adelle and Lewis.

Adelle was at her wit's end. She was scared and didn't know where to turn. She wasn't getting the answers to her questions, and this elevated her frustration levels. Lewis gave her some medication to help with her nerves.

As the weeks passed, Trevor's hair grew at a faster rate. His fingers grew an additional inch, his palm size increased further, and his feet increased in both width and length. Many days he was bedridden with pain. Every joint, muscle, and bone hurt him. He wanted to pause this transformation, but there was no stopping the mutation. The bones would grow faster than the tissue surrounding them. His skin and the muscles felt as if they were going to split or tear apart. Once his legs, arms, and feet stopped growing, the pain would subside.

Trevor noticed that even his eyes were getting larger, his ears and nose were getting pointier. His voice changed somewhat, and his tongue grew an inch longer. Some of his teeth even fell out. In less than a week, longer and sharper teeth replaced them. The new teeth, two on the top and two on the bottom, were actually fangs, thicker than the other permanent teeth. When the new teeth came in, they pushed the others closer together and made many of the old teeth crooked. Of course, this concerned Trevor privately, but he kept that secret to himself. He didn't want to upset his wife even more than she was already. He did everything in his power to keep his mouth closed and his teeth hidden.

Adelle was so heavily medicated that, even though she was very upset and concerned about what was happening to her husband, at times she felt as if she were living a nightmare. Many nights she would wake up and think all the events from the past six months, and even the past six years had been just a dream. Then reality would set in and she would panic. Over the weeks and months, Adelle began to accept her new life, but she was in a constant struggle with her role. She started to drink at night and then in the morning, even though she knew she shouldn't because of her pregnancy. The drinking didn't mix well with the medication she was on, and her personality changed for the worst. Trevor attempted to keep her away from the alcohol, but Adelle always had some stashed away somewhere.

The only rock in her life was Garrison. She loved him so much. For so many years, she had wanted a child of her own, and when Garrison came into her life, she had been overjoyed. Yes, Garrison had some issues with biting the dog and her husband, but otherwise he was a perfect little boy. He was smart, handsome, and good. He was respectful, brilliant with the violin, and she thought someday he would really be a special person who might help change the world with his intelligence. Adelle always had high hopes for her adopted son.

Garrison loved his mom as well, but Carolyn was a bigger part of his life than Adelle. This was not lost on Adelle. She knew that Garrison was closer to Carolyn. The problem was that she could do nothing about it. She needed to be more involved with Garrison's life. She knew that part of the decision to hire Carolyn years ago had been to help take care of Garrison and to free up more time for Adelle, so she felt a lot of guilt when she thought of Carolyn being more of a mother figure than she was. It hurt her deeply, and she knew it was her own fault. There was nothing she could do about the past, but she wanted to change the future.

Lewis, meanwhile, was afraid of Trevor and didn't know what he had gotten himself into, but he continued with his work. He was in so deep that he couldn't go to any of the authorities, such as the police or some of his fellow doctors. How could he explain this to anyone?

Lewis thought that even if he attempted to notify anyone aside from the people living in the house, Trevor would kill him and do it in a horrible and painful way. He was in way over his head, dealing with something he knew nothing about. He had a little boy whose intelligence was almost surpassing his own. He was medicating an unstable patient to keep her calm. And the half man, half monster roaming the house, who was paying him handsomely, was transforming from a normal man into a thing that he had never imagined he would see, much less meet, in his life. Some days were better than others and in a twisted way, Lewis enjoyed some of the challenges that were ahead of him. He worked feverishly every day and read many journals to attempt to get to the bottom of what was happening to his patients. Over the years, he had grown close to each one of the Seawicks. He even at times felt like part of the family.

Adelle was now entering her fourth month of pregnancy. The baby had grown to almost full size, which astonished Lewis and the family. The ultrasounds still depicted a grotesque baby. Lewis was concerned that Adelle would give birth any day, and he made further arrangements for the birth to take place at the Seawick Estate. He brought in a hospital table and other instruments needed for the delivery. He prepped Carolyn on what to do and how to assist him during the birth.

As the time of birth neared, Adelle became very sick. She started having trouble keeping any food or liquid down. She felt terrible, and was extremely tired and achy all the time. She even noticed that she was losing some of her hair when she washed it. The unborn child kept her up most nights. It kicked and moved constantly in her womb, to the point where Adelle thought it was going to break through her abdominal wall. Sometimes she had trouble walking because the baby was either kicking or leaning on some nerve close to her back.

Adelle's stomach was huge. She looked as if she were carrying triplets. The times the baby would stop kicking or trying to get out were far and few between, but when these moments occurred, Adelle made sure to take advantage of them by relaxing and getting some sleep.

Even during those moments, it was hard for Adelle to get any rest. She saw what her husband had turned into, and she could not get his physical change out of her head. It haunted her. The thought of having his hideous baby inside her repulsed her even more. Many times, she thought of having the thing aborted, but she couldn't bring herself to do that to any living thing. Even to a creature that no one had given birth to in the history of humanity. Adelle knew this was still hers and Trevor's baby. Never in her life had she ever been at such great odds on any issue.

One night, Lewis was finishing some work in his basement lab on the estate. It was late, going on around eleven o'clock on a Friday night. He turned out all the lights and went upstairs. He was going to fix himself a drink, and he had gotten a few feet from the bar when he heard some commotion upstairs. Trevor was yelling, and Lewis quickly ran upstairs to see what the problem was. As he got to the hallway on the second floor, he headed toward Adelle's bedroom. He saw Trevor, who immediately told him that Adelle's water had broken.

The sounds of the controlled panic of everyone in the house awoke Garrison. He began to cry as he stepped out of his room and into the hallway. Loren escorted him back to his room as she tried to calm him down.

Carolyn came on the scene and tried to comfort Adelle, who was not doing well. It had only been five months, and now her water had broken. She knew something wasn't right, but in a twisted way, she was glad that this had happened. Maybe it was for the best. Maybe the baby would end up not surviving the labor if it was so premature. Lewis, Carolyn, and Trevor helped Adelle to her hospital bed in the basement and helped prep her for the delivery. The walk was a long one, but Adelle was doing fine on her way to the bed.

Everyone was quite nervous. Lewis checked Adelle, and she was five centimeters dilated. Adelle's pains were getting stronger, so Lewis administrated an epidural to help with the pain. Trevor was in the room with Lewis and Carolyn. Carolyn had some previous experience with deliveries and was confident about what she was being asked to do.

Trevor came over to the side of the bed where Adelle lay quietly. Lewis prepared the area and made sure everything was in order. When the contractions started, everyone was tense, but they all went about their specific jobs. Trevor supported Adelle through the contractions, and she had a calm and confident look on her face through the event.

As the contractions became closer and closer, Lewis told her that it was time to start pushing. The delivery was very short but not easy. The unborn child wanted out as fast as possible and rushed things along for everyone.

Trevor held Adelle's hand as he stood near the table. He was very upset and nervous. He wasn't used to doing this. He felt weak in the knees through the whole process. He wasn't excited because there was the thought in the back of his mind that the child might not live through the birth. Not knowing what the child might look like kept Trevor's emotions in check but for the same reason added to his concerns. Trevor's senses were working overtime during the process. His newly discovered and heightened senses of smell, eyesight, and awareness made the experience a more stressful one than he could have ever imagined.

Trevor attempted to console Adelle, but he was more interested in what was going to pop out from between her legs than in the support she needed at the moment. Adelle felt alone even though her hand was going numb from Trevor's tight grip. Lewis broke Trevor's concentration by saying that he could see the child's head. Lewis encouraged Adelle to push through the delivery. Trevor looked down. As he did, Adelle noticed the expression on his face: one of horror, fright, and disgust. Trevor acted as though he was startled to death, but then he quickly encouraged Adelle to push. Adelle was so upset she forced herself up into a hunched position as best as she could to see what Trevor was looking at.

Lewis yelled, "No! Trevor, keep her down!" as he fought with the baby's head. The head was completely out. The child started to move, almost as if the baby was helping the doctor. The head moved back and forth, its mouth opening then closing. A violent scream tore from Carolyn's mouth as she watched the baby emerge, and she quickly turned away.

The baby started to cry, and moments later, its call for help developed into a high-pitched growl. Out came his left arm as he placed his hand on Adelle's inner thigh. Adelle felt the hand and thought it was strange for a baby to do that, but she was too busy pushing to ponder the hand for long. His right arm came out, and he placed his right hand on his mother's lower belly. He was pulling himself out of the womb.

Lewis was so stunned at the sight that he stopped pulling and let the baby do most of the work. Lewis's eyes widened. He'd had some idea as to the extent of the deformity, but seeing it was believing it. The child's head was long and very thin. The hair was thick on top of his head. The eyes were twice as large as a normal baby's eyes. The ears were large and pointy, and the bottom portion rounded off just below the opening of the ear. The baby had teeth, and the ones that were immediately noticeable looked to be very sharp. The baby cried out in a high-pitched, almost whistling growl that changed into a sound like a normal human cry and then reverted to the growling noise. The baby's nose was long, and the mouth was wide and farther back on the face, closer to the ears than normal. The arms were two to three inches longer than a normal newborn's. The neck was long and thick. As Lewis took note of all the differences, the rest of the child's body slid out of Adelle like a snake coming out of a hole in the earth. Covered in blood, the newborn child's legs were longer than normal as well. The body was long and very hairy. The hair was covered with blood and vaginal fluids as it clung to the skin, as if the body were covered in Vaseline.

Adelle collapsed onto her back on the bed. Trevor was still holding on to his wife's hand. He wiped the sweat from her forehead as he snuck peeks at his unusual child who was fighting Lewis and Carolyn.

The baby had started fighting with the umbilical cord as Trevor attempted to cut it. He told Carolyn to help with the arms, but she didn't move. She could hardly look at the child that had just been born. Lewis, in a stern voice, commanded Carolyn to hold the arms down.

Carolyn obeyed uncomfortably. As she touched the baby's arm, it moved its head toward her hand. She pulled back.

Lewis was furious. He told her again to hold the arms still, and again she obeyed, but this time she didn't let go of the arm. She could hardly look at the baby and the situation just a few feet from her face. Lewis finally cut the cord and told Carolyn that he was going to work on the baby. He told her to clean up Adelle.

Lewis picked up the child to clean him off as best he could. The newborn seemed to be fighting the doctor's movements with his long arms and legs. Lewis asked for Carolyn's help once more. He had thought he could handle the baby, but the moving arms and legs had proven too much. Lewis and Carolyn attempted to clean the child, which was not an easy process. When they finally got the baby cleaned up, Carolyn attempted to console the child and comfort him the best she knew how.

Meanwhile, through all of this, Trevor noticed he had put his hand to his mouth, the same hand that had once been holding Adelle's.

Adelle was attempting to see her baby, but Lewis kept getting in the way. Adelle wanted to see her child even though she knew he was deformed. She could not help it; she wanted to see what she and her husband had created before it died. When Carolyn finished cleaning up the newborn, she made her way towards Lewis and handed him the baby. Lewis reluctantly took the oddity in his arms. Carolyn raced over to clean up Adelle so she could help Lewis out with the baby.

Trevor, still standing by his wife, looked on in amazement. He witnessed everything and was amazed by what he saw. He couldn't believe that he was seeing his only biological child for the first time. Thoughts of Garrison were not with him during this. The event partially disgusted Trevor, but he felt something inside him calling out to the newborn child. The child's wide, large-shaped, deep, piercing black eyes were open. Trevor felt that he needed to comfort this child. He was drawn to the child and obsessed with what he saw, what he had created, and he was curious to get a closer look at the hideous monster that had come out of his wife. All thoughts or feelings of not wanting this child had vanished for the time being. He was drawn to the baby as a thirsty man is drawn to water after being trapped in the desert for days.

Adelle's eyes were now on her husband. The fact that he was not holding her hand or comforting her or even paying any attention to her was not lost on her. This act of basic rejection, at least the way she saw it, was very difficult to experience.

Trevor slowly walked over to Lewis as he was busy trying to calm the baby, which was fighting him every step of the way. The child looked at Trevor, bent his head until his long chin touched the top of his chest, twisted a little from side to side with his long arms and legs, and then stopped moving. He then raised his chin and opened his mouth to cry. As he cried, the eyes closed tightly, and the cry turned into that disturbing high growl. He almost sounded like a distressed wolf in the woods being attacked by another animal. Then the child stopped its crying and closed its mouth.

Adelle yelled, "What is going on? What was that noise?" No one in the room paid any attention to her questions.

Moments later, the baby's eyes grew wider and his face stretched. Without any notice, large amounts of black liquid exited from his rear end and from his mouth. The child then moved his arms and legs around and growled as if he was in discomfort. Carolyn and Lewis were in shock. Carolyn backed away from the child as Lewis stood there for a moment and then asked for more towels to clean up the mess.

Trevor reached for his son's arm. The child moved around on the table and quickly grabbed for Trevor's hand but missed because of Trevor's nervous withdrawal. Trevor was startled at first, but he moved in closer and allowed the child to grab his hand for comfort. The growling stopped, replaced by a calm but scared whimper. Large tears formed in the baby's eyes, as well as in Trevor's.

Adelle, for the first time, saw the whole of her baby. She was terrified by what she saw lying on the table, and to have her husband hold its hand with his was boggling her mind. She couldn't believe what she had witnessed. She was in a trancelike state, with her eyes fixed on the action.

Trevor looked over at his wife and noticed she was staring at him and the baby. Trevor knew that he had forgotten his wife for a few minutes in all the commotion. He didn't think it was that big of a deal, failing to realize that he had left her out of seeing their baby for the first time. Trevor smiled at Adelle from a distance as if he had done nothing wrong.

Adelle looked at the child, then back at Trevor with a scared and confused expression on her face, and then she looked upon her child one more time. Her face turned to pure horror as her eyes widened, her eyebrows rose while she pressed her lips tightly together, trying not to scream. She was filled with surprise, shock, and a longing for companionship, but mostly with the pure emotion of fear. She couldn't believe that something that looked like that had come out of her, and she was confused because Trevor was acting as if nothing was wrong with it. She felt like she was trapped in some twisted *Twilight Zone* episode. She took a deep breath and let out a scream that could be heard all over the grounds of the estate.

Lewis attempted to calm her down, but Adelle was in a total panic. She was screaming uncontrollably. She had her hands up to her face, and then she thrust her hand up into her hair as she cried and screamed. Lewis continued to fight with Adelle, trying to calm her down. He had Carolyn lie on top of her as he got some medicine in a syringe. He ran over to Adelle and jammed the needle in her arm. In less than five seconds, she stopped screaming and slowly calmed down as sweat poured from her face, neck, and shoulders. Meanwhile, Trevor didn't move, nor did the baby as they watched the whole exhibition. It was as if they were in their own little world.

As Garrison was playing with Loren, he heard his mother's screams, and he ran past Loren and through the hallway, down the steps to the basement door. As he tried to enter, he discovered the door was locked. Loren ran after Garrison to stop him. Garrison was yelling for his mama as Loren pulled him from the door.

Adelle lay there on the hospital bed while breathing heavily, with a scared look on her face. She started to control her breathing, then closed her eyes and fell asleep as pure exhaustion overtook her body. She had collapsed on the hospital bed with tears rolling down each side of her face.

Meanwhile, Carolyn ran over to the door and yelled to Garrison that everything was fine and that he didn't need to worry. Loren then got control of Garrison and took him upstairs. He knew something was wrong, he just didn't know what exactly it was.

Later that night, Trevor and Lewis moved Adelle to her bedroom in the basement. She was still out of it from the medication. Lewis reassured Trevor that she was going to be fine. He then told Trevor to check on the baby to see if it needed anything. Just as Trevor was walking down the stairs, Garrison ran after him.

"Daddy, I want to see my newborn brother. Can I see him? Can I see him, Daddy?"

Trevor said, "Of course you can, but, Garrison, the baby is not... does not look like you or me. He is a little different in appearance."

Garrison looked at his dad in a rather funny way and said, "Why does he look so funny, Daddy?"

Trevor attempted to explain in his best words that sometimes some kids didn't always come out of their mommies' bellies the way they should. Some were not born with all their fingers or toes. Garrison seemed to understand, but Trevor furthered his lecture to his son as they made their way to the basement steps. He told Garrison how his baby brother looked and asked him not to make fun of him or treat him any differently.

Garrison thought it was cool to have a brother who looked different from him. In fact, he was even more excited to see his new playmate.

Trevor and Garrison went down into the basement to check on Carolyn and see how the newborn was doing. Carolyn was caring for the child by keeping an eye on him and making sure he was doing okay.

She was getting more adjusted to the sight of the baby and in fact felt sorry for the young boy. She was going to bring the new one upstairs after she finished cleaning him up. The little one was resting in a small bassinet as she continued to clean up the area. Trevor explained to Carolyn what he had told Garrison about his brother's appearance. Carolyn asked Garrison if he wanted to see his brother, and Garrison anxiously said yes.

Garrison looked inside the bassinet and saw his brother for the first time. He only saw his head because the rest of his body was covered in a blanket. Garrison was a little shocked by his brother's face. He said, "Daddy, my brother looks like a dog."

Trevor said, "Now, Garrison, that is not nice. I never want you to say anything like that about your brother again. Got that?"

"Yes, sir. But he does look like a dog or some kind of animal."

Trevor said, "Okay, that's enough. We need to go upstairs now."

"Don't worry, Trevor," Carolyn said. "I'll look after the baby. Go on upstairs and take care of Garrison. Then why don't you get some sleep? I have the baby resting now, and he should be out for a while. You need to rest while you can."

Trevor went upstairs with Garrison and walked him to his room. He tucked his son into bed. He told him goodnight and asked him to go to sleep. Then Trevor retired to his study, poured himself some Kentucky bourbon, and collapsed in his chair. He downed a couple of hard swallows then stared at the spot on the floor where Garrison's incident had happened. He wondered what the newborn was going to be like and how he was going to care for it as well as Garrison.

Just then, Garrison appeared at the entrance of the office and walked slowly toward Trevor. Trevor adjusted his posture somewhat as the boy approached him. Garrison spoke to his dad in a slow but precise delivery. "Daddy, I am really excited seeing my baby brother. I am sorry that I called him names. I did not mean to hurt his feelings because I love him. I promise I will be a good brother to him."

Trevor's eyes filled with tears. He had wanted so much to have a normal family, but now he knew this had been only a wishful dream. Before Trevor knew it, Garrison was at his side, with his arms wrapped around his dad's arm. Trevor was nervous, remembering the bite on his wrist, and he was apprehensive about any of Garrison's physical actions. Then, as Garrison's hug lasted for a while, Trevor placed his large right hand on Garrison's blond hair. He stroked his son's hair while tears flowed down his own cheeks. He bent over and hugged his son for the first time since he was born, while Garrison uttered the words, "I love you so much, Daddy."

Trevor cried uncontrollably as he rested his cheek on Garrison's forehead. His emotions were working overtime not only because of the birth but also because of the action-packed months that had led up to this monumental day. Trevor put Garrison back to bed. He met Carolyn in the hallway and wished her a good night's sleep, then told her that he would stay up for a while to take care of the newborn. Carolyn told Trevor that Lewis was going to watch over the baby and that he ought to get some rest while he could. Trevor nodded and walked her to her bedroom door. He then checked in on his wife, who was fast asleep. Trevor was himself tired but knew that he could not get to sleep. He decided to rest in his study for a few hours.

A few quiet hours passed, but during the middle of the night, the child awoke. It howled and growled as it furiously thrust its arms and legs around in the crib. It seemed the young boy was in pain, and Lewis thought that he might not make it through the night. Lewis didn't say anything to Trevor or to Adelle, but usually deformed children like this didn't make it through the first night. The baby's head was very thin and long, so the brain was also misshapen. Lewis had thought this would cause instant death at birth, but perhaps instead, that death would occur later on in the night.

Carolyn's nerves were shot, but after hearing his cries, she rejoined Trevor and Lewis. From time to time during the night, the cries of the new arrival awakened Garrison. Carolyn would assist Garrison to keep him calm and to help him go back to his room to sleep.

The next morning, Adelle finally came to her senses as she arose from her sleep. With some help from Lewis and Loren, she was able to stand and walk a little in her room. She wanted to see her baby, but she had major reservations. Loren told her to take her time, but Adelle thought that the baby probably didn't have much longer to live, and she wanted to see her child before he died. She didn't think she could live with herself if he died before she saw him up close and personal.

"How was his night?"

Lewis didn't want to tell her, but she was impatiently waiting for an answer. "He didn't have a good night. He was restless and was in a lot of pain. He didn't get much sleep."

Adelle felt pity for her son because she knew he was in so much pain. She began to take the lead as a mother and said she wanted to see her child. "I want to see him."

Lewis reminded Adelle and reconfirmed with Trevor on the spot, "I don't know if this is a good idea. In most of these cases these types of deformed babies don't live long after delivery. In fact, him living through the night was a miracle." Lewis then went out and wheeled the bassinet into Adelle's room next to her bed. Adelle could have walked, but Lewis wanted her to rest on the bed for a while.

Adelle closed her eyes and took a deep breath as the bassinet came closer to her, until finally she mustered up enough nerve to look. She then saw her child for the second time. This time he was clean but still looked horribly deformed, and her heart wept for his condition. Adelle then began to comfort the young child as best she could, but it was very difficult for her. The noises coming from the young child disturbed her at first, but Adelle grew accustomed to the unnatural sounds.

Trevor, who was in the room, finally spoke up. "Adelle, I know this is a shock to you, and it is a shock to all of us, but this is our child. I know this is not the child we expected, but it is our child. We need to love it as long as it is alive. That is the least we can do for our baby. We need to come up with a name for him."

Adelle knew her husband was right, but her heart was just not there for this child, and that made her very sad and disappointed with herself. She knew that she should love this child no matter what it looked like, but she hadn't come to that point yet. She thought that maybe she felt this way because she didn't want to get too close to a child that would probably end up dying any hour. But she knew down deep in her soul that there was very little love for this child in her heart.

Trevor and Adelle agreed upon a name for their newborn baby. He would be Adam Winthrop; Winthrop was Trevor's middle name and Trevor's father's first name. Trevor wanted to keep the Winthrop name in the family.

A couple of days passed, and to Lewis's surprise, Adam continued to live. In fact, after a few days it seemed that Adam was not only surviving but growing—and growing at an outstanding rate. A few days turned into a few weeks, and Lewis charted Adam's daily growth rate. His development in that time was amazing. He was as big as most one-year-olds, and he was not even a month old yet.

Trevor and Adelle were upset and concerned. They couldn't believe that the little monster had not only lived but flourished and gotten stronger each day. Since day one, they had prepared themselves for the worst, but now it had been almost a month, and the opposite of Lewis's warnings had happened. Instead of mourning the death of their son, they had a healthy and rapidly growing boy on their hands. Now reality was sinking in as the shock and awe wore off. They had another son to take care of, and what a responsibility it was going to be. Both Trevor and Adelle were happy that Adam had survived, and weren't convinced of the fact that he was going to expire soon.

Lewis was growing increasing tired of the couple's misplaced hopes in their son's chances for survival. He told them the brain was so misshapen that he could not understand how Adam had even survived the birth, much less continued to grow at this rate. The couple shared his concern. Trevor and Adelle insisted that Lewis find the underlying cause of what had caused the deformity. They had many questions that Lewis just could not answer at the time. The blood work was off the charts. Like Garrison and Trevor, the type of blood was nothing like he had ever seen in medical school or any case study he had read in his life.

Lewis wanted desperately to go to the leading research universities in the country to see if they had any answers, but Trevor and Adelle were against letting their secret out. Trevor didn't want it ever mentioned outside the grounds of the estate until he could find a cure or at least know what they were dealing with. This upset Lewis because he didn't have a clue as to where to turn for the answers.

CHAPTER 8

Prerequisites

Garrison was getting bigger by the day and growing as fast as a weed. He was a good six years ahead of the normal growth rate for a child his age. He was also getting more intelligent by the day and was now reading at a college level. He already had mastered many advanced subjects and he continued to study college level material. He still played the violin like no other before him, as his hand-eye coordination had only gotten sharper. He was growing and maturing, and he was gaining better control over his emotions.

At almost two months old, Adam had doubled in size and was starting to walk. His approach to walking was not normal, though; he would bend his legs and place both arms down in front of him with his hands on the floor. He would walk on both his hands and legs, and then he would stand to walk on his feet only for a few steps. This was upsetting to Lewis and to Adam's parents. Lewis had to place Adam in a room in the basement for fear he might hurt himself and possibly others. With his lab supplies out in the open, Lewis was concerned that Adam might hurt himself with an instrument or chemical that might be lying around. He had a cage constructed in the basement with thick bars on all four sides and the top. The cage was not just a precaution but something the family had to construct. No one knew what Adam was capable of now or would be down the road. Lewis and Trevor were concerned that he might escape, and that wouldn't be a good thing. How would they explain him to the authorities? Adam didn't like the caged bedroom. He wanted to be free and didn't like to be enclosed.

In a very short time, Adam began to speak, learning with some help from Trevor and Carolyn. Garrison tried to help Adam, but Adam never really cooperated with him. This irritated Garrison; all he wanted was to help Adam, and Adam seemed not to want his help.

Adam had been growing at an alarming rate both physically and mentally. In just months, he was talking in full sentences, but it seemed, at least at this stage, that his intelligence might not be on the level of Garrison's. He was slower in his delivery of speech and cognitive thinking. Of course, Adam was a different type of person than Garrison was at this age. Garrison was more human whereas Adam was lesser of a human and more like an animal.

Adam had grown additional teeth. The newly formed teeth were razor sharp and large. He attempted to bite everything and anything when he was hungry. Carolyn was very careful not to get bitten. She even went to the extent of putting a modified muzzle, made for a dog, on Adam during his baths and playtime. At first, Adam didn't like the muzzle but after several attempts he learned to accept wearing the devise. Adam's hair began to grow longer and faster not only on his head but on his arms, chest, and legs as well.

Adam longed for his mother's love, but Adelle was never around as much as Carolyn because Adelle felt a deep guilt and disgust in her soul about bringing Adam into the world. She was upset at herself for not being a good mother to Adam because of the fear and repugnance she felt toward him. It bothered her, but she could never bring herself to be close to him. She still could not get over having had an animal slide out of her vagina. It repulsed her to no end to think that she had carried this beast inside her for five months. Her mind would always drift toward her husband, and she would wonder what he had inside his sperm to be able to create such a thing. Then she would think about her precious Garrison and the way he had started this whole process, but even with his involvement, she loved him more than anyone she ever had, including Trevor. Adelle felt as if she had been on autopilot with everything that had transpired over the last nine or so months. She had experienced so much and felt so much pain during that time that it seemed every day she was shocked more by reality. To see her own son run around in a caged cell on all fours, growling like a rabid dog, was too much for her to handle. Then to have him speak in a deep hissing voice and to think that she had given birth to a monster was beyond anything that she could accept with a sound mind.

With his rapid growth and development, Adam was taking more notice of his surroundings. He was trying to figure out how he fit in. He didn't understand why he was not allowed to sleep in a normal room or be as free as his brother. He also noticed the difference in the way he and Garrison were treated by his father and especially his mother. He didn't understand why he wasn't placed on a pedestal like Garrison and why he was not as free as Garrison to roam around the grounds of the estate.

Most adults underestimate the intelligence of kids, as well as that of animals. Children and animals notice adults' behaviors or personality oddities. They are like prisoners in cells watching the guards as they pace from one area to another or stand watch. In this case, Adam was not a normal child. He knew there was something special about him. He didn't know why he was so different from everyone else. He did somewhat resemble his father, but he looked nothing like his mom or his brother, or even Lewis, for that matter. He knew that he acted differently as well. He knew he was different from others both in physical appearance and in others' treatment of him, and this upset him significantly.

Adelle was in a constant state of emotional stress that she didn't even see Adam for long periods of time, sometimes as long as days. She didn't want to think about what she had brought into this world. She didn't really love Adam, and certainly not like she loved Garrison. She knew that Adam sensed this feeling.

Adam longed for his mom, but he was closer to Carolyn, and in a twisted way Carolyn loved Adam. At first, she was scared to death of the baby, but after spending so much time with him, she ended up loving him as if he were her own. Carolyn took care of Adam more than his mother did because Adelle's mental well-being was shaky at this point. In fact, her nerves had been shot ever since the birth. Not only was she dealing with a deformed child that seemed almost half-human and half-animal, but then she was seeing her husband change right before her eyes, not to mention trying to cope with the issues with Garrison, making Adelle almost suicidal. Lewis continued to administer medication for her nerves, which made Adelle very tired and forced her to take long naps throughout the day.

One day, Trevor and Garrison went outside to walk near the wooded part of the estate grounds. Garrison was picking up some rocks on the ground and throwing them with a high rate of accuracy toward a tree here and there. Trevor thought it would be fun so he picked up a rock and looked up at a limb about thirty feet up on a tree, about sixty feet from where they were standing. He twirled the rock around with his fingers and then threw it. He saw it as it left his fingers, and he could swear that he watched it turning as it flew toward the limb. It twirled through the air, and he heard it hit the limb, solidly in the middle. He even saw the indention the rock had made in the limb, and he heard the rock fall toward the ground and make a small thud as it stuck in the soft mud. As Trevor saw what he had done, he knew that a couple of months ago this feat would not have been possible.

Trevor then picked up another rock and aimed at another limb on a different tree. This time his target was about ninety feet away and fifty feet up. The result was the same as before; the rock hit almost exactly where he was aiming. Trevor repeated this three more times, and every time the same result occurred. Trevor was excited and amazed by his newfound skill.

He noticed Garrison was attempting the same exercise but was not faring as well as his dad. He only hit about half of the targets that he was aiming at. Trevor showed him how to throw the rock with more accuracy. He gently took a rock, placed it in Garrison's hand, and told him to first visualize hitting the target. He told him to focus, to trust all his senses, and to allow them to work as a unit. After a few attempts, Garrison was doing much better.

Trevor noticed, as no other time in his life, the many different smells of the forest. He didn't have a complete understanding of what he was sensing. Even though he had grown up in the area, this was the first time in his life that he had noticed so many conflicting smells and how hard it was to differentiate them all. Among the smells of the trees, the flowers, the grass, the weeds, and the dirt, he could even smell the different animals that lived in the forest. He was shocked to discover these new smells.

Then he noticed the different sounds the forest was making. He heard the leaves as the wind brushed past them, but he also heard the branches as they swayed from left to right or up and down. He could hear as many as three dogs barking from the other houses, which were located far from where he was standing. He could hear movement in the forest, and he swore that he could sense animals watching him. Never had his instincts been this highly tuned to what was taking place all around him. His mind was in a constant state of fluctuation in the attempt to take in all the information that was hitting his sight, his hearing, and his other senses. So much noise, so much to see, so much was happening at once that it was so hard to take everything in and process his surroundings. He felt new and alive as he had no other time in his life.

Trevor stood there, taking all of this in and trying to understand what he had been missing all his life. This newfound wonder at having been transformed into a computerlike animal with feelings. As he looked down upon his smiling son, shifting his weight from one leg to the other, he thought to himself how much time he had wasted by not experiencing the world and its natural beauty. He viewed some of these irritations as disadvantages that he would have to deal with under this seemingly new way of experiencing the world.

Garrison spoke up. "Daddy!"

"Yes, Garrison, what is it, son?" Trevor asked as he looked at the trees that surrounded them.

"Daddy, it is a good thing, you know?" Garrison said while looking up at his dad. Trevor looked down at his son with a bewildered expression. Garrison continued. "Do you smell all of those different smells, Daddy? Do you hear all that noise? I have heard them. I have smelled all of them. I have been able to all my life. I don't understand why others don't hear or see or smell them. But now you do see it all, don't you, Daddy? You do hear it all. You smell it all, don't you?"

Trevor muttered almost under his breath, "Yes, Garrison. I do know what you're talking about. I don't understand it, but I have never experienced anything like this in my life."

Garrison smiled and laughed as he ran over and picked up a rock and came back to his dad. "You're welcome, Daddy. It's fun once you get the hang of it. Here, throw this rock at that squirrel in the tree behind me. I bet you can hit it now."

Trevor was startled by his son's words. He gently shook his head as the rock was being pushed into his hand. Trevor was bewildered. *Could Garrison have known what he was doing when he bit me that day?*

"Yes, Daddy, I knew what I was doing."

Trevor knew full well he had not spoken aloud. He dropped the rock in surprise, and Garrison quickly picked it up again and placed it into Trevor's now willing hand.

"Go on, Daddy. Throw the rock at the squirrel."

Trevor looked up and spotted the squirrel on a tree about seventy feet from them. He was shocked that Garrison had even known the squirrel was there, but down deep in his soul, he knew it had been his son's instinct working in overdrive. In fact, he had known where the squirrel was too. Without a moment's hesitation, Trevor raised his hand behind his head and threw the rock. He watched it turn end over end as it sailed through the air at a rapid pace. He was fixated on the rock until it hit the squirrel in the back of the neck. Immediately, the squirrel went into a spasm and lost its balance. It fell helplessly to the ground and started to flop around like a fish out of water.

"Good shot, Daddy. You got him," Garrison said proudly.

Trevor was amazed that he had hit the animal, and he noticed that he was moving toward his prey as if he had done this a thousand times before. He couldn't even remember telling his legs to run to the scene.

Garrison ran ahead of his father saying, "Come on, Daddy. Hurry up before he runs away."

Trevor jogged toward the half-dead animal. Garrison picked up the squirrel, and Trevor yelled, "Garrison, be careful. Put that thing down now!"

Garrison, instead of listening to his father, held the animal out with both hands. Trevor raced toward him and stopped about three feet from his son's outstretched arms. Trevor looked at the squirrel as it attempted to escape Garrison's grasp. Garrison had the squirrel around the neck and the back of the legs. It was scratching Garrison's hands, but that didn't seem to bother Garrison in the least.

He looked up at his father and said, "Come on, Daddy. It's okay."

Trevor had never been this nervous in his life. His hands were shaking and sweating profusely, and his knees felt weak. The blood was pumping through his body at a rate he had never experienced while his mind jumped from one of his senses to another. He could hear the squirrel struggle while seeing it thrash around in Garrison's hands. All of Trevor's senses were working overtime. Each of them was heightened to a level of sensory appreciation that he had never experienced in his life.

Trevor reached out to take the squirrel as Garrison handed the animal to him. He replaced his son's hands with his own and grasped the animal around the neck and the back of the legs. The sharp claws dug into his hands and wrist. This heightened Trevor's newly discovered anger.

Then Garrison said, "Go on, Daddy. Don't stop now."

Without a moment's hesitation, Trevor opened his mouth, lifted the squirrel, and bit into its side, all the while looking into Garrison's eyes. Garrison smiled and batted his eyes rapidly as if he approved. Trevor felt the body of the squirrel tense up and react violently to the bite. He smelled the wild, fearful, and gamey smell the squirrel gave off and enjoyed the squeal of the animal's pain as he continued to bite into it. Trevor took another bite, and another, attempting to break more of the skin under the fur. Then he stopped and looked at the now dead squirrel. He started to cry. Suddenly, an unnaturally loud scream came from his mouth. He then released the carcass and allowed it to fall to the ground. Through his outreached hands, he viewed the fall as if the squirrel were in slow motion.

As the corpse hit the ground, it bounced twice, and Garrison raced to pick it up. He began to bite into the wounded side. Trevor stood with his mouth open. His saliva was flowing from his jaws; it ran down the edges and sides of his mouth as he watched his son break off a piece of the meat. Using his fingernails, Garrison ripped the skin back to expose the muscles. He bit into the exposed muscle and pulled like a dog on a chew toy. Trevor stood there salivating over the scene. He slowly knelt next to his son. He looked like a scared and starved child who had not eaten in days.

Garrison offered the remains to his dad once more, and finally Trevor, with a tear in his eyes, reached down, picked up the animal, and quickly sank his teeth into the wound. Even though it had disgusted him in the past, Trevor now finally understood what his son had been going through all those years. Trevor loved the smell, the taste of the muscles and tendons; they were chewy but tasty. He loved the musky scent of the animal and the gamey odor of the open carcass. The blood with the added aroma of the muscles was intoxicating. His adrenal glands were working hard, and he could feel his heartbeat not only in his chest but throughout his body. The pleasure was greater than the best sex that he had ever had in his life. He felt so powerful, so unforgiving, and so wrong that it heightened his passion for the meal. He knew that Garrison didn't know any better: he was acting on instincts and not on reason. But Trevor knew what he was doing, and a small part knew it was wrong for him to act the way he did, but a larger part loved every second of the act. He was feeling so many emotions it was hard to process all of them. Now he knew he was like his son, and down deep inside Trevor's soul, he loved it. He had never felt this alive in his life.

Trevor looked down at his son once more and then offered the rest of the animal to Garrison with a smile of acceptance. Garrison had never felt more deeply the love of his father than at that moment. From that moment on, their relationship became closer and more loving than ever before.

CHAPTER 9

Evolution

Trevor and Garrison continued their odd eating behaviors over the next couple of weeks. Trevor bought some traps, as many as five at one time; he would put them out in the forest on the estate. A squirrel, raccoon, opossum, rabbit, or even a fox occasionally would find its way into those traps. Trevor would then call for Garrison and they would secretively either go into the forest or bring the animal into the basement of the house to dine. Usually Trevor used bait to lure the animals into the traps. They learned quickly that captured animals tended to bite or scratch their capturers. Trevor ended up buying gloves that covered most of the forearm for both him and Garrison.

Garrison thought it was fun and exciting. He especially enjoyed the taste of foxes, whereas Trevor preferred raccoons. Both really enjoyed the muscles and tendons of the animals so much that they usually used the rest as bait for the next capture. They liked the feel of chewing on the muscles, and the blood was a delicacy that enhanced the flavor of the main course. Garrison had more trouble with the muscles because his teeth were not as sharp as Trevor's four newly acquired fangs. Sometimes Garrison brought a small pair of scissors in order to cut the muscle into bite-sized pieces.

They had an agreement between them not to tell anyone about the meals. Both knew all too well that no one would understand their practice. They understood each other and thought it was fine to continue as long as it didn't hurt anyone. Trevor certainly didn't want Adelle to find out, and neither did Garrison. Garrison didn't want to disappoint his mom. They wanted to keep this from Lewis as well because he would be upset and would want them to stop.

During this time, Lewis and Adam had been getting to know each other. Lewis had Adam perform many physical and mental tests to gauge his progress. The transformation that Adam had made over four or five months had been amazing for Lewis to witness. He videotaped and documented every test and every milestone that Adam achieved. Adam was now developing more skills and was behaving considerably well. The only problem with his attitude was that he wanted to spend more time out of the cage with his father.

Trevor and Garrison were getting very good at eating in the basement and cleaning up after themselves or cleaning up outside before they got into the house. So far, Lewis had not caught on to their practice, but one day when he went strolling into the basement, he could not believe his eyes. He saw Trevor and Garrison hurrying to get into the bathroom, and both of them had blood on their faces and hands from one of their feasts. This greatly disturbed and frightened Lewis, so much so that he threatened to call the police and wanted to call in more doctors on the spot.

Trevor quickly pointed out that Lewis was just as guilty as they were, or at least the courts would look at it that way. Trevor said that he was not hurting anyone and that there was no difference between hunting deer to eat and capturing forest animals.

Of course, Lewis disagreed, but down deep he knew that if this news got out, his future as a doctor would be uncertain. Trevor paid him handsomely to be the family's doctor. Lewis didn't want to give that income up. Additionally, Lewis was in so deep that he didn't see a way out, and he was concerned for his own safety if he should rat them out.

On the other side of the issue, Lewis wanted to know more about their odd behavior. He questioned Trevor and Garrison about why they enjoyed this type of cuisine. Both were blunt in their answers. They said they craved the muscles; they liked the texture and the aroma of the animal. They enjoyed the way the animals contorted their helpless little bodies, the way they would roll in their hands or arms before and after the bite. They enjoyed the sounds they made and the odor they gave off. The two could smell the fear in the animal, and that smell was like an aphrodisiac to them.

Lewis was horrified when he heard this coming from their mouths. Of course, Trevor and Garrison sensed the fear and attempted to calm the doctor down as best they could. At times, Trevor's eyes seemed to tell a story of shame. He knew what he was doing was wrong, but a part of him desired it and thought nothing was wrong with it. Garrison had no remorse, no ill feelings regarding his past or current actions when it came to eating animals alive. He considered the practice normal. He couldn't understand why his mother and the others in the house didn't join in. Garrison was confused about why his dad had told him to keep this little secret from others and not to ever let anyone know what they were doing.

After a week of consulting with Lewis about his newfound diet, Trevor wanted the doctor to get to the bottom of what was happening to him and to his son. Trevor was not necessarily scared but concerned. He was troubled over his growth. He had grown a few inches since the bite. Of course, Trevor was more concerned with what might lie ahead of him and what other physical changes might take place. Trevor told Lewis that he thought he needed to direct his research toward Germany, the place where Garrison was from and thus the source of the problem.

In Trevor's mind, his logic was solid since he had had no health issues until Garrison bit him. Maybe Garrison carried some kind of disease that somehow affected the human brain, causing it to exhibit the symptoms that Trevor and Garrison were experiencing.

Trevor was equally interested in finding out why their senses had become heightened. Being the businessperson he was, Trevor wondered to himself whether, through research, the source of their changes could be used as a miracle cure someday. He imagined a medical breakthrough that would bring untold and astonishing riches in the future.

Trevor explained this to Lewis and informed him that he would obviously ask Lewis to take the credit for this venture and that he would share in the profits. Lewis had to agree with Trevor's thinking. Trevor was right, as he usually was about money and business ventures. This was a perfect opportunity for Lewis to make a name for himself, to become immortal in the medical field. Maybe there was a cure or a way to correct the disease or whatever was happening to Trevor and Garrison. If he could control some aspect of their chemical makeup, there were untold riches in the venture. He imagined discovering the exact chemical makeup of Garrison's body. He imagined what it could do for the sick or the old—cause them to never get sick or improve their eyesight, hearing, taste, feeling, awareness. This was the fountain of youth to some degree. It was an opportunity to heal as God had when he was on the earth. Lewis knew that in the end, this would also create money, lots of money, and fame for him.

Trevor knew that if he dangled the money-and-fame carrot in front of Lewis, the doctor would never go to the police or share his potential discovery with another scientist, thus ensuring total secrecy and security.

Trevor's obsession with security and exclusiveness in society had worn on Lewis. He ended up calling some people in Germany, especially Sonja, and made plans to visit the place where Garrison had been found to see if he could turn up any information that he could use in his new partnership.

Lewis attempted to convince Trevor to tell Adelle what was going on. Trevor didn't want Adelle to know what he was doing to animals. He thought it would set her back psychologically. No, this secret had to stay a secret. Lewis finally agreed. He started to think more about the situation. He said the only good that had come from it all was Trevor's improved relationship with Garrison. They were closer now than ever before.

However, Lewis was concerned about Adam. He was worried how Adam played into all this newfound friendship. He bluntly told Trevor that he believed Trevor had all but abandoned Adam, and certainly Adelle didn't spend any time with her son at all. Carolyn was the acting mother to the child. Trevor felt bad about what he had done to Adam, and he told Lewis that at times he didn't see Adam as human. Lewis looked at Trevor and asked himself whom Trevor thought he was kidding. Trevor was basically half-man and half-animal himself, thanks to his personal metamorphosis.

Trevor knew what Lewis was thinking and answered the unasked question aloud. "You think I am just like Adam, don't you, Lewis? You think I am an animal myself."

Lewis shook his head. "No, Trevor, I did not say that."

"But you do, Lewis. I can almost read your mind. Whatever has gotten into my system, I can feel what others feel. I can sense things that I have never sensed before. You cannot fool me, my friend. You think I am a monster just like my son." Then Trevor grabbed Lewis's shirt, pulled him up off the ground by a foot, stared into his eyes, and said, "Admit it, man."

Lewis was shocked as he hung in midair. Before he could say anything, he was released from Trevor's grasp. He stumbled back a few feet and regained his balance. He stood there in stunned silence.

Trevor turned away to walk out of the room, but as he left he said, "Sorry, Lewis, but don't ever make me angry again." He stopped at the doorway and added, "You're right. I need to pay more attention to my other son. I will correct the situation." Then he left the room.

Lewis fell back onto the edge of his desk. His heart was racing a mile a minute as he attempted to gather his thoughts. He had never been so frightened, but at the same time, he knew Trevor wouldn't hurt him. Trevor needed him too much.

Trevor had always had an odd personality, even during his early years. He had a mind of his own, and many people attributed this to him being mostly alone through a large part of his life. When his parents died, Trevor needed to grow up fast, and he had learned not only how to take care of himself but how to entertain himself. He was so used to being alone that he had the freedom to do what he wanted when he wanted. Therefore, it wasn't surprising that he wouldn't visit Adam for days upon days.

This bothered Adam, and he wondered why his dad never visited him or played with him. He would ask these questions of Lewis, which made Lewis uncomfortable.

The next morning, Trevor told Garrison that he thought it would be nice to take Adam out for a walk. Garrison didn't like the idea; he wanted Trevor to spend all his time with him. Trevor insisted that he and Garrison needed to spend more time with Adam to make him feel that he was part of the family.

They went down to the basement and found Adam outside the cage with Carolyn. Adam had learned not to bite and had continued to improve both physically and mentally. He was acting more like a five- or six-year-old even though he was not yet one. As Trevor and Garrison approached, Adam looked at his dad with caring eyes. Trevor told him to get up and come outside with him and Garrison. Adam was very excited. Trevor told Carolyn to stay in the house and relax. As much as Carolyn was surprised that she was going to get a break, she welcomed the much-needed rest.

The trio went outside. Garrison had brought a small ball to play with, and he and Adam kicked it around. Trevor had some trouble with the sight of Adam running. Adam ran not only on his feet but on his hands as well. He walked upright, but then as he picked up speed, his hands would drop down and meet the ground. Adam's shoulders were shaped more like a dog's than a normal boy's. The boy also panted with his tongue hanging out of his mouth at times. Aside from his oddities, Adam possessed some incredible traits. One of his best was his incredible quickness.

Garrison was equally talented. He never missed the ball while kicking it around. Each kick was dead center, and the ball went exactly where he wanted it to go. Adam seemed to have more control over the ball once he got the hang of kicking it and having it kicked back to him. Adam learned very fast how to stop the ball with his body as he jumped in front of it. He would then quickly get on his feet and kick the ball back to Garrison using the same perfect motion as Garrison's kicks. Trevor stood there, very proud of both of his sons but troubled by Adam's strange appearance. He had changed so much over the past few weeks. His appearance changed daily, in fact. Each passing day he added more hair to his body while his remaining hair grew longer. His face became thinner whereas his snout and ears grew longer.

Trevor continued to watch his two sons as they kicked the ball around the back lawn. As time went by, the game started to get competitive and rough. Not too long into it, Garrison decided to slow the play down and placed his foot on the ball. He looked at Adam who was pacing back and forth with saliva pouring out of his mouth. He had a daring smile on his face that suggested his desire for Garrison to bring it on. Garrison noticed this posture. He smiled back at Adam, then aimed the ball at Adam's head and kicked it hard. Adam saw the ball coming toward him. He hit the ground with his hands and moved his legs up behind him to kick the ball to Garrison with his heels. Garrison jumped up, stopped the flight of the ball with his chest, and gained control of it. Then he kicked it as hard as he could toward Adam. This time Adam jumped two feet straight up in the air and caught the ball between his feet midair. As he came down, the ground jarred the ball loose, and he became very angry. He picked the ball up and threw it as hard as he could at Garrison. Garrison caught the flying ball with his hands, creating a loud *pop*. Adam stood there with his hands by his side, growling. Garrison cocked his head, smiled, dropped the ball, and kicked it in midair right toward Adam. Adam caught the ball with his left hand and instantaneously threw it back in an almost unbelievably fast motion.

When the ball left Adam's hand, he rushed toward Garrison with pure anger and hatred on his face. Trevor knew they were about to get into a fight, so he ran after Adam. Garrison caught the ball and was preparing to throw it back at Adam, but Adam was rapidly closing the distance between them. Garrison couldn't get his throw off in time as Adam lunged at Garrison and tackled him. His hands came down on Garrison's shoulders, and his feet hit Garrison's knees. Garrison fell back hard. The two fought on the ground and would not let each other go. Adam was growling with his mouth open just a foot from Garrison's face, while Garrison was staring into Adam's eyes with a crazed expression.

Before they knew it, the boys felt Trevor's strong hands on their arms as he separated them from each other. After a few moments, Trevor got them under control and told them they must get along or they would both be going back to the house. The boys calmed down but traded glares back and forth.

The three walked toward the edge of the park where the tree line separated the well-manicured lawn from the forest of trees and small bushes. Garrison's attention turned to the first trap. Then Trevor caught a whiff of a trapped animal.

Adam quickly moved his head toward the trap to see what Garrison was looking at and why. He spoke in a slow, growling, almost hissing voice, "What's that smell?"

Trevor didn't want to introduce Adam to his and Garrison's habit so he spoke up. "It's nothing, Adam. Let's move on."

Adam looked at Trevor and said, "No, Daddy... I... I want to see what's out there." Adam took off running, and after a few yards, he hit on all fours as Trevor yelled for him to stop.

Garrison and Trevor ran toward Adam, chasing him in hopes they would catch him before he found something he shouldn't. Adam ran fast, and at the edge of the forest, he found the cage. A small gray fox was trapped inside. Adam stopped and circled the cage as Trevor and Garrison reached the scene.

Adam said, "Daddy... what's this?"

Trevor was growing more nervous as the situation escalated. Garrison broke the uncomfortable silence. "It's a captured fox, Adam. What do you think it is?"

Adam looked at Garrison with hate-filled eyes and snarled his response. Trevor wanted to remove Adam from the area, but he knew the secret was out.

Adam bent down close to the cage and sniffed the scared fox's odor. He liked the smell. He opened his mouth and licked his lips with his long tongue. Then he asked, "What are you going to do with this animal?"

Trevor didn't say a word. Garrison answered instead. "We'll eat him," he said.

Adam turned to Garrison and smiled with his eyes fully wide. "Really? You eat them after you catch them?"

"Yes, Adam. Do you want to see for yourself?" Garrison asked. "Why yes, Garrison." Adam backed away from the cage to allow his brother to retrieve the fox.

Trevor still just stood there, not moving a muscle. He knew what was going to happen, but he was frozen in place. He felt as if he were watching a movie. He didn't want to deal with the reality of what was taking place before his very eyes.

Garrison got down on his knees and lifted the opening of the cage. He reached inside carefully to pull the fox out. As he did, the fox bit his hand. This sent Garrison into a small rage; he hated when animals bit his hands or his wrists. He got very angry when they scratched him on the forearms. Even more aggravating for Garrison was having Adam laugh at his discomfort. Garrison finally pulled the fox out of the cage as it fought for its life. He put his left hand around its neck while his right hand held the tail near the body. The fox's paws flailed and scratched Garrison's forearms badly.

Adam approached Garrison and reached out for the fox. Garrison quickly moved it away. Adam went for the fox again, and Garrison got up quickly and headed toward his dad. Adam, who was frustrated and ready to attack, quickly followed. Trevor was caught in the middle. He had started something with Garrison, and he had thought it was going to be their little thing, just between them. Now, another person had crashed the party. Trevor had to let Adam into their inner circle. He knew that he couldn't say no to Adam and let Garrison have his way with the animal. At the same time, he was concerned that Garrison might be upset about having Adam in on the treat.

As the boys started to push each other, Trevor once more had to separate the two. He finally spoke up. "Now, boys, don't fight over this fox. There is enough here for everyone. Adam, stand back and watch Garrison. He will show you how it's done."

Adam obeyed the order, stepped back, and kept his eyes on the fox. Garrison looked down at the struggling animal and quickly bit into the side of the fox as it contorted in fear. Adam let out an excited yell and spun around in a circle. He stepped quickly toward Garrison. Garrison extended the fox and offered it up to Adam to show him what he had done.

Garrison didn't intend to share his meal with his brother. The animal was in intense pain, and spasms shook its body violently in response. It wanted to get away, but Garrison's strong hands wouldn't allow for its freedom.

Adam had never felt this much adrenaline flowing through his body in his young life. He absorbed the moment at hand. He reached out with his hands and gripped the fox in the same place as Garrison. He looked up at Garrison as he sank his teeth into the back of the fox just inches from Garrison's bite.

Furious, Garrison pulled the fox away from Adam's mouth, leaving behind a piece of the fox's flesh. As he pulled it away, the fox's claws dug deeper into his forearm, and he had to release the fox. The animal quickly limped away, and before Garrison knew what had happened, Adam leaped into the air and fell on the runaway fox. His right hand came down on the fox's neck, pinning it to the earth, while his left hand took hold of the back end. He bit into the wound as he twisted the fox's head 180 degrees. Garrison and Trevor could hear a popping sound as its neck broke. Adam ate wildly at the middle of the fox, pulling at the muscles and tendons, peeling them away from the animal and ripping them out of its carcass. He devoured the animal as if he had not eaten in days.

Adam didn't want to share his feast, but Trevor ordered him to give some to his brother and his dad. Adam reluctantly agreed and ripped off a piece from the other side of the fox. He threw the rest of the animal at Garrison's feet. Garrison was upset that Adam didn't leave the best part to them, but Trevor controlled Garrison and told him that the next time he would teach Adam to share better.

When the three returned to the house, Lewis was outside going for a short walk. He noticed the three covered with blood from their mouths down to their hands. He caught Trevor's eye, but the other man didn't even blink. He told the others to get inside the house before Adelle caught them in their present condition.

As Lewis caught up to Trevor's long stride, he said, "What the hell is going on, Trevor? Did you take Adam out to perform more of your sadistic sacrifices?"

Trevor stopped, looked down at Lewis, and said, "You mind your own business and get in there and help me clean the boys up before anyone sees us. Garrison has some deep scratches that need medical attention."

"You cannot keep up this behavior, Trevor," Lewis said. "Now you are bringing Adam into this. You don't know what he is capable of. We don't know what he's going to do one day to the next. He is uncontrollable, man. Imagine if he got out in the wild. We couldn't call the authorities. He would be lost forever, and who knows what he would do or where he would go."

Trevor looked deep into Lewis's eye and nodded. "I understand what I did wasn't a smart thing to do, but what is done is done. I will take the leash the next time."

"The next time? There is not going to be a next time."

Before Lewis could continue, Trevor swung his bulky head around to face him and said angrily, "This is my problem. These are my sons. I will do what I wish, when I wish, and you will not order me around. Do you understand that, Lewis?"

With that said, Lewis came back down to earth. He nodded in agreement, concerned over the possible harm that might befall him.

With a groan, Trevor grasped Lewis's shirt in both hands, picked him up a couple of feet in the air, and looked him eye to eye.

Lewis could smell his bad breath as Trevor spoke. "Do you understand, Lewis?"

Lewis quickly and nervously said, "Yes. Yes, sir, I understand."

With that, Trevor roughly put him down and, as Lewis's feet hit the ground, pushed him a little. Lewis fell. Trevor turned and went inside. Lewis just sat in the courtyard shaking; he drew his legs up to his chest and held both sides of his head in his hands.

Later that night, Trevor walked into the massive great room where Lewis was on his laptop trying to find some answers to this horrible nightmare. Trevor said, "Lewis, I spoke to Sonja the other day, and she will be expecting you next week. She had more information on the area where they found Garrison. I want you to go to Germany and see what you can find out. If you find anything—and I mean anything—of use, I want you to report back to me and only me. Do you understand that?"

Lewis agreed. "I understand, Trevor. I am sorry for upsetting you earlier today. I just don't want Adam getting loose. He could cause a lot of problems for us, especially for you and Garrison."

"I agree," said Trevor. "Thanks for the warning. I wasn't thinking clearly this morning. I need to control my emotions better. Don't worry, I will take care of the boys in your absence." With that, Trevor left the room and went to check on his wife upstairs.

Trevor knocked on Adelle's bedroom door. Adelle answered as she was wiping tears from her face. Although Trevor had changed so much, she grabbed him eagerly and held him with both arms as she said, "Oh, my love, I missed you so. I have been so confused. I don't know where to turn or what to do. How is Garrison?"

Trevor said, "Garrison is fine, and so is Adam."

Adelle responded, "Oh, Adam. Yes, of course, Adam. So, he is... he is doing well?"

"Adam is doing fine. He is growing faster physically and mentally than Garrison did at his age, or at least physically. I think Garrison is way more advanced right now mentally, but you never know what is going to happen down the road."

Adelle pushed Trevor slightly away and walked toward her bed. "Of course, we don't know what Adam is going to do. I am sorry, Trevor." She began to cry again. "I am so scared of that... that thing!" Her tears increased as she continued in a harsh, loud tone. "I know it's terrible to say, but I cannot love that thing that I gave birth to. I feel like I brought some kind of evil into this world."

Trevor knelt in front of her as she sat on the bed. "I know it's difficult for you to accept. I had problems with Adam myself. Hell, I even had problems with Garrison, but you know we have grown so close over the past few months that I think we are really coming together as father and son."

Adelle replied, "Yes, yes, I know you guys have grown closer, and I am so glad. I want you to love him as much as I do."

Trevor said quickly, "I do, Adelle. I love him, I love you, and I love Adam. I don't know what is going on here, but Lewis is going to Germany next week. He is going to meet up with Sonja and maybe get some sort of answer regarding this situation. Maybe he can find a solution to my problem, or to our problems. But Adelle, I've never felt better in my life. I feel so alive, and I am filled with so much energy. The feeling is incredible. Just like you, my love." With that, Trevor moved his hands down Adelle's legs and looked into her tearful eyes. His hands went back up her legs and under her nightgown. He moved his hands to her inner thighs and roughly spread them apart. He said, "Don't worry. Enjoy life and accept it as a gift, not as a punishment. We will find the underlying cause of this, and I promise you we will have a normal life someday. All of us."

With that, Trevor pushed his wife back and pleasured her orally. Trevor's long tongue moved rapidly at first, and then he slowed his licks to a tantalizing pace. He mounted Adelle and quickly slammed his manhood into her tight tunnel.

Adelle knew there was something unholy about what she was doing, but she had no choice. Her guilt was making her physically ill. She knew that she was making love to a half animal, half man, but part of her didn't care at that moment and she knew she couldn't stop her husband. Thus, she accepted her position and tried to get through the incredible, powerful, and exhausting intercourse that lasted most of the night. It had been a long time for both of them. For a moment, Adelle tried to forget her problems and she let herself go to her husband. At this point, his appearance didn't matter, nor did she care because she had no choice in the matter. She tried hard to forget her husband's form and only remember him as he had looked when they were first married. They fell asleep in each other's arms for the first time in many, many months.

CHAPTER 10

Revelation

*L*ewis packed his bags and made his way to Germany. When his plane landed in Berlin, he met up with Sonja. She drove Lewis to her office to pick up all the information that she had collected through the years. Many investigations had taken place in the attempt to find Garrison's parents, but there had been no leads and no one had come forward with any information regarding "Der Kleine Wald Bursche," or in English, "The Little Woodland Lad," as they called the boy.

Sonja took Lewis to his hotel south of Berlin. It took them many hours by car to reach their destination. The forgotten town was so small and out of the way that even many of the local farmers didn't have much knowledge of the area. The locals kept to themselves and rarely ventured out of their town, which was the nearest to the woodland area where nearby hunters had found Garrison. The area was remote, and the forest was so thick with trees that in midday anyone caught in it would think it to be nighttime. The area wasn't hiked often because of the density of the forest and its hilly terrain. Few hikers had gone very deep in the woods because of what the local legends said about the forest being alive with many different animals. Some say they had been known to attack hunters and hikers alike, but no one had made reports like that in the last twenty or thirty years. All the locals had heard the stories about the forest being haunted, and few if any of them would even think about venturing too far into it.

Lewis spent the first couple of days attempting to find the hikers who had discovered Garrison. One of them was out of the country on vacation, but Lewis made arrangements to meet the other one to discuss what he had witnessed. Lewis had all of the copies of the police reports plus local newspaper reports and articles, but he wanted to meet the person who had found Garrison, the little boy who had changed the Seawicks' lives forever.

The first person Lewis spoke with was the first police officer at the scene. His name was Josef. He spoke in broken English, but he was fluent enough that Lewis could understand him.

"I can remember the Woodland Lad like it was yesterday. I received a call about a young baby that was found in the woods. At first, I did not believe the call was legit. When I walked to the scene one of the hikers was still holding the boy." He looked at Lewis and Sonja with sad eyes. "The boy had been crying, was obviously very hungry, with marks all over his face, legs, and arms. Bug bites and scratches covered his body. The two hikers were both male, in their early twenties. They were visibly shocked when they discovered the boy. They said they looked around and yelled for anyone who might have been there. They could not believe that someone would leave a baby alone in the forest. Then the reality of the situation hit them, and they knew that someone had intended to leave the baby for good. That was when they called the police. They gave precise instructions of their location in the forest, but the dispatcher told them to meet the police at a major road nearby and take the baby to the local hospital. That is when I first saw the baby. I waited for additional backup. When the ambulance and a small army of officers showed at the scene, the paramedics took the baby from my arms. The hikers then took me to the exact location of where the young boy was found. Me and a couple of other officers investigated the scene. The hikers told me they saw some barefoot human footprints at the scene, but by the time they got back to the location where they found the baby, it had started to rain. The footprints had washed away before the police could take any pictures or make a cast of the prints in the soil. We talked to everyone from that area in front of the forest, but the locals did not give us much information. It was common practice not to venture into the forest, especially that deep of an area."

The next day Lewis met with one of the hikers named Franz. Franz told the same story as the police. He did, although hesitatingly, say that when they discovered the baby, he had felt they were being watched. The men circled the small area for any signs of someone who was looking after the baby. The area was one of the few areas, if not the only one, that had some clearance from the trees. In almost all directions when they were hiking in the forest, when they looked up, all they saw was a dense cover of leaves over their heads. In this area, the sunlight came down like a waterfall and filled the surrounding space with much-needed light. The baby was lying on the ground almost in the middle of this waterfall of light. There was a small stream a few yards away from the abandoned child. Franz said that he had gone deep into the forest, but they had seen nothing but trees and had heard only the rustling of the leaves and the normal noises of the forest. That was all that Franz said about the situation, just as what was stated in the police report. He did say that the footprints had upset them because they had been so large.

Lewis spoke with many in the town and attempted to gather as much information as he could about "The Little Woodland Lad." Everyone was very happy to hear that the boy was safe and sound. Even to that day, no one had a clue as to what had happened the day the boy was found. Lewis reported what little he learned to Trevor. He did have some interesting information, and he wanted to collect some samples from the local area before he came back home. Lewis told Trevor that he would fill him in when he got back, but he needed to run some experiments.

Trevor was very annoyed that Lewis would not tell him what he had found. Lewis always told Trevor everything, but this time he was keeping something from his employer. Trevor knew whatever he was keeping from him must be a major find. This excited him, but he was not accustomed to people refusing to tell him the complete story.

After a week, Lewis came home, and Loren picked the good doctor up at the airport. When Lewis arrived at the estate, he went straight to the laboratory to run some tests. When we got down to his lab, he saw Garrison, Trevor, and Adam all playing. Adam had grown, very much so. Garrison was his normal self, but Trevor now had a slight bend in his back. He had let his hair grow on his arms and around his neck more than he had before Lewis's trip.

They were all very excited to see Lewis, except Adam. He had never really cared much for the doctor. The doctor always seemed to hurt him by drawing blood or studying him, asking him questions, or testing him constantly. Adam didn't like these things.

Lewis asked to see Trevor alone and told him that he had discovered something that might be of major interest. Trevor and Lewis went to Lewis's office in the basement near his lab.

Lewis closed the door and said, "I thought you might find this very interesting. When I interviewed people in the village, I noticed something strikingly familiar. No one looked their age. I spoke with this one lady who was around sixty, or so she told me, and I swear she didn't look a day over forty. From the police officer to the local people, everyone was youthful in appearance and more active than most people their age. I don't understand it. It's so puzzling to me. I noticed there were some drugstores around the area. When I went into one of their stores, and there were few of them to begin with, I noticed they didn't sell much medicine, pain relievers, or antihistamines. I asked the owner or manager of this one store, and he told me that people around there just didn't get sick so they didn't stock the store with those types of things. They sold mostly food, household supplies, and drinks instead. So obviously my thoughts came back to Garrison. The child has never been sick a day in his life. He has never even had a cold, Trevor. So, with that information and having seen the natives of that area, it made me think something might be in the food or the water or maybe the air. I collected some samples from these areas. I need to do some research on them. It's going to take a few days, maybe even a few weeks." Lewis sat down and looked up at Trevor, who was very interested in the news.

Trevor said, "So you think there is something in the food or the water that might make people appear younger and be immune to illness?"

Lewis said, "I don't know yet. Yes. Maybe. I don't know."

"Lewis, do you realize the possibilities this might present?"

"Yes, I do, Trevor," said Lewis. "I understand full well the possibilities. That is why I am so excited."

Trevor straightened up, walked to the other side of the room, and said, "So, do they know the answer? Are they keeping this secret for themselves? Are they profiting from this somehow?"

Lewis shook his head. "They don't have a clue, Trevor. I didn't volunteer anything. The town doesn't have many people. It's a village in the woods. In fact, this town is almost surrounded by the woods, thick woods. So thick you cannot even see the sun if you walk inside the forest. I mean, what you have in your backyard is nothing compared to what I saw in Germany. On top of this, these people hardly leave the area. They have their own farms. They all work at the same mill that has been there since God knows when. They are very self-sufficient people that really don't need outside help."

"Amazing," Trevor said quickly. "Please continue, and don't let me stop you. Thanks for the information."

Lewis continued with his research. He studied his samples of water and some food, both packaged and not packaged. He sampled and studied some vegetables that had been grown in the area. He took soil samples as well as plants from the area. After a few days of research, he was a little confused. This was a field he knew little about. With strict orders from Trevor, he didn't ask for help. If there was something to this idea, some diluted fountain of youth, Trevor wanted to find the secret so his company could profit from the phenomenon. Lewis thought that if he had actually discovered something that would help improve the health of people or that could be used to serve humanity, he would be a very rich man someday. His name would be in every medical textbook ever printed.

After a few days when all his tests were done, he discovered something. He wondered why no one else had discovered it. He was perplexed about this. If he had discovered or noticed it, then why hadn't others before him? Maybe there was nothing there to begin with. Many areas in the world had strange anomalies. Maybe this was one of them.

Lewis noticed a common element in all the plants, trees, food, and water from the sampled area. It was the same chemical that showed up in Garrison's, Trevor's, and Adam's blood work. Lewis's heart was pumping over this new information. He told Trevor of the news, and it made Trevor excited and happy. The next question was where the chemical had originated. Trevor and Lewis knew that somehow Garrison had transferred the chemical to Trevor, but how did Trevor transfer it to Adam by way of Adelle? Was the transport agent Trevor's semen or some other bodily fluid? And what about Adelle?

Adelle had not been affected, at least not to their knowledge. This puzzled them both. They were also bewildered by the question of how the chemical had been transferred from Garrison to Trevor. Obviously, the bite was a suspect, but the question was how. Lewis decided to take a closer look at Garrison's teeth. Maybe the chemical came from there, or maybe it was somewhere in the saliva. There had to be some vessel that transported this chemical from Garrison to Trevor.

Another issue with this strange substance was that it changed its structure over time. Under the microscope, this seemed to be the case, not only with the new samples from Germany, but with Garrison's, Adam's, and Trevor's blood work. Lewis had a couple of theories. Maybe the chemical changed when the temperature changed. Maybe something in the body or a shift in the person's mood would cause the chemical to alter itself. Did it change with heat, or did it mix with another chemical in the body that might trigger a reaction? With Garrison, it seemed that he had attacked the dog and Trevor when he was annoyed or mad. Trevor had noticed a change in his own body when he got excited or had a sudden energy rush.

After a few weeks passed, Trevor wanted Lewis to go back to Germany to continue his research because they now had something to go on and could pinpoint the area of the chemical or infection. Lewis said that he was going to do some deep hiking in the forest to see what he could find. He had not had the time on his last trip there, and he had not understood what he was dealing with. He left the next morning for Germany with Trevor's best wishes.

During this time, Trevor and his sons were living life as usual. Often they would go out with Adam on his leash, and they would either hunt animals or get the animals that were captured in the traps they had set. Their eating habits did not change. Adelle was getting better with her increased medication, prescribed by Lewis. Garrison continued his violin playing, and he studied various subjects every day.

Adam had the biggest change in his appearance and his personality. He was learning to control his anger and was developing his motor skills to astonishing levels. When he was allowed, Trevor took Adam in the backyard and they threw the ball back and forth. In the beginning, Adam had some trouble catching the ball, but after a few days of practice he caught every ball thrown at him. His personality was becoming stronger as he was growing more confident in his abilities to learn from his environment.

Adam's physical appearance changed rapidly. He was getting larger and stronger. His arms and legs were getting longer, and his back was more curved and muscular.

Trevor had never felt better in his life. He was excited by the possibility of Lewis finding out the secret to what in Garrison's body had made him into who he was and what in Trevor's body had forced this physical and mental change on him, not to mention what had caused Adam to turn out the way he had. For Trevor, the potential discoveries by Lewis were endless and valuable for all concerned.

When Lewis landed in Germany, Sonja again picked him up at the airport. Lewis, per instructions from Trevor, was to explore alone in the forest. Sonja found a small cottage that one of the locals used only half the year. The other half of the year, the person lived in France. This was odd considering that most of the local people never really ventured outside the area. Most of the locals worked at a nearby mill. They had everything they needed. Over the years, nonlocal people rarely visited this area. Lewis was an outsider, but oddly he was accepted, especially the last month he was there.

After a good night's sleep, Lewis got up rather early and took a long hike into the woods. He made sure to let Sonja know which direction he was going. He had his cell phone fully charged and his backpack filled with extra supplies. Sonja drove him to the road nearest to the forest and dropped him off. She insisted that Lewis not go alone, but she couldn't find anyone willing to hike with him.

Lewis was having second thoughts about his adventure. He thought that maybe this was not a good idea after all. He was not as young as he used to be, but telling Trevor no was not an option, nor was the thought of missing something that could change the world. Lewis wanted to go on alone. He didn't want someone else to share the discovery. Trevor insisted on this, and that was all Lewis needed to know; he was going alone on this hike. Lewis carried a small sleeping bag, a rifle, a small tent, and food for a few days in his backpack. He started into the woods.

Lewis went straight for the place where they had found Garrison. This area was easy to get to, but it still took him about an hour of hiking to reach. Lewis had heard of the Black Forest in Germany, but this place had to be bigger and even darker. When he came to the place where Garrison had been discovered, he looked at the surroundings to gather his wits. He noticed a small, overgrown trail. At least it looked like a trail to him. He took the path to see where it led. He noticed some broken branches. The farther he went on the trail, the darker it got in the forest. The trees seemed to have grown into each other even more since the previous month's visit.

Lewis went deeper into the forest, and every now and then he would collect samples. After a few hours or so of walking the trail, it suddenly ended. He was having a hard time seeing, so he took his flashlight out and looked around. As Lewis shone the flashlight around, something reflected its light. Then he heard something move. It was running away. Lewis stood still, focused the beam back to where he had seen the reflected light, and slowly moved the flashlight toward the running sound. He was scared, but thinking it was some kind of animal, he attempted to get closer to the area where he had seen the reflection.

When he got there, he looked down and saw some tracks. He was not an expert in identifying tracks, but he knew they had come from some kind of animal. Lewis took his rifle and held the flashlight and rifle as one.

He cautiously walked deeper into the forest. He heard many sounds from the forest. He couldn't help but keep looking up at the trees that blanketed the sky over his head. He felt as if he was walking uphill. He began to notice the plants around him. They seemed to be larger in scope and size than normal. As he walked, his feet sank deeper into the forest's floor. He thought this was because the ground was so fertile. Maybe that was the reason the brush and plants were so large. He wondered how the plants could grow so large when they received very little sunlight.

A few minutes later, as Lewis continued his long journey, his cell phone rang. As soon as the first ring finished, it seemed as though the entire forest moved and scattered to find a place safe from the noise. Then the second ring started, and the forest seemed to calm down. After the third ring, Lewis answered without looking down at the phone.

"Hello," he said as he looked around, surprised by the now silent forest.

On the other end, Sonya said in broken English, "It's been a while until I hear from you. You are doing good?"

"Yes, thanks, Sonja. I am pretty deep in the woods here. I feel like I have been hiking for hours. According to my odometer, I am about four miles from the spot where they found Garrison. Thanks for calling. I need to get off the phone. It is late and getting darker. I wish I didn't have to spend the night in his god forsaken place, but I don't have a choice. I made it this far. I cannot turn back now."

Sonja said, "Be careful, Lewis. Call me when you get out. Good-bye."

As Lewis hung up, he noticed the forest seemed to settle back into its normal level of noise and activity. He wanted to go back, but he thought, *Just a little farther, and I will stop and go back.* Before he knew it, he was a mile or two deeper in the forest. He was very tired, but for the sake of science, he pushed on through the rough and thick brush. There were few wide-open spots in the forest. He used those areas to make good time by picking up his pace. He heard a lot of water running and from time to time had to cross a small stream. He was getting used to the sounds of the forest, but he was still concerned that maybe he had hiked too far into the woods and might run out of daylight. Lewis didn't even want to think about how the forest looked during the night, but he did have a flashlight with extra batteries in his backpack.

Lewis stopped here and there and collected more samples of plants, leaves, soil, tree bark, insects, and worms. As he was putting some of his samples in his backpack, he heard a strange and different sound, a sound he was not used to hearing. He listened for a moment and he heard something move in the forest around him. He stopped what he was doing and looked around. He was a little frightened and picked up his rifle. He kept hearing something moving all around him. It would stop and then start up again. He first thought it might be a pack of wolves or wild dogs. He became very concerned about his situation. He knew that he might encounter something like this when he went into the forest, but it was too late now for him to change that decision. He was miles into this oasis of trees with only a cell phone to connect him to the modern world. He felt like an alien from another planet. He felt so alone.

Panic coursed throughout this body, but he quickly forced himself to regain control over his feelings. The last thing he needed was to panic in the middle of nowhere. He adjusted his backpack and slowly moved back toward the trail in order to get out of the forest. As he was walking away, he kept looking to his left and his right, then turning around to see what was behind him. Suddenly, he tripped and fell backward on his backpack. His gun was still in his hands, but he dropped his flashlight. He gasped and heard more activity from the forest for a moment then the noise died down. He gathered his emotions, got up quickly, and brushed the dirt off his clothes and supplies.

Suddenly he heard a voice with a thick German accent say, "Are you hurt?"

Lewis about jumped out of his skin. He struggled to get control of the rifle lying across his legs. He finally got it with his left hand while his right hand struggled with his flashlight. In a panic, he quickly pointed the light at every angle around him.

"Who's there? Who said that?" he shouted eagerly.

"Don't be afraid. It is only me," the strange, unseen voice said in broken English.

"Show yourself! Where are you? Who are you? I have a gun!" Lewis informed the voice.

"Yes, I see you have the gun but what use is it to you? Lay it down on the ground," the voice said while laughing. Then the unseen man came out from behind one of the large trees about twenty feet in front of Lewis. Lewis quickly pointed the flashlight at him, and as he did, the man raised his oversized hand to shield his eyes and spoke. "Put the lights down now!"

Lewis kept the light on the man. His mind was racing. He looked closer and noticed that the only clothing the man wore was a small piece of worn cloth around his waist. He had no shoes on his extremely oversized feet. The man was huge. Had to be seven-foot-tall or so, built strong, with long blond hair and extremely large hands, feet, arms, and legs. His skin was white, extremely pale, but very dirty. His head was deformed and very large; he stood with a slightly hunched back.

The man spoke again but was more forceful with his tone. "Please, put the lights down now!"

Lewis reluctantly lowered the light to a spot about halfway between the man and himself. He looked down at the rifle lying on the ground.

Again, the man spoke. "Thank you. Don't worry. I will not harm you."

Lewis was nervous, but he didn't want to scare the man by reaching for his gun. He stepped backward, and before he knew it, he was farther from his gun than before.

The man spoke up again and broke Lewis's concentration on the rifle. "So, you not from here, no?" He laughed hard as he walked toward Lewis with a long stride. "Are you with the authorities?"

Lewis was confused. He muttered, "No... no, I am alone. I am a doctor." As soon as he said those words, he thought that he might have sealed his fate by telling the man he was alone. "I... I mean, my... my party will be here any minute."

The man smiled and lowered his head to his right. He said, "Why's you lie? You are alone. I know this to be fact. I will not harm you, Lewis."

Lewis was shaken. He asked, "How do you know my name?"

The man said, "That is what the voice that you carry in your pocket called you."

Lewis said, "How do you know? How did you hear?"

The man replied, "I hear everything in the forest. The forest is my home. Now..." He started to walk toward Lewis at a more normal pace. "You say you are not the authority but doctor. Why you are here?"

Lewis cleared his throat and said, "I am doing some research for a friend. A few years ago, a baby was found in this forest, and—"

"Small baby!" shouted the man. "When was boy found?"

"About six or so years ago," said Lewis.

The man placed his hand over his mouth and uttered these words: "How old was the boy when he was found?"

Lewis said, "We don't actually know exactly how old he was, but he was a newborn, maybe a few days old."

The man stared down at the ground for a moment and then said, "Please come with me, Lewis. Come with me. It is fine. I will not harm you."

Lewis was feeling a little better now in the presence of this large man, but he certainly didn't want to go with him to God knew where.

The man said, "Please. I have someone I want you to meet. It's regarding the baby."

Lewis knew that he had to go with the man; maybe he knew something about the story behind the abandonment of Garrison. He went but kept his distance, staying about ten yards behind him all the way. Knowing this was strange territory for Lewis, the man walked somewhat slowly to allow him to keep up. They walked deeper into the forest.

After another mile or so of a mostly uphill journey, Lewis thought he was going to die. Then he noticed a large cave with smaller trees, brush, and moss growing on top of and around it.

The man stopped and said, "Please stay here." Then he turned and cried out, "Zelda! Zelda, come here! Hurry!"

Lewis noticed some movement inside the cave then saw a massive figure emerge from the opening. It was a woman, one of the biggest that Lewis had ever seen. She was shorter than the other large being but stood about six feet nine. She wore only a small piece of cloth that covered her breasts and the lower part of her body.

The colossal women spoke in German. "What's wrong, Wolfgang? Oh, who is this gentleman?"

The man said, "Zelda, this man is a doctor. I found him in the woods. He said about six years ago they found baby in the forest."

The woman's mouth opened wide as she braced herself on the side of the cave opening. She looked down as she hung on every word from her husband.

The hairy beast-like man continued, "He said the baby was a few days old." Then he looked at Lewis with a wild-eyed smile. "So, good doctor friend, may I ask this question? What kind of clothes this baby was wearing? What color the blanket was?"

Lewis looked from the monstrous man back to the large woman. "I don't know. I don't know the answers to these questions. Look, I am here on behalf of a friend. He adopted the child they found in these woods. There is a space near the front of this forest where the trees don't cover the sky like they do here. There is a small creek with running water, and the baby was found…"

The woman broke out in tears and screamed in English, "*Stop it! Just stop it.*" She ran over to a frightened Lewis and grabbed his shoulders with her big hands, her very long fingers gripping him around and under his arms. "What color was the hair, the eyes?"

Lewis nervously said, "A blond. His hair was blond… is blond, with blue eyes. He had cuts and bite marks all over his body. He was lying there crying about three or so feet from the creek. It was in all the papers in town, and all throughout Germany. Do you know anything about this baby?"

The woman loosened her grip on Lewis, looked down, and cried some more. She gathered herself and sat down on the ground. She looked over to the man and then quickly looked away, shaking her head. The large man knew she was hiding something, and she knew that she needed to let him know the rest of the story.

"Wolfgang, many years ago when we had our last child, I told you I would take care of it. After so many of them, I could not stand to murder another one. So, I went deep in the forest and found this place, a place where my son would be found."

Lewis's mouth hung open, and his senses were on fire. He realized that he had found Garrison's birth mother. He thought it was impossible that this was even happening. He allowed the woman to continue her story.

"When I was walking with him, I heard something in the forest. I heard voices for over two long days. I would rest him down on ground, leave him, and come back to you. Those two nights, I would sneak out and check on him. The third day, I heard more voices. I lured the hunters into the area where I lay my son down. It was the hardest thing I have ever done."

The man stood there in silence for a moment then slowly walked toward her and spoke. "So, this boy is our son, no? I thought you were going to take care of it."

The woman said, "Wolfgang, I could not. After killing our last three children, I just not could do again."

Lewis was taking all this information in, astonished at what he was hearing. He didn't want to interrupt.

The man looked over to him. "Well, allow me to introduce ourselves. Apparently, you met our son what I not knew was alive. My name is Wolfgang, and this is my wife, Zelda."

Lewis said, "It's a pleasure to meet both of you. Let me explain why I am here, please."

Zelda got up and said, "Please come in. We do not get any visitors, so the house is a mess, but please come in. We will not harm you, sir. We are peaceful peoples."

Wolfgang spoke up. "Please come in. We will not harm you. Please tell us about our son."

Lewis was very nervous and didn't want to go inside. He thought they would harm him, but he couldn't run away. Even if he had the opportunity to run from them, he was so exhausted from the miles and miles of hiking, he couldn't make it even if it meant his life. On top of these obstacles, the air would probably slow him down more than his exhaustion. It was thick and heavy. Each breathe he took was a struggle. The air smelled as if the forest had just undergone a rainstorm. Thick, heavy, and musty odors dominated every inch of the area.

Lewis left his rifle on the ground and put his flashlight away. He let Zelda and Wolfgang go inside first, and then he slowly followed. He stopped at the edge of the cave and looked inside. All he saw was darkness.

Wolfgang said, "If you wait a moment, I will start the fire so we see better."

Lewis waited outside the entrance for a few minutes, which seemed like hours. Zelda walked up to him and said, "So my son is still alive?"

Lewis said, "Yes, yes, he is, if this baby is really yours. I mean, I am confused. Why are you... what... why are you living here?"

Just as Lewis finished, he saw the fire burst into flames as Wolfgang got it started in his fireplace. Lewis looked around and saw a rather normal room with very large furniture. The floors were dirty, but the rest of the house was surprisingly clean—or cleaner than at first expected. Then Lewis noticed a swastika painted in a framed picture, as well as what looked like some old and rare artifacts. There was a small, oddly shaped lampshade on top of an oil lamp over in the corner. There was obviously no electricity in this home. It looked as if they had moved in a hundred years ago and had not changed a thing in the house.

Wolfgang said, "My name is Wolfgang Von Ritzmitter. I know this looks strange to you. I know how my appearance disgusts you, but there is explanation."

Lewis eagerly spoke up. "No, your appearance does not disgust me. Believe me, I am used to your appearance, or something like it. This is amazing. You don't understand my excitement. So I have this perfectly clear, you are the parents of that baby they found in this forest?"

Zelda said, "Yes, we are." Wolfgang paced around, visibly irritated. His large feet slammed to the ground, causing the dust and dirt to move across the wooden floor. He squeezed his hands into fists as he moved his eyes around the room. Zelda was nervous, and she thought she had better start explaining her side of the story.

Lewis was still scared. He thought they were going to kill him, but thought that if he could talk to them and maybe earn their trust, they might spare his life.

Zelda looked at Wolfgang as she began to tell the secret that she had kept from her husband for more than six years, and to explain to him about the first few days of her abandoned baby's life. She had Lewis sit down at their table near the fire.

Wolfgang wanted to speak and ask her many questions. He had thought Zelda was going to kill the baby after it was born, so he was surprised that the baby was alive.

Lewis was scared. He was wondering how Wolfgang was going to react to what Zelda had to say because the other man looked to be not only confused but also pissed.

Zelda began her story. "The day I found out I was with child was a horrible day for us. We did not want to bring a child into this world. To live in the forest and eat off the land was not what we wanted for any child. After the first birth, Wolfgang took the child and killed it. He picked up the child by leg and slammed the baby down on ground. When the second child came along, he killed that one too in the more pleasant way. He killed that one by twisting the neck. The third child, he kicks it hard. It fell on ground when he put his boot through its head. We did not want to have child from the beginning, but things happen. After the change, I was able to bear child, but before no child was born."

This information puzzled Lewis for a while and, quite frankly, disturbed him greatly, but he was making the obvious connections between Zelda's situation and Trevor's.

Zelda continued. "So, when fourth child came, I could not bear to see another murder. So, I took the baby into the forest. I laid the baby down in place where hopefully someone see him. Two day goes by and nothing, but on the third day, I heard people come back. I lure them by making sounds. Then they take the baby. I am sorry I lied, but I could not bear to see another killing."

Wolfgang nodded in approval and understanding, but he was not pleased. "I understand but I am disappointed that you were not honest with me."

Zelda said with a wounded heart, "Sometimes you are not the most caring or understanding person."

They stopped talking and both looked at Lewis. He was sweating and very nervous. He was thinking, *If these two could kill babies, what would they do to me?* He began to speak. He told them why he entered the forest. He told them about Garrison, how he had been found, how he had been taken care of by the police and the local orphanage. Lewis told them about Trevor and Adelle, and the couple's desire to adopt the boy and the way they ended up doing that. He told them of Garrison's high intelligence, his accomplished motor skills, and his incredible health. He told them about the dog incident. He told them about how Garrison bit his father and how his father had changed physically and mentally. He told them he was confused by how Garrison was physically normal, but his father was disfigured physically since the bite. He told them of Adam and explained that Adam was basically half-animal and half-boy. Among all the information that Lewis presented, this was the area that Wolfgang seemed to be most interested in.

As Lewis was explaining the events of the past six or so years, Wolfgang got up and walked the floor many times. Wolfgang looked many times at Zelda. She made eye contact half of those times. They spoke in German between them after Lewis again pleaded with them not to hurt him.

"I assure you that I was not expecting to find anyone living in this forest. I want to make it perfectly clear that I am not interested at all in turning you two in to the authorities. I am only interested in finding the reason as to why Garrison acted the way he has during certain moments throughout his life. I am reaching for some answers as to how he had changed his father into something strange and beast-like. I am here to find out the cause of these problems and maybe find a cure. I implore you not to kill me and allow me to go so I can continue with my research."

Wolfgang and Zelda seemed shook up but also annoyed by the notion that they would harm or even kill Lewis. They told him that he was free to go when he wished and that no harm would come to him as long as he would not harm them. Wolfgang was concerned that Lewis might notify and bring the authorities to this place and have them arrested, but Lewis was very convincing when he promised not to tell anyone the whereabouts of their location. Lewis was only interested in finding a cure and finding the root cause of the situation. Lewis nervously asked them about their own personal appearance because it was exactly like Trevor's. He wanted to know the cause of their condition.

Wolfgang told Lewis that they would not hurt him and that this visit from him was quite a shock to them. Wolfgang sat down and asked, "How many people have been affected?

"Just two people at the moment. The boy and the adopting father."

"Two is too many. It is very important for them not to spread the mutation to others."

Lewis was surprised when Wolfgang said the word *mutation*. Wolfgang started to reveal the secrets of what Lewis had been after for years. He started from the beginning, when he had been a young scientist looking for a job after graduation. In 1931, his former mentor and employer, Professor Hans Wundrak, was offered a position with the Nazi Party to form a group with other scientists. The professor was famous in all of Germany for being the leading expert on human molecular biology and the study of reproductive cells. Professor Wundrak asked Wolfgang to join him as his assistant. At the time, everyone was excited about the new leadership of Adolf Hitler.

The intellectual groups were segregated into many parts; Professor Wundrak and Wolfgang were assigned to the reproductive-cell research team. They worked on the project named "Weiter Leben" or "Continued Life." The project had two objectives. One was to find the genetic structure of the perfect human and to learn to reproduce that genetic structure before birth. The perfect human would be immune from diseases; have certain hair, skin, and eye colors; and have no physical or mental deformities. The second objective was to find some kind of remedy for any physical and mental deformities and to cure diseases that didn't have cures at that time.

Professor Wundrak and Wolfgang spent years studying the problem. They worked tireless hours studying the DNA structure not only of humans but of animals and plants, work that led to their discovery of a new chemical formula. After many years of adding and subtracting numerous types of chemicals, they came close to recreating a formula that would enhance the DNA structure. This formula could help change the basic structure of many different organisms' DNA. They named the newly found chemical the Leben Formula—or, in the inner circles of the Nazi Party, Formula L. Wolfgang made it perfectly clear to Lewis that only he and the professor knew the makeup of this chemical mixture. He did not reveal it to anyone else.

The purpose of their study was to see the effect the formula would have on all living organisms. They wanted to better life for the German people. Hitler wanted to find the secret of life. He wanted someone not only to discover the secret of life but to find the perfect human and animal molecular structure. Hitler was also interested in changing a human's or an animal's molecular biological structure. He wanted a chemical or a drug that would make the human body incapable of being invaded by disease. Hitler told everyone, especially Professor Wundrak and Wolfgang, that they would have unlimited subjects to experiment on, namely the Jews who were captured.

The professor and Wolfgang were excited to start testing on human subjects. They would use animals and plants to see the different effects, if any, the formula would have on their molecular structure, as well. After the tests, they would collect and analyze data, and then hopefully they would come closer to the ultimate goal of the project.

After a few years of research and testing on animal and plant subjects with the Leben Formula, the professor and Wolfgang heard of a village at a nearby forest. The forest was very dense and hardly any of it had been completely explored, for one reason or another. Some of the locals were afraid of the forest and said that strange animals occupied it. Others said the forest was so dense and thick that hiking through it was almost impossible. The village was extremely small. It had one grocery store, one drugstore, and one factory, which made tires and other rubber products for a few companies in the bigger towns and cities nearby. The school was also the church, and most of the people stayed close to each other, helping whoever needed assistance.

This small and not-well-traveled town was called Renn. The town was so small it didn't show up on most of the countrywide maps. The locals had a reputation for not venturing outside the town. This practice started many years ago when the founders of the town wanted to get away from the bigger cities and live a life in the country with clean air and good, friendly people. The only odd thing about this area was that people didn't seem to grow as old as they should. Many of the villagers looked as if they were twenty to even thirty years younger than their actual age. Another strange component to this town was the lack of sickness. The drugstores had less and less use for medicine as time passed. There were a few sick people in the town, and many people had passed on, but for the most part, everyone seemed to be very healthy.

The professor and Wolfgang were interested in the town for obvious reasons. They explored it and ran many tests on the numerous samples they collected. They didn't have any inkling as to what they were after, but they had to start with something. After a few months of tireless research, they came up with nothing. Was there something in the villagers' diet? Was something in the air causing them to fight off sickness better than the other towns throughout Europe? The research was long and exhausting. Both Wolfgang and the professor invested many hours.

One day, the professor suffered a major heart attack in the lab and died immediately. From that day forward, Wolfgang was on his own, without a mentor. He was allowed to continue the work on the "Weiter Leben" project. He wanted assistants, so Hitler assigned a few people to him. Before returning to the village, Wolfgang and his assistants studied the molecular structures of not only the human beings but plants and animals as well. They attempted to coordinate what they already knew with what was going on in the small village.

When Wolfgang had exhausted all possibilities in the village, his work took him into the forest. He went exploring in the deep, thick, dark woods the natives had feared since the beginning. As he walked through the thick underbrush, he would stop to collect as many samples as possible. He took all the samples back to his lab and had his assistants run tests on them.

Wolfgang had a theory that maybe the answer lay deep in the forest—maybe a plant, or a certain stream or spring of water. Maybe something was somehow getting into the drinking water of the people, or maybe the people were breathing something airborne. There had to be an answer to why these people were so healthy and young looking. All the villagers had small gardens or ate what was growing in the area. They drank water from wells that tapped into springs. Springs appeared all over this area, from what Wolfgang had been told. He was convinced the secret was organic and these people were ingesting something that was helping them keep young and healthy.

One day during his research in the forest, Wolfgang stumbled on something by accident. He collected samples from a tree located so deep in the forest that it had taken him a couple of days just to reach the area. Most of the land was uphill, the ground seemed to be very rich, and the soil dark and moist.

Wolfgang hiked deeper into the forest. After a difficult night of camping out, he went even farther in. After a few hours had passed, Wolfgang was exhausted. He wanted to go home. As he was about to turn back, he saw something strange around one particular tree. He walked closer to get a better look and discovered that some kind of moss was growing on the ground around this very large, stately tree. The trunk was larger than that of any other tree he had seen in the forest. The moss had a yellowish-green glow with a hint of white haze on the top. Wolfgang had never seen anything like it. He reached down to feel the moss. The texture was like silk. He attempted to pull up a portion with his fingers, but he couldn't pull the moss away from the ground. He pulled out his knife and cut some of it. He had to apply some pressure for the knife to get through the moss so he could examine it more closely. After he got the moss loose, he noticed a large white root buried deep in the ground. He dug around the root with his knife, and after a few minutes of digging and pulling, trying not to injure the root, he finally got it free. The root was a good foot and a half long, in the shape of a large carrot. At the end there were five smaller roots. Wolfgang decided to pull on one of them that had been growing away from the tree. As he pulled on it, the ground below was gently breaking. For fear of harming the root, he pulled out a small shovel from his gear and started to dig around the root. Wolfgang dug for a long time, and before he knew it, he had dug about ten feet from the starting point. He continued, and finally he came to the end of the root, or so he thought. The root seemed to go straight down into the earth. He pulled gently on the root at first, and then he started to pull harder and harder. Finally, it began to give way. After an astonishing six to seven more feet, he finally pulled the entire root out of the earth.

Wolfgang immediately noticed a good portion of the root was slimy and wetter than a typical root in this area. When he looked down, he saw a small puddle of water at the bottom of the long hole where the root grew. He thought there had to be a spring under him. After a burst of energy from this creditable discovery, he cut four sections of the root with his knife, making sure not to further injure the root system.

He gathered all his plants up as best as he could. He had to wrap the root system around him so he could better carry the moss back to his lab. He was worried that it might die before he could get back, so he hurried as best he could. He had to spend another night in the forest. He was lucky to find a small river, and he decided to camp near it for the night. He placed the roots in the flowing stream in hopes of keeping them alive. He made sure to mark his territory in case he needed to get back to this place at a future date.

When Wolfgang returned to his lab, he was covered in dirt, but he had kept the moss alive. That very night, he took a sample of the moss and ran a battery of tests to see if he could find anything unusual about its chemical makeup. He obviously knew something was different about the plant physically. His theory was that somehow the moss's roots might have affected the drinking water of the village, thus maybe explaining why the villagers lived longer and had fewer physical illnesses than normal.

Wolfgang was busy analyzing the plant, and he wanted to see what effect the Leben Formula would have on it. On a whim, Wolfgang, with the use of a dropper, placed a few drops of the formula on the root of the moss plant. He studied the results under his microscope. He saw some astonishing changes. He didn't have a clue what would come from these changes, but there had been a reaction like no other.

While Wolfgang was telling his story, Lewis attempted to hang on every word and not let one sentence get past him. He wished he had his notebook, but he didn't want to ask permission to get it from his backpack.

Wolfgang continued with his story. He told Lewis that because of the experiment, he thought he had accidently discovered a part of the molecular structure in the human body that in theory would prevent human illness. The moss from that tree had a different structural makeup from most mosses in the forest. Wolfgang went back numerous times to countless different trees, and all of them were the same, but this one particular tree, large in size, massive in structure, and strong in stature, was the only one with this particular kind of moss growing around its base. At the time, he didn't understand or know why the moss formed around only that tree. Still, Wolfgang was careful not to rob much of the moss because it was obviously a limited commodity and was potentially very valuable for the future.

Many weeks went by as Wolfgang attempted to grow the moss in a controlled environment, but after a few days, the moss would lose its color and even its texture and die. He concluded that he didn't water the moss enough. In his controlled environment, he replanted the moss in wetter soil and watered the plant regularly. At the time, he didn't yet know that the plant needed a continuous supply of water to keep it alive. He eventually discovered that the chemical makeup of the moss had some of the same characteristics as the villagers' drinking water. The drinking water came from a spring that the entire village used. The town used numerous springs for wells, and each home had a well in its backyard.

Wolfgang knew he was onto something big here. For that reason, Wolfgang's research was at a fever pitch. He wanted to see if the new chemical substance would assist an animal in growing as it did with the plants. The only way to test that was to experiment on animals, but Wolfgang didn't stop with animals. He had access to humans, and lots of them. With so many Jews in captivity at the time, his human subjects were limitless.

Wolfgang went on to speak about the numerous experiments that were performed on rabbits, foxes, squirrels, hogs, pigs, chickens, and of course, the Jews. As he spoke, he had a lifeless face, his voice was unemotional, and he spoke of these events as if he were explaining a cooking recipe. The moss, most notably the grass part of the plant, was compounded with a special mixture of chemicals that Wolfgang created and then quickly injected into animal subjects. At first, the subjects would experience intense pain, then they would start a rapid growth spurt. In all cases, the bones would grow faster than the skin would, and the skin would split in two. Many times, the bones would be visible to the naked eye. Not only would the bones grow too fast for the rest of the body tissue but even the eyes, ears, mouth, teeth, and some organs would grow too rapidly in many of the subjects. This caused these areas to split or rip apart while the animal was still alive, thus causing the subject extreme discomfort and pain. In most cases, the leg muscles would tear in two, exposing the bones.

In the first week, the human subjects' joints would ache and they would experience terrible discomfort. Some of the subjects would experience more distress than others. After a couple of months, they would cry out in more pain. They would scream loudly as their legs, arms, neck, head, shoulders, and back began to grow. As had happened with the animals, in some cases the bones would grow too fast, causing the skin and muscles to rip and pull away from the growing bones. This was especially a problem with the fingers, arms, and legs, but especially with the back. In the beginning, Wolfgang was frightened of his subjects, mostly because of the unknown. He would have them placed in cells and bound with chains around their necks, ankles, and wrists.

At first, the process was messy. Somehow, the first batch of the formula was too strong, and the reaction was fast and violent. Some of the subjects' pain was so great they would experience cardiac arrest or pass out and die of exhaustion. Some would go crazy because of the lack of sleep the pain caused. The loss of blood was great, and subjects would sometimes bleed to death. On many occasions, the SS guards would take the subjects and place them in a special large cell near the lab to die on their own. They would dispose of them later. With some of the subjects, the eyes would get too big and split in two, causing extreme pain and discomfort. It had been a challenge to keep the subjects alive through the experiments.

Wolfgang began to laugh and smile when explaining the suffering of his subjects to Lewis. He had tested children as young as one, and elders of ninety years or more. Some of his subjects were in good health, while the others were not. Some of these unfortunate people could not walk, see, or hear, and some were mentally ill. If Wolfgang wanted a subject that had a certain deformity but couldn't find one, he would force the deformity on his subjects. He would blind them, pour acid in their ears, or place a pen inside the ear to deafen them, or he would break their backs in order to cause paralysis. Wolfgang didn't know exactly how many subjects he used, but the numbers were over one thousand humans and a few hundred animals. He would do anything to see how his formula would react with all types and forms. He wanted to see if the formula could cure these ills or deformities. Wolfgang constantly found himself adding or subtracting chemicals or doses of solutions from his original formula.

After three long years of experimentation, Wolfgang finally developed the correct formula so the subject's muscles grew at the same rate as the bones. He found the perfect mixture of each chemical plus the right amount of moss. He discovered just how much of each chemical should be added to the formula so the muscles would not split because of the rapid growth of the bone. When he finally perfected the formula as best as he could, he would use the sickest Jew they could find and inject the formula.

Many of these subjects had discomfort but not the consistent pain of those from the very first batch. The discomfort would come and go, and the process would be long. Typically, in a few months the subjects were cured, and according to the subjects themselves, they had never felt better in their lives. The only remaining issue was the deformity of the physical body. The transformations were grotesque, and often the subjects were unrecognizable at the end.

The other problem Wolfgang encountered was that Hitler ordered the subjects to be destroyed for fear of them banding together in opposition of the Nazis. Hitler ordered the subjects to death before the total transformation was complete.

As Wolfgang was explaining this to Lewis, the only time he shook his head or showed any emotion was when he described the side effects of the formula. After countless attempts, he couldn't prevent the deformities from affecting the subjects. The deformity was rapid growth rate and increased size in all extremities, including the head, eyes, mouth, and ears. Rapid and extreme hair growth followed. Although the subjects wouldn't live very long after the mutation was complete, thanks to Hitler's orders to exterminate them, Wolfgang believed that, according to the cell structure, the newly formed organisms might live forever.

Wolfgang paused and sat back in his chair as he stopped to drink some water Zelda had poured for him. She offered some to Lewis, but he declined. Wolfgang picked the story back up.

After months and months of testing the infected subjects, he noticed their senses were keener, they had more awareness of their surroundings, and they had taken on the instincts of an animal. After further testing, he found that their adrenaline was reacting with the formula that was flowing through their bodies. The studies showed they were hungrier than normal. They also seemed to be more intelligent. They would perfect certain tasks presented to them. They also seemed to become more agitated than normal. One of the subjects got loose and attacked a chicken. He bit into the chicken with his teeth, then pulled and pulled like a mad dog until it was dead. He attempted to eat the chicken before being tied and bound. This was common in all the subjects, including animals.

Wolfgang began to feed certain animals to the subjects. For some reason, the subjects loved to feast on any animal, whether it be a live fish, a squirrel, a fox, a chicken, a snake, or any animal found in the forest. Wolfgang wanted to get to the root of what made the adrenaline interact with the formula to make the subject more aggressive and hungry for animals. In addition, the adrenaline and the solution tended to accelerate the growth of the mutation. The angrier, more emotional, or more stressed the subject got, the faster the mutation developed until it was complete.

Hitler was extremely pleased with the progress they had made over the years. Hitler and Wolfgang knew they had found a formula for perfect health and a way to cheat death. Hitler wanted to be injected with the formula, but Wolfgang wanted to do more testing. Hitler was impatient, but Wolfgang argued that he couldn't allow his fuehrer to suffer the mutations the formula caused. This angered Hitler, but ultimately, he accepted the answer and allowed Wolfgang to perform more tests to perfect the mutation process.

Wolfgang was now one of Hitler's favorites on his Third Reich staff. Hitler kept Wolfgang's work a secret from the world. He told no one of the experiments. There must have been some rumors, Wolfgang thought, but as with the Jewish situation, most people kept information to themselves. On the rare occasion that someone even hinted at any top-secret information, that person would be eliminated. Some had even been thrown in with the Jews for extermination.

Wolfgang sat back and looked around the cave. He raised his hands up in the air and said this was all built for him by his fuehrer. The cave had been constructed in the fall of 1938 under the orders of Hitler and a few of his men. He had wanted a safe place for his most secret but prized scientist who discovered the key to eternal life. He sent an expedition of five men out into the forest at least five miles or so from the nearest town. One of the men found the large cave. They reported to Hitler, and he had a small crew dig out the remaining dirt and rock. They dug deeper into the floor of the cave and discovered a long passageway that twisted down to a small cliff. Over millions of years, water had poured through this passageway and emptied outside the cliff into a large pond. The men constructed a wooden floor to cover the ground. In some parts of the cave, they put up wooden walls and used plaster to protect them from moisture and the temperature changes throughout the year. They installed a trap door to the side of the newly constructed floor to provide access to the passageway. In the passageway, the men dug out the extra rock and dirt and made a lab for Wolfgang. The lab was not as large or nice as the one he had in town, but it worked for him. The lab was very seldom used by anyone. Down below the passageway, the crew discovered a large spring, and they constructed a well to provide access to fresh water. Inside the unfinished part of the passageway, they installed a generator that produced steam using water from the spring under that portion of the cave. The generator produced enough energy to charge batteries, so some of the machines could work for short periods in the complex.

Through the years, Wolfgang collected many test tubes, candles, and lab instruments, as well as many chemicals he had found. He had special hiding places all throughout the cave, especially in the far end. He collected iron poles, blowtorches, oil, gas, rope, sleeping bags, clothes, and other supplies that he thought he might need in the future. He put a stove, a bathtub, and a sink inside the cave. Even if they never used it, other members of the Nazi Party would be able to use the cave if the war didn't progress the way they hoped. He also constructed a fireplace, as well as a bedroom in the back part of the cave. Another room was for ammunition, guns, small bombs, grenades, and other items that could be used for protection.

Hitler had wanted to protect the man who had invented this most special formula. Hitler eventually wanted the formula for use on the men in his army. He wanted his soldiers to live forever. He wanted some of the German people to be injected as well, so they could breed the perfect human race he longed for. The formula was not perfected yet. All Hitler had needed was time, but time had not necessarily been on their side.

Wolfgang stopped his story, and got up from his chair and walked over to the fireplace. He looked down and said it was a shame they had run out of time. Lewis sat there in his chair. He was afraid to move because he didn't want to interrupt Wolfgang for fear of stopping this incredible tale. Wolfgang continued.

The Allied Nations had been closing in on Berlin. Wolfgang couldn't believe that Germany was going to lose the war. Hitler was nowhere to be found. He had lost contact with him. Wolfgang went into hiding in the woods with his wife. For some reason, the Nazis didn't destroy the cave. The couple made a doorway of brush and rocks to cover the entrance. Wolfgang was forty years old when Nazi Germany fell. The SS, per Hitler's orders, destroyed Wolfgang's lab. Hitler didn't want the Allied Nations to get possession of the formula. Hitler knew the formula would make any nation the ruler of the world if they learned its secrets and could mass-produce it. Wolfgang was smart though. He had smuggled out many gallons of the formula from his lab and hid them throughout the forest. To this day, they were still buried deep in the forest they called home.

Zelda continued the story while Wolfgang went over to their kitchen area and pumped water out of a well inside the cave. Zelda said that when they were first trapped in the cave, Wolfgang had had only three choices. He could die in the forest over time, turn himself over to the Allies, or inject himself with his own formula. Obviously, he had done the last.

Wolfgang walked back to his chair and sat down. He pointed to his massive left forearm and said, "This is where I injected myself with the newest batch of the formula. It was the most promising batch up to then." In a week, the pains had started in all his joints. In less than a month, the hair began to grow all over his body. Then his extremities started to grow at an alarming rate. He was in some pain and discomfort, but it was bearable. His head, eyes, ears—everything grew. In about three months, the mutation was complete. During the last stage, the extra hair that had grown all over his body fell out, with the exception of hair on his head, chest, armpits, and pubic area. The hair on his arms and legs fell out completely. That had been almost a hundred years ago. Wolfgang and his wife were still alive and had not aged since the injection.

Lewis mustered a few sentences to tell them his friend, Trevor, was in the stage where the hair was still on his body. Everything else had happened to his friend just as Wolfgang had described. But Lewis explained that Trevor had not been injected but bitten by his son... or rather Wolfgang's son. He asked how that could be. He also wanted to know why it had taken Trevor so long to mutate. Wolfgang explained that the formula had been somewhat watered down because of the youth of the boy. The mutation process would take longer.

Wolfgang said that in the later stages of his research, he had found that as the subject's adrenaline reached a certain level, it mixed with the chemical solution. The combination caused a reaction, resulting in an increase of saliva production. Wolfgang believed that the mixed formula came through the gums, so maybe when the boy bit the man, the saliva got into the man's bloodstream. In the final part of his research, he inspected the teeth of the mutants and found that some were almost hollowed out. Maybe the chemical mixture came through the hollow part of the tooth, or maybe it seeped around the gums. Wolfgang said he had run out of time before he could determine the answer. Wolfgang himself had only four teeth.

Lewis was getting more excited, and he interjected what he had found in his three subjects. With all this new information, everything was beginning to make sense, and he thought this had to be the only answer for how the formula was transferred. Lewis wondered why it was through saliva alone. Wolfgang said that it had to be in the bloodstream but that the adrenaline had to reach a critical level in order for the formula to be transferred. Somehow, the formula could not be transferred through normal saliva, sweat, or any other agent. In addition, the formula must come through the mouth. Wolfgang believed that not only was the increased level of adrenaline key to infecting a subject but also the temperature of the formula had to be elevated when it was transferred. The formula was useless until the right temperature was reached.

This newfound knowledge was fascinating to Lewis, but as the conversation slowed down, he wondered again if he would be allowed to leave with his life. He didn't know why Wolfgang was sharing all this top-secret information with him, especially after all those years keeping it hidden from the world.

Wolfgang sensed his fear and answered the unspoken question. He said that he could not go out in the world looking like this, a mutant. If he had only had more time, he could have improved his and his wife's appearances. He'd needed more time to perfect the formula, but Germany had fallen and thus ended the research. The Nazis destroyed all his labs and his subjects, all of them. They destroyed most of the formula that was in the lab itself. There were too many side effects, and for this reason alone, they decided to destroy everything that dealt with the formula. They even eliminated the newer subjects that had not lived long enough to undergo the transformation. Hitler had ordered mass killings of all the subjects.

Hitler had gotten cold feet at times with the project, even before he gave the order to eliminate all the test subjects. Wolfgang seemed very upset that Hitler hadn't given him enough time to test the subjects through the completion of the mutation process. Many times, Hitler had killed the men and women before the mutation even began. He was concerned that they might turn on the Nazi Party and become an issue for the country. Wolfgang had to convince Hitler to keep them alive long enough for the testing to be complete and for the mutation to run its full course. In some cases, Hitler listened to him, but he only wanted them alive for a few months, until the mutation ran its course. Wolfgang had never seen the full and final effects of the formula until he used it on himself and his wife. Wolfgang was very interested in what one of their offspring would look like and how the child would act through time. With the knowledge of his son, Garrison, he felt that his research was branching again into the unknown. He kept reassuring Lewis that his life was safe if he didn't notify anyone of their presence in the forest.

Wolfgang continued with his story. Zelda and Wolfgang escaped to the cave to hide out for as long as it took. Many of the Nazis didn't know about the cave. The ones who did, Hitler had killed. For some reason, Hitler didn't order the destruction of the cave itself. Wolfgang didn't know why. The only reason he could think of was that Hitler, in the back of his mind, thought he would eventually use the cave for himself.

Wolfgang himself killed five SS men who threatened to keep the doctor in captivity. Wolfgang and Zelda had a lot of trouble getting away from the SS and the Nazis. They had to run from building to building and hide behind lots of rubble from the bombings as they fled. They ended up stealing a car and somehow made their way out of the city. They soon ditched the car outside the city limits because they had run out of gas. They spent a few days traveling by foot, trying to get to the forest where the cave was located. They didn't ask for any help along their journey in fear of bringing a stranger to the cave. The travel into the forest was even longer and harder. The cave was hidden well, deep inside. They had to cover four to six miles of wooded and hilly terrain to reach their safe haven; it took several exhausting days.

A few months after he changed, he injected Zelda with the formula. Zelda wanted to live forever with her husband, even if it meant living in the forest and being separated from the world. She didn't have much family still alive, and the ones who were alive had fled to America in the last years of World War II.

Lewis was still concerned about his safety. He kept asking himself why Wolfgang was telling him things that had been kept private for so many years. He finally got up the courage to ask that question. "Why are you telling me this story after all of these years?"

Wolfgang laughed and said, "No one has come this far into this forest for me to tell this story." Then he got very serious and said, "Why did you come so far into the forest?"

Lewis told Wolfgang the truth. He explained that he worked for the baby's father. He told them in more detail about Garrison, Trevor, and Adam.

Wolfgang was very interested in Adam. He had never experimented with mating a mutant with a nonmutant. He found the information about Adam to be fascinating.

Lewis also explained the possible financial riches that could result from this disease, chemical, or whatever it was that Garrison had flowing through his body. He made a desperate plea to Wolfgang for the formula, saying that he would share half of all profits and keep Wolfgang's and Zelda's identities a secret. Wolfgang wasn't interested in riches or fame. He and Zelda had been in the forest now for over a century, since the end of World War II. They were used to this lifestyle. Obviously, neither had aged nor would age; they would live forever unless someone killed them or they killed themselves.

Lewis asked a question about food. Wolfgang and Zelda said at the same time that they lived off the land. They killed and ate the animals they could catch. The pond also held many fish. In addition, they ate berries, small plants, and the roots of plants in the forest. Sometimes Wolfgang would go into the town where Lewis had started his journey and would take some food from the locals' fields. He always worried about footsteps and being seen, so he was extra careful whenever he made his trip, but those days were far and few between.

Wolfgang discussed life after he and Zelda moved into the cave. Their bodies could withstand the bitter cold of the winters and the brutal heat of the summers. That was one of the many advantages of the formula: the body could adapt to extreme climates. The forest provided the proper amount of food. They had stored many packages of all types of vegetable seeds inside the cave. They replanted them in the forest. Some of the seeds grew, and some did not. Wolfgang had discovered that he could remake the formula at his lab in the cave, but after so many years, he had run out of the chemicals needed to create it. He did use a mixture of something he was working on with the water and the moss plants, and somehow when he fed this water mixture to the seeds, more times than not they germinated. In many cases, the plants grew and produced larger than normal vegetables or fruit. Wolfgang had a problem keeping the animals out of his makeshift gardens here and there in the forest. The lack of sunlight was a large problem for him.

Wolfgang had continued his experiments in the cave for years. He would make cages for the animals he trapped and would run experiments on them. Wolfgang performed experiments on turtles, fish, roaches, worms, frogs, birds, spiders, snakes, and other forest animals. He would sometimes go to the edge of the forest and collect stray dogs and cats from the village. He told Lewis that he had discovered some interesting new material over the years. He said that if he had time someday, he would go into further detail on his latest experiments, but he did go into some detail on a few.

He was ultimately attempting to perfect Formula L after the war, but he had lost a lot of materials and supplies when his lab was destroyed. He tried to work on lessening the effects of the mutation, but his lab was not equipped to handle this large of a task. He did attempt some new experiments on tissue regrowth. He would cut a leg off a frog and inject the subject with a new formula to see if the frog would regenerate the missing limb. Most of the subjects died before the test was complete. Additionally, with the limitation of his new lab, he couldn't work as effectively as he would have liked.

Something that Wolfgang wanted to perfect in the future, besides the original Formula L, was the mixing of human and animal DNA. If he could add the most attractive parts of the human and the best parts of a certain animal, the resulting subject could be very useful for military or even everyday purposes.

"Imagine," he said, "if you had a man with eyesight that was off the charts, or a human that was as strong as a cow, or both. The subject would make a powerful weapon in combat."

Of course, he didn't have the technology in the cave to attempt this process, but he did play around with the formula. Conversely, adding or taking away some chemicals either proved too painful for the animals, which ended up dying in their cage, or killed them in minutes. Wolfgang told Lewis that Adolf Hitler would have been so proud of him for his current research and for his work to achieve the perfect human.

The forest was peaceful for Wolfgang and Zelda, and they considered the outside world to be very boring. Wolfgang never really liked people that much, and he enjoyed his time in the forest. He was deeply in love with Zelda, and they had made a wonderful life together.

From time to time, a few hikers would enter the area, but the two of them were never discovered. Wolfgang and Zelda could hear footsteps from long distances, so if anything were to approach them, they would hear it before they were seen.

As the conversation died down, Zelda mentioned that it was getting dark, and she suggested Lewis stay the night. Lewis got up and unpacked. He didn't have a choice. He showed them his cell phone, and he called Sonja to notify her that he was okay. The signal was very weak. He didn't tell her of Wolfgang or Zelda. Wolfgang and Zelda were shocked by the cell phone. They couldn't believe something like that had been invented. Through most of the night, Lewis explained the world the way it was now. He attempted to explain how different it was from 1945. He recounted as many world events from the past decades as he could.

Lewis also took notes so he wouldn't forget anything. He and Wolfgang sat together and recapped what they knew. Both men wanted to learn from each other. It was amazing: a German scientist who created Formula L on one side of the table and on the other side a man from the States who had seen and was experiencing the effects of what the formula had created.

Wolfgang was fascinated by the fact that Lewis had experienced the effects of the formula. He was most interested in Lewis's opportunity to witness the long-term effects of the formula on a living subject. Not only had he witnessed one being affected but he had seen the birth of a human with the formula inside him in the earliest stage of the mutation. If that wasn't enough for Wolfgang, Lewis had not only witnessed that but had also seen a subject transfer the formula to a normal human being. This was shocking to Wolfgang, and he loved every minute of their conversation.

They went into great detail about how the formula changed a human being into part animal and how it increased the senses in the subject's body. They also discussed how the subjects changed both in their personalities and in their physical makeup over time. How their talents for hunting, their reflexes, and their hand-eye coordination had improved since the infection. They also discussed the transfer of the chemical to an unaffected human by way of a bite—not just any bite, but a bite of anger or other emotion that increased adrenaline to the point where it reacted with the formula inside the body. They discussed at even greater length whether when an infected man mated with an uninfected woman, the offspring would be more animal-like and more uncontrollable. But they concluded that when two infected humans mated, they would create a more normal human without the physical mutation but with the same heightened senses and the appetite of an animal.

Wolfgang had no thoughts of killing Lewis, but he had known Lewis feared for his life from the beginning. After talking with Lewis for hours on end, he felt that he could trust the man. Besides, he was very interested in finding out what would eventually happen to all of Lewis's subjects. If it even did end. In the name of science, Wolfgang had to keep Lewis alive. Lewis was now the most interesting man Wolfgang had met since the war. It was amazing that, almost one hundred years after Formula L was invented, it would affect people a half a world away in America. Zelda wanted Lewis to live because she wanted to see pictures of her son in the future. Obviously, Lewis did not carry any pictures, but he told them he would return with more information.

Wolfgang didn't give him the formula or tell him the chemical make-up of the discovery. He told Lewis, "I am concerned the other man, your superior, will use this formula for his country and make America even stronger than she already is. I know you are close to finding the secret to the formula, but in all probability, you will never discover the complete formula. I just wanted to let you know that, Lewis." Wolfgang smiled at Lewis as he was enjoying the empty and defeated look that was on his face. "If you bring others to the cave, I would kill them all."

Lewis understood. He knew that if he returned to the forest, it would not be long before either Wolfgang or Zelda knew someone was coming. Lewis reassured them he had no interest in others finding them. He wanted a cure. Wolfgang laughed and said there was no cure or antidote for the formula. The process was irreversible. The only way to stop the infection was death.

Lewis asked if he could make a second call from his cell phone. He ended up getting through to Sonja and told her that he was fine and that he was going to stay the night in the forest. His cell phone was the best on the market, and he had great reception, but this deep in the forest, the signal was spotty. Lewis attempted to get some sleep but only managed a few hours. He was too afraid and too excited to sleep.

The next morning, he ate some food from his backpack and went on his way. He told them that he would come back, bring them pictures of their son, and report to them on the condition of all of his subjects. He assured them that if he ever returned, he would be alone. Wolfgang feared Lewis would tell what he had learned. As Wolfgang pondered this, he understood that he had to keep Lewis alive in the name of science. He knew that without Lewis and his research, Formula L would never be studied unless Wolfgang made himself known to the world. Of course, this could never happen because he and Zelda would never be accepted in normal human society. Wolfgang was very impressed with the work Lewis had done so far, and he was especially interested in Lewis's three different subjects.

After Lewis said his farewells, he attempted to walk at a normal pace, but he caught himself jogging a few times. He wanted to get out of the forest and away from Wolfgang and Zelda in the worst way, but then again, a part of him wanted to stay and learn more. He knew that he had to go, and they had seemed to want him to leave. After a good day of hiking, Lewis was about to faint from exhaustion, but he kept going. He found the energy to keep moving, mostly out of fear of them following him. Before he knew it, he was losing daylight and the forest was getting darker and darker. He finally made it out before the sun was down. He fell to his knees as a rush of freedom filled his soul. He felt as if he had cheated death itself. He was shaking like the leaves in the forest as the wind brushed across them at all angles.

He called Sonja and asked her to pick him up. He waited about thirty minutes, though it seemed like thirty days. He kept his eye on the forest, afraid that one of them had followed him or was going to come after him while he waited. Every sound he heard, he thought it was one of them, but much to his relief, he saw nothing. For the first time in his life, he was scared but also very excited to get back to the States and tell Trevor all about his trip and his discoveries. Then he saw the headlights in the distance, and he knew it was Sonja. His cell phone rang, and it was her on the other line, making sure it was him that she saw.

Once the car pulled up, Lewis threw his backpack and supplies in the back. He was dirty, smelly, and noticeably frightened. He got in the car, and closed and locked the door. Sonja asked, "What is wrong? Are you okay?"

Lewis kept looking at the forest and quietly said, "Please drive. Everything is fine.

Lewis spoke nothing of Wolfgang or Zelda. The only tidbit of information that he shared was that he was tired and a little scared because he had gotten lost but that he had collected many good samples. Sonja drove to Lewis's hotel.

After taking a long shower, Lewis called Trevor and told him that he would be leaving for home the next day and that he had some good information. He told him he would talk with him when he got back. Then he crashed in this hotel room for a much-needed night's sleep. He was too tired to stay awake. The next morning, he got ready for the travel back to States, and Sonja drove him to the airport.

CHAPTER 11

Factuality

*B*ack in the States, Adelle was getting better thanks mostly to her medication. She was more relaxed about her current situation. She was more tired than she had ever been in her life, and she took many long naps throughout the day. The medication made her very relaxed, and she didn't seem to care about many of the things that she had cared about before.

Trevor decided that it would still be in everyone's best interest if he continued to place a leash around Adam's neck when they went outside. The leash was for when they took a walk or went out to play. Adam didn't seem to mind, although he couldn't understand why his brother didn't have to wear a leash.

Garrison, Adam, and Trevor continued their outings in the forest; these outings were becoming not only a pleasure but also a habit. As the days went by, they were eating less regular food and more of the animals caught in the traps in the forest. Carolyn couldn't figure out why they were never hungry, but she chalked it up to their condition. She didn't seem to be very worried for her safety; she and Adam were closer now than ever. Her relationship with Adam was making Garrison somewhat jealous though.

Loren picked up Lewis from the airport and drove him to the estate. As soon as the car pulled up, Trevor was there to meet him. Lewis got out of the car, and Trevor showed him his arms. All his hair had fallen out in less than two days. His chest hair and leg hair were gone as well. Lewis looked at Trevor with a blank expression and didn't mention the issue. He told Trevor that he needed to see him in his study after he unloaded the car. Trevor knew something was up by his tone of voice and because he could sense something was wrong, that Lewis had some major news to share. Surprisingly, Trevor was patient and allowed Lewis to unpack. Trevor told Lewis he would be in his study waiting for him.

Trevor was sipping on some cognac when Lewis entered the study. Lewis closed the door behind him and walked at a rather fast pace to the chair in front of Trevor's desk. Trevor looked up from his drink and followed Lewis's every move without saying a word or moving a muscle. Lewis put his hands together on his small notepad, glanced down at the floor under the desk, and then looked up into Trevor's eyes.

He said, "I found Garrison's birth parents."

Trevor's mouth fell open and he leaned forward on the desk. "I'm sorry, what?"

"I found his birth parents," Lewis said again. He explained everything to Trevor. He followed the notes in front of him strictly. He left nothing out. He told Trevor about the village, how healthy and young everyone felt and looked. He told him of going into the forest and collecting many samples. He told of him Wolfgang, Zelda, their past, and all the many experiments they had performed. He told him of their physical appearance, the formula, the cave, everything. He left nothing out.

Trevor sat there through all the stories. Many times, he leaned back in his chair, looked out the window behind him, and then leaned on the desk, hanging on every word. He honestly hadn't thought Lewis would find anything; he had actually thought the trip was going to be a lost cause. After Lewis finished his dissertation, Trevor breathed a sigh of relief and sat back in his chair.

He said, "So, there are actually people like me out there in this world?"

Lewis quickly answered, "Yes, there are, Trevor. But there are only five that I know of at this moment. You, Wolfgang, and Zelda all share a similar appearance. Garrison is the more normal looking one, obviously, and, well… Adam is unique. What I learned from Wolfgang coincides with my studies as well, and it all starts with this Formula L. Once it's injected in a subject, the mutations begin. After three months, the total mutation process is complete. If the mutated subject bites a normal subject, the normal subject mutates as if they were injected from the start. The same process occurs. Just like what happened when Garrison bit you. Now, what I find even more fascinating is what happens when two infected subjects mate and the woman gives birth. Wolfgang didn't test this because he ran out of time, but in his own personal experience with three offspring, all of them came out rather normal as compared to the mutated subjects. The other three murdered brothers of Garrison were just like Garrison. Or so I think they were. At least from what Wolfgang said, they looked more… normal. When two infected subjects mate and bear an offspring, they produce a Garrison. Which is to say, a normal-looking boy with no physical mutation but a rapid growth rate, rather long extremities, and a very high intelligence, not to mention an unworldly immune system. Then you have the third circumstance, as in your case with Adam. You were infected from Garrison's bite, but Adelle was not. She got pregnant, bore Adam, and… well… Adam is Adam, more animal in appearance, with more mutation than you have."

Trevor shook his head. "Okay, you said this Wolfgang person has this Formula L in his possession?"

Lewis said, "Yes, he does, or that's what he told me. He said he had a few gallons hidden throughout the forest. He was almost proud of the fact that no one else knew where the formula was located. I certainly wasn't going to push him for more information on that subject. Trevor, I was scared for my life."

Trevor quickly answered, "Oh, I understand, Lewis. I totally understand. It must have been a very traumatic experience for you. But what you are telling me is that he found the secret to life. So, will I live forever? What about Garrison? Adam?"

Lewis said, "I don't know, Trevor. I mean, Wolfgang said he was about forty when he injected himself, and that was in 1945. He is now over a hundred and thirty years old. He said in his studies, he believed the subjects would live forever unless an unnatural cause killed them. I believe Garrison and probably Adam are the same way."

"So, the son of a bitch actually pulled it off," said Trevor.

Lewis responded, "Pulled... what do you mean exactly?"

"This guy, out of the blue, just happened to invent a way to cheat death and find a cure for all illness. I bet he doesn't have a clue how much potential money he is sitting on with that little secret of his."

Lewis didn't want to push the issue too much, but he said, "I wouldn't want to be the one who attempted to take it from him, Trevor."

Trevor whipped his head around. "Who said I was going to take it from him? Maybe we can arrange a deal with each other. With his know-how and my financial backing, the world could be ours. What power we could possess together."

Lewis quickly rose from his chair as Trevor walked around his desk. Lewis was getting a little nervous, but he mustered his courage and said, "Trevor, this creature doesn't negotiate with people. He is a very evil..."

Trevor gripped Lewis by his shirt, pulled him away from the chair and off the ground by a foot, and looked him in the eye angrily. His breath was horrid; it smelled like rotting meat mixed with the cognac he had been drinking. His eyes were black as coal and had a misty glare to them as he spoke to Lewis. "Do you think I am a creature, Lewis? Am I not human anymore? Do we disgust you, Lewis?"

"No. No, Trevor, please put me down now!"

"You are not in a position to tell me what to do or when to do it. Do you understand, Lewis?"

"Yes. I understand," Lewis said nervously.

"*I am still a man, Lewis!*" Trevor shouted. He released his hold on Lewis, and the doctor stumbled back a few feet. Trevor walked toward the window, placed his hands on the window seal, bowed his head, and started to cry.

"I am so sorry, Lewis. Ever since... Hell, ever since I was bitten, I feel like every day I am losing control of my emotions. I don't know how Garrison does it. He has lived with this, this virus in him all his life. Maybe he can control it better than I can. But as the days go by, I feel more out of control. I am so sorry, Lewis. Please forgive me. Please help me. I sometimes love the way I am, and then at times like this, I wish I was dead."

A surprised and somewhat relieved Lewis said, "It's okay. I should have never said the word *creature*. You must understand. I have never been through that kind of stress before in my life. I felt as if I was on an alien planet. We can work through this, Trevor. Should we tell Garrison about all of this?"

Trevor shook his head. "I don't know. I don't think so, not yet."

Lewis said, "Fine. Well, if that is all, I need to get back to the lab."

Trevor turned around and picked up his drink. "You have had a long trip. Why don't you relax for a few days?"

With that, Lewis walked out and Trevor sat down in his chair and again looked at the spot where his son had murdered Snowy. He sat there thinking about how much his life had changed in just a short time.

Lewis didn't rest; he went back to his lab and started his experiments. While he was in the basement, he could see and hear Adam eating a small, undistinguished-looking animal. Lewis's stomach had been upset over the past few days, and the sight and sound of Adam and his meal made the poor doctor vomit on the spot. Adam stopped, looked up, smiled, and went back to eating. As Lewis was cleaning up his vomit, he wondered how long he could live with these animals and all the strange habits that surrounded him. He felt trapped and wanted to escape, but he knew he could never leave without being pursued either by Trevor or by one of his hirelings. Through all the pressure and stress, there was a part of Lewis that wanted fame, money, and recognition in the scientific world. These facts alone kept the doctor sane and in control of his feelings.

The relationship between Garrison and Lewis developed rather well over the next few months. Garrison had been growing taller, getting more mature. His proficiency in the violin had reached an epic level. Many of Trevor's friends from the Louisville Orchestra wanted to invite Garrison to be their guest violinist. Loren and Lewis handled most of the arrangements since Trevor didn't want to be seen in public. His appearance would harm his business and of course would raise many questions. He always spoke with his acquaintances on the phone. Many of his corporate relations conducted their business with Loren. Loren was the main force in all his business affairs. She carried out every order from Trevor regarding any business activity or decision.

After numerous phone calls, Loren set up a date with the orchestra for Garrison to perform as the guest violinist at one of their concerts. This was a momentous event for the Seawick family. Trevor was very proud of his son, and he listened to many of the records that were taped at the practice sessions. Adelle couldn't be prouder, nor could Loren and Carolyn. The first time Garrison walked onstage at the Louisville Orchestra, Loren, Lewis, and Adelle were in their private balcony seats. A Seawick had held those seats for decades. Lewis secretly recorded the performance so he could bring the tape back for Trevor to watch. Garrison would be going onstage after intermission. He was to play Mozart's Violin Concerto No. 5 in A Major, K 219. This piece was one of Garrison's favorites, and at his request, the maestro had agreed to enter it into the program.

When it was time for Garrison to take the stage at the tender age of seven and a half, he walked into view of his mom and bowed his head with a huge smile on his face. Adelle couldn't hold back the emotions. She was so proud of her son. She was also proud of what he had accomplished at such a young age. Garrison now stood six feet tall with long arms and legs proportionate to his body. His hair was golden blond with not one hair darker than any other. His eyes were the deepest blue, his skin was pale white, and his shoulders were broad. As he walked, his head never bobbed up or down or sideways; it stayed perfectly still like that of a runway model. He walked out to loud applause and the rustling of people in their seats, whispers about how tall this young man was and how handsome he looked, what stage presence he had. He was in total control of himself, the orchestra, and the audience.

As the show began, all eyes were on the young prodigy. Garrison, as if he owned the orchestra, nodded to the conductor, and the concerto began. Garrison got ready for his part, lifted his instrument, rested his chin on the violin, and raised his right hand and arm all in one fine, fluid motion. He began to play. Each draw from the bow was perfectly balanced, and the tone of the violin was pitch-perfect. He played as if Mozart himself possessed his body and shared a part of his mind. Nothing in the world could have sounded as beautiful as this moment.

Adelle had tears running down her face. She was so proud of her only son, the love of her life. No thoughts of Adam existed in her mind or her heart at that moment. It was as if, for a short twenty-eight minutes, her life was perfect, as she had always dreamed it to be.

Garrison played hard and well, with no mistakes. When the last note faded, the audience gave a standing ovation for the young prodigy. Everyone knew that a performance like this one didn't happen but once in a lifetime. This was not only Louisville's finest but also one of the world's superior violinists.

After the performance, many people showered massive praise on the young boy. This pleased Garrison, and he was very happy to perform in front of such an accepting audience. Weeks after the performance, the Seawicks were getting many calls to have Garrison perform for this orchestra, and for that orchestra, in this city and in that city.

Adelle wanted a normal life for Garrison, or at least as normal as she could get for her son. She also didn't like the amount of time that Garrison was spending with Adam. She spoke many times with Trevor and Lewis, asking them to limit their time together. Garrison didn't want to be around Adam anyway. They had uncomfortable feelings toward one another, as most brothers do. As one brother becomes better or more popular, the lesser brother begins to grow envious. Certainly, this was the case in the Seawick family. Adam didn't like all the attention Garrison received, especially not from his parents. It irritated Adam and made him more upset and angry.

During this time, Trevor wondered if he could start to play the violin on his own. He thought that with his newly found talents, maybe this gift would be bestowed on him as it had been bestowed on his son. Trevor had hoped that God would have blessed him with the innate skills of a violinist. He thought, *Why not? If God could smile on Garrison, why would he not smile on him?* So, he ordered a fine violin from one of the local stores, and when the violin and bow arrived at the house, he was very excited. He even allowed Garrison to show him the finer points of violin playing.

Trevor thought he would pick the skill right up like Garrison had, but to his disappointment, he failed miserably the first time he attempted to play. He practiced hours on end, and he improved with time, but he never reached Garrison's level. He was jealous of the fact that he couldn't play as well as his son, but he understood how special Garrison was, so he couldn't be too hard on himself. Although it was a disappointment, at least he could play. He played well, and his development over those couple of months was like twenty years' worth of practice.

After many discussions, Lewis and Trevor decided not to tell Garrison about his original parents. Garrison had been doing wonderfully with his schooling. He was in high demand as a featured guest violinist and had numerous concert appearances. He loved to perform in front of so many people. In his personal life, his relationship with his father was better now than ever before. Trevor and Lewis didn't want to interrupt Garrison's development in any way. They thought telling the boy about his birth parents would set him back, and decided that they would tell him of his original parents when he was older. Then maybe someday he would recreate Formula L, sell it to the government, and make an untold fortune for the Seawick corporations. At least this was the long-term plan that Trevor and Lewis had for the young boy.

Lewis continued with some experiments and research on his own but finally concluded that he couldn't reproduce Formula L. He lacked the necessary knowledge of chemistry. Trevor realized this quickly and talked with Lewis. They thought that maybe it would be a good idea for Trevor to pick up a chemistry book or two, learn what he could about chemistry, and attempt to recreate the formula himself. Lewis also tried to teach himself, but it was almost an impossible task to master or even complete. He tried his best though, and he did learn a lot of new information in a very short time.

Throughout this time, Lewis continued to analyze the specimens that he had collected during the trip. After months of research, he found very little that surprised him. He documented everything on the computer, made note after note, wrote paper after paper on not only what he experienced but what he knew about the metamorphosis that had touched his life then became his life.

Garrison, like his father and Adam, was now partaking in odd eating habits on a daily basis. Trevor was finding it more difficult to keep this dirty little secret from Adelle as each day passed. He found himself lying to her more and avoiding her on more occasions. His breath always smelled nasty because of his diet, and his hands seemed to always be dirty or cut up in some way.

Meanwhile, Adam's growth had leveled off. Physically, he had become more animal-like in appearance than a human. Mentally, his speech had improved at alarming levels. He was now talking in complete sentences with better diction. He was becoming more aware that his dad didn't pay as much attention to him as he did Garrison. This upset Adam, and he started to resent Garrison not only as a brother but also as a person. He grew angrier through this phase of his life.

Lewis had been studying Trevor closely after the physical change was complete. He had thought Trevor would one day be as intelligent as Garrison, but as time passed this seemed not to be the case. Lewis, even though it was hard for him to say this to Trevor, had been keeping track of Trevor's intelligence level. Since the bite, it had increased, but not to the level of genius. On the other hand, Garrison's intellect surpassed genius-level. Lewis wondered if somehow the formula had been diluted through Garrison's bite. Maybe when the formula went through the teeth of the infected subject and entered into the noninfected subject, it lost its effectiveness. If this was truly the case, Trevor would never reach Garrison's intellectual level. This caused great concern for Lewis. How was he going to tell Trevor this news without upsetting him?

Lewis began to pay more attention to Garrison, and they were becoming closer to one another. He showed the boy all the samples that he had collected on his trip to Germany, leaving out many of the nasty little details. Garrison knew that Lewis was trying to find the underlying cause of what made him the way he was and what was in him that had caused his dad's mutation. Garrison was just now starting to show signs of not only knowing what he had done to his dad but feeling sorry for his actions. Many times, Lewis, Adelle, and even Trevor had to console Garrison and tell him that it was not his fault. They all told him that something was going on that no one totally understood but that maybe someday they would understand what was going on inside of his body.

Garrison was growing more inquisitive about his situation. More and more, he wondered why he was so special. He had a hard time understanding why he was so tall for his age, and why he was so smart compared even to people much older than him. He couldn't understand what had happened to Adam or why he was such a monster. Garrison and Adam never got along, and Adam knew that Garrison routinely called him hurtful names.

At a very young age, Garrison knew that there was something not quite normal about him, but he kept this to himself. Now he had been told that his dad was the way he was because of his bite. This really bothered Garrison. Adelle, when she could, always consoled Garrison and made him feel as if it was not his fault. She told him that these things happened at times and that he just had to plow through these problems, accept them, and try not to let them dominate his life. That was what she was doing, and that was her only advice to him.

Garrison loved his mom with all his heart. He thought she was beautiful and insightful. Their relationship was very special to both of them. Garrison knew and sensed that his mom didn't like Adam, and this excited him to some degree. He had never liked Adam, so to have someone else feel the way he did made Garrison feel less alone in his hatred for his brother. Garrison also didn't like the fact that his dad was spending so much time with Adam. This was something else that Garrison and Adelle had in common.

As Adelle felt better each day, she wandered around the house more. She began to become very suspicious of her family. The problem was that they would all disappear for hours on end. Of course, Adelle had no clue as to where everyone was during these long, absent periods.

Lewis was busy working in his lab and writing up reports on what he had learned each day. Loren was busy handling the business, with Trevor's guidance. Trevor and his two sons were usually off in the woods or in the backyard; if they were not eating, they were playing games. Sometimes these games got very rough, and Trevor had to separate the boys from nasty fights. The mansion had a small walk-out area toward the back of one side. It had served as the servants' quarters when the house was constructed. Now, especially over the past few months, the service area had been transformed into a fully functioning lab for Lewis.

Adam was moved into a larger bedroom that was located close to Lewis's lab. The former bedroom was twenty feet in depth and another twenty feet in width. Trevor had the cage delivered and constructed inside the bedroom. The back part of the cage was drywall, with the concrete wall of the basement behind it. The left side had steel bars that rested up against the drywall. The front part of the steel cage sat back in the room about ten feet from the door. The total area of the cage was about ten feet deep and about twenty feet in width. The non-caged area of the room was for medical supplies and equipment for Adam, as well as a small desk. Lewis often took blood from Adam, as well as hair, urine, and fecal samples. The bathroom was located next to the bedroom, and the walls of the bathroom were caged as well. Trevor knew of Adam's great strength, and he feared that he would start tearing into the drywall and attempt an escape. At the time of construction, Trevor had been concerned the workers on the cage might ask questions, but to his surprise, they had done their job and gone on their way with no fuss. Lewis had overseen the project and told the workers that the cage was for pet monkeys his employer intended to train. This had seemed to go over very well with the workers. Lewis had also had an operating table delivered to the estate when Adelle was going to have her baby. That same table now rested in Lewis's lab.

Lewis made Adam's bedroom as comfortable as possible. He had the latest and the best television with DVR and all the video games a boy could ever want. Adam was very fond of his home and didn't mind that he was behind bars most of the day. He knew that his temper sometimes got out of control, and he accepted that he had to live this way. When he was out of his cage, Lewis always had a chain attached to a collar around his neck. Again, Adam didn't seem to mind, but he would at times ask why Garrison wasn't wearing a chained collar. The chain had a small wire threaded through the thick links. On the handle at the end of the chain was a button that when pushed would send a shock through the wire to the animal whose neck was on the other end. This kept Adam in control when Trevor took him outside. Adelle hated the idea of the chain, but she understood that it was a necessity.

In the lab, Lewis and Trevor had tile installed for flooring. Both thought it was an easy way to clean up any spills or messes. The tiled floor had a drain in the middle that went directly to the sewers. Lewis bought a large table for four grown adults, the kind of table that came up to the average person's hip and required long-legged chairs. This was the table where Trevor and his sons took part in their eating festivities. Lewis made a point of not being in his lab when the three brought in their food.

Lewis had the entire lab and bedroom videotaped twenty-four hours a day. He wanted to capture anything and everything on tape and to document Adam's behavior patterns and potential changes. He reviewed as best he could the hours upon hours of footage. The video cameras only recorded if the camera detected movement.

For many weeks he watched the numerous tapes of all three eating their dinners or snacks. Trevor and Garrison were a little daintier than Adam. Adam ripped and tore his prey apart, creating more of a mess than his brother or his father. Lewis documented a very important part of the tapes: the three didn't always eat all of their prey. They preferred the muscles of the animals. Each of the three had his own way of separating the muscle from the body of the victim. Garrison and Trevor would pick more with their teeth and then strip the muscle gently away from the bones with their hands. Adam was messier and did more of the separation using his teeth. The muscles were very tough, especially for Trevor and Garrison. Garrison sometimes used a pair of scissors and gently cut the muscle tissue into small, bite-sized pieces.

Lewis used this opportunity for experimentation. He discovered that when they bit into the tissue, a small amount of a strange chemical came out of a few of their teeth. After taking samples from the many bites, Lewis discovered that the chemical was the Formula L, or at least that is what Wolfgang insisted it was. Along with Formula L, some other substance came from either the teeth or gums and caused the exposed muscle to break down while in their mouths. In one of his experiments, Lewis witnessed the chemical soften the muscle tissue to the point where the muscle turned into a basic piece of meat for them to swallow. Lewis always made it a point not to physically touch any part of the remains of the animals. He took extra precaution in the most extreme ways not to be infected by Formula L.

The forest behind the estate had plenty of animals, but Trevor didn't want to deplete the area of life, so at times he would purchase small animals like chickens, hamsters, rats, rabbits, dogs, cats, and frogs from the local pet shops. Trevor had a vast array of connections through the town, and he used them when he could. Numerous storeowners didn't know where the deliveries were going. Trevor owned various small farms nearby and had the animals delivered to a number of them.

Then, as needed, Lewis would pick up the animals and bring them back to the estate. Lewis hated this part of his job, but he was not in the position to debate it.

Trevor, Adam, and Garrison didn't live on wild animals alone. Their diet also consisted of vegetables, lettuce, sushi, and other items. Adam, out of the three, didn't have a taste for the various alternatives to meat, whereas Garrison and Trevor only consumed live animals as a delicacy or a treat. Adam preferred live animals for his regular diet.

A normal day would consist of Garrison and Trevor sitting down at the dinner table with Adelle and having a nice quiet meal. They would discuss the events of the day. Trevor and Garrison were always mindful not to tell everything to Adelle. At times, Lewis would join in on some of the meals, but those opportunities were few and far between.

Adelle was becoming more suspicious of Trevor's most recent behavior, as well as Garrison's. She started to question them about their whereabouts and actions throughout the day. However, she could never get a solid answer from them. Adelle kept herself busy, mostly through some charities that she had associated herself with throughout the years. Her friends knew something was wrong with her. She was not the same Adelle she had been years before. Some of her friends called the house and asked to speak with Trevor. Trevor never had time for Adelle's friends and never returned any of their calls.

As the days went by, Adelle grew more curious as to the experiments that Lewis was performing in the basement. She would go downstairs from time to time, but when she passed Adam's room, Adam would quickly stop what he was doing and yell out in a loud but low, almost hissing voice, "Mama! Mama! Please visit me, Mama!"

Adelle would quickly pass the bedroom's entrance and run to the lab area to find Lewis. When Lewis was there, she felt somewhat comfortable, but when he was not, she dreaded the walk back past Adam's room. As she passed the room again, Adam would scream out in a louder voice, "Mama! Where are you going? Please come back and play with me."

For many reasons, this greatly disturbed Adelle, and it was the primary limitation on her trips down to the basement. She had never liked the basement from day one. It was the absolute worst area of the estate for her. She didn't like the darkness caused by the lack of windows, and she always felt claustrophobic in that area of the house.

CHAPTER 12

Everlasting

few months passed, and snow invaded the forest. The animals were low in number because the cold forced many of them to live deeper in the forest. One cold and snowy morning, Adelle looked out her bedroom window and noticed an increased number of tracks in the snow, running from the house to the edge of the forest. She also noticed some reddish discoloration in the snow that didn't seem to be part of the natural landscape. Normally, Adelle was a passive person who didn't pay any attention to something like the image she had just seen. However, this morning she was feeling more aggressive and inquisitive. She first thought some animal had either dragged something out of the forest and placed the dead animal in the snow, or dug up something from the snow-covered ground. However, the area of the discolored snow was too large for that to be the case.

Adelle quickly changed her clothes, put on her coat and shoes, and went outside. She walked to where the tracks lead to the forest in the backyard. They went from the walk-out entrance of the basement to the edge of the forest. As she was walking, about one hundred yards from the house, she came upon the first brownish-red spot in the snow. It looked like blood, but she wasn't sure. The wind was beginning to pick up as she stood out in the freezing cold, attempting to figure out what had made the spots.

As Adelle continued to investigate, it began to snow lightly. She walked farther and noticed more of the discolored snow in front of her. It looked as if someone had wiped his or her hands off in the snow. She found the discoloration in multiple areas. Adelle's mind was racing, and her thoughts quickly turned to Garrison. *Something must have happened to him*, she thought. She quickly ran back to the house, slipping every so often along the way. She felt her heart in her throat; she knew something had happened to her favorite son. She finally made it back to the walk-out entrance, but the door was locked. She knocked and knocked on the door, but no one answered. She looked around, and all she saw was footsteps everywhere in the snow. She didn't have her keys on her, so she couldn't get inside the basement. The door was thick, and just inside the entrance was a large area that was used as a mudroom. Apparently, no one could hear her knocking, and thoughts that something was not right were swimming rapidly in her head.

After repeated attempts to get someone's attention inside, Adelle ran around to the back. As her foot hit the patio, she slipped again and fell hard on her side. The fall shook her a little, and after she took a few moments to gather her thoughts, she got up and raced into the house. Loren was walking down the hallway, and Adelle yelled in a panic, "Loren, where is Garrison? Is he all right?"

A startled Loren said, "Of course he is all right. He and his father are down in the basement with Adam."

"Thank God. I thought he was hurt. I was outside, and I tried to get inside the basement, but the door was locked, and no one answered when I knocked," Adelle said. Then a puzzled look appeared on her face. "What is with the snow?" She stopped and looked around the room.

After a pause, Loren said, "Well, they are all in the basement. At least, they were the last time Lewis saw them. Lewis came upstairs to pick up some reports for Trevor. You know how they love that basement. They seem to live down there lately."

Adelle walked slowly out of the room and laid her coat on a chair as she passed. She walked to the basement entrance, which was massive. The hardwood stairs measured about eight feet wide. The walls were made of wood as well, and they had massive decorative wood carvings that were square in shape on each side of the walls. A high sheen radiated on the wood from the shellac. What little light that hit the area reflected off the walls and floors.

Adelle listened intently for any voices or sounds but didn't hear a thing because both doors at the bottom landing were closed. She was scared out of her mind for some reason she could not explain, but she finally mustered up the courage to go down to the basement. Adelle still hated that basement. She was like a small child afraid of the dark space, and she always had an uneasy feeling when she entered that part of the house. Most of her uneasy feelings had to do with Adam and his caged-in living quarters. She knew the cage was necessary but hated for him to be locked up like some wild animal.

Adelle waited at the basement entrance and looked down the many steps that eventually ended at the landing. Oversized doors stood at each side of the landing. The left door was an entrance to many rooms. This area was mostly made up of bedrooms with attached bathrooms and walk-in closets, an open family room, a walk-behind bar, and a theater that could seat over twenty people. It was mostly a party area. The right door was the entrance to Lewis's lab and living area. This part of the basement had been remodeled many times over the past few years, most notably in the last few months. Adam's bedroom was also located on that side of the house. Toward the back of the area were a large kitchen and family room, with more bedrooms and bathrooms filling the remaining part of the basement.

Adelle began her descent down the dark, wide steps, focusing on one step at a time. She hadn't turned the lights on upstairs because she wanted to see what her family was up to in the basement. Many times, when she went downstairs, she thought they were hiding something from her. She continued her dark journey down the steps. She wanted to turn the lights on, but she didn't want to draw anyone's attention to the fact that she was there.

In the back of her mind, Adelle knew something was wrong. She surmised there was some deep, dark secret being kept from her. She had felt this from the beginning but had chosen not to pursue the truth about what was going on behind her back. She knew that Trevor was acting stranger and stranger by the week. The incredible physical and mental change that had happened to him was unworldly. She found it difficult to comprehend how Trevor was dealing with his new look, and she felt both scared of him and sorry for her husband.

Garrison was the love of her life, but she knew that he was different. Adelle didn't want to dwell on the fact of how different her little boy was because too much thought on this issue disturbed her greatly. From the day he bit the dog to the day he bit into her husband's wrist, she had known her little boy was special, and not in a good way. Even with this knowledge, she loved him with all her heart.

Adelle had had a very stressful past few years. She had waited for so long to get pregnant. When she found out that she was going to have a child of her own, she had been ecstatic. Throughout Adelle's pregnancy with Adam, her emotions had gone from pure love at the moment's notice of existence, to almost pure disgust at the moment of birth. The fact that she didn't love her only natural-born child haunted her daily. She had never in her life had to deal with such emotions; in fact, no human had ever had to deal with any issue like Adam.

Over the past few months, Adelle had known something was happening behind her back, and she had to know what was going on. If she didn't find out, it would eventually drive her crazy. Adelle had ideas, but she never thought too long or hard about those ideas. She didn't like or want to think about her worst nightmare: losing her entire family to something that she didn't understand and couldn't defeat if it confronted her. She and Trevor had grown apart these past few years. She had to stop this from happening. She had to save her family from whatever force was trying to drive them away from her. It was time for her to make a stand. All these thoughts flowed through her mind at all angles and at breakneck speed as she stepped closer to the door on the right.

As she stepped on the landing, Adelle looked up and turned to see the full view of the very steps that she had used for her descent. The only light that was showing came from the first floor. Adelle didn't want to make any noise or have her presence known. This was out of her character, but she was afraid she wouldn't find out the truth if she went about it any other way. She was afraid of what she might find, but she was more afraid that her findings might disappear if her presence was known.

Adelle took her eyes off the stairs and turned her attention to the door. Usually, Lewis locked the door, so she was afraid she would not be able to get inside. Suddenly, she heard someone walking toward the door on the other side. Her heart skipped a few beats; she didn't want to be caught there. She quickly but softly glided over to the door on the other side of the landing. *Thank God*, she thought when the door opened. She went inside and cracked the door so she could see who was coming out. She pressed her ear up against the doorframe so she could better see and hear.

The door opened, and Lewis appeared. He stood by the door for a moment and then went upstairs with his coat on his arm. His heavy footsteps hit each step like the marching of a Nazi soldier. Each step he took made Adelle's heart beat harder. She gingerly opened the door and saw only the bottom part of Lewis's legs walking up the steps. She quietly stepped out onto the landing, taking care not to be seen or heard. She quickly looked at the other door and then back up the stairs. She waited for Lewis to finish his ascent. He finally made the turn at the top of the stairs and was out of sight. She listened intently for the footsteps to fade away to silence.

Adelle dashed over to the door to the lab. Her heart was beating as fast as it had ever beaten in her life. She thought the door was locked, but to her surprise, when she looked down, she saw it was not fully closed. Apparently, Lewis hadn't closed the door all the way. Adelle placed her hand on the doorknob and pushed the door slightly open a few more inches and looked around, but she saw only part of the lab. She heard some strange sounds coming from the room, around the corner of the long wall nearest to Adelle. She opened the door just wide enough that she could get her thin and somewhat frail body through. Scared out of her mind, she thought about a possible escape route as she eased the door open with her right hand. An odd smell floated in the air.

Adelle couldn't figure out what the smell was, but the farther she walked along the wall of the lab, the stronger the smell got. She heard a voice; it sounded like Trevor's voice, but she wasn't sure because it was muffled and she couldn't understand what was said.

Adelle gingerly walked near the wall. She was rapidly coming upon Adam's room. She prayed that he wouldn't be in there. As she approached the room, she very slowly attempted to look inside without being seen. She awkwardly bent her neck around the opening of the room. Her palms were sweaty from nerves, and her legs were getting weak from stress. Adelle looked inside Adam's room and saw nothing. Cold shivers went up and down her spine. She was relieved that he was not there, but she wondered where he was. She couldn't believe that she had allowed such a thing to enter the world through her legs: a child that was half-human, half-animal, a child that hissed and growled and had to be put inside a cage. No one on this planet understood what Adelle had gone through over the past year. Many times, she wished she had aborted the thing, but her religious beliefs had prevented such a decision.

Adelle inched closer to the place where the wall ended. She was certain she heard something, but no words were being spoken. It sounded as if people were eating. As she came to the end of the wall where it turned and opened to the large room that Lewis used as his laboratory, she saw her entire family sitting at a large and very tall table. They had a studied look and were extremely quiet, aside from the chewing sounds.

Suddenly, Adelle saw Adam pick up what looked to be the hairy leg of some kind of an animal. Adelle's mind, eyes, ears, and total attention were focused on the sight, as if a hunter with binoculars finally had seen his prey and stopped to look and adjust the sights for a better look. She noticed the blood all over the table, all over Adam's hands and mouth. Her attention then turned to Garrison, and she saw that he had blood on his hands and face as well. She saw her favorite son pick up a small, hairy paw or ankle, and she watched him place this forbidden object into his mouth.

Without any control, Adelle walked slowly into the room. Her eyes looked at Adam, then at Garrison, and then she saw the back of Trevor's head. She started to take deep breaths, each one deeper than the last. Her eyes were wide open, so much so that it made blinking impossible. Her hands came up to her face, and she screamed as she stepped closer to the feeding table.

After the first scream, Trevor turned around, a surprised look on his bloodied face. Adelle looked at her husband in total terror and let out another blood-curdling scream. She took deep breaths, inhaling just as hard as exhaling. Losing control of her emotions, she ran toward Adam, who sat eating quietly without any emotion at all. Trevor got up quickly from his seat. Adelle's eyes cased every inch of the bloody table. Parts of what looked like a deer were scattered over it. Trevor was now standing, but he appeared to be in shock, unable to say a word to his troubled wife. Garrison stopped eating and laid a deer hoof down in front of him.

Adelle was screaming as loud as her voice would allow. The screaming disturbed everyone except Adam, who continued eating. After her initial screaming and breathless panting, Adelle struggled to get words out. "What are you doing? What the hell are you doing? Give me that." Adelle ran over to Adam and reached for his right arm with both of her hands.

Trevor yelled, "*No!*"

Adam, with his catlike reflexes, moved his large head toward Adelle's left arm. With his mouth open as wide as it could go, he sprang toward her and bit directly into the middle of her forearm. Adelle gasped at the sight but felt nothing at first. Then sharp pains went up her entire arm and into her shoulder. Adam growled as he grabbed his mother's arm with his hands and adjusted his bite so he could go deeper into her arm. He positioned his legs to push off from the chair, but in so doing, he knocked them hard onto the floor, with Adelle screaming in pain and sheer panic.

Trevor grabbed the scissors that were lying on the table. With one quick movement, he plunged them into Adam's upper shoulder, causing Adam to release his hold on his mother. Adam reached back for the embedded scissors as he hissed and growled at his assailant. He pulled the scissors out of his back and watched as Adelle lie on her side on the tiled floor, holding her arm. Meanwhile, Garrison jumped out of his chair and went to help his mother get to her feet.

Adam turned his attention to Garrison and said, "Get away from the bitch! She's mine!" Adam leaped toward his brother, tackling him to the ground. They held onto each other with an intense hatred that filled each of their hearts. Neither one gave in to the other. Garrison and Adam were face to face on the ground. Adam attempted to move in on Garrison's neck, but Garrison fought to prevent him from achieving his goal. Trevor went over to help Adelle and see how badly she was hurt.

Adelle pushed him away, telling him, "Stop Adam from hurting Garrison. They are fighting."

Trevor turned his attention to the fight. Garrison and Adam were rolling around on the floor of the lab. Garrison was struggling because Adam's arms and legs were longer than his own. Both kids were angry at each other. They were unleashing months of pent-up rage.

Adam released the full weight of his anger toward Garrison, a brother that he had never liked, a brother who got all the attention from his parents, a brother who was free from a chain and a jailed cell. The months seemed like years to Adam. Although his relationship with his dad had changed in the past few months, Adam still harbored very ill feelings toward his parents, but especially toward Garrison. Garrison didn't care to speak or play with Adam. Garrison felt that he was better than Adam, and in many instances, he was. The brothers were like night and day in both appearance and intellectual processes. Adam was a fighter, a scavenger, and everything he did was based on instinct alone, whereas Garrison was more refined. Garrison possessed a higher intellect, and he was a connoisseur of the animal world instead of just a killer who enjoyed the kill more than the taste of his prey.

Trevor moved in and attempted to separate his two sons. Neither one would let go of the other. A much larger and stronger Trevor finally took both of his arms and, with his powerful hands, separated the two from each other. A second later Garrison got loose from his father's grasp and charged under his arm to tackle Adam while Trevor was still holding onto Adam's shoulder. Adam looked slightly confused; his father wouldn't let him go. Trevor took his free hand and placed it on Adam's shoulder to secure him even more while Garrison grabbed and punched him. All the while Trevor was screaming at Garrison to stop. Trevor was attempting to control Adam in fear that Adam was the better fighter and was stronger than Garrison. Trevor pushed Adam down and placed a foot on his chest. In one quick motion, Trevor grabbed Garrison and held him back, all the time yelling at the boys to stop fighting and to control themselves.

Adam's chain was still around his neck, but during the battle the leash had come loose, and it now lay on the floor. Adam noticed he was free. While he was still on his back, he quickly pulled the leash with his hands as fast as he could. Finally, he captured the entire length of the leash. While this was going on, Garrison yanked himself from his father's grasp and with all his might ran toward Adam. Adam was sitting on the floor, his hands filled with the chain. Garrison leaped into the air and tackled Adam. The collision knocked the back of Adam's head hard on the tiled floor. Adam tried hard to wrap the chain around Garrison's neck and almost succeeded, but Garrison pushed him away at the last second. As he did, Adam rolled over and got back on his feet. He looked angrily at his dad. He thought Trevor had sent Garrison after him. Garrison got up and went after Adam for a third time. This time Adam was ready.

As Garrison ran over to him, Adam stretched his long arms and grabbed Garrison by the throat with his left hand. With his right hand, he grabbed his brother's shoulder and pushed him back about ten feet. Garrison was almost airborne as he fell onto his backside, and he slid on the floor when he landed. During this battle, Trevor went after Adam's leash to attempt to regain control of him. As Trevor bent down to pick it up, Adam dashed toward him and bit deeply into his arm. Adam's teeth were so sharp and long, some of his teeth bit through the tissue and hit the bone in his father's forearm.

A shocked Trevor froze as he tried to collect his thoughts. He attempted to pull away, but that reaction only ripped more of the skin. He yelled at Adam, ordering him to release his arm and back off. For the first time in his existence, Adam didn't listen to his father. Trevor hit Adam on the head with his free arm, but this only made the teeth slide down his arm, cutting more of his flesh. Trevor screamed in pain. He pulled on Adam's hair in an attempt to release himself, but it was a waste of effort.

A half-dazed Adelle ran over to Garrison as he lay on the floor, bleeding from a cut on his head received during his fall. She yelled at Adam to release his bite from his father. She raised her voice in such anger that Adam was surprised. The tone enraged Adam even more. He released his bite from his father and went after his mom with a fiery anger that was almost unworldly. Just as he leaped into the air to reach her, Trevor stepped on the chain. The chain yanked Adam down, momentarily choking him. Adelle stood there with her hands covering her face, crying, screaming, and shaking. As Adam figured out what had stopped him, he turned around and again went after Trevor feverishly. Adam's mind was not at all rational at this point. He was lashing out at anyone he felt to be a threat, as any trapped animal would.

Adam jumped toward Trevor's head. Trevor instinctively covered his face with his right hand while holding his left arm out to stop Adam's forward motion. Adam attacked Trevor's injured right arm close to the initial wound. Adam pushed down his father's outreached hand. As Trevor stumbled back, Adam, in an attempt to hang onto his father, shoved his thumb into Trevor's right eye as he tried to wrap his hand around Trevor's head. Adam's thumb went deep into the eye socket.

The combination of the pain from his reinjured arm and now his eye was unbearable for Trevor. With all his strength, he tried to throw Adam off from him, but Adam was still clinging on with all his might. Trevor managed to push Adam off for a few seconds, but not without a price to pay. As he pushed Adam away, his son's teeth clamped down harder, digging into the bone in Trevor's forearm. As Adam attempted to gain a better hold on his dad's arm, he bit down and Trevor pushed him even harder than before. Adam pulled and ripped a large patch of skin and meat away from the arm.

Amid all the action, Adam's long thumbnail remained embedded in Trevor's eye. As Adam quickly pulled his arm back to gain a better hold on his father, Trevor's eye popped out of his head. The badly injured eye hung from the socket, still attached by the optical nerve. Trevor reached for his wounded eye, exposing the side of his neck. As Adam's back legs hit the floor, like a spring he jumped again at his father, but this time he went for the exposed neck with his mouth wide open.

Adam's jump was so well timed that he made perfect contact with Trevor's neck. Adam's teeth embedded themselves deeply into his father's neck. Adam wrapped his long fingers around and dug his claws into Trevor's arm while his other hand held Trevor's head. He pushed the top part of his father's head down toward his shoulder, trying to expose more of the neck. He bit more rapidly around the neck, attempting not to miss any exposed, clean area.

Trevor tried to get his son off him, but with so many areas of his body now hurt, he was finding it more difficult to fight back. When he pushed Adam away, it made the bite worse because the razor-sharp teeth ripped through the skin and muscle. Adam bit faster and tried to go deeper into the side of Trevor's neck. After every successful attack, Trevor moaned loudly.

Garrison and Adelle screamed at the sight and attempted to go to Trevor's aid, but before they could reach him, Adam repositioned his bite, bit down as hard as he could, and pulled like hell. He stopped and pulled again as hard as he could, shaking his head from side to side. Finally, a part of the skin, meat, and muscle partially broke away. Adam got a better grip and ripped that dangling chunk of meat out of Trevor's neck. Blood went everywhere, gushing from the open wound. Trevor finally pushed Adam off as he fell backward onto the floor.

Adam got up and came back for more, but suddenly a gun went off. The shot hit Adam in his right shoulder. The force stunned him for a second. Then a second shot landed in Adam's stomach. Garrison and Adelle both stopped in their tracks. Their eyes darted around the room to see who had shot Adam. To their surprise, the shooter was Lewis.

When Lewis left his lab, he had made his way out of the house, gotten into his car, and set out on the road. As he was driving, it dawned on him that he had left his notebook in his lab. He turned around and went back to the estate. When he got out of the car, Carolyn was on the phone attempting to call him. She told him there was a disturbance in the basement, but she was too afraid to go down there to investigate. Lewis rushed to the basement. When he arrived, he had seen Adam on top of Trevor, and he had immediately gone for the tranquilizer gun that he had hidden in one of the drawers in his laboratory.

After the two tranquilizer shots were fired, Adam fell to his knees, groaning and growling as he looked at Lewis, and then the tranquilizer took effect. He braced himself with one hand on the floor and pulled the darts out of his body with the other hand. He crawled a few feet toward Lewis before he passed out.

Meanwhile, Trevor was on the floor with blood pouring out of his neck. Adelle and Garrison ran over to him as he writhed slowly from the pain coursing throughout his body. His eye was dangling from his optical nerve, his neck was noticeably misshapen from the deep bite, and blood covered most of his upper body. Adelle stood over the sight and let out another blood-curdling scream. Garrison knelt by his father's side and laid his head on his dad's shoulder while putting his arms around him, being careful not to hurt him more. Adelle shook as she attempted to control her screaming. Trevor let out a loud moan and gasped for air. Adelle fell to her knees, placed her hand on his arm, and watched her husband gasp.

Trevor looked at his wife with his one good eye and mouthed the words, "I love you." He closed his eye tightly, and with his mouth wide open, he made one coughing sound then went limp. Trevor expired in front of his family.

Adelle started to cry, and then she noticed her hand on Trevor's arm. As she looked at her arm on his, she noticed her forearm was bitten and bleeding. She looked down at Trevor again and then looked at her son. Her breath was erratic. She looked up, and her eye caught Lewis's as he attended to Adam. Adelle shook violently all over and screamed uncontrollably. At that point she knew her life would never be the same again; she was now infected. Her emotions were at odds with each other. She was fighting with the reality of the loss of her husband, she had witnessed her husband's most brutal death, and she was concerned for her own well-being. The feelings and thoughts hit her from all angles.

Lewis didn't know where to start. Adelle was crying uncontrollably, and Garrison was lying down on the floor with his father, who was now dead. He knew he had to secure Adam as soon as possible. He ran to the hospital bed and wheeled it over to Adam, who was lying motionless on the cold, tiled floor. Even though Adam was very young, his weight was more than Lewis could easily handle. After repeated attempts, Lewis got Adam on his back on the same table that he had been born on just a year prior. Lewis strapped Adam's arms by his side and secured his legs. He thought that the leather straps would hold Adam after he woke up from the tranquilizer. Lewis didn't know how long it would take for Adam to wake up. The formula, even though it was young and still developing in his body, was a weak version of what Garrison and Trevor had in their system. Still, Lewis had concerns about how fast the formula would work on neutralizing the effects of the tranquilizer. He also secured Adam's large head in place with a leather strap, making sure it was well fastened.

After securing Adam, Lewis had to calm Adelle down. He went over to one of the drawers in his lab, pulled out a syringe, and filled it with a sedative. He approached Adelle and quickly pushed the needle into her arm. In a matter of seconds, she stopped crying and passed out.

Through all this activity, Garrison was still lying with his dead father in a pool of blood on the floor. Garrison didn't move. Lewis bent down, placed his hand on the boy, and told him to get up and help him take care of his mom. Garrison did as ordered, and they carried Adelle to another room in the basement. Lewis cleaned and attended to the bite on her arm. Garrison just stood there looking at her. He was emotionless and didn't move a muscle. Blood covered his body, most of it his father's. Garrison didn't say a word for the longest time, and Lewis thought he was in shock. The doctor shook his head many times, knowing that Adelle was now infected. Garrison noticed his concern. Then he finally spoke.

"Mom was bitten. So, will she be like Adam now?"

Lewis glanced up at Garrison, then looked down and continued to clean Adelle's wound. He said, "I would not say like Adam. More like your father."

Garrison looked down at his beautiful mom with great sorrow and sympathy. "She never wanted to be like us. She never asked for any of this. Can you make her better? Can you make her normal again?"

Lewis quickly glanced over at Garrison. "No. No, I cannot. There is no medicine to reverse the mutation."

Garrison asked, "How is it, Lewis, that I do not look like my brother or my father? Will my mom look like them?"

Lewis stopped cleaning Adelle's bite and rested his hands on the bed. He looked at the boy and said, "Garrison, you are now the man of the house. Your father loved you very much. So does your mom. They want the best for you. You must stay focused, Garrison. You need to control your anger and your thoughts. You have to take care of your mother now."

Garrison replied, "I know that, Lewis. I will. But you did not answer my question."

Lewis quickly said, "According to my research and what I know, somehow you were affected with this mutation. It has made you taller, accelerated your growth, and made you wiser than most. When you bit your father, it mutated him physically and mentally. However, you already know that, don't you? What you don't know is that after you bit your father, your mother got pregnant when your father was still infected. As you can see, apparently that combination does not set well.

Adam was born. I can't say what's going to happen for sure, but if I was going to take a guess, your mom will take a similar path to your father. I am thinking the full mutation will take about three months."

Garrison bent down, laid his head on his mother's arm, and cried. Through the cries, Lewis could only make out the repeated phrase, "Mommy did not ask for this." Garrison controlled himself and looked over at Adam who was lying there in the leather straps. He said, "It is all his fault. He is to blame. He killed my father, and now he made my mom sick."

Lewis quickly went over to Garrison, placed his hands on the boy's shoulders, and said, "Garrison! Look at me, Garrison. Look at me! You cannot blame Adam. He doesn't understand what he has done. He... he is just an animal, or part animal. He doesn't think rationally. I'm not asking you to forgive him, but please, don't make things worse for yourself or for your mom. Your mom needs you now more than ever."

Garrison calmed down somewhat as he embraced Lewis. He knew that he was alone now and that he had to grow up fast. He was young but smart for his age, and he knew what kind of responsibility awaited him in the near future. He knew he still had a lot of support in his family. He viewed Loren and Carolyn as part of the family, and now Lewis was starting to join that group. Garrison trusted Lewis more than ever before. He was forced to put his trust in him now that his dad was gone.

Then the silence broke. Suddenly, Lewis and Garrison heard someone screaming. Carolyn had mustered up the courage to enter the basement to see the source of the noise. She didn't like her view. All she saw was two people in hospital beds while another man lay in a pool of blood. It was like something out of a horrible slasher film.

Lewis ran over to Carolyn and attempted to console her, but she pushed him away. He raised his voice and told her what had happened. She was crying uncontrollably, feeling guilty for not following Lewis into the basement sooner than she did. At that moment, she blamed herself for what had happened. Lewis finally convinced her that it wasn't her fault and that she had to get control of herself. He needed her help.

Carolyn saw Garrison and ran over to console the boy, who still had his head on his mother's arm. Carolyn loved Garrison as if he were her own child. She hugged his shoulders while he continued to look at his father's body on the floor. She found the courage to look at Trevor's body and saw what an awful sight it was. She pulled Garrison up, they embraced, and she told him that everything was going to be okay. Then she heard Lewis tell her that he needed to tell Loren about the situation.

Lewis told Garrison and Carolyn to stay with Adelle while he went over to the phone. He called on the intercom system for Loren to meet him at the entrance to the basement. He told her that he had something important to tell her. Lewis needed some help cleaning up the place and taking care of Trevor. He couldn't call the police. He didn't want the horrible secret out in public view. He was in a panic because he didn't know what to do next. He had to control himself. He asked himself how he was going to explain the death of Trevor, one of the richest and most prominent men in America. He needed help, he needed time, and he needed to think. He had Adam, Garrison, and Adelle to take care of. Then he had the issue of what to do with Trevor's body. Added to all of this, Carolyn was now in the picture. Lewis looked at Trevor's lifeless body once again. The blood was still leaking from his awesome frame as his body lay on the floor. The blood was spreading out around his body, getting thicker and harder.

Someone knocked at the entrance of the basement. Lewis ran over to the door. He didn't want to shock Loren. He told her what had happened. Loren, a person who had always been in total control of her emotions, listened to Lewis's every word. She grew more shocked as the story progressed but spoke not one word. When Lewis finished his story, he told her that he needed to control the media coverage. He couldn't let any pictures of Trevor go public. No one could know of his condition. Too many questions would be asked, and the publicity would not be positive for Seawick Enterprises and all the businesses they owned and operated. Loren agreed. As the conversation continued,

Loren wiped many tears from her eyes, but she remained calm. She had to for the sake of the family. That is what Trevor had trained her to do over the many years of service. After filling Loren in on the events that had just transpired, Lewis asked her if she was prepared for what she was about to see. Loren said yes and entered the room. Obviously, she could never prepare herself enough for what she saw. Her eyes filled with tears and they started to flow down her cheeks as she saw poor Trevor's body lying in a pool of blood. She couldn't help but think back to the day the Seawick family had hired her. Trevor had been a fixture in her life for decades. She had watched Trevor grow from a little boy into an adult. They had grown closer since Loren began helping Trevor with his business activities. She couldn't believe this once so innocent little boy had gone from being so cute, smart, and kind to part monster in just a short time. Ever since the change began with Trevor, she had wanted to leave but hadn't been able to. It was not the money. It was her love for Trevor. He had been like a son to her.

Loren was one of those people you could trust with your life. She did her job, and she didn't require any supervision. She was paid extremely well, and Trevor had rewarded her with not only a large salary and bonuses but also a small share of the company. Loren loved Trevor and the Seawick family. She knew that he loved her, but he had never really come out and said the words over the years. Loren felt as if Trevor had put her in control of the company businesses out of pure convenience, but she also appreciated that he had trusted her with all the high-level information through the years. She had felt a little slighted when Carolyn came on the scene years ago, but she loved running the business and being the main liaison between Trevor and the shareholders. Loren had always been a constant fixture in Trevor's life.

Now the problem was how to break the news to the press and how to keep Trevor's appearance out of the papers. Lewis needed a fresh set of eyes and a clear mind to help him make these tough decisions. Of course, first things came first. They had to take care of Garrison and Adelle. Adam was in restraints for now, so he was secure. Something had to be done with Trevor's body, and it needed to happen fast. Loren and Lewis pondered many ideas. The authorities would want to look at the body, and that was not an option. They would see a horribly disfigured creature and immediately an investigation would ensue. Adam would be discovered, and that would be very difficult to explain. This type of press was not what the Seawick companies would want. The body needed to be disposed of, but how could they explain the situation to the police?

Carolyn finally got Garrison out of the room and cleaned him up; then she went to clean up Adelle as best she could.

The obvious problem was that the identity of Trevor must not be made known to the public or to any authorities. Therefore, the body had to be destroyed somehow. Lewis came up with an idea. He knew a man, a friend of his, who owned a crematorium. He believed that his friend could handle the details and get the body cremated rather quickly and quietly. This would solve the potential identity crisis that might develop. The key obviously was not to have the cremator see the body. Lewis contacted his friend, who went by the name of Joel.

Joel was an odd, overweight man, small in stature and rough in appearance. He had a productive business cremating animals, dogs, cats, birds, and all kinds of pets. The city sometimes asked him to dispose of the homeless or any unidentified body found dead in the streets or wherever. Lewis had befriended Joel through a mutual friend of theirs, and an odd relationship had developed. The mutual friend was a young doctor in medical school who sometimes would pay Joel to let him practice surgical techniques on some of the dead clients.

Lewis called Joel and asked if he could call in a favor. He wanted a cremation casket to be delivered to the estate. He explained that the body was horribly disfigured due to illness and that the family didn't want to have anyone see the body. Joel was a little surprised by the request, but after hearing what Lewis was willing to pay for secrecy, he was willing to deliver the casket without further questions. Lewis asked that the casket be delivered first thing in the morning. Joel agreed.

Lewis had to hurry to clean up the area. With Loren's help, he moved the body onto a table. He placed the half-eaten carcass of the deer in large plastic bags. He told Loren that later he would bury the deer in the forest. He cleaned the table and placed a large plastic bag on it. Then he had Loren help him with Trevor's body. They placed the lifeless creature on the table. Lewis took some gauze and wrapped up Trevor's neck and all the wounded areas of his body. He told Loren to tie up the legs with some rope that he had gotten out. He wanted to fix the arms to the body. Lewis was worried about Trevor's length. He was six feet, six inches in length, and Lewis wondered if the casket was going to be long enough. He didn't want to call Joel back, so to make sure the body would fit inside the coffin, he knew he might have to make some adjustments. As Loren was busy with Trevor's body, Lewis cleaned up the floor. He didn't want a drop of blood to be seen by anyone. The casket was going to be delivered early in the morning, but he was going to place the body inside the casket himself. He didn't want anyone to see Trevor's body even though it would be wrapped up.

Lewis didn't have a body bag and didn't have the time to get one, so he used some plastic trash bags cut in half. With Loren's help, they taped the plastic bags around Trevor's body extremely well. When they got through with the task, Loren and Lewis began the process of cleaning up the dried blood on the tile floor. It took hours upon hours. They poured the mopped-up blood down the toilet, down sinks, and even down the bathtub drain.

In the middle of the cleanup, Adam woke up, and he was not happy. He growled, yelled, and demanded that someone release him. Lewis gave him a sedative, and Adam went back to sleep. Lewis wheeled and pushed him into his cage in his bedroom, then went back to work, cleaning up and preparing for the casket.

Lewis and Loren had no sleep that night. Before they knew it, Joel and his coworker were knocking on the basement's door per Lewis's instructions. Lewis let them inside, but they only made it a few yards. Lewis told them to place the casket down and to leave. He would put the body in the casket. He told them to come back in a few hours. They did as instructed. Lewis, with Loren's help, carried the body to the casket. Because Trevor's body was very heavy, they had to set it down from time to time. The first time they placed the body down on the floor, they said that they hoped the body wouldn't leave any blood marks. Thank God, no blood marks were showing after they picked the body up. Loren made sure to be very neat and clean about the preparation. They got the body to the casket and laid Trevor down beside it.

Lewis shook his head. His worst nightmare was realized. The body looked to be too big for the casket. He didn't know what to do. He thought most caskets were around eighty inches long. Lewis ended up measuring the casket, and it was seventy-nine inches, or six-foot seven inches long. Apparently, Trevor, still growing before his death, was now taller than six feet seven inches. Lewis could order another casket, but he didn't want to raise even more suspicion. He didn't know what to do. He told Loren to help him see if they could force the body inside. Loren picked up the feet while Trevor picked up the shoulders, and they placed the body inside. Loren had some trouble with the lower end, so Lewis ended up picking up that part of the body and putting it inside for her. The body fit for the most part, and Lewis was relieved. They had to tilt Trevor's head to the side for the fit to be perfect.

They closed the top of the casket, and Lewis said that he was going with the body to the crematorium. He called Joel and said that he was ready to go as soon as possible. Once Joel arrived, he and Lewis picked up the casket and drove it to the crematorium. Lewis was as nervous as a cat. He wanted this to be over as soon as possible. The drive was long and slow, too slow for Lewis's liking. Finally, after an hour of traveling, they stopped the car and got out. They unloaded the casket and carried it inside. Joel made many comments about how heavy this individual was and how he must have been a large man. Lewis just nodded in agreement.

Inside, Joel had one of his assistants waiting with the large furnace already lit. They placed the casket on the rails, and Joel stopped to say a few words. Lewis impatiently stood there, trying not to cause more suspicion than he already had. After Joel stopped speaking, which to Lewis seemed to take an eternity, he walked to the end of the coffin and gently pushed some buttons, and the casket started to move into the furnace. Lewis watched every second of the experience while thoughts ran through his brain. Lewis was tired, hungry, and mentally spent. He had not slept in over a day, he had not eaten in what seemed to be forever, and he just wanted the event to end. He had to dispose of the body, and finally it was happening before his very eyes. Lewis started to think about Trevor and all that they had gone through over the years.

A tear formed in Lewis's tired eyes as he watched the casket burn. So many thoughts, so many memories, so much evil; at least in his mind it was evil. Trevor had scared Lewis in such a way that Lewis viewed him as evil. Trevor had liked his new body, his new state of being, and that had greatly concerned Lewis. Lewis knew that Garrison was different, but at least he looked normal, which had not been the case with Trevor.

Before Lewis knew it, flames engulfed the casket. Lewis had finally disposed of the body. Now he had to break the news of Trevor's death to the press. He had it all planned out. They would notify the press of the death and say that an early cremation had taken place. They had some friends on the police force and some with the local paper. If they called in some favors, there would not be a major investigation into the quickness of the cremation.

After the coffin finished burning, the ashes were removed and given to Lewis. Lewis drove home and placed them high on the mantel in the great room. He then went to his room, showered, and went straight to bed. The next morning, Lewis met with Loren, and the two of them made all the necessary contacts. Loren carefully worded the press release to say that Trevor had suffered from a major heart attack and had been cremated immediately. No funeral or memorial service would be necessary. The press release was sent out, and before long, the phone was ringing off the hook.

Loren was busy handling the multitude of calls that were pouring in as word got out about Trevor's death. She had to hire a few security guards to control the press. The press sometimes made their way onto the property, and they didn't hesitate to knock on the door to get someone to answer. The paparazzi were also out in full force. If any newspaper reporters came to the front door of the house, it was Loren's responsibility to get security to escort them off the property. Many stayed outside the estate and took pictures, wrote stories, and issued television reports with the estate as a backdrop. The news spread all over the nation. Loren called as many people as she could. Most of those people were business contacts, and she made them feel as comfortable as possible with the promise that business would continue as normal considering the current circumstances.

Meanwhile, Carolyn was occupied with Garrison and Adelle, and Loren had to inform Adelle's parents of Trevor's death. Adelle's parents could both speak some English, but it was very broken. Loren told them that Trevor had had a massive heart attack and that they didn't need to come because there would be no funeral service. Throughout the years, Adelle seldom visited her parents, going back to her days at Harvard. She had never really been that close to her parents, which was odd considering that Adelle was an only child. When Loren told them the news, Adelle's parents insisted that they would at least make a trip to see how she was holding up. Loren informed Adelle of the conversation, and she immediately got on the phone and called them.

Adelle was shaken but very strong. She didn't want to see her parents. She didn't want to see anyone, for that matter. She was shocked and depressed and didn't want to have to lie all over again to more people. She couldn't relive the events around Trevor's death again. After an hour-long conversation on the phone, she finally convinced her parents not to make the trip. As the days passed, Adelle suffered a major setback emotionally and had to go back on her medication. Meanwhile, Adam had to be sedated heavily in his caged bedroom until Lewis could figure out what to do with him. Garrison, on the other hand, was recovering, but he missed his dad.

A few weeks went by and Adelle's condition improved only slightly. She was very depressed. She missed her husband. She wanted her old life back, not this new life of depression, horrible dreams, and images that were burned into her brain forever. She attempted to forget all the terrible nightmares by way of the bottle. She drank and drank until she couldn't stand up at times. Lewis warned her not to drink with all the medication that she was on, but she didn't pay any attention to the voice of reason. Adelle soon found out that the more she tried to forget, the more she remembered. Her only solace was Garrison. She loved that boy with all her heart, and he was the only one that kept her from losing her mind.

On the other hand, Garrison had changed as well. He missed his father. For many years they had been far from each other, but over the past year they had grown almost inseparable. Now Trevor was gone. This hurt Garrison maybe more than anyone else because his father was the only person in the world who understood what he was feeling inside. Only his father knew what he was going through, the thoughts, the sudden pains, the feeling, and the reality of being so different from others that no one else could even come close to understanding. Garrison had lost his dad in that fight, a fight that his brother had started and that had ended in such a brutal way.

Garrison's rage toward Adam was growing, swelling inside his soul day by day, week by week. The hate filled every inch of his heart, and not once did Garrison do anything to stop the hate from reaching his soul. He had never liked Adam, and now he hated his brother with all his being. Garrison had loved being the only child. He hated to share anything, especially attention from his parents. Now the thing that he most hated in this world had killed his father. The same father who at one time didn't like Garrison and had let him know it. But in such a short time, they had found something they could share, and Garrison knew that in the future, their love for one another would have grown into something special. Then that thing had come along, and Trevor had taken him on one of their hunting trips in the forest. In Garrison's eyes, that was supposed to be a father-and-son-only trip. Then Adam came on the next hunting trip, and then the next one, and the next. This was very upsetting to Garrison, who believed that he, and only he, could give his father the gift: the gift of change.

At the time of the bite, Garrison had had no clue as to what was flowing through his system, but after he bit his dad and he started to change, Garrison knew that he had something special flowing in his blood, his body, or his soul. He couldn't place the source or even understand what was taking place in him, but he saw his father's emotional and physical changes. In the end, Garrison knew his dad had loved the change. Garrison didn't understand what he had done to his father, but he knew he had done something, something special, and something that only he could do. He knew that Lewis had more knowledge of what was going on in their lives, more than he let on. He knew that eventually his father would have told him the secret about his transformation. His dad would have told him some day, but now he was dead and the secret had died with him. Only Lewis knew the secret now.

Through all of Garrison's mourning, his thoughts were becoming clearer, especially regarding the trip Lewis had taken to Germany. At that time, Lewis's personality had changed. Garrison believed that his dad's personality had changed somewhat as well. Garrison wanted to know what had happened on that trip. What had made Lewis so jumpy and so short with his answers? He knew Lewis was hiding something, and he had to find out the truth. *Maybe the truth has something to do with me*, Garrison thought. Maybe Lewis knew something that he wasn't telling Garrison. If so, what was the secret?

Garrison's mind was so advanced for such a young boy. He had a knack for reading people. He could study them and at times could guess what they were thinking, where they were going to go, or what they were going to say next. Garrison used to play games with himself. He would watch his father, and certain moves from his dad dictated to Garrison what his dad's next move would be. Like every time his dad sat on the couch, Garrison noticed that he always gently tapped his right foot on the floor and then moved his left foot just before he got up. He would study his father during breakfast as well. His dad would take two or three sips of coffee, hold the cup in his hand, and then place the cup down on the table. He would do this most of the time when he was not disturbed or interrupted by his wife, Loren, Carolyn, or the phone. Garrison used to keep track of the number of sips of coffee in his mind, and he would play games using percentages. In his mind, he would take mental notes of Trevor's weekly average sips of coffee before he would refill the cup or not fill it up at all.

Garrison never told anyone of this because he liked to keep secrets. He liked to keep little tidbits of information to himself. He never liked to show his hand to anyone because he felt it made him weaker. Garrison used his type of behavior when he hunted. He could tell when an animal was going to move, in what direction, and how fast. The problem that Garrison felt with all of this was that after studying animals, or people for that matter, he never understood why they didn't study him the way he studied them. Garrison was more than just a special little boy; he was too intelligent for his own good. He realized that Lewis knew something, and he needed to find out what secret Lewis was keeping from him.

Time passed rather slowly over the next few months. The press's involvement in the death waned slightly. The Seawicks' business interests were virtually unaffected, considering all of the press. Loren was well respected, and she knew as much as Trevor did about the numerous financial interests of the entire Seawick fortune. Garrison was now becoming more interested in the businesses. Loren was pleased for him to have even a remote interest at such a young age. Garrison's high intellect served him extremely well throughout most of the training process. He didn't have the experience, and it showed, but he was an astute and fast learner. He seemed to be more aggressive than his father, but overall Loren saw many of his father's characteristics in young Garrison.

Lewis was very busy during this time. His main concern and time-related project was Adam. He personally constructed and installed in Adam's cage a device that would retract the chain that was around Adam's neck. A large wheel rotated the chain around a pulley when manually operated. As the wheel turned, the chain wrapped around the pulley and shortened. Lewis installed the device so he could clean the cage. Adam, meanwhile, was doing well. It seemed that he was calmer and could be reasoned with more than before the attack on Trevor. Lewis made sure not to purposely anger Adam and tried to befriend him. For the most part, the plan was working rather well. Lewis didn't want Adelle or Garrison in the basement. He was afraid that Adam would be violent with them, and to be honest, neither Adelle nor Garrison wanted to see Adam.

Adelle still wasn't doing as well as the others. She was getting the familiar sharp pains in her joints and was suffering acute headaches. The pains left her body as fast as they arrived. She knew what was happening. She had seen it firsthand with Trevor. Now she was one of them, and she knew it wasn't going to be pleasant. She sat alone for hours on end and thought about what her future held. Adelle knew well the three or four months of hell that her husband had had to endure before his horrific change was complete. She spoke at length with Lewis about what she should expect from the pending mutation.

Lewis, against his better judgment, told Adelle what he had found out about the mutation, but he didn't tell her about Garrison's birth parents. He knew that if he told her, that information alone would send her off the deep end. He informed Adelle that since the bite had been deep and the teeth had gone into the tissue, the potion, or whatever it was, was in her bloodstream.

When Garrison bit Trevor, he bit the wrist and broke the skin. Trevor endured three months of suffering until his body was finished mutating. Lewis told Adelle he believed that likely the same would happen to her. This really upset Adelle. She asked for a cure, but there was no cure. Lewis said he had worked feverishly to discover a way to reverse the mutation but had found no solution.

Lewis really wanted to tell Adelle about Garrison's birth parents. He wanted to tell that horrific story to someone, anyone who was willing to listen. As a doctor and now a scientist, he wanted to tell someone about this new species, but he couldn't. No one would believe him, and he was afraid for others' lives, as well as his own. He had to protect Garrison as long as he could. He didn't want Garrison to turn into a monster like Wolfgang and Zelda. He also had to think about the family business and the way any information that came out would affect profits or the good name of the Seawick Enterprises company and the many other enterprises that had sprung from it.

Adelle was deeply depressed and very frightened. She had always been a beautiful woman, and now she would become a hideous creature. She thought she would never be able to go out in public again or have any friends. This depressed her to no end.

Adelle also deeply missed her husband. Almost every night her own screams awakened her as she recalled images of Trevor's death. Her sorrowful heart grew with hate mixed with a large amount of loneliness. She hated Adam with all of her being. Adam was not her son, even though she had given birth to him. She hated him. He was a monster to her, and she made it clear that everyone in the house must feel the same toward him. She knew that she could not call the authorities because they would ask too many questions and the respected name of Seawick would be damaged for decades.

Adelle was becoming more unstable. At times, Carolyn and Loren caught her talking to herself, sometimes arguing with herself in a rather emotional way. One day, Loren caught her talking to herself about a vase that was misplaced on the mantel. Loren thought she was talking to someone else because she heard two different voices. Instead, it was Adelle throwing her voice as the conversation became an exchange of two different trains of thought. If Loren didn't know better, she would think there were two people in the room. This was happening more often as the weeks went by. Sometimes Adelle would talk to inanimate objects or speak to a chair as if someone were sitting and listening to her. Many of those conversations were calm and unimportant in nature, while others were rather loud and dictatorial. These actions spooked Carolyn. She thought Adelle was talking to Trevor's ghost, but the odd thing was, she never heard her bring him up in private conversation with others. Lewis tried to speak with Adelle about her issues, but she denied that she was demonstrating any abnormal behavior.

Garrison continued playing his violin. Many times, he was invited to play along with the Louisville Orchestra during their practices. He was even offered a few jobs with the orchestra, but he turned them down. He loved playing the violin. It made him feel normal and in control. Garrison knew that he was different. He would think back on the many meals that he had had with his father and his evil brother. He enjoyed those meals and really had a powerful desire to continue them. While most kids Garrison's age would want ice cream or candy, Garrison wanted the taste of a freshly killed animal's muscle with blood dripping from the tough tissue. Lewis was concerned about Garrison, and he spent more time with him than ever before. The two grew closer after Trevor's death. Garrison needed and desired a father figure in his life. He missed his father so much. He felt sorry for the way he had treated his father at times while he was alive, and he would give anything to bring him back to life just to say he was sorry for his actions.

Garrison rarely came down to the basement to visit Adam. These visits normally upset Adam greatly, and he would growl and hiss at Garrison. Lewis was very angry about these visits, and he spoke harshly with Garrison about them. Lewis was concerned about totally losing control of Adam, but he especially didn't want Garrison to take on any of Adam's aggressive and evil characteristics. In fact, Lewis and Garrison had hundreds of conversations about this very subject. Lewis told Garrison that he had an awesome responsibility ahead. He had to be the new face of Seawick Enterprises and take part in all its business activities. Garrison was very receptive to the idea and was more than willing to accept as much responsibility as he could. Lewis, when speaking about Adam, always used a tone of disgust. Garrison liked this because he felt that Lewis was on his side and not Adam's side. Garrison felt 100 percent confident that he could trust Lewis.

What did upset Garrison was the fact that he knew he might one day have to care for Adam. Lewis rarely brought this subject up, but from time to time he did, and Garrison made it perfectly clear he wanted nothing to do with Adam in the future. Lewis knew this was a major problem because his worst nightmare was for Adam to get loose and bite someone, or even several people. That would spread the formula, and it could easily get out of control. This could never be allowed to happen, and Lewis knew he needed to secure the situation before his death.

Another issue that was concerning Garrison was the condition of his mother. He knew that Adam's bite would cause his mom to change over time. This angered him to the point of complete hatred for his brother. He couldn't believe that he could do such a thing, not only biting his mom but murdering his father on top of it. Garrison was a peaceful child by nature, a good child with a good heart. He had his moments, but he had never thought of killing his own father; it just never crossed his mind. He viewed Adam only as an animal, not as a human being. Garrison knew one thing: he was never going to take care of that animal while he was alive.

Garrison's diet of animals didn't disturb him at all; in fact, he thought it was natural until Lewis told him that it was abnormal. Garrison's diet had changed, but his desire for a raw meal was growing inside him. Lewis tried to encourage him to eat cooked meat, but Garrison didn't like it that way. He felt the same about chicken and fish as he did about red meat. Even the thought of eating cooked meat repulsed him. He liked his meat. The muscle of the animals, the tendons, and the ligaments were the parts that he preferred. He liked the smell of the animal and the way it struggled as he bit into his prey. He loved the way the animal twisted and turned in his hands, and he loved the way his teeth sank into it. He felt like god because he had so much control, so much power over any animal that he captured. Garrison also liked the taste of blood, but it had to be warm and fresh. He didn't really like the blood when it was cold.

Garrison attempted to explain all of this to Lewis, but the doctor just could never grasp Garrison's point of view. Trevor understood what Garrison was feeling when discussing this strange and unusual condition they now shared. Up to this point in time, no one in this world had experienced what Garrison had gone through throughout his life. Trevor was the only one that finally comprehended what was going on in his son's heart because his own condition had begun to change. That was the thread that had kept the two together. Garrison knew that his dad had loved the fact that he had changed, and he knew from his dad's point of view that he had changed for the best. He accepted the fact that his father hadn't cared too much about his outward appearance as long as he gained more intelligence. He knew that his dad had loved to play the violin and that after the change he had been better at it. He had loved his son for this and only this reason. Garrison knew that his own father had used him so he could benefit from the misfortune that had befallen his son. The problem was that the misfortune in Trevor's eyes had turned out to be the best thing that ever happened to him. Garrison knew it, and so did Garrison's mom.

CHAPTER 13

Crossroads

*M*eanwhile, Adelle's life was starting to become more interesting. At 3:23 a.m., she woke and started to scream loudly in pain. Her pains were so sharp she could hardly catch her breath. She attempted to control her breathing for fear of passing out or having a heart attack. Her heart felt as if it were going to burst out of her chest. Her head felt as if it were going to explode. The sweat was pouring out of her body from head to toe. Her vision was blurred when she first woke up, but a few minutes later, everything was clear. She was scared. She was partially out of it because of the intense pain that would not leave her body. The pain would not stop, would not ease; just constant pain, combined with pressure and stress from all parts of her body. Parts of her skin felt as if they were being pulled in opposite directions. Her skin felt so tight, and she swore she felt it tearing and ripping apart. Normally her pains would last for a short while and then disappear, but not this time. This particular night the pains were constant and refused to leave her alone.

Just then, Carolyn, whose room was down the hall, knocked on her door. "Adelle... are you okay?"

Adelle, breathing heavily, wailed with all the effort she could muster, "Yes, I am okay. Just leave me alone!"

Carolyn obeyed her command and let her be. She walked fast down the hall and closed her door. She knew that Adelle was her boss and that she had better do as told. She wanted to tell Lewis but thought better of the idea. She thought the pains should go away soon because that was what had happened with Trevor. Carolyn crawled back into her bed and said some prayers for her friend.

Adelle got up and sat on the edge of her bed. She was afraid to walk. She felt as if her joints were going to split in half. She took her pillow and covered her mouth as she screamed into the soft silk cover. She moaned and cried for hours on end. Eventually, the pains eased and finally stopped. She collapsed onto her side and fell asleep from total exhaustion.

At 10:23 a.m., Carolyn knocked on Adelle's door, but there was no answer. She opened the door and saw Adelle lying on the bed sleeping. She felt sorry for Adelle because she knew the night had not been a pleasant one. Carolyn closed the door and went downstairs to find Lewis. She explained the terrible night to him, and he listened with great interest. Lewis understood more than anyone could imagine. He said he would talk to Adelle when she got up.

Lewis had told Adelle about the mutation, so all of this was expected, but given her condition, he thought he needed to inform her on a daily basis. Whenever he talked to Adelle, it seemed to console her, even if the exchange was not pleasant. Lewis estimated that she had about two more months before the total mutation would take effect. Lewis's samples from the glands around Adam's teeth looked different from the samples from Garrison. This worried Lewis because he didn't know what kind of metamorphosis would occur or how bad it would be for Adelle. Since Adam had been born with the formula from one parent and the other parent was normal, he was more of an animal than a human. Garrison's parents were both infected with the formula, and Garrison turned out more normal compared to Adam. Lewis was in unchartered territory with Adam. He never had seen anything like Adam. Garrison's original parents were not that badly mutated. Lewis wished he had some samples from Wolfgang and Zelda, but he had not been in a position to ask them when he met them in the forest.

Adelle knew in the back of her mind that she was in trouble. She knew that she would end up like her husband and maybe worse. She had been bitten by a monster, whereas sweet little Garrison had bit her husband.

At 11:43 a.m., Adelle woke up wet with sweat and felt as if someone had beaten her badly. She rolled over onto her back and enjoyed the feeling of being relatively pain-free. She moved her arms toward her face and noticed bruises in the joints of her fingers and wrist. She noticed the same in her forearms. She looked closely at the bruises and touched some of the black-and-blue areas. They were sore, as if someone had beaten those areas with a baseball bat. Her heart rate increased because she knew that the changes were beginning to take place.

This was one of Adelle's worst nightmares come true. Trevor's change had physically revolted her at first, but after a few weeks, she had made herself get used to the idea. Even when they made love, it had been disgusting for her, but she had gone through with the acts. She had had no choice because she couldn't say no to Trevor. Oh, there were so many nights that she had had the same experience, too many to count, and she didn't care to recall them. She had hated the hair on her husband. It had been everywhere, so revolting that she had wanted to vomit during every encounter.

Now she was going to be like what her husband was, changing from a perfectly normal human being into some unexplainable, unholy manifestation. Even God would have difficulty understanding how His creation could develop such an evil facade. Like a person with great beauty who was now ugly, Adelle didn't want this fate to befall her whatsoever. She wanted a way out of this blanket of evil, and she knew somehow that there was a way. She couldn't think of the alternative. She couldn't go on with life if she looked like a monster, even though she might enjoy some of the advantages to the change. She liked the idea of being smarter, being better able to sense things around her, and quite possibly doing things that she couldn't before, but she couldn't accept the idea of being a monster.

Adelle knew that she needed to see Lewis and tell him what had happened the previous night, but she was afraid to confront her own fears. She attempted to get up from her bed. She swung her feet over the side. As they hit the floor, they were very sensitive for some reason. Adelle looked down and saw that her feet had gotten a little bigger. When she placed a foot in her slipper, the fit was tighter than normal, and part of her heel hung off the back. This exercise hurt her feet. Adelle felt a stinging sensation up her legs. She looked down and saw that her nightgown was an inch shorter on her. She began to cry because she knew what was starting to happen to her body. She knew that she would never be normal again. The process had already started.

She got up gingerly, and while holding onto the bed, she removed her feet from the slippers and walked over to the bathroom. She was a little dizzy and somewhat bewildered from the bad night's sleep. Each step sent pain up and down her legs. The sensation was like trying to walk on a foot that was asleep. After a few steps, the pain seemed to ease. She knew that her body had changed, but she didn't understand why the change had happened so fast. With Trevor, the pains were more frequent, but the change was slower, a little more gradual, it seemed. In the back of Adelle's mind, she knew that something was wrong and that maybe her transformation would be more severe than Trevor's because Adam, not Garrison, had bitten her. This made her even more nervous and upset than ever.

When she got to the mirror in the bathroom, she noticed that her face had changed a little. It seemed that her face—and her head, for that matter—had grown. Her chin looked to be pointier and her ears seemed to have moved up her head a little. The change would probably not be that noticeable to someone who had not seen her for a while, but it was certainly noticeable to her this particular morning.

Adelle slowly got dressed and went downstairs to speak with Lewis. She needed to ask him not only about her pains but also about what had happened during the night. Lewis met her in the kitchen and noticed the change right off. Adelle rushed to his open arms, hugged him, and started to cry. She said through her tears, "Lewis, I don't want to end up like Adam. I didn't ask for this. I don't want to be a monster like my husband or like Adam."

Lewis understood and patted her back as she cried hard in his arms.

Garrison witnessed all this unfolding before his eyes while he was eating at the table. His anger toward Adam grew, and he was getting more upset by the thought of what his brother had done to his father. Oh, how Garrison hated Adam. He hated him so much he couldn't think clearly.

Lewis finally calmed Adelle down so they could talk. "Look, I know you're scared. I am here to help you. I am working on a cure, but I haven't found one yet. I was with Trevor every step of his transformation, so I have some experience with this metamorphosis."

However, Adelle quickly pointed out, "It was Adam, not Garrison, who bit me." She knew that her transformation would be harder, more painful, and more drastic than Trevor's because of Adam's condition. Lewis knew this to be true, or had figured out as much.

Adelle was beside herself. She left the kitchen and ran down the hall. Lewis followed her, afraid of what she might do to herself. She made it to the great room before he finally caught her. He placed his hands on her shoulders and shook her rather hard.

"Listen to me! I will help you through this. You are not alone!"

"I am alone! This is not happening to you, it's happening to me! You don't understand, I am so scared. I see what it did to my husband. I don't want that to be me. I don't want to turn into that."

"I understand. Listen, I will help you through this. In the meantime, I will work endlessly to find some way to stop this process from developing further."

Adelle finally got control of herself long enough to listen to Lewis's words of encouragement.

Meanwhile, Garrison was not far behind, and he peered out from behind the hallway wall to spy on his mom and the good doctor. He felt very sad for his mom, and he had great sympathy for what she was going through. He had seen the fear in his dad's eyes, but Trevor had never let his emotions be known for the most part, unlike Adelle, who wore her emotions on her sleeve. Garrison knew this was going to be a tough road for his mom to travel. He hated when his mom was upset. It had always bothered him, even at an early age.

At 2:37 p.m., Adelle was sitting on the couch looking out over the room with a blank stare on her face. A million thoughts were going through her head, and most were of Trevor. She contemplated how he had suffered before and during the change. She couldn't believe that just a few years ago, he had been this very handsome, kind, and giving man, and then in a blink of an eye, he had changed into something completely different. What bothered Adelle almost as much as the transformation was how she had allowed him to make love to her during and after his physical change. This had haunted her since it began. She had felt so dirty and so unholy making love to something that was part animal. It had disturbed Adelle to the point that it made her sick to her stomach. She had hated the fact that he was so withdrawn from the rest of the world. He hadn't wanted anyone to see him in his condition. Now she understood what he had gone through. She didn't want people to see her in her current condition. Adelle had never considered herself a ravishing beauty, but she didn't consider herself ugly by any stretch of the imagination.

Lewis was concerned about Adelle physically, but he was more concerned about her emotional well-being. He tried hard to think of a way out of this bad situation for his friend. Obviously, he knew from Wolfgang that there was no cure and no way of reversing what had started. He didn't want to experiment on Adelle because he didn't want her to endure more pain and stress. Lewis spent many hours in the basement trying to come up with something, but he found no answers. Sometimes when he was downstairs, he checked in with Adam. Adam was always lonely, and he considered Lewis his only friend, but he hated the fact that he was locked up behind bars and had a chain around his neck. He wanted to go outside, chase something that ran on four legs, and eat it. Lewis fed him regular food, and Adam hated the diet. He wanted raw meat.

Downstairs, Lewis unlocked the door and then made sure he locked it behind him. He went to check on Adam, who was playing with some of his toys. At times, Adam could be a very happy little boy; at other times he was a terror of an animal. Lewis sat down and racked his brain, trying to come up with something, anything, to cure Adelle or slow the eventual transformation. He came up with nothing. All he could think about was Wolfgang's statement: There was no cure once the process started.

Adelle was still sitting upstairs where she could hear Garrison running around on the second floor. He was with Carolyn, who was going to teach him some math that he wanted to review from the previous week's studies. The house grew quiet, which was not a good thing for Adelle. The quieter the house became, the lonelier it grew. Silences like this gave her time to think about her husband's transformation. She thought about his death, the way he'd died, and the way he looked when he died. She also thought about the happiness they had shared for many years before Garrison, and she thought about their life together and how nice and peaceful everything had been before she found Garrison. Adelle thought about how much she loved her son, but at what price? Garrison's entry into her life had been a wonderful thing, the most wonderful thing in her life at the time, but it turned out that it might have been the worst event in her life. For the first time, she felt resentment toward Garrison, and she allowed that feeling to grow into dislike. She started to cry again, and as each moment passed, she hated herself more and more for thinking such a thought. Even the idea of the slightest negative thought about her most precious child, the most beautiful and perfect little boy in the world, disturbed her greatly.

Adelle wiped the tears from her eyes, and with a powerful rage, she got up and looked around the room. The hate was filling up her heart; she could not control herself any longer.

Most people believe the human body or human spirit can only take so much. After time, so much stress, so much anger, so much sorrow usually works its way out. When the emotions come out, there is no control over them. Only action will make the feelings inside speak their point of view. It is God's way of giving the human spirit relief, whether it be a spiritual or a physical relief. God knew what he was doing when he created the animals and us. He made us all personal controllers of our own feelings, and those feelings need to be acted out, or the lack of control dominates the mind, heart, and spirit of the animal or human. It's been said by many that the connection between human and animal is not as far off as many would think. After all, we are all animals. We act out, we lash out, and we reach out to our emotions. For some, the control might be steady and long-lasting dominance over a particular object or emotion. For others, the control might come in waves. We all experience the control of our feelings in different ways. When we don't control those feelings and instead allow the animal buried deep inside us to gain control over our true selves, we as humans get ourselves into trouble. Some humans say things they don't mean, or they say something they believe but that hurts the listener. Sometimes, humans act out their emotions, not only through actions but through words as well. This is when humans are at their most dangerous and, simultaneously, most vulnerable state.

A couple of weeks went by, and Adelle's pains increased in length and frequency. This time, she noticed more changes to her physical appearance. Her head was getting noticeably bigger and longer, and her nose and chin were growing pointier than before. She had more facial, arm, and leg hair, and she had grown approximately four inches taller. She still looked human, and the real transformation had not yet taken place. Adelle's pain was intense. At times, it was so bad that Lewis had to come into the bedroom and sit with her on the bed until it subsided. She was becoming more frightened. She began to notice more sensory changes in her body. Her sense of smell was becoming more acute. She could smell things around the house that she hadn't noticed before. She hated this aspect of the transformation the most. Her hearing was getting better, and this irritated her to no end. She couldn't sleep at night, even when the night was pain free. She heard everything, and she couldn't stand this gift either. Her eyes were getting better. Everything was getting clearer, and she could see in the dark better than ever before. Adelle was a changed woman already, and she hated every minute of her change.

Adelle was still depressed and scared, but her newfound aggressiveness was becoming a safe haven for her to some degree. She wanted to do things that she never would have done before all of this started, but at the same time, her feelings of depression and loneliness controlled her and stopped her from doing anything out of the ordinary. This constant conflict of feelings caused great stress in her life. She was constantly battling the two extreme feelings every waking moment. One second she had the energy of five healthy and strong women, but the next second her depression zapped all the new energy from her soul. Trevor had given into the different feelings and let himself freely enjoy the new life. Adelle didn't allow herself this freedom or this pleasure. She was more concerned about the end result, even more than Trevor had been while he was going through his change.

One morning when Adelle woke up, she felt something unusual inside of her mouth. Something was pressing against the inside of her cheek. She ran her tongue over it. She tasted blood, and she got up and spit the item out in her hand. It was one of her teeth. She looked at the tooth and again started to cry, but this time the cry was in anger, not in despair. She thought that she'd had enough. She didn't know what to do, but she knew she had to do something. She had to at least act as if she was doing something about her condition. Getting to the source of one's problems was usually the best answer in most cases. She thought about it for a while and decided that speaking with Lewis wasn't helping the situation, and she didn't want to involve Garrison in any way. She didn't want to upset him. She couldn't speak with the other girls in the house. She didn't really like Carolyn. The woman had grown too close to Garrison for Adelle's liking. She was afraid that she might say something out of line if they spoke and the conversation went the wrong way. Loren was always busy, and she was too much of a businessperson for Adelle. Adelle had never really liked business, and she felt that Loren was too consumed with the family business to offer any help with her problems. That only left Adam. She needed to speak to him. The more she thought about it, the better the idea sounded to her. The source of all her stress seemed always to come back to Adam and his actions. The feeling of anxiety that came over her was very powerful, and she just had to speak with him. She had to see him and unload her feelings on him. She had to let him know how she felt and how he made her feel.

Adelle went to her bathroom and looked in the mirror. The person in that mirror was not the one she had known all her life. It was some stranger, some awful, ugly, demented stranger who had invaded her body and changed everything that was Adelle Seawick. She opened her ever-expanding mouth and saw the hole in her gum where the tooth had fallen out. She took a closer look and saw something white in the pit of the gum. It looked like another tooth. Adelle brought her long fingers up to her other teeth and attempted to wiggle all of them to see if any others were loose. Sure enough, another tooth on the other side of her mouth was loose. She also discovered two other loose teeth on the lower jaw. She knew that Trevor had lost some teeth when he went through the transformation. She knew she was well on her way to the midpoint of her conversion. Adelle got herself ready and went downstairs for some breakfast.

At 9:15 a.m., Adelle was sitting at the breakfast table eating an apple and thinking about Adam and Lewis. She knew that Adam was in the basement in his cell, and she knew that Lewis had the key to the basement door. She wanted to pay Adam a visit. Her hatred had overtaken her fear of him. She was starting not to be as afraid of him as she had been his whole life. She wanted to talk with Adam and ask why he had done such a terrible thing to his father. She wanted to know why he had bitten her and whether it was purposeful or accidental. Adelle had never really had a meaningful talk with Adam. He repulsed her, he scared her, he made her feel as if she had done something wrong to the human race by allowing such a monster to live in our world.

Her mouth was watering, which made her swallow more than normal. Her soul felt alive inside her body, begging for release. However, something was trapping her soul and not allowing it to go as it banged on the door of freedom. She had to see Adam. The feeling was swelling deep inside her, and she couldn't control her emotions. The only thing on Adelle's mind was speaking with her other son. The son who was the root of all the evil in her life, the same son who had turned her world upside down since the day he was born. She had never felt this passion, this desire, this aggressiveness toward anyone in her life. It scared her but only to a certain degree. She wanted more. She wanted to fully explore her feelings and not bottle them up as she had done all her life. Adelle had always been a conservative person, a caring person, a careful person, not some free spirit who wanted to run throughout the world and visit every experience with joy and excitement. This feeling of exploration and aggression was all new to her.

Adelle waited patiently in the great room for Lewis to come down for his morning visit to check on Adam. When he came down from his bedroom, he walked toward the basement. Adelle got up quickly from her seat and met him before he started down the stairs. "Lewis, we have to talk. I want to talk to Adam."

Lewis looked at Adelle and noticed right off how her appearance had changed seemingly overnight. The change was subtle but noticeable. He was a bit nervous as he said, "You know this is only going to upset you, Adelle."

"I know, Lewis, but I have to speak with my son," she replied firmly.

He nodded and invited her to accompany him downstairs. As they approached the door to the right of the landing, Lewis reached into his pocket for the key. He unlocked the door and stepped inside. He held the door open for Adelle.

Adelle stopped at the threshold of the door. She looked inside and was visibly nervous. Her hands shook to a point that she had to place them under her armpits to calm them. Her stomach felt nauseated as she broke out in a cold sweat. It had been almost two months since she had been in that part of the house. She finally found the courage to step inside, and she walked quickly past Lewis. She wouldn't allow her body to stop her forward progress.

Lewis knew this was hard for Adelle to go through, and he wanted to be as supportive as possible. He walked in front of her, turned, and went inside Adam's room.

Adelle heard Adam moving around, and finally she heard him say something, but she couldn't make out the words. As she approached Adam's door, she was dazed by his stench. The smell was not pleasant. His odor was very musky, like a dog's smell after running in a rain shower on a hot summer day. His breath was horrific. Adam hardly brushed his teeth, and his heavy breathing in his caged cell filled the air with his foul breath.

Before she was in sight, Adam said, "Mother, is that you?"

Adelle stopped and said, "Yes, Adam, it's me."

"Come here, Mother." Adam got up and walked toward the bars.

Adelle closed her eyes and took a deep breath. She then opened her eyes and walked with both of her hands gripped tightly into fists. As she entered the room, she saw Adam. He had grown, but he otherwise looked the same as he had two months ago. She noticed that he was taller than Lewis. Adam's head was lengthy and narrow, with long hair growing out in all directions. His eyes were close together and placed far from the nostrils of his doglike nose, which had moisture dripping out of the nostrils. His mouth was well below his oversized, protruding nose. The wide mouth seemed to curve deeply across his powerful, thick jaws. His ears were hairy, pointed at the top, and they came down to a small ear lobe. The ears were higher on the head, above the eyes. His neck was long but thick, and his shoulders were wide and strong. His arms and legs were many inches longer than any human's, and his feet were extremely large with a deep arch.

Suddenly, Adam smiled at her and asked, "Where have you been, Mother? Playing with Garrison? Seeing if he is okay? I bet he isn't behind any bars like me. Why do you love him more than me?"

Adelle pursed her lips and said angrily, "Well, at least he didn't kill his father or bite his mother."

Adam growled and slammed his body into the cage as he wrapped his hands around the thick bars. Lewis jumped back and almost stumbled over a chair. Adelle jumped and let out a short scream.

Adam looked at her and hissed, "Didn't your perfect child bite his father? Hmm! Maybe if we had a decent mother, we wouldn't go around biting our... loved ones."

Adelle said, "Don't compare your actions to Garrison's."

Adam snarled. "Everything was fine until you interrupted us, you bitch. Sometimes I have trouble with my emotions, and you, you confused me. I loved my father, but I got confused. It's all your fault, Mother. You caused me to kill him. You caused that to happen, not me. And that other son of yours just let it happen, didn't he? He laid there with you on the floor, and neither one of you stopped me, did you, Mother? Why don't you ask your little precious Garrison why he didn't stop the fight?"

Adelle stepped closer to Adam and said rather heatedly, "That is no way to talk to your mother."

"Mother!" Adam shouted as he slowly turned his large head and looked from Lewis back to Adelle. "You are a sorry excuse for a mother."

Adelle shouted, "Shut up! Shut the fuck up, you... you fucking monster!"

Adam raised his head a few inches, opened his mouth, and growled as loud as he could, showing all his long and thick teeth with saliva dripping from them.

Adelle was reduced to tears as she covered her face with her hands. Lewis stepped toward Adam and told him to settle down and keep quiet. Adam didn't obey Lewis's command; in fact, he hissed and growled at Lewis.

Adam yelled, "You never wanted me, did you, Mother? Why did you have me if you didn't want me? You treat me like I am some monster. You even call me a monster. Well, from where I am standing, you are the monster, Mother, not me! You and that freak of a son you have. Perfect little Garrison with his perfect, white, angelic face. You both make me sick."

Adelle was still crying, but she was screaming at Adam between breaths. She was hyperventilating, but she was still trying to get her point across. Adelle had to come to peace with this or at least come to terms with what had happened to her husband, her son, and now herself. She asked, "Why did you kill him? Why did you murder him? Why did you mutilate him, you fucking monster?"

Adam got more upset. He pushed himself back from the bars of the cage and walked around. He got on all fours and slowly trotted around the room, jumping up on his bed and jumping back off, all the while looking directly into his mother's eyes. He was still hissing and growling at her. He was salivating all over the floor as Adelle continued to yell at him.

With all her strength, Adelle continued questioning and interrogating her son. "Why did you kill him? He loved you so much. He wanted you to feel normal."

Adam stopped, rose up on his feet, and walked slowly to the bars. He looked deeply into his mother's eyes and said, "Daddy did not love me. He didn't want to be with me. He never loved me like his precious little faggot, Garrison. When dear Daddy was changing into a... better person, he acted like he loved me, but I knew it was all an act. I sensed his loathing toward me. He knew I was better than he was, and he hated that fact, just as he hated the fact that his little perfect Garrison was even better than him. He let himself change. He wanted to change. He wanted to be like me and not like you people. You people are inferior to me. Garrison is inferior to me. Let me out of this fucking place and I will show you how imperfect you people are."

Lewis spoke. "Shut up, Adam. You have said enough. You will never leave this cell as long as you live."

Laughing, Adam said, "As long as I live? How about as long as you live, dear Doctor?"

Adelle spoke with great passion in her voice. "You are crazy!" As she started to sob, she said, "You are a crazy, sick, demented creature that should have never been born. I hate you!" She stepped back and cried uncontrollably.

Lewis had had enough, and he went to open his drawer. Adelle watched his every move through her tears. When he opened the drawer, she noticed the tranquilizer gun. Lewis loaded up the gun and walked over to Adam. Adam pleaded with Lewis not to shoot him, and he began to run around with the chain on his neck. Lewis moved over to the pulley that had the chain wrapped around its wheel. As he cranked the pulley, the chain pulled Adam to the side of the cage, shortening its length. He had the chain pulled back to about three feet from the wall. Lewis opened the door to the cage and stepped in. He pointed the tranquilizer gun at Adam and pulled the trigger. He shot him three times with the tranquilizer, and after a few moments, Adam fell limp on his bed.

All Lewis heard was Adelle crying uncontrollably in the background. He was very concerned about Adelle's mental state, and he said to himself that it had been a huge mistake to bring Adelle down into the basement to talk to Adam. He had known it was a mistake from the start, but this was Adelle's home, and she was still his boss.

Adelle was so upset she could hardly control her shaking hands and legs. She thought her legs would give out from under her, she felt sick to her stomach, and her head was killing her. She had to get out of the room. She had to get out of the basement; she felt so confined in that area of the house. She raced out of the room and up the stairs with a fury. Lewis cried out for her to stop and wait for him. She paid no attention to him.

Lewis was aggravated out of his mind. He had to make sure to lock the cage door so Adam would be more secure. After locking it, he ran after Adelle but had to stop and lock the basement door. He began to run upstairs as fast as he could, but when he got to the third step, he fell and hurt his ankle and his lower leg. He got up rather slowly and got control of his bearings, then continued his climb up the steps, this time with a limp.

Adelle had a good head start on Lewis. She was up the stairs and across the great room before he got to the top basement step. Lewis was calling as loud as he could for her. Loren came running out of her office. Carolyn and Garrison came from upstairs and ran down to the foyer to see what the problem was. Lewis was running from room to room in an attempt to find Adelle.

"What's wrong?" Loren yelled to Lewis.

"Have you seen Adelle? She was in the basement a minute ago and came running up here, and now I can't find her," Lewis said as he ran into the kitchen and noticed the room was a little out of order.

Loren asked, "What was she doing in the basement?"

"Never mind that now. Just help me find her." Lewis saw the kitchen door was slightly open. He ran as fast as he could, but his ankle and leg were really hurting. As he stepped outside, out of the corner of his eye, he saw something on the edge of the woods. Adelle was kneeling on the ground. Lewis yelled, "Adelle! Adelle! Don't move. I'm coming." Loren, Carolyn, and Garrison poured out of the house and followed Lewis.

Garrison was yelling, "Mom! Mom!" Carolyn and Garrison knew something was wrong. They didn't have a clue as to what had happened in the basement, but they knew Lewis was upset. When they saw Adelle kneeling on the ground outside, they knew something wasn't right.

Lewis got about ten feet from Adelle. He was so out of breath he couldn't speak. Carolyn stopped next to him and said, "Adelle, what are you doing out here? Are you okay?"

Adelle knelt on the hard-grassy ground, looking out over the forest with her back to everyone. She rocked back and forth only slightly. Her tears couldn't be seen, but her sobbing could be heard by all. She began to speak softly but got louder as she said, "Leave… me… *alone*… and take Garrison inside. *Now!*"

Lewis finally caught his breath and stepped toward Adelle. He said, "Adelle, let's go inside."

Adelle turned around, still on one knee. It was then that Lewis noticed the blood covering her wrists and hands. Blood was on her face and on the front of her dress. In her left hand was a large bloodied kitchen knife. She had slit both of her wrists.

Garrison screamed out, "Mommy! You're bleeding!"

Adelle started to cry hard as she rose to her feet and pointed the knife at Lewis, with both bloodied hands gripping its handle as tightly as she could. She screamed, "Stay away from me, all of you. Garrison, get inside now! I don't want you to see this."

Lewis said, "Adelle, this is not the way out. I can help you."

Adelle replied, "Help me? Help me? What the fuck do you mean, help me? You couldn't help my husband, you couldn't help my son, and you certainly couldn't help that monster you have locked up in that basement you call your lab. You are a monster too, you bastard. You're sick. Sick in the fucking head, you demented fuck. You let them eat live animals. How fucking sick is that, you crazy…" Adelle stopped and lowered the knife as she looked down and over to her right. She cried hard and closed her eyes. She raised her head up to heaven and said breathlessly through the tears, "I never asked for this. I don't want to be a monster like them. Forgive me, God."

She raised the knife to her exposed throat. She closed her eyes, swallowed hard, and quickly slid the knife from one side to the other with great pressure. Adelle heard many screams, but the one scream that she heard the loudest was from her son. She dropped to her knees. The pain was intense. She could feel the blood emptying from her neck. It was warm, and she could feel it flowing down her breasts. The feeling was silky as the blood flowed freely. Her hand released the knife, and as it hit the hard ground in front of her, her hands went to her throat automatically. The feeling of her hands on her throat made the wound sting even more. Adelle's eye caught her son's as time stopped for a moment.

Garrison's eye went from horror to sorrow in a matter of seconds. He cried out, "Mommy! Please do not die. I love you."

With that, Adelle closed her eyes and fell to her knees. The jolt caused more pain in her neck as the blood from her wound splattered before her. Adelle knew these were her last moments on earth, but she didn't care. The pain was so intense. Every move she made caused more pain. She couldn't help but to move because the pain was attacking her from so many directions. She started to feel a little dizzy, and each breath she took caused more discomfort as more blood escaped from her body. Adelle was hurting and getting very tired and lightheaded. She looked down at the ground and fell on her side, further hurting her wounds. As she rolled onto her back, the wound opened up more, causing more distress, so she rolled back onto her side with her hands still on her throat. No matter what position she was in, she couldn't stop the pain.

Adelle could smell the dirt and grass with every breath she took, knowing full well that the next breath might be her last. She tried to remember the scent because it might be the last thing she would ever smell or see in her short, young life. Her head had a light feeling as she felt strange hands on her shoulder. The hands were Lewis's, and she knew at that moment he could do nothing to save her. He also knew that she wanted to die, and he allowed her this wish. He didn't even attempt to salvage her life. This was Adelle's only way out; she and Lewis knew this to be true.

As Adelle lay on the cold ground, Garrison ran up and placed his arm around her shoulder. He lay on the ground beside his mom, facing her with his eyes glued to her beautiful but dying blue eyes. Neither one looked away as the blood gushed out of Adelle's neck and onto the ground underneath her. Garrison felt the warm blood as it squirted onto his arm and parts of his face. He mouthed the words "I love you" to his mom as she gasped for air. Her open mouth widened slightly after each breath she took, but Garrison noticed the repeated breaths were coming further apart.

Garrison said his last words to his beautiful mom, "I love you. Good-bye, Mommy." With those words spoken, Adelle took her last breath and expired.

Garrison continued to hold his mom with his hand on her shoulder. For as long as he lived, Garrison would never forget the blank stare on his mother's face. He loved his mom with all his heart. She was the only person in the world who accepted him for who he was and never made any mention of him being different. His mom loved him, and he knew it; he had felt it, sensed it from the start. Garrison didn't have many friends, nor did he have many people who loved him. His dad had loved him, but only for a handful of months, and even then, Garrison had felt his dad was just using him to gain knowledge of his condition. He knew his dad had had many unanswered questions about his mutation, both during and certainly after his change. Garrison knew that his dad had wanted someone to confide in at that time. Then his dad had brought Adam into his world on a more regular basis, something Garrison didn't like one bit. Through all the bad moments that had happened in Garrison's life, the only person who had been there from the start was his mom. He had always thought, as many little boys think, that his mom was beautiful. He loved the way her hair seemingly floated in midair as she walked. He loved the way she smelled, the way she spoke, the soft and gentle voice, a voice of reason that he so desperately needed all his life.

Those images would always be present in his mind, but they were clouded now with hate. Hateful passion now dominated his heart. His hatred was for only one person: his brother, Adam. Nothing in this world, human, animal, or inanimate object, drew the ire from Garrison's soul more than Adam. Garrison would never forget that last image of his most scared mother, her face covered with blood and a look of pain that he had never seen in his life. Not only had that brother of his taken his father, but now in just a couple of months, he had taken his mother as well. He knew that his mom couldn't take the pain of changing into something grotesque, something unworldly and unholy. Adam's bite had changed his mom into an animal. Garrison's heart almost exploded with pain as he thought about what she must have gone through all those years, especially the last couple of years, dealing with an issue that was extremely difficult for anyone to cope with or begin to understand.

Garrison had begun to blame himself even before this most recent episode. He often asked himself what his life would have been like if he had never bitten his father or never attacked and killed that dog. At a very young age, Garrison knew the consequences of his actions. He knew that he had changed many people's lives through his decisions and actions. He knew now that he needed to be more responsible than most because the power he had was immense. He had the power to literally change not only someone's life but also a person's physical appearance and mentality. Whatever he had in him, he knew now that he could cause great pain or great joy, depending on how a person viewed the situation. He also knew that his brother couldn't be trusted—ever. He needed to do something about his brother because Adam would never be able to control his feelings and thoughts, and there would be severe consequences that could endanger others' lives.

Garrison felt that he could control himself. He had worked on controlling his anger, his emotions, and his thoughts. He had his mother to thank for that but also Carolyn. Carolyn had always taught him how to control himself and how to concentrate when he had trouble focusing. He loved Carolyn a lot, but he loved his mom more. The only issue he had with his mom was that he wished she had paid more attention to him. He was at a point of no return. He was alone now with no parents to guide him in his life. He knew he had Carolyn, Lewis, and Loren, but they were not his parents and never would be. His parents were dead, and he felt alone.

Lewis bent down and knelt on the hard ground next to Garrison. He placed his hands on the boy and said to him, "Garrison, I am so sorry about what happened. Please, let's get up. Clean yourself off and I will take care of things here."

Garrison said, "Will you clean up my Mother?"

Lewis replied, "Yes, of course I will. I will clean her up, but I need to call the police. Everything will be fine."

Garrison got up and walked with Carolyn back to the house. As they walked, Garrison kept looking back at his mom lying on the ground. He didn't want to let go, but he knew that he had to. Then his emotions took over, and he cried hard as he walked into the house.

Loren looked at Lewis and said, "Okay. What are we going to do about this? Are you going to call the police?"

Lewis looked at Adelle's body and studied her face, arms, and legs. He said, "The mutation is not that drastic. I think it is safe to call the police. I don't believe they will ask many questions. With this coming so close to Trevor's death, we have to present a body to the authorities this time. Right?"

Loren agreed. "I think you're right. Do you want me to call some of the policemen that we have an association with now, or do you want to wait?"

Lewis quickly said, "Call them now and act like you are upset. I don't want to touch the body. We need to tell the truth of what happened but leave the... issue... a secret. I will consult with Garrison and Carolyn so they will keep the issue to themselves. Adelle has gotten larger, but her looks won't raise any questions. At least, I hope not."

Loren went inside and called a police officer named Jim Callet, whom they'd had an association with over the years. She told Jim what had happened, and he said he would personally come over to see the situation. Jim said he would bring a few of his men over. He was greatly disturbed to hear about Adelle's death. He was more upset for Garrison. Jim had known Trevor well, and he couldn't imagine anyone going through the death of his father and mother less than two months apart.

Jim arrived at the estate with four other police cars. Lewis and Loren escorted the officers and county coroner to the backyard. They saw Adelle's body, and Lewis filled them in as to what had happened. Loren played the role of distraught woman very well. Lewis controlled the storyline. After the police consulted with Lewis, they interviewed Garrison and Carolyn. Everything went according to plan.

Garrison knew that he didn't want the family secret let out into the world. He understood that his family name was on the line, and that was very important not only to him but to his parents as well. All Garrison wanted in his life was peace and a normal life. He didn't want to be treated differently. So, when the police asked him their questions, he made sure not to tell them anything about the transformations of his parents, and he was careful not to let on about the existence of Adam.

Jim's men took the body away in an ambulance. Lewis and Loren followed Jim down to the police station to provide further information about what had happened. Jim assured them that everything would be fine and that the death would be ruled a suicide. Jim wanted someone to issue the official announcement for the news and the papers. He did remark about Adelle's height and the amount of hair on her arms. With so much blood everywhere, her small facial deformities were not an issue.

Loren said that she would make a statement to the press. They didn't want the press at the estate. Garrison had gone through enough these past couple of months; he didn't need a mob scene outside his house. Jim told Loren that he would have a police officer stationed outside the estate for a few days to chase off any photographers or reporters that might attempt to get a story out of this unfortunate situation.

In the early-morning hours, just moments after Loren issued the press release, she called Adelle's parents in Germany. As if there was not enough stress and pressure on Loren, she had to be involved in another issue that was not in her job description. It was a very difficult job for Loren to do, but she handled it professionally, just as she handled everything regarding the Seawicks' affairs. Adelle's parents were beside themselves, and Loren could only imagine the pain on the other end of the phone in a land far away. They said they would come to Louisville as soon as they could, and Loren didn't attempt to talk them out of the visit this time. Of course, that created another problem for everyone in the house. How would they explain Adam?

Loren consulted with Lewis on this issue, and of course, Lewis was beside himself. He couldn't believe all the problems that he was encountering. One problem after another; they never seemed to stop for the doctor and this family. He didn't know what to say or do about the Adam situation. He thought that maybe he could make up a story about how one of Adelle's friends took the baby out of town or how one of the Seawicks took him for the weekend. He didn't know what he was going to say or do about the situation.

Adelle's death didn't change any of the Seawicks' business relations. The control of the estate would still be in Loren's hands. Total control would be turned over to Garrison and Garrison only when he reached the age of twenty-one, but with some limits. Loren would control the estate and all the businesses as she had over the past year. She would also take custody of Garrison and Adam. Trevor had told Garrison a while back that he would leave everything to Adelle and to Garrison. Garrison, according to Trevor's and Adelle's wills, would get everything. He would inherit all the businesses and be in substantial control when he turned twenty-one, and by the time he was thirty, he would have complete control over all the Seawick assets. Everyone knew that Adam wasn't capable of handling the estate or the Seawick's business affairs. Garrison had his own plan for Adam but knew that Loren wouldn't agree to the course of that plan.

Trevor had always wanted Garrison to control his fortune, and he had told Loren to help educate Garrison about all of the different businesses in the Seawicks' portfolio. Loren made all this information public in her press release.

Adelle's parents arrived in Louisville the next day. This was only their second time ever in the United States, the first time being Adelle and Trevor's wedding. Loren picked them up at the airport. Wilhelm and Greta hugged Loren, and both cried on her shoulders. Loren was not expecting this type of emotion from them because the last time they met, they had been very standoffish. Loren took them back to the estate so they could rest.

As they went in, they were very tired from the long trip. Lewis met with them and introduced himself. He told them he was the family doctor, and expressed his sympathy to them. Wilhelm and Greta were honored by the Seawicks' hospitality. In the background, the Vonsicks saw Garrison. For the first time, they were seeing their grandson, but they couldn't believe their eyes. They ran over to Garrison and hugged and kissed him as if he were their own child. Garrison loved the attention and, like the young man he was growing into, he offered his condolences to the couple. They both returned the kind gesture by remarking how sorry they were for the loss of his parents and his brother in such a short time. When he heard this, Garrison gave them a bewildered look. He looked over to Loren and Lewis, but they were just as dumbfounded as he was. Garrison didn't correct his grandparents but continued with the moment at hand.

The Vonsicks went to their room and cleaned up before dinner. As they went upstairs, Lewis motioned to Loren, Carolyn, and Garrison to step into the dining room. In a low voice, Lewis asked what had happened. Loren said she thought they said they were sorry that Garrison had lost his baby brother in a possible miscarriage. They had all heard the same thing. This was such a blessing. Now they didn't have to explain Adam. They all were thinking the same thing about what Adelle had done. She must have told them the good news at first, but when she found out Adam was disfigured, she had told them she'd had a miscarriage. So maybe Adelle had planned to have an abortion, or at least had thought about it at the time she told her parents about the issues Adam would have after birth. Lewis stated emphatically that Adelle had never asked or even inquired about an abortion. This was a true mystery to them all, and its secret had died with Adelle. They would never know why Adelle had told her parents the lie.

Adelle had a closed-casket funeral, and the visitation was limited to family members. The funeral itself was small and private. Adelle's body was buried next to her husbands on the grounds of the Seawick Estate. Their final resting place overlooked the valley of trees near the edge of the forest. The grass hadn't even taken root on Trevor's gravesite yet, and now the ground had to be disturbed once more. The area where Adelle had died looked strange; the grass had grown almost overnight in a rich, dark green. The grass had grown taller than in other areas of the yard. This was of great interest to Lewis, and he could hardly wait to run some samples on the new grass.

Garrison witnessed the burial with his three friends–Lewis, Carolyn, and Loren. Other than the funeral director and a few workers, no one else was present when the coffin descended into the vault. Garrison wanted to see the coffin being lowered into the ground. He felt compelled to watch the funeral to the end because he felt he needed closure. He saw the men close the cement box as they lowered the heavy cap to permanently encase the coffin against the outside world. Garrison witnessed the dirt shoveled over and around the structure. Carolyn was standing nearby in case he needed a shoulder to cry on, but the little boy never shed a tear. He stood and watched the whole process unfold before his eyes. He never became choked up or even felt like breaking down to cry. He was past all of that now. Garrison was a strong-minded young boy who was wise far beyond his years. He had learned to control his emotions, and thus he had learned to control his body physically.

As he watched the men scoop shovelful after shovelful of dirt onto the top of the vault, all Garrison could think about was himself. He knew that Lewis understood more than he let on. He could sense it as he could sense anything and everything around him. That was part of his gift from god. He knew people. He could read them through their body language or their tone of voice or their reaction to a question. Garrison needed to find out what Lewis knew. He believed that Lewis and his father had been keeping something from him, but he couldn't put his finger on it. Garrison saw and heard each shovelful of dirt land inside the hole. The hole, to Garrison, symbolized a mother's womb. He knew that the dead would lay in peace until god called for their souls to be lifted up into his heavenly arms. He could hear the dirt as it rolled down the sides of the grave. He could smell the earthy, moist ground in the air after every shovel released its grip on the dirt being sent to its permanent home, the earth's womb. He heard the wind through the trees as if nature's own symphony were playing for the two dead souls. Was this his punishment from the uncomfortable holy being? Did god not want to allow a creation of his to experience perfection? Or was this run of bad luck for Garrison a warning from his holiness himself, a punishment for being perfect? Garrison knew it was not his fault, and he grew angry at the thought of being punished for something he had no control over. Garrison was not pleased with this god, and in his view, this forced punishment was wrong.

The next morning, Garrison woke up early and got dressed. He went downstairs, picked up his violin, and went outside to visit his deceased parents. The earth still had a damp, musky odor around the gravesites. Garrison looked over the forest while the tombstones were still in his sight. He took in all of what the forest allowed. He played a Mozart violin sonata. He played the violin part while the piano accompaniment played in his head. He remembered every note from the piece that he was going to play at the Louisville Orchestra as a guest performer in a few weeks. While the tears rolled down his cheeks, he played every note as if it would be his last. He didn't perform this demonstration of extreme virtuosity for his dad; he did it for his mom. She had always loved to listen to her son play, and this small sonata was in her honor.

All the members of the house heard the violin playing. Everyone knew he was playing for his mom. Wilhelm and Greta were shocked by the sounds their grandson was making with the instrument. They had known he was good and they had heard his CD recordings, but to hear his playing in person was very special to them.

Garrison hadn't played the violin as much as he would have liked over the past few months, but he really didn't need to practice. He was perfect, perfect in every way, when he played the violin. He knew it, his mother had known it, and his father had known it even in the early stages of his playing. Garrison wondered if he had offended god with his perfection, not only with his proficiency on the violin but with his intelligence or with his motor skills or with any other skill that he had perfected during his lifetime. He knew he was highly intelligent. He was smarter than anyone he knew. He could pick up any subject and master it in very little time. He found this to be fun. It was developing into a hobby for him. As time went on, he knew that the time for playing around was limited. He knew that he had to learn the family business, and he was ready to take on the challenges that were waiting for him. He respected Loren, and he promised himself he would wait his turn per his parents' wishes. He informed Loren of one request. He wanted to meet the investors, the managers, and all the people who ran the Seawicks' interests.

Lewis, meanwhile, dug up a few samples of the ground where the grass had grown so fast and lush, where Adelle had died. The grass in that area continued to grow faster than the rest of the lawn. He took the samples to his lab and analyzed them. The roots that had been exposed to Adelle's blood were twice as long as the normal roots that surrounded the infected area. The mutated formula had obliviously been in Adelle's body, and it had caused the grass to grow faster, stronger, and deeper in color. Lewis had seen this in the forest in Germany too. He took many notes and pictures, and he videotaped the findings, recording them, along with the other volumes of work that he had accumulated.

After some very emotional good-byes, the Vonsicks left in Loren's car on their way to the airport. They told Garrison to keep in touch with them and told Loren to make sure that Garrison called them on a regular basis. Garrison and Loren agreed, and as the car pulled away, Garrison waved to the only grandparents he knew. They had come and gone in such a short time, just like so many of the people he had loved in his life. This made Garrison sad but also angry. It seemed as if people tended to either leave him or die as soon as he got close to them. Of course, he had Loren, Carolyn, and Lewis. They had not left him, at least not at the moment. Although he was close to them, he longed for someone related to him so he could have some contact with his family lineage.

Lewis and Loren planned to keep Adam sedated as much as possible when people came to visit. The floors in the estate were very thick, and for the most part, it was hard to hear any noise coming from the basement. To be on the safe side, Garrison, Lewis, and Loren didn't want Adam to draw any attention to him and the basement. He would be very hard to explain.

Months went by, and per Garrison's wishes, he met with many of the people that ran the Seawicks' business interests. All the important players in the family business came away astonished by the boy's intellect, and were impressed by his maturity level. They were complimentary of Trevor and Adelle. This pleased Garrison and he felt it was a greater honor to be a son of two such respected individuals.

CHAPTER 14

Truthfulness

Something had been bothering Lewis for a while now. He knew that he needed to tell Garrison about his birth parents, but he feared that Garrison would be angry or, even worse, that he might want to see them. Lewis never wanted to go back to that forest again. He felt he had cheated death the last time. He was also concerned about what they might do to Garrison. Would they kill him if they saw him? Would they befriend him? Would Garrison want to live with them or have them come and live on the grounds of the Seawick Estate? Lewis was confused and scared. He had to reveal this nasty little secret to somebody, but he didn't trust anyone with the information, not even Loren. He thought that when Garrison got older he might tell him. That sounded good to Lewis, although he knew the longer he waited, the angrier Garrison would be. Lewis loved Garrison as an uncle would love his nephew. He only wanted what was best for the boy, and he wanted to keep him safe and secure. But mostly, he wanted Garrison to be mentally stable. He was afraid that someone with Garrison's wealth, power, and intellect would be impossible to reason with if he ever lost control of his good judgment.

Meanwhile, Garrison could sense the stress that Lewis was under and started questioning him on why he was so preoccupied. Lewis blamed it on Adam, who was not improving. Adam wanted out of his cage. He was going stir crazy being locked up all the time. He wanted the freedom to go outside and explore the world around him. He wanted to kill something, anything, so that his desires would be satisfied. He also wanted to see Garrison and questioned why he couldn't play or talk with him. The truth was he hated Garrison deeply, but he wanted to interact with someone his age, or at least someone who was not as old as Lewis. Everything about Garrison annoyed him to no end. He hated him, and he let Lewis know it. Lewis tried to talk some sense into him, but it was a lost cause. Lewis knew that he had to keep the two separated. He talked to Garrison about Adam many times, but Garrison didn't want to have anything to do with him. In fact, Garrison had, on many occasions, suggested eliminating Adam altogether. When he did, Lewis and Loren quickly reacted in a very unsettled way. They told Garrison that Adam was his brother and that it was wrong of Garrison to advocate such an idea. Garrison would always agree with them, but down deep, he knew that something had to be done with Adam.

A couple of years passed, and during this time, Garrison's life was greatly improved, aside from the thoughts of his brother hanging over his head. He was about to play in front of a sold-out audience at the Louisville Orchestra. He had intended to play a Mozart sonata, but the orchestra asked him to play a more difficult piece. Garrison agreed, and at a moment's notice, the program was changed. The orchestra honored the memory of Garrison's parents by making the opening night of the season a tribute to Trevor and Adelle Seawick. The most special guest violinist was Garrison Seawick, to perform Mozart's Violin Concerto No. 3 in G major, K 216.

Garrison had most of his friends and his business managers there on opening night. He had practiced with the orchestra for a while. Most of the time practice was a bore to Garrison. He knew when to come in with his violin parts, but the orchestra needed the practice. Garrison understood, but it annoyed him. He made many in the orchestra nervous because of his proficiency in the violin and the power he had by his massive wealth. Garrison also knew the complete details of the musical works to be played, so he knew if someone played off key or made a mistake. Many of them viewed the young boy as a prodigy beyond anything most of them had seen or heard, including such individuals as Mozart, Strauss, or Mendelssohn. Garrison carried himself as an individual who was always in total control and who knew exactly what he was doing all the time. He never made a mistake and was impatient with others who did.

The opening night of the concert, the young Garrison Seawick took the stage. The most anticipated performance was about to commence. He walked out to a thunderous applause with his violin in his left hand and the bow in this right. He walked quickly between the members of the orchestra and made his way to the area in front of the conductor. As he walked about midway to his destination, he raised his right hand with the bow and waved it around to the audience. The audience loved the showmanship and applauded even louder. He stopped at the microphone and took a bow to the crowd and conductor. The audience settled down, and the conductor organized the members of the orchestra. Garrison nodded approval to go forward with the opening bar of the concerto. The orchestra played.

Garrison's mind was on his mother, and it soon turned to his father. He contemplated everything that had happened over the past year or so. He felt an odd sense of freedom during the start of the performance. Everything seemed to be in the past now, with the one exception of his brother, but he tried not to think about that person in his life. He always said that life was too fragile to become upset over a small, unimportant event or person that wanted to disrupt a good life.

When it was Garrison's turn to play, the crowd grew silent. He drew his bow and played well. He played as he had practiced, with great intensity and flare. His face contorted at certain sections of the movement. Many said that he moved with the violin as if he were making love to the music. Even at a very young age, the passion and emotion that he displayed on every note made the experience very special for the listener. After the first movement, which was lively and bouncy, he settled down into the slow and romantic second movement. Some musical scholars have called this movement the "Minor Miracle." It certainly was when Garrison played the piece. Hardly any noise came from the audience as he played.

The movement was like Mozart himself, simple yet complicated, and if not played correctly, the very essence of the piece would be lost on the listener. Tears rolled down Garrison's cheeks as he played. He was remembering his parents, especially his mom. The movement was elegant, silky smooth, and brilliant like his mom had been when she was alive. The third movement was a joyful release of whimsical fun, a release that Garrison's soul needed after the poignant second movement. The piece ended with perfection, and the audience rose and gave young Herr Seawick a much-deserved standing ovation.

As Garrison took his bows, he looked through the audience to see where everyone he knew was sitting. He obviously didn't see everyone, but out of the corner of his eye, he saw a very attractive girl about his age. She had long, curly blonde hair with striking blue eyes. She was dressed in cheap clothes, but her beauty made her look as if she were covered with diamonds. This was the first time young Garrison had noticed a girl in his youthful life. He could sense that she liked him. She looked at him with star-filled eyes, and her mouth hung slightly open in wonderment. He more than glanced at her but had to turn away and walk off the stage. She noticed the glance from the maestro. Garrison came back after the audience wanted an encore, and he saw her again applauding with the people around her. As many have said in the past, a woman who loves classical music is a woman filled with great desire and passion within her spirit. Words cannot describe women; only a composer's music can outline a woman's essence and describe her inner core.

Garrison walked off the stage and went in the back. He wanted to get out to the audience to meet this girl, but he had responsibilities backstage. After the concert, he met with the members of the orchestra and many of the orchestra's board of directors. Overall, the night was a huge success, but Garrison couldn't get the image of the cute little girl out of his mind. He wanted to call the front office of the orchestra and ask them if they had any records of the seat holder's name, but he never pursued it.

Even to this day, Garrison often wondered why he didn't investigate who that lovely creature was in that seat. Maybe it was the understanding of his situation that wouldn't allow for him to court anyone, especially someone as striking as that person, into his different world.

A few months went by, and Lewis asked Garrison to sit down with him. He had to tell him and Loren about what was flowing through Garrison's body. Lewis knew through Wolfgang that those who had Formula L in their systems would live forever. He only had Wolfgang as proof, but he felt that he couldn't tell Garrison about Wolfgang. He was afraid of Wolfgang's warning never to let anyone know of his and Zelda's existence. He had to honor their wish to be kept secret, especially from Garrison. They hadn't wanted him to begin with, so they had given him up. They had killed their own children before Garrison, so Lewis knew they were very dangerous creatures. *Creatures* was a good word for them too, because they looked more like creatures than humans. Their image still haunted Lewis at night.

Somehow, Lewis had to explain to Garrison that it was his belief that Garrison might live not only for a very long time but forever. That he would never grow old or sick. He would never die unless something ended his life unnaturally. Of course, Lewis had known this for a long time now, but he wanted to find the right time to tell Garrison. Lewis had seen what Formula L had done to the Seawick family in just a year. His responsibility now was helping Garrison. He had to share what he knew about the formula, but he knew that Garrison would question him to no limit. Lewis knew Garrison would want proof. He would ask for the chemical breakdown of the formula. That was how Garrison was when it came to situations like this. He gave Lewis headaches with his constant questioning and deep conversations on any subject. Lewis thought maybe if he told Garrison the truth, the boy would accept it and go on with his life, but he knew that was not going to happen. Oh, what should Lewis do? What an awesome responsibility he had to bear. He could hardly breathe at times, it weighed so much on him.

One day, Garrison came down and knocked on the door to the right of the basement entrance. After what seemed to be a long time, Lewis answered. He didn't want to let Garrison in at first, but this was Garrison's house, so he had to abide by his wishes. Garrison walked in and said he wanted to speak with Lewis. Lewis's heart sank because he knew what Garrison was going to ask. He decided to be proactive and take Garrison outside because he was afraid that Adam would overhear their conversation.

Adam did hear, and he could smell Garrison as he talked with Lewis. He hissed and yelled, "Garrison! You little maggot, come here. I want to talk to you."

Garrison's rage was strong inside him, but he had learned to control his anger. He stepped toward Adam's room, but Lewis took hold of his right arm and said, "This is not a good idea, Garrison."

Garrison looked down at Lewis's arm and said, "Please let go of me. I want to see what he has to say."

Lewis reluctantly let go of Garrison's arm. Garrison walked slowly and confidently into Adam's room. He looked at Adam with a smile on his face and began to speak. "So, Adam, do you like your little room?"

Adam was very upset, and he slammed his body into the cage bars and extended his right arm, attempting to grasp Garrison, but the bars prevented him.

Garrison snickered and walked to within a foot of the outstretched hand. He bent forward and sniffed it. He said, "Who did you kill today?"

Adam angrily said, "Come a little closer, and it will be you, you freak of nature!"

Garrison's smile widened, and he cocked his head to the left as he looked into Adam's yellowish-green eyes. "Freak of nature? Me?" he asked. He turned away and walked out of the room.

Adam yelled, "Come back here, you freak! Come back here, old brother of mine!"

Garrison laughed as he passed Lewis. He walked toward the basement door saying, "I will be waiting for you outside, Lewis."

Lewis followed Garrison out of the basement. He closed and locked the door, and they walked out to the backyard. They stopped in the courtyard. The sun was out, shining brightly. The trees created some shade near the pool. In the distance, on the spot where Adelle had committed suicide, the grass was still greener, thicker, and taller than the grass around it. Garrison walked near the pool and asked if that location was okay with Lewis.

They sat down, and Lewis started the conversation. "I know you have many questions, Garrison. I need to be honest with you. I hope you trust me, because what I am about to say to you will shock you. I was hired to help you. You know your parents were very upset when you bit that dog in your father's library. They were very disturbed by your actions. I performed test after test after test, and I came up empty. I thought you had some mental issue, but when you bit your father, it changed the scope of my research. Your father changed physically and mentally. You know the story. Your dad wanted me to find out what was going on with him. Why was he changing? He knew it had something to do with the bite from you, but he never condemned you, Garrison. He loved you very much although he never showed it much. He was so preoccupied with his business dealings, and when you bit the dog, he was afraid of you. He never said that to me, but I could see it in his eyes and in his actions toward you. I know you are special. I know you can sense it as well. I have seen some very strange things in my life, but what I have seen these past few years leaves me absolutely speechless. I have gone over this in my mind every day and every night. I wake up in cold sweats. When your father was killed, I lost not only a friend but the only person in this world that shared the secret I have. You are the most amazing boy I have ever seen. You are not even ten years old yet, and you act like a thirty- or a forty-year-old. You are the smartest human being that I have ever met in my life, and I have met some of the most brilliant men and women that were ever born in this country. Your capacity to learn is unworldly. Your father and mother saw this in you at a very young age, and that's why they brought me into the picture. At times, I wish they had never contacted me, but I would have missed one of the biggest, most incredible finds in the history of the world."

Garrison was glued to Lewis's every word. Lewis was upset, but he tried to hold it together. He didn't want to tell Garrison, but he needed to tell him. He needed to tell someone or the secret would eventually kill him from the inside.

Lewis moved to the edge of his seat while Garrison sat without moving a muscle. Garrison knew that Lewis was going to explain some things that he had wanted to know for a long time.

Lewis continued. "Your father wanted me to investigate your past. Garrison, I don't know how to tell you this. This is going to shock you, but your parents didn't want you to know until you got older. Garrison, you are adopted."

Garrison's eyes got very big, and his mouth opened slightly. He hadn't known. In fact, he had never even thought about the possibility.

Lewis went on to tell Garrison about how he had been found in the woods in Germany. He told him about the fertility problems his parents had had, and then he told him of the adoption. Lewis paused. He was sweating profusely.

Garrison noticed Lewis's fear and said, "Lewis, it's okay. I am fine with it. I never thought I was adopted. I don't know why my parents never told me."

Lewis swallowed hard and said, "They were going to tell you, but they were waiting for you to get older so you could completely understand. Then as you grew up, you had some issues. You grew and developed so rapidly. Your father wanted me to find out about your family history. We thought at the time that we might stumble on something important that we might be able to use to help you or to understand what was happening to you. I mean, Garrison, it is not normal for anyone to grow as fast as you have grown or to have developed as fast as you have. After you attacked that dog, your parents were distraught, but the main issue for your father was his own change.

He knew it had something to do with you biting him. He thought if I could learn more about your family history in Germany, maybe we could find some answers, perhaps a way to reverse the process. Believe me, Garrison, I didn't ask for this. I was a doctor, and in just a few months, I was pulled into something that I had no experience with and, for that matter, something no one has had experience with in the history of mankind. I feel that I am going crazy, Garrison. After your father's death, I have had no one to consult with, I have had no one to talk to. I am alone, stranded on an island with no communication with anyone."

Garrison leaned forward on the edge of his chair. "So, Lewis, what did you find out? What do you know that you are not telling me?"

Now Lewis couldn't hold back. He had to tell Garrison the entire story. Either Garrison was going to respect him for coming clean with his information or he was going to fire Lewis on the spot.

"Garrison, I have come to love you. I respected your father and your mother. I was... I mean, I am... paid handsomely for what I do and for the services that I hopefully provide. But I am helpless because there is no cure. When I went on my trip a couple years ago, I went to Germany. I coordinated a meeting with your Aunt Sonja. See, Garrison, you were found in the woods near a small village. The village isn't even on the map. Sonja called your mom one day and told her about a newborn baby boy that was found in the woods by some hikers. That baby boy was you, Garrison. The authorities took care of you, but they never found your original birth parents. Your dad thought it would be a good idea for me to explore to see if I could learn anything that would aid in fighting the changes happening to him. Your dad was desperate, Garrison, desperate for a cure. As it turned out, he liked being the way he was. Well, to make a long story short... Oh, God, please forgive me for what I am about to say. Garrison, I must ask your forgiveness, but I want more than anything your understanding, if that is possible. Remember that at the time I had orders from your father, and he was looking out for your best interests. He was going to eventually tell you himself, but he never got to. Garrison, I found your birth parents."

Garrison was shocked. He moved around uncomfortably in his chair then got up. He started to cry; he couldn't control these emotions that were hitting him so fast. Both of his parents had died before his very eyes, he had a monster for a brother, and now this. He walked away from Lewis, but he didn't know where to go. Lewis got up fast, followed Garrison, and tried unsuccessfully to get him to look at him.

Lewis said as fast as he could, "Garrison, stop, please look at me. Garrison, I know this is a shock to you, but there is more to this story, and I am afraid to tell you."

Garrison stopped moving and regained control of himself. His ears rang as if a large bell had gone off inside his head. He listened; he knew that Lewis had more information.

Lewis walked Garrison back to his chair and bent down beside him to tell the true story. He said, "Garrison, what I am about to tell you will disturb you. I found them... or actually, they found me... in the forest. Deep inside of this forest, I came across some interesting-looking plants. As I was taking some samples, I heard something move in the forest. Before I knew it, I ended up meeting your birth father. Garrison, it pains me to say this, but he is just like your dad physically. I was scared out of my soul. I thought he was going to kill me. In fact, I knew he was going to kill me, so a part of me asked some very difficult questions of him."

"Your birth father was one of the most important and most secret scientists that Adolf Hitler had working for him. He discovered a formula called Formula L. Your father... I mean, your birth father... accidentally discovered the secret to life. He discovered a formula that basically stops you from getting old. He uncovered the fountain of youth. Your birth father is well over one hundred years old, but he doesn't look over forty. He told me that he believes that he will live forever. He's also never gotten sick since he injected himself with the formula. Your mother is also alive. She was injected with the formula as well. They had four babies, three of whom they killed. They killed their own babies, Garrison, your brothers. Then you came along, and your birth mother couldn't kill you so she left you in the forest in a place where you could be found. She got lucky. You got lucky when you were found. Your birth father didn't have a clue that you were alive, and to be honest with you, I doubt your mother knew you were alive either. Your birth father's name is Wolfgang, and your mother's name is Zelda. Wolfgang told me that, according to his studies, when they bore an offspring, that offspring would live forever, and your appearance will remain at a certain age forever. In other words, Garrison, you will never grow old. He said to me that the age at which you will stop growing will depend on nature, but he was thinking around thirty or forty, somewhere along that timeline. Garrison, you have never been sick a day in your life. Everything he told me has come true so far. He also told me that this formula was going to be used to make the perfect race of humans. This explains why you are a master at the violin and why you are so much more advanced than anyone I know. You can grasp concepts that men four, five, six times your age cannot grasp. Intelligent men with IQs off the charts. I don't think you will turn into… well… into an animal. You haven't done so in all these years. Wolfgang believes you will not turn into an animal, but if you bite someone, that would turn them into what your father turned into."

Garrison was stunned. He didn't know what to say. Finally, he got his thoughts together and said, "What happened to Adam? What…"

Lewis interrupted Garrison. "I know what you are going to say. Apparently, when someone is infected with the formula and they mate with someone without the formula, they create a child like Adam. Wolfgang wanted to perfect his formula, but Germany was losing the war and Wolfgang ran out of time. He and his wife hid in the forest to escape imprisonment or worse. Your father, Trevor, wanted me to find a cure, but according to Wolfgang, there is no cure. I have to believe him. This formula is so beyond my comprehension. Listen to me, Garrison. Listen to me well. Wolfgang and Zelda are bad people. They were going to kill you when you were born. They have no regard for life."

Garrison interrupted Lewis's rant and asked what his parents were like.

Lewis said, "They eat live animals. They look like what your father looked like before his death. They are extremely tall and have immense strength. Please, I beg you, please don't go after them. Please don't see them. I promised Wolfgang that I wouldn't tell a soul about him, but I told your father because I thought he had a right to know. I am so sorry that I didn't tell you, but your father didn't want me to tell. He was intimidating in his final months. He would have killed me if I told you. I wanted to tell you the first thing, but after the death of your parents, I knew I couldn't tell you. But I know you want to know the truth. I don't know if I did the right thing or not. Please forgive me. I don't know what to do." With that, Lewis totally broke down and couldn't control his emotions. Years of stress came out all at once.

Garrison sat there trying to process all this new information. He had never thought in a million years this would happen to him. He couldn't believe it, but everything was making sense now. He knew Lewis was telling him the truth, and he understood why Lewis hadn't told him.

Garrison placed his hand on Lewis's shoulder and said, "I understand and respect the position you took. You were following my father's wishes. Lewis, you are all I have—you, Loren, and Carolyn. You people are my family. You always have been and always will be. Is this all the information you have for me? Is this everything?"

Lewis collected himself, nodded rapidly, and said, "Yes, yes, that is everything. I have nothing more to report."

Garrison said, "Well, what a day this has turned out to be, huh?" With that, he smiled and helped Lewis to his feet. He asked Lewis if he was all right before he went toward the house. Garrison reassured Lewis that he had no ill feelings toward him or toward either of his fathers. He also stated emphatically that he had no interest in meeting the parents who had left him to die in the forest.

As Garrison walked inside, Lewis fell into the chair that Garrison had been sitting in, and he collapsed. Lewis again lost control of his emotions and cried as hard as he had ever cried in his life. This was too much emotion and drama for any man to be able to handle well.

Garrison took the news of his adoption and his newly discovered birth parents surprisingly well. Lewis, after he composed himself, told Loren the complete story as well. Garrison ended up telling Carolyn. They all met over dinner and made a pact not to let this information out to anyone. Garrison was starting to take more control over his new family now. Lewis felt that the weight of the world had been lifted off his shoulders. He told Garrison that he would work on finding a cure, but Garrison told him not to worry about it. He liked the idea of living forever. Garrison then told Loren and Carolyn about his taste for animals. They were appalled and didn't understand or approve. This new information was too much for either of the women to take in at once. Garrison told them that he would continue with this on his own terms. He missed the nightly meals but said he would control the feedings. Garrison had a way about him that was very convincing, making him able to control people and their actions. Garrison knew that he had a little something over his newly formed family; that something was fear, and he was going to use it but in a nonthreatening and nonviolent way.

Garrison was tired of trying to love someone or to chase after someone who didn't love him back. He had felt that way for years, so he had no interest whatsoever in contacting his birth parents. Lewis assured Garrison that, at least to the best of his knowledge, Wolfgang and Zelda would never come after him. They had no interest in seeing him or in meeting with him. They wanted to be left alone, and that was fine with Garrison.

CHAPTER 15

Isolation

*G*arrison and his family were getting along very well. He started his schooling with Carolyn again. He was thinking about testing into college, but Carolyn thought he was too young to go. He was learning so much from reading textbooks and reports on the computer. He also spent many late nights with Loren, talking about the family businesses. He was a fast learner who proved to be very innovative. Despite what he told Lewis, Garrison did think a lot about his biological parents. He thought about what they looked like. He kept thinking about what Lewis had told him: that they resembled his father. Garrison couldn't believe that they looked like his dad. If so, how in the hell did he get to look the way he did: fairly normal? This blew Garrison's mind. It didn't make any sense to him.

What did make sense to Garrison were his appetite and his music. He went back to the forest and set the traps that his father had set many months ago. He missed the tastes the forest had to offer him. He continued to dine on live animals. He ate anything that made its way into the traps. The adrenaline rush that he got from seeing a trapped, scared, and feisty animal would make his senses keener than they already were. The extra rush he experienced when opening the cage and sinking his teeth into the wild game was orgasmic to Garrison. He loved the smell of fear the prey gave off, and this feeling of power made him happy. He was one with nature, which felt like home to the lonely boy.

Garrison continued to play his violin while studying more of Mozart's works. He had a knack for memorization, and he was especially good at memorizing musical notes. The members of the Louisville Orchestra were so impressed with him that they offered him a place on the Board of Directors. Garrison gladly accepted the offer. He knew he was a great advertisement not only for his business but also for the orchestra. He wanted the orchestra to succeed, and he thought this would help sell more season subscriptions. Garrison and the family business were also large donors, and that, Garrison believed, was really behind the whole appointment—that and the fact that publicity of him and his talents would help the orchestra gain notice throughout the country. Garrison was fine with being used in this situation.

Lewis and Garrison grew very close. They would talk about any subject under the sun. Lewis found Garrison to be one of the most interesting people he had ever met. Garrison's knowledge was beyond anything that Lewis had experienced. Lewis was very smart himself, and Garrison found Lewis to be the only person he could speak with who could understand the wide array of subjects they discussed.

One of their most frequent subjects was Adam. Adam was getting more hostile and belligerent as the weeks and months went by. Both Lewis and Garrison understood he was in this mood all the time because he was a prisoner in his own bedroom. He wanted out. Adam wanted to hunt, to kill, and to eat something. On several occasions, Garrison caught a small squirrel or a raccoon and placed the animal in a cage. He then placed the cage in Adam's cell after they pulled the chains around Adam's neck back toward the wall. Adam never said thank you, but he did appreciate the gesture.

Garrison never ate in front of Adam or with him. Garrison preferred to eat alone. He perfected his own way of eating his prey. Many times, it was the thrill of the hunt. Sometimes he would pick up rocks, throw them at an animal, and chase it down and field-dress the animal in his own special way. He noticed the more animals he attacked, the better he got. Over time, he had gotten stronger and wiser in his hunting. He made sure he was never caught by any of the neighbors.

Garrison made a few appearances in churches around the city. He performed violin concertos at these small concerts. He didn't make a lot of money off these concerts, but he enjoyed playing for people who loved music as much as he did. He got so involved with the orchestra that he even had a few of the guest performers stay at the estate. When this happened, he would hire local professional chefs and have some of the best meals presented to his guests. At times, he would do the same for his special friends like Lewis, Carolyn, and Loren.

Garrison was getting more interested in biology, not so much because of his condition but because he enjoyed learning about the human body and the makeup of the many animals that he studied. Garrison worked hard in his studies and his violin playing, but to him it was not work. Many times, he thought that his new family worked too hard, and he always gave them the time off they needed or wanted. He especially knew that Lewis needed to get away since he was the one who dealt with Adam the most, and Garrison didn't want to have to deal with his brother on a full-time basis. Garrison needed to keep Lewis around for as long as he could. He knew that he couldn't just go out and hire someone off the street to take care of a nauseating animal like Adam. Lewis had to be the one to take care of him because the alternatives were not acceptable to Garrison.

Heeding Garrison's advice, Lewis started a weekly ritual that would get him out of the house on a more regular basis. He started to go out on his own for dinner at least a couple of times throughout the week. He had done this a lot before Trevor came into his life, but as the years passed, he had gotten out of the habit. Most of the time he frequented the same restaurant, but other times he tried new restaurants throughout the city.

One night, Lewis was out late getting dinner. After dinner, he stopped by the grocery store near the estate and stocked up on some items that he liked, such as potato chips, beer, pretzels, and cheese. Lewis didn't have much of a social life, and this was his way of getting out of the house for a while. He used the self-check lane and went to his car where he placed his groceries in the trunk and proceeded to get behind the wheel. The night was cooling off, and not a cloud was in the sky. He heard footsteps far behind him and then a scream. It sounded like a woman's voice.

He turned around and saw a figure attacking a woman. The two were struggling in the parking lot. The woman screamed for her assailant to let her go. It seemed as if the attacker was after her purse.

Lewis, without thinking, yelled, "Hey! What's going on?" He trotted toward the commotion. Then he heard a loud noise that reverberated through the parking lot. Lewis jumped at the noise as his left shoulder flew backward. He felt a burning sensation in his shoulder. Then suddenly he felt another burning sensation on his right side near his stomach as he heard another loud noise. Before he knew it, he felt the ground pressing against his side and his head hitting the cement. He was out of it. He didn't know where he was, and all he heard was people screaming. He looked up in a daze and saw an unfamiliar face saying something he couldn't understand.

Finally, after repeated attempts, Lewis made out what the young man was saying to him. He could understand just a few words. "Hey, buddy, are you okay? Just lay there until help comes."

Lewis didn't understand what had happened to him. In the background, he heard the wheels of a car make a high squealing sound as the engine raced loudly. The kind young man who first came to his aid said, "Man, you are shot. Did you get a good look at who did this to you?"

Lewis wanted to say something, but his breath was short and he was in a state of shock. He couldn't form the words to express his thoughts. In fact, he found he had no thoughts at all. His body was numb, and he could barely move.

The ambulance came in a short time, and the EMTs attended to him as Lewis started to regain some control over his voice and thoughts. He told one of the guys working on him who he was. Then the police came and attempted to ask him some questions as the emergency workers were placing him on a stretcher. They told Lewis that he had been shot twice and that he was lucky to be alive. Lewis told them his cell phone was in the car. He told them to call Loren at the estate. The police did what he asked and contacted Loren.

Loren was very upset on the phone, and she told the police that she would be at the hospital as soon as possible. She raced through the house to get to her room. She needed to get her keys and purse. She saw Carolyn and told her, "Lewis has been shot. I am going to the hospital."

From his room, Garrison heard everything. He came out quickly, very upset, and started crying. He again lost control of his emotions. Loren told Carolyn and Garrison to stay at the house. Garrison refused; he wanted to go with Loren to see his friend in the emergency room. Loren refused him again, and Garrison angrily demanded that she take him. Against her better judgment, Loren said that Garrison could come, but she wanted Carolyn to remain at the house in case they needed her. Loren and Garrison raced to the hospital. When they reached the emergency room, Lewis was being prepped for surgery. Loren met with the doctor, who said that Lewis would be fine but that they needed to get the bullet out of his side. The first bullet had gone through his shoulder, causing damage to some tendons.

Garrison and Loren were relieved to hear that Lewis was going to be fine. They allowed the medical team to work on him. There was a police officer there, and he asked Garrison and Loren some questions, but they didn't have a clue as to what had happened. The officer filled them in as to what they believed had happened. The lady who was attacked was in the other room with a head laceration. She wanted to speak with Loren and Garrison. Her name was Deanna.

Deanna was a thin, older lady in her fifties with salt-and-pepper hair. She first thought that Loren and Garrison were the wife and son of the gentleman who had tried to help her. She told Loren and Garrison that if not for Lewis, she didn't know what would have happened. After the guy shot Lewis twice, he whipped the pistol around and hit her on the head. Deanna fell to the ground and before she knew it, her attacker was gone. Nothing was stolen. Deanna seemed to think the man who assaulted her not only wanted her car but wanted to kidnap her as well.

She didn't know why because she didn't have a significant amount of money.

Loren and Garrison stayed at the hospital for several hours. The doctor came out and told them Lewis was in recovery and he would be fine. They had had to perform extensive work on his shoulder, and digging deep to get the bullet out of his side. Overall, he was very lucky the bullets didn't hit any vital organs. Loren asked Garrison if he wanted to go back home, and he told her no. He wanted to see Lewis after he woke up. A few hours went by, and Lewis finally awoke from the anesthesia. The doctor told Lewis what had happened to him and what they'd had to do to repair his wounds. Lewis was pleased that he was still alive, and he was very happy to see Garrison and Loren there by his side.

Lewis immediately told Garrison to find his pants and to reach into his right pocket. There was the key to the basement. He told Loren and Garrison that Adam needed to be taken care of and that he obviously wouldn't be there to take care of him. Loren said that she would take care of Adam, but Garrison quickly interrupted and said he would handle the situation. Garrison stared at Lewis and told him that both he and Loren would take care of Adam. Lewis was afraid of leaving a boy in charge of an animal like Adam, especially considering the history between the two. Loren said that they would take care of Adam, but she made Garrison promise to behave himself. Lewis interjected that he didn't want any trouble from the two of them. Lewis then asked Loren to leave the room. He needed to speak with Garrison alone. Loren closed the door as she reluctantly left the room.

Tired, Lewis said to Garrison, "Garrison, I am serious. I… you don't need to cause a scene with Adam. Just make sure you feed him. That is all I ask of you. As soon as I can get out of here, I'll retake control of Adam. I want you to listen to me closely. If Adam gets out of control in any way, here is what I want you to do. In my desk, the first drawer to the right is a small bottle. The bottle is filled with a sedative. I have a bunch of syringes in the second drawer on the same side of the desk. Put the syringe in the bottle and pull the syringe back to fill the shot about three quarters of the way. Make sure you pull the pulley back as far as it will go to make sure Adam is close to the wall. I sometimes have to jam the needle in Adam's leg. Make sure you don't get hurt. Adam is very strong. Remember, Garrison, only do this if he gets out of control. You might wait until he falls to sleep to give him the shot. Tell him I will be back when I can. Can you do this for me?"

Garrison nodded and said, "Don't worry. I will follow your orders."

Lewis said, "Now, on my key chain is the key to the basement door. It's this one." He pointed to an oddly shaped key. As he pointed to another key, Lewis continued, "This key is for the desk drawer. Garrison, remember, I cannot help you while I'm laid up in this hospital bed. So, it is very important that you don't start anything with Adam. Just ignore him. Go in there, feed him, and get out. And for god's sake, please remember to lock the door."

"Yes, sir," Garrison answered.

"I knew this day would come. I just didn't know when," Lewis said. "I'm not always going to be around for you, Garrison, so you're going to have to take care of your brother. I know you have differences with him, and that is an understatement, but you need to do this for me." Lewis was getting very tired. He closed his eyes to take a break.

Garrison said, "Don't worry, Lewis. I will follow your instructions." He stepped out of the room to let Lewis rest.

Oh, what a responsibility Garrison had now. He must feed his brother and take care of him. For a little boy who was not even ten years old yet, this was a big responsibility, one that he accepted with great honor and respect. Garrison went home with Loren. During the drive, he fell asleep in the car. When they arrived, he went straight to bed, and Loren filled Carolyn in on all the events of the night.

The next morning, Garrison got ready as he did every morning and went downstairs for his breakfast. While he was eating, Loren came down and greeted him. After their breakfast, Loren wanted to escort Garrison down to the basement to see Adam. Loren preached to Garrison about remaining calm in Adam's presence. She told him not to start any arguments with his brother. Garrison was a little put out by all the coaching from everyone. He knew how to act, and he knew he would remain under control. Loren and Garrison descended to the basement and stopped at the door on the right. Loren opened the door and gave the key to Garrison. They went inside, and Garrison half ran to Adam's room. Adam was awake. He got up from his seated position and angrily said, "What are you doing here?"

Garrison told Adam about Lewis being shot and said that he was in the hospital. He told him the doctors said that he would have to stay in the hospital to recover for about five to seven days. Adam was actually worried and concerned about Lewis. Garrison sensed his emotional pain. He told Adam that he and Loren were going to take care of him while Lewis was recovering. Then when Lewis returned to full strength, he would reclaim his position as the caregiver.

Loren saw the two getting along and said that she was going upstairs to take care of a few things on the business end. She told the boys to behave. She knew she had to trust Garrison and that he must be given the opportunity to prove to everyone he could handle stressful situations. For Loren, going down to the basement was very stressful, and seeing a monster like Adam was even worse. It was the last place she wanted to be. Garrison knew this was all a test, and he prepared himself for the challenge.

Loren left the two brothers. Adam was still a little depressed. Garrison prepared Adam's breakfast and placed the dish of food on the tray near the cell. Garrison said that he would go into the forest this morning and would try to find something that Adam would like. Adam was very surprised by Garrison's kindness. He even began to thank Garrison for his nice intentions. Garrison left Adam and went outside to the back of the house, and before he passed his parents' resting place in the ground, he came across the spot where his mother had died. The grass was still greener, longer, and thicker than the grass around the area, but he noticed that the area had also gotten larger.

Garrison walked into the forest and picked up a small rock. He walked a little farther in the woods and then stood still. He listened and watched for any movement. He heard something behind him, and as quick has he could, he turned around and threw the rock. It missed a small squirrel by inches. Garrison found another rock nearby. The same squirrel was still sitting on a branch very high in the tree. Garrison cocked this arm back and waited for the perfect moment, then threw the rock as hard as he could without making much of a sound. The rock whistled through the air and hit the squirrel in the back. The animal fell and landed hard on the ground. He ran over to his prey and watched the squirrel flop around wildly on the forest's floor. He looked around for a stick and found one that was about four feet in length. He whacked the squirrel hard on its head in an attempt to kill it for Adam. He took the dead squirrel and went back to the house, then went down to the basement and gave the squirrel to Adam.

Adam slowly took the squirrel from Garrison; he looked very surprised that Garrison had kept his word. Adam told Garrison, "Thank you." He turned and began to eat the squirrel.

Garrison said, "I knew there was not time to set a trap and that you liked live animals better. So, enjoy and I will see you later in the day." Adam was very thankful.

As the day passed, Garrison went down to the basement again and checked on Adam. Adam had finished his meal and laid the massacred remains on the floor outside the cell. Garrison went over to clean up the mess. He picked up the mostly eaten carcass and placed it in a garbage bag, cleaned his hands, and then came back. He pulled up a chair and said to Adam in a calm voice, "Adam, I need to ask you a question. Did you love Mom and Dad?"

Adam went over to Garrison and said bluntly, "No. They never loved me or accepted me. So, no, I didn't. All they talked about and wanted was you. I am the monster. You were the angel. You were the perfect one, and I am the imperfect one. Or so they tell me. I don't think I am. In fact, I know that I am better than you."

Garrison didn't show any emotion but asked, "Why did you kill my father?"

Adam hissed and jumped around in the cage, but Garrison didn't move a muscle. With a deep and very raspy voice, Adam said, "There you go again. He was my father too. Why did you say *your* father? *He was my father too!*"

Garrison got up slowly and said, "You're right. I am sorry. I wondered why you attacked him and killed him."

Adam said, "I don't know. Mother was screaming, and it upset me. I was annoyed. I thought our father was going to hurt me. So, I reacted. I acted on instinct. Instinct is all that I have, you know. It is the very essence of what makes me who I am. Don't you understand that, dear brother of mine?"

Garrison looked down and said, "I think I understand."

Adam, who couldn't control his anger, slammed his body into the bars of the cage and said, "I hate you, brother. I cannot help it. I despise you with all my heart. I cannot help it, but I want you dead just like our father, just like our mother, and hopefully, just like my dear doctor, Lewis. I won't stop until I make your life as miserable as mine, you fucking piece of shit."

Garrison smiled, but he was getting a little angry.

Adam continued. "Yes. Yes, I feel your anger, brother. You are no different or better than I am, you cocksucker. You are like me. Only you are whiter, weaker, sissier than me. You are the weaker brother, and I will prove that to you, you stupid son of a bitch."

Garrison stood up, turned around, and said, "I am better than you, and I will prove that to you someday, but now is not that time, Adam. I will be back tomorrow, and I will prepare you a very special meal. You have a good night."

Adam looked at him in bewilderment and got very angry. He was yelling at Garrison as he slowly walked out of the room, "Don't you patronize me, dear brother. *Come back here!*" Garrison continued to walk over to the desk. Adam heard something but couldn't make out what he was doing. Garrison walked past the room and went down the hallway. Adam continued to talk but now in a lower tone. "Where are you going? I am not finished talking to you."

Garrison stepped out onto the landing, closed the door, and locked it. He placed the key in his pocket, and with a smile, he looked at the door and placed his hand on it. He slowly slid his hand down the door and then walked upstairs with a very large smile on his face, as if he knew something the world didn't.

The next morning after breakfast, he told Loren that he wanted to see Lewis after he fed Adam. Loren said that would be fine. Garrison first went into the woods to one of the traps that he had set the day before. Sure enough, the trap contained a small raccoon. Garrison picked up the trap and walked it to the house. He went in the basement entrance from the outside, but before he went in, he placed the trap down on the ground. He reached inside his pocket and pulled out a syringe. He filled the syringe up about three-quarters of the way and jammed the needle into the raccoon. The raccoon ended up dying. Garrison went inside and placed the raccoon in Adam's cell, where his brother immediately started to devour the carcass.

As soon as he bit into the raccoon, Adam tasted something funny. He couldn't place where he had tasted the flavor before. Garrison knew that Adam would eat on the raccoon for a while. He couldn't help himself. After fifteen minutes, Adam wasn't feeling well. Garrison then pulled the pulley back as far as he could and went back to the desk. He got out another syringe and filled this one up all the way. He went back to the room and opened the cage door. Adam was acting a little strange. Garrison walked up to Adam, who was swinging his arms around slowly, trying to fight Garrison, but he was too drugged to be of any danger. Garrison slammed the needle in Adam and shot him with a full dose of the sedative. Garrison then closed and locked the door of the cage and went upstairs to see Loren. They proceeded to the hospital to see Lewis.

Lewis was glad to see Garrison. Garrison told him that he and Adam were getting along well. He told him that Adam was sleeping and that everything was fine. This was a warning sign for Lewis. Lewis was concerned that something had happened, so he asked Garrison if he had had to use a sedative on Adam. Garrison said no and continued to talk about how well they were getting along. Lewis knew something was going on and continued to question Garrison, but Garrison didn't waver. He insisted that everything was fine, and he told Lewis not to worry.

Lewis did worry, but he was to the point where he almost didn't care. He was tired, and he liked not having to take care of Adam. Adam disgusted him. He hated him, but he knew that he had to take care of him. It wasn't as if he could send him off so someone else could take care of him. It was all on Lewis. The thought that kept Lewis up most nights was that Adam was going to live forever. He worried about him getting loose someday. He worried that if the truth ever came out about Adam, Lewis would probably go to jail. It would ruin his career as a doctor. Lewis wanted his normal life back again, but he didn't know how to get it back.

Lewis knew Garrison all too well. He knew that Garrison was up to something, but he knew that he couldn't control the boy. Neither could Loren, so when Garrison left the room, Lewis told Loren to leave Garrison alone. He told her that he felt as if he could trust Garrison and that she didn't need to worry. He told her to go on about her business and said he would deal with the issue when he got back. Loren consented. She didn't want any part of Adam. He scared her, and she didn't like going down into the basement with him. She hated the fact that he was even in the basement. She wanted to build a separate building on the grounds to house Adam, but she never developed that particular idea.

Loren and Garrison drove back to the house. It was getting late. Garrison had his supper with the two ladies. He then took a plate of food and went down the steps to the basement. He opened the door to the right of the landing and went inside to Adam's room. Adam was out like a light. Garrison placed the plate of food down and looked over at his sleeping brother. Garrison, without any emotion, went over to a hospital bed sitting in the corner of the room. Garrison looked at the bed from all angles, trying to figure out how it worked. It was the same bed that Adelle had been in when she bore Adam. After he studied the bed, Garrison walked over to the closet in Adam's room where he knew Lewis kept some restraints. He found two long restraints, took them out, and placed them near the bed. He also found four small restraints, two for the hands and two for the legs. He wheeled the bed around and moved it closer to the cage door. He then noticed the bed was too big to fit inside the cell.

Garrison went over to the pulley and released the chain to the longest length. He then unlocked the door of the cell, stepped inside, and went over to Adam. He made sure Adam was still out by gently kicking his foot. There was no reaction so Garrison took hold of Adam and rolled him over onto the floor. He grabbed Adam's feet and gently dragged him across the floor to the bed. The bed was as low as he could make it. Garrison sat Adam up and lifted his brother onto his shoulders. This took a great effort from Garrison since Adam was almost his same size. He sat Adam down and moved him so that he fit in the middle of the bed. Garrison took all of Adam's clothes off with the exception of his underwear. He was surprised to see so much hair all over his brother's body. Almost every inch of it had at least some hair on it. The hair was long but not very thick. The hairiest parts of his body were his arms, legs, and pubic area. His chest was thick but rather narrow and not as long as the other parts of his body. The chest hair was wavy and thick.

Garrison took one of the long restraints and placed it over Adam's chest. The second long strap went over his thighs. Garrison proceeded to take the small restraints and wrap each ankle to the end of the bed. The other small restraints were for Adam's wrists, which he strapped down tightly on the bed. Garrison made sure that all the straps were securely fastened so they wouldn't come lose. He stepped back and looked at his work, and he was pleased. The chain was still around Adam's neck in case the straps didn't secure him. Next, Garrison found some duct tape. He unrolled long strips of it and placed them over Adam's mouth. Garrison knew there was no way his brother could get loose from this setup. He turned the light out and closed the door. After locking the door, he went upstairs to get a shower.

The next morning Loren was going to the hospital, and Garrison said that he would stay home. After breakfast, Garrison studied for a while with Carolyn but said he wanted to take some food down to Adam. Carolyn said that would be fine and she went upstairs to clean. Garrison got the food together and went downstairs. He could hear some noise, and he knew that Adam was awake after his long-forced nap. Garrison thought that Adam must be a little scared after waking up and finding himself restrained on a hospital bed. Garrison chuckled, went into the room, and turned the light on. There was Adam, trying to move. He stopped and attempted to look at who had come into his room.

Garrison calmly put the food down on the desk and went over to see his brother. He didn't say a word. As he walked over to Adam, he saw one angry eye looking at him as Adam attempted to say something. Garrison walked up to the edge of the bed. Adam's arm was restricted, but he was trying to reach toward Garrison. Adam's body was floundering around on the bed, but the two long straps restricted most of his movements. Garrison looked down slowly at the arm, and it looked as if Adam was going to break his arm off. Garrison bent down and placed his left hand on the hairy head of his brother.

Garrison placed his right index finger to his lips and said in a sing-song voice, "Hush, little baby, don't say a word. Your big brother thinks you're nothing but a turd. Please don't move or you'll be in some pain. Try not to worry or you'll go insane."

He stopped rubbing Adam's head and started to laugh. He turned and walked out of the room, closing the door behind him. Garrison could hear the bed move by way of Adam's strength as he tried to get out of his bondage.

Adam was scared. He had never been this restrained in his life, and he didn't know what his big brother was going to do to him. He tried hard to get loose from his bonds. He pulled and jerked as hard as he could, but nothing broke loose. He was secure in his capture. He was not used to this or fond of it at all. He wanted to be let go so he could have the taste of freedom.

To Adam, time seemed to linger on for an eternity. The door was closed, the lights were out, and soon he just gave up. He relaxed himself as best he could. He was getting extremely hungry, so hungry in fact that his stomach was making noise. He had not eaten in about a day and a half. He could smell the food that Garrison had brought down. Later, in the day, the door opened and the lights came on. Adam attempted to move, but he couldn't see what was happening. Then Garrison appeared in his line of sight and he felt the bed move. Garrison lifted the head of the bed to where Adam could see better instead of lying flat as a pancake.

Garrison spoke, "Adam, I apologize for the straps, but Lewis ordered me to place them on you so you cannot escape. He made me promise him to make sure you behave. Kind of like a dog on a leash, huh? You have caused enough problems in all our lives. You do not need to cause more problems now, especially with Lewis being shot. You know, Adam, Lewis made a comment to me the other day. He said, 'Garrison, it's nice not to have to worry about Adam.'"

"Adam, you understand that you killed my father, right? I say 'my father' because he was my father, not yours. You never appreciated him. Oh, don't get me wrong. At times, I hated him when I was younger. He viewed me as a little problem in his life, and at times he feared me, and at other times he was jealous of me. He was jealous of my intellect, my mastery of the violin, and my perfection. He was jealous of my ability to memorize and solve complicated problems. Oh, believe me, I showed off to him at times, and I knew it aggravated him. So, I was not a nice little boy at times, but I never killed him. See, Adam, he always viewed you as a monster, and he was correct in that assessment of you. When I bit my father, he started to understand what I went through and what I was going through. We grew close very fast. We fell in love with each other because we shared so much. We were cut from the same cloth, so to speak. Oh, my intelligence and my skills intimidated him, but after I infected him, he seemed to improve and get better. He was smarter, stronger, and better overall. I made him into something better than he was before. I kind of feel like god, you know? I began to love him more as each day passed because we understood each other. He finally understood me and what I was feeling inside my heart. I always understood what he was feeling inside his soul. Do you know what I mean? For the first time in my life, I finally had someone that knew what I have gone through all my life. I always felt that I was alone, and I hated that feeling. Then finally I had someone in my life that understood me. I guess I ought to thank you for bringing us closer in a twisted sort of way. He could see the contrast between you and me. Hell, after he had you, my oddities were minute compared to yours. For the first time, he was not afraid of me."

Garrison leaned over and looked down at Adam. "Then you, of all people, killed the one person that finally nodded in approval of me. You are the reason my father is dead. Not only did you kill him, but you purposely mutilated him. You made him suffer and hurt badly. The pain you caused him before he died had to be unbearable, and to think that I had a front-row seat."

Garrison walked over to a box that he had brought down from upstairs. He looked over to his quiet and subdued brother lying on the bed and said, "Not only did you kill my father before me but in front of my mother as well. It… upset her. It made her more confused than ever before. She was dealing with me, my father, and you. She had to deal with all of this in the span of just a few years. You, my brother, were the root of everyone's problems. If it was not for you, we could have made it work. Instead, I lost both of my parents. I have nightmares every night. I have no one to share my true feelings with except you, and that is unacceptable to me. You know, I have always given you a chance, but you have always attacked me either verbally or physically. Oh, do not get me wrong, I have never liked you or accepted you as my brother. You disgust me, you irritate me, and you are the cause of everything bad that has happened to me recently. You have caused pain and suffering to my parents and to my friend, Lewis. Loren and Carolyn do not even like to be around you and, of course, who can blame them? So, it is up to me to correct the problem, our little Adam problem."

Garrison reached into the box and took out an old sewing kit, which contained a smaller box filled with needles and another small box filled with sewing pins. He took the needles out of the box and separated the larger from the smaller ones. Garrison got out the heaviest thread he could find in the sewing box. He threaded the first needle and made a large knot. Then he threaded the second needle, spaced the two about five inches apart, and tied another knot. Garrison continued this until he had knotted ten of the large needles on one thread. He cut the string and laid it down on the desk. Next, Garrison took a box of small pins with flat heads. He placed them down on the desk next to the thread of needles. He turned around and looked at Adam.

Adam was very nervous and he tried to speak, but the duct tape made talking impossible. He lay there and accepted his position, but he was concerned. He didn't know what Garrison was going to do.

Garrison went over to Adam, bent down, and whispered in his ear, "You filthy, pathetic subhuman. You took the two people that I loved the most in this world away from me. You created nothing but stress and strain for all of us. You ruined my life, but only up to this point. Now you will suffer as I have suffered, as my mother suffered, as my father suffered at your hands. You will now feel what real pain feels like. Like my mother, who was in so much pain, and her only request was for the pain to ease. Just lay there and think about them for a while. Think about what you put them through during your short, wretched span of existence on this planet. You were a nagging pain to them and to me physically, emotionally, and mentally."

Garrison walked away from the bed and out of the room. Adam again attempted to get out of his restraints, but it was no use. Garrison came back with a hammer that had a long but thin head, the type mostly used to hammer small nails. He went over to the pins and picked them up. He placed them on the portable cart. He walked over to Adam and picked one of the pins up with his right index finger and thumb. Garrison looked from the small pin to Adam with a big smile. Adam was very upset. One brother could smell the fear, while the other could smell the hatred and the extreme desire to hurt and inflict pain.

Garrison, without saying a word, placed the pin in his left index finger and thumb. He picked up the small hammer and bent down to Adam's flexing right forearm. The forearm was moving about an inch from left to right, up and down, in a rapid, jerky movement. Garrison put the hammer down on the bed and moved the pin from his left hand back to his right hand. With his left hand, he gripped Adam's wrist and pushed it down on the bed. That stopped the jerky movement. Garrison calmly took the pin and inserted it two or three inches into Adam's forearm, forcing the pin toward the elbow. Garrison continued to gently hammer the pin deep into his flesh at an angle. In great pain, Adam yelled loudly through the duct tape. Snot and nasal drainage dripped from his nose and sprayed out with every deep, painful breath that he took.

Garrison hammered the pin deeper into his brother's arm. The pin went in easily, and Garrison realized he wouldn't have to use the hammer. He wanted the pins to go in at an angle so that the farther the pin went in, the deeper it would embed itself in the forearm tissue. The more Adam moved, the more pain would be inflicted upon him. Garrison replaced his left hand with his right hand on Adam's wrist. He placed the second pin about one inch from the first one, again sliding the pin deep into the forearm. Adam was writhing in pain. His whole body was jerking, trying to release any part of his body.

Adams forearm was about fourteen inches long, thin but very strong. Garrison continued to place the pins in Adam's arm about one inch apart. He went in a straight line up to the end of his forearm. Garrison counted eight pins. He started over near the wrist and went over about an inch to the left. He placed the pins in the forearm going in the same direction as before, making sure the pins were going in at an angle. Garrison continued this activity on the other part of the forearm. Again, eight pins along the length of the arm and right up to the end of the forearm. Garrison had a total of twenty-four pins in Adam's arm when he was through.

Adam was beside himself and in a lot pain. His fear had turned to anger, just as Garrison had predicted. Adam moved around, and the more he moved his arm, the more pain he caused himself. After many minutes of intense pain, he learned not to move his arm. The pain was still there, but it wasn't as bad as it had been when the pins were first entering the flesh. Every movement he made in his arm caused his pain sensors to light up. He would try to relax the muscles, but that moved the pins even more and thus caused even more pain. Every move he made caused Adam to suffer even more.

Garrison calmly moved the cart around to the other side. Adam was now crying hard, tears flowed down the sides of his head. As Garrison held Adam's left wrist down on the bed, he picked up another pin and, instead of putting it in pointing toward Adam's elbow, he put it in across the forearm, with the head of the pin facing the body. As before, he embedded them at a slant. Garrison placed fourteen pins for the first row. Then for the second row, toward the outside of the body, Garrison placed the head of the pins away from the body. He placed fourteen additional pins between the two established rows, but as in the previous arm, these pins pointed up the arm toward the elbow. That made thirty-two pins in this arm alone and fifty-six pins in total for both arms.

Adam lay there feeling each pin as it slid through the skin and muscle. Every move he made caused agonizing pain. He couldn't relax or make the pain go away. Adam was trying to concentrate on not moving or flexing any of his forearm muscles, but he was unsuccessful. Garrison pushed the cart back and turned around to leave. He could hear Adam moving and jerking around in pain on the bed. Garrison went over to the desk and looked in the top drawer. There was a ruler there. He picked it up and walked over to Adam.

As he looked at Adam, he said, "Shut up and stop making all that noise, you dirty animal." He raised the ruler up, brought it down on Adam's right forearm, and repeated the beating, increasing the speed after each strike. After twenty or so slaps with the ruler, Garrison went over to the other forearm and proceeded to do the same, only this time he smacked Adam faster. He hit the arm as fast as he could count, around thirty times.

Adam was in an extreme amount of discomfort. His forearms were bleeding, his body was drenched in sweat, and his breathing was very deep. The duct tape made breathing very difficult for him. Garrison noticed this, so he went over to the sewing box and got out a pair of scissors. He walked over to the scared and helpless Adam, opened the scissors up, gripped the hair on the top of Adam's head to secure it in place, and then jammed one of the sides of the scissors between the lips, breaking the duct tape. The hole was about one inch wide, and Garrison made sure the opening was big enough to allow more air to flow. *After all*, Garrison thought, *I do not want to kill my brother.*

Garrison left Adam literally crying on the bed in incredible pain, pain such as he had never felt in his life. Garrison locked the door to the basement and went upstairs. He studied for a while with Carolyn, and after supper he again took a plate of food downstairs.

Garrison entered the door on the right of the landing. When he got to Adam's room, Adam was still awake but exhausted. Garrison closed the door and put the food down on the desk. He went over to Adam and removed the duct tape from his mouth; he was not gentle with it.

When the tape was removed, Adam immediately pleaded, "*Please*. Please, Garrison, help me. Take these pins out of my arms… ohh… ahh… oh, *please*."

Garrison took the plate of food up from the desk and said, "Shut up, Adam, and eat your dinner."

Adam started to say something, but Garrison forced some food in his mouth. After about five minutes, Garrison stopped feeding his brother and got more duct tape out of the drawer. Adam was pleading with him vigorously to let him go, saying that he was sorry for what he had done. Garrison attempted to put the tape on his mouth, but Adam wouldn't hold still, so Garrison grabbed the ruler again. After loud pleas from Adam not to do it, Garrison hit both forearms again. Adam threw his head back on the bed and opened his mouth wide from the pain. Garrison put the tape over his mouth, this time without holes to help him breathe better. Garrison got out two syringes full of tranquilizer and rammed the needle into Adam's leg, followed by the second in the same area. Adam fell limp and went to sleep. Garrison thought the tranquilizers would keep him calm for twelve or so hours. He left the room, locked everything up, and went outside to play.

The next day after breakfast, Garrison studied some of his classwork with Carolyn. Afterward, he went down to the basement. He walked into Adam's bedroom and found Adam surprisingly awake and crying from the pain. Garrison imagined that when Adam woke up, he had probably forgotten about the pins in his arms. As Adam moved them, an unimaginable pain had sent shockwaves throughout his deformed body.

Garrison picked up the ten sewing needles that were tied to the long, thick thread. He walked over to Adam and, with no eye contact, placed the first needle in the large muscle between the shoulder and the neck, just above the collarbone. Garrison pressed the needle in as far as it would go, gaining help from the small hammer. Adam was beside himself. He pleaded with Garrison to stop, but Garrison continued. The second needle went in about an inch away from the first. It was closer to the shoulder, just under the collarbone. The third needle was another inch below but to the right of the second needle. The fourth needle was down from the third one, going toward the nipple. With this needle, Garrison only went about halfway into the body. The fifth needle was directly in the nipple and also went in the body about halfway.

Garrison retrieved the scissors, cut the thread, and repeated the same procedure on Adam's right shoulder and chest. The first three needles were hammered into Adam's body as deep as they would go. Adam writhed on the table. The pain from the forearms to the newly planted needles was overwhelming, too much for him to take. He was crying as hard as he could, making unreal sounds of pain and sorrow while begging. He attempted to plead for relief from the pain, but the pain was so intense he couldn't form the words, which Garrison would have ignored, regardless. Garrison instead made the cries worse by pushing his fingers under the thread that was attached to each needle.

Garrison only used three of his fingers on Adam's left side. He pulled slowly. As he pulled, Adam screamed through the duct tape, his head rising off the bed while his arms shoved up against his restraints. He was in even more pain now because he moved his arms as Garrison tugged at the thread of needles. Garrison stopped and decided to pull each one out individually. He had trouble with some of the needles, but most of them came out with only a little struggle. Adam was crying hard. He was in pain, but through all his torture, he was also getting mad. He wanted the pain to stop, and he especially wanted his demented brother to stop torturing him. He was going out of his mind with pain.

It took Garrison a while to get the thread of needles out of both sides of Adam's chest. Garrison said, "I believe that is enough for the day, Adam. I will be back tomorrow. I know you are hungry, but I am sure your pain is your first thought."

Adam looked at him with bloodshot eyes. They looked tired, as if they wanted it all to stop, but there was a touch of anger in them.

Garrison asked, "Do you want me to stop?" Adam nodded his head as fast as he could. He squinted his eyes to plead with his brother to stop the pain.

Garrison laughed. "Do you hate me? Do you want to hurt me as I am hurting you, Adam? If I let you go, would you do the same to me, you fucking animal?"

Adam shook his head left and right as if to say, no, he would not do any harm to his brother.

Garrison said, "Well! I don't trust animals. I believe that you would hurt me, and you could never be trusted. I believe that your intention has been from the very beginning to try to hurt me since your pathetic ass was born. You are a disgusting animal, you subhuman piece of crap." He placed his left hand on Adam's forehead. Adam's head fell back on the bed hard as he moaned from the jerking that had woken up the pain in his forearms and chest even more.

Garrison looked deeply in his eyes and said, "Be honest with me, you animal. You would love to do what I am doing to you right now, wouldn't you?" Garrison was yelling as loud as he could. "Answer me, you fucking animal. Answer me!" Garrison grabbed Adam's shoulders and was shaking him and moving him up and down on the bed. He quickly removed the duct tape from his mouth.

Adam yelled in a pained, tired, but angry voice, "I hate you! Get me out of this fucking setup, you stupid fuck! Yes, I would do the same to you. Of course I would hurt you. Do you think I haven't been thinking of this all my life? You crazy son of a bitch, I would be doing worse to you. I should have killed our mother as I did our father. I should have ripped out both of her eyes and fed them to her. I hate you, I hated her, and I hate everything about this place."

Garrison lost control. With his right hand, he went after Adam's neck and got a perfect grip. He squeezed as hard as he could. Adam was starting to choke, so Garrison released his grip. He picked up more of the duct tape and taped up Adam's mouth again.

Garrison picked up one of the threads of needles and clamped his other hand down on Adam's right ankle. He proceeded to jam the first needle into the middle of the ball of Adam's foot. Then, in a straight line, the second, third, fourth, and finally fifth needles went down Adam's foot toward the heel. The needles only went in about halfway. Garrison released his grip and went over to the other foot. He held the foot in place, and this time he had to sit on the leg while he repeated what he had done to the previous foot. Then Garrison walked to the sewing box and pulled out more needles, the longest and thickest he could find. Still working on the left, he held the lower leg in place as best he could. Garrison placed a needle inside the back part of the ankle between the bone and the Achilles tendon. Garrison went over to the right foot and repeated the procedure. Then he went to work on Adam's hands. Again, grabbing the largest and thickest needle that his mother had had, Garrison took up the hammer. He placed the needle in the middle part of Adam's hand. Adam had his hand closed in a fist, which hurt him even more. Garrison pushed the needle between the clenched fingers and hammered the needle into the middle of the hand. The needle went in the palm, through the hand, and out the top. Garrison repeated the exercise on Adam's other hand, with the same painful result. Adam was so completely overwhelmed by the pain that he couldn't think straight.

Garrison was losing control of his thoughts. He fought back the incredible urge of his natural instincts to attack his brother. He stepped back and left the room. His heart was beating a million times a minute. He had to regain control of his senses and his emotions. Garrison knew even at this young age that he had to control himself or he would end up doing something regrettable. The formula, or disease, that flowed through his body caused him to react negatively or aggressively when angered. But he also had the ability to call upon his senses to do very special things. His ears, hands, and eyes could do unworldly things at levels that no human had achieved in the history of humanity. However, Garrison knew the one emotion, the one sense, that he had to control was his anger. Sometimes the anger caused him to lose control and become more animal than human.

After a few moments, Garrison got control of his anger and went for the tranquilizer shots. Again, this time he placed only one of them in Adam. Soon Adam was out like a light, and Garrison looked at the sight before him. Down deep, he loved what he saw. This thing, this creature that lay helpless before him, this abomination that had taken his parents' lives and made his young life miserable, was now going through the same pain as Garrison. He thought that Adam needed water and food to keep him alive. He knew that Lewis was going to come home in several days, and he was anxious about how he was going to explain all of this to the doctor. Lewis was going to be very angry with him, and rightfully so. Garrison knew that he had to tell Lewis the truth, but he also was not through with Adam. He thought about making up a story that he could get away with for a short time.

Garrison went upstairs and called Loren. He told her that he wanted to see Lewis, and she said that would be fine. She told Carolyn to bring him to the hospital to visit. When Garrison arrived, he quickly went to Lewis's private room. Garrison asked how he was doing, and Lewis told him that he was sore but feeling great. Garrison wanted to speak with Lewis alone, so he closed the door and sat down next to him.

Lewis could tell something was wrong. Garrison told Lewis that he had had to use the tranquilizer shots on Adam because he was getting too wild. He told him that he had done it safely by jumping on him to hold him down while the chain was pulled as close to the wall of the cell as possible. Lewis was very concerned, and he told Garrison that his actions were not smart. Garrison proceeded to ask Lewis some questions.

"Lewis, please don't take this the wrong way, but have you enjoyed your time away from Adam? I mean, let us be honest with each other. When I am away from him, I feel better. Since you have been in here, I have taken care of him, and to be honest with you, I do not like it. I do not like being around him. I cannot imagine what you have gone through all this time, basically alone. I understand it is very stressful and tough to handle emotionally and physically."

Lewis hung his head and began to show a little emotion. "It is a very difficult situation. I must admit, this time in the hospital has been much needed for my nerves. Oh, I think about him and especially you. Oh, please, Garrison, be careful. Please don't let the monster hurt you."

Garrison got up and walked over to the window. Lewis watched his every move. Garrison looked and acted so much like his father had when he was alive. The way he walked, even talked, and the way he carried himself made a large impression on Lewis. He even admired the way Garrison was in control of the situation. For that moment, this young boy brought back many memories of Trevor for Lewis, memories of how Trevor would have handled himself in this type of situation. It impressed the old doctor.

Garrison took a deep breath and began to speak. "Lewis, you have to trust me on this. I hope... no, I pray to god that you see it the way I see it. I hope you understand that sometimes a family must take care of certain family issues. Sometimes, if certain issues are not dealt with, those very issues might end up not only controlling other issues but also affecting things that should not be touched."

Lewis was very quiet, not moving a muscle as he rested on the bed.

Garrison continued. "Life would be easier without some of the issues that have developed. Sometimes problems are just that: problems."

Lewis asked, "What are you getting at, Garrison?"

Garrison turned and smiled. "Tell me the truth, Lewis. Having Adam out of your life would make your life easier, now wouldn't it?"

Lewis cocked his head a little to the left. "Yes, I suppose it would. In fact, it definitely would. Garrison, what are you planning? Did you do something to Adam while I have been in here?"

Garrison smiled and looked over to the window. He said, "Lewis, he is a monster. He killed my father, he has caused me mental pain through the years, and he might as well have put that knife to my mother's throat." Garrison laughed like a much older man and turned away from the window. He put his index finger up to the side of his face and continued as he walked over to Lewis's bed. "Lewis, let's say there is this bully at school. He will not leave you alone. He is unreasonable and emotionally unstable. He is an angry child whose father beats him at home, so he lashes out at others who are weaker than him. He does this because he believes it is in his nature to do so. He learned this from his father, who instilled his sense of reason and understanding. No matter how many times you defeat this monster, he will still come back to bully you. You try and try until you either give up and allow him to win or you take more drastic measures. Why battle something that is uneducated, dim-witted, and unintelligent? Many great leaders of war will tell you that if your opponent cannot be reasoned with, you should eliminate him. Think about it, Lewis, and when you get back to the estate, we will continue this discussion and hopefully reach a conclusion on this issue."

Lewis was shocked by what he had heard. He acted as if he didn't understand what Garrison had been trying to convey, although he knew what Herr Garrison was saying; he had been very clear about the meaning of his message.

"What are you saying, Garrison? Please don't do anything you might regret."

Kevin C. Popp

Garrison continued to smile as he put his hand on Lewis's bed. "You are not a stupid man, Lewis. I am not a stupid boy. Don't treat me as being stupid. Please do not do that to me. I hoped that I had earned your respect enough for you not to treat me as if I am some normal grade-school kid trying to diagram a simple sentence. Please, I ask you not to insult my intelligence."

This response surprised Lewis, but he knew that Garrison was right. "Okay, you're right. You're right. You have earned the respect that you so covet. So, I guess I should say, are you saying you want to kill, remove, and erase Adam from your life?"

Garrison smiled widely, tapped the bed with his hand, and jumped back. He said, "Exactly! That is exactly what I am saying."

Lewis swallowed hard. "Okay, fine. Please listen to me and don't do anything to Adam. Don't kill him, Garrison. Wait for me to get home, and we will continue this conversation. You're right. Like you, he will never die. He will live forever. I don't know if I can take that for the rest of my life. My biggest fear is that he'll escape. Can you image if that happened? Can you image something like that running loose in this city? How could he be explained? The police would look further into the death of your father and your mother. Hell, they might even pin it on me. I was there through the whole thing. I was an accomplice to it all."

Garrison raised his hand and said, "Do not worry, Lewis. He will not escape. At least, not at the moment. Don't you think I have been thinking the same thing all these years? I have a business to run. I cannot take the chance that he might escape. One day he might, and I agree that would be a terrible thing for all of us, especially for the family name and the family business. All of the goodwill we have accumulated could be gone in a second because of one little problem that was not attended to."

Garrison walked to the door. "Do not worry, Lewis. Nothing will happen to Adam's life while you are in this hospital. Get better and we will continue this discussion when you get home. Have a good night, Lewis."

Lewis sat there and watched Garrison step out of the room. He watched the door close behind him. He looked away and then down at his legs. He knew that he couldn't control Garrison, and he knew that young, smart boy was up to something if he had not already done something. A part of Lewis was glad that Garrison had said what he had. However, another part of him was upset that the vicious circle kept going around and around. And somehow, he was always in the middle of the circle. Maybe this time he needed to let things play out, listen to what the boy had to say, and see what was on his mind. Maybe his ideas would be good solutions to the problems they currently faced. Lewis wasn't looking forward to taking care of Adam for the rest of his life. He knew he only had twenty to thirty good years left in his own life, and the thought of taking care of that monster all that time was unacceptable to Lewis. He couldn't even entertain that thought without getting sick to his stomach. When he thought about it for even a moment, about how it would be years from now, it made Lewis contemplate suicide. Lewis knew he couldn't match Adam or Garrison in life expectancy.

What worried Lewis more than anything was what would happen if Adam killed Garrison or if Garrison died some other way. Adam would be alone. Who would take care of him or keep him in his controlled setting? Who would be willing to even attempt to take care of him? What if he escaped? What if he bit someone and that poor and unfortunate person transformed into a monster as Trevor had or as Adelle had been about to? No one would have a clue as to what was happening to them. They would kill themselves, die of shock, or worse yet, continue the string of transformations. If one infected person changed, that person could bite another, and that person could bite another, and so on. When did it stop? Or the better question: How long would it take for the entire world to fall into utter chaos? Maybe the noninfected would end up killing the infected ones eventually. But at what cost? Many people's lives would be in shambles. Lewis couldn't allow this to happen.

Lewis knew he could control Garrison somewhat, or he at least had a chance with him, but there was no chance with Adam. Adam was a lost cause, and the older he got, the less control Garrison or Lewis would have over him. Eventually Adam would have to be stopped. Lewis knew the two brothers would never reconcile their relationship, and even if they did, Adam couldn't be trusted. He was more animal than human and couldn't be reasoned with on any level. And, for that matter, he would never even care to accept the awesome responsibility of the power that he possessed. One bite from Garrison had permanently affected the Seawick family. The current situation, if not totally controlled, would get to the point where it might endanger the human race. A new species had been created, and that was what scared Lewis the most.

He also worried about Wolfgang and Zelda. How long were they going to stay in their small area of the world? They would live forever, not just for five hundred years or for a thousand years but forever. Eventually they would come out into the world, and they would not be accepted. All it would take to cause total chaos would be for them to infect a handful of people in a large town or small city.

Lewis thought that maybe what Garrison was suggesting might not be such a bad idea after all. That maybe it would be a blessing for Lewis to not have to deal with Adam ever again. With him dead, Lewis wouldn't have to worry about him attacking anyone and spreading the god-awful formula that should never have been invented or discovered in the first place. Lewis thought that maybe Garrison was the ticket to his own personal freedom and that this was the only way to get away from the curse. A part of Lewis wished Garrison would even do the dirty work for him.

Loren and Garrison went back to the estate and had dinner together. Garrison was worried about Adam not getting any food or water. So, he again fixed a plate of food and walked downstairs to the door on the right of the landing. Adam was just coming to when Garrison took the duct tape off his mouth. Adam was still groggy from the tranquilizer. He was going to say something to Garrison, but he soon found food in his mouth. Adam was grateful through the pain because he was very hungry. Garrison fed Adam as if he were a baby, with one forkful of food after another. He gave Adam some water. Adam was still in great pain, but at least he was rested. He pleaded with Garrison to take the pins and needles out of his body, but of course, Garrison ignored his requests. Garrison got out from the desk drawer two tranquilizer shots and gave them to Adam. Adam liked the tranquilizers because at least he didn't feel the pain when he was unconscious. Unfortunately, the formula that was in Adam fought to conquer the chemicals from the tranquilizers. Thus, the effect of the shots only lasted for a short time.

The next morning, Garrison went down to see Adam after breakfast. He took another plate of food but didn't intend to feed Adam again. Garrison went directly to Adam's feet and quickly took all five of the needles out of both. After every pluck, the pain shot up Adam's leg through his side. Garrison laid the thread of needles down. Adam's pain increased after the needles were out. Next, Garrison removed the two large needles in each foot between the Achilles tendon and the bone. He left the room momentarily, and when he returned, he was carrying a box. He reached into the box and pulled out a pair of shaving shears. As he turned the shears on, Adam tensed up, causing more pain. Garrison glided the shears over Adam's legs. Hair flowed off the small cutting blades. Garrison worked intently to make sure all the hair was removed. He swept up the hair on the floor with a broom and then used the vacuum to clean what he had missed.

When the cleaning was over, Garrison went over to the box and pulled out two long, four-inch nails with a thickness about the size of a medium screwdriver. Garrison pulled a stool up to the end of the bed. He got out the small hammer and went over to Adam's right foot. Garrison sat on the stool and used his right knee to hold Adam's wiggling foot in place. He took one of the nails and placed it on the skin between the Achilles tendon and the anklebone. Garrison used the hole that the large needle had already made. Adam attempted to look, but every move he made sent shivers of pain throughout his body. Garrison aimed the hammer at the nail as he pressed the nail hard to the small opening in the skin. He brought the hammer back and, with one hard blow to the head of the nail, sent the nail through to the other side. Adam raised his hip up in the air as far as it would go, and his eyes opened as wide as they could. Garrison backed his leg off the foot and got off the stool. He moved the stool to Adam's left foot. He took the other nail and again pressed it hard between the anklebone and the Achilles tendon of Adam's foot. The hammer hit the nail hard, and the nail went through to the other side, just as in the last foot. Again, Adam was beside himself in pain. Garrison backed off the bed and placed the stool out of the way as he enjoyed the painful, loud moans his lesser brother made. Adam now moaned and cried constantly. He couldn't stand the excruciating pain. He was begging Garrison to stop, but the duct tape over his mouth made his pleas inaudible. Adam writhed around, but the more he moved, the more pain it caused him. Garrison was enjoying every minute of his agony.

Adam was breathing heavily, and Garrison was concerned that he might die from the stress and pain alone. Garrison, being the forgiving boy that he was, went to get another tranquilizer shot. Adam loved the shots, so Garrison showed Adam the shot as he was squirming around on the bed. Then Garrison decided to have some more fun. He placed the shot on the bed near Adam's head before leaving the room. He was gone for a while before he returned. Adam couldn't make out what Garrison had in his hand. It didn't matter anyway; he wasn't thinking straight, nor was he in any position to do anything about what was going to come next.

Garrison pulled out one of their father's darts. Trevor hadn't played the game often, but he had kept an expensive set upstairs. Garrison tossed one of the darts in the air. It came down just inches from Adam's right shoulder. Adam knew that Garrison could hit him at any place on his body if he wanted to, with his uncanny hand-eye coordination, the same hand-eye coordination that Adam shared with his brother. Garrison tossed the second dart high in the air, and it hit one inch from the right side of Adam's neck. The third dart was in the air in no time, and it hit two inches from his left ear.

Garrison had one dart left in his hand as he walked closer to Adam, saying, "Sorry, old brother of mine, but my aim is a little off today." He picked up the three darts, walked away, and turned his back toward Adam. After he got about eight feet away, Garrison turned and smiled. He looked at Adam's upper thigh and said, "Adam, I am going to throw this dart into your leg. If you do not move a muscle, I will put the other darts down. If you move at all, the other three will enter your leg within ten seconds. So, let us begin."

Without much of a break, Garrison cocked his arm and threw the first dart. It hit directly in the middle of the thigh. Adam moved violently and tensed up, making matters even worse for him.

Garrison said, "Oh, Adam. That sure was a stupid thing to do." As fast as he could, he fired the remaining three darts. Within ten seconds, all of them went into Adam's thigh. Garrison went over and pulled them all out, one by one, slowly. The last one he pulled out at a slant to make the pain more severe.

Garrison walked over to the sink in Adam's bedroom and cleaned himself and the thread of needles. He walked out of the room to Lewis's lab. He looked around and saw the coffee pot that Lewis used to make freshly ground coffee every morning. Garrison filled the coffee machine up with water and turned it on. He placed the coffee pot on the plate and waited for the water to heat up. The process took about four to five minutes. Adam was still making lots of noise from the pain, and it was getting on Garrison's nervous. At first, he had loved the sounds of the excruciating, throbbing, burning pain of his brother. However, he had grown tired of them. When the coffee pot was filled to the required level, Garrison took it and went into Adam's bedroom. He closed the door and put the coffee pot on the tray next to Adam.

Adam was moving around even more now, and before he knew it, Garrison took out a pair of scissors. He went down to Adam's crotch, cut his underwear in the front in two places, and removed the cloth. Adam was moving back and forth making absurd sounds that annoyed Garrison to no end. At first, Garrison didn't want to look down at Adam's penis. Then he picked up the coffee pot full of scorching hot water and held it over Adam's bare penis, and Garrison's blank expression transformed into a wild smile. Of course, this didn't please the little guy. Even though Adam was part animal, he was also a man like any other man on the face of the planet. The one area that he didn't want anyone to harm was his penis. Adam was moving from side to side. Garrison looked at Adam and said, "Hey, Adam, look at me."

Adam looked at Garrison as his brother slowly tipped the coffee pot to allow about a cup of hot water to escape. The hot water slowly poured out of the pot, and as it covered Adam, he made the most interesting sounds that were difficult for even Garrison to hear above the screams. Garrison laughed at Adams's predicament but stopped suddenly. He wanted to hear Adam's cries of pain, his earth-shattering screams of intense, mind-blowing hurting. Garrison knew all too well what kind of anguish he had given his brother. Garrison witnessed the blisters that formed on Adam's penis and his inner thigh. Adam was in so much pain from the hot water that he didn't care what Garrison did to him next. Garrison sensed this, and that was the reason he stopped. To add to the pain at this point would be foolish to some degree. Adam wanted the pain to stop, and the only way that goal could be achieved was through death. Garrison understood and was forced to stop the torture. He placed the coffee pot down on the tray and picked up the tranquilizer shot in the desk drawer. He administered the shot, and in a few seconds, Adam was out like a light. Little did he know that the formula would react with the tranquilizer and eventually reverse its intended conclusion.

For some added enjoyment, Garrison went over to the sewing box and got out a long piece of thread. With a needle, he threaded a button as best he could. He made quite a few loops through the button. He wanted to make sure it would be secure enough that the thread wouldn't break. He made sure the thread was about ten inches long. Garrison picked up the needle and thread with the button on the end. He walked over to Adam. He lifted Adam's right pinky finger and pushed the needle through the fatty tip of the pad. He threaded the next two fingers and the index finger. He moved all the fingers down the thread and made sure all of them were together. He cut the thread and tied up the loose end many times. Adam wouldn't be able to get his fingers open with knots on one side and the button on the other side. This was added torture for Adam, something that Garrison needed to do to his lesser brother.

As Garrison was leaving the room, he looked at his brother lying on the bed. He sensed the same pain he had felt since he had started this exercise. He knew that he had put his brother through intense suffering. None of this would bring his parents back to him, and he knew that, but Garrison needed this release. He needed this revenge to help his soul rest easier throughout the day. Garrison was getting closer to feeling that he was even with his brother, but the pain of seeing his parents die before his very eyes would always haunt him. As Garrison went upstairs to prepare for the next day, he knew that he had to end this, but he didn't know how. However, Garrison knew one thing for sure: he was getting bored with these little games he was playing with Adam. The cries of excruciating pain were not pleasing to Garrison's ears anymore, but he wasn't finished with the games. Garrison felt deep down in his heart that Adam hadn't suffered enough.

CHAPTER 16

Obstructions

$\mathcal{L}$oren was so proud of Garrison for the way he had handled the stress and difficult circumstances that he had faced in the last few months. Carolyn was very proud of him as well, especially of his willingness to stay focused on his homework and studies through these difficult times. Garrison was thankful for all the praise. After breakfast, he and Carolyn began to study. When Garrison studied, he didn't waste any time. Everything was business for him. He didn't joke around or move, and he certainly didn't play during study time. He was very studious and wanted to learn new things. Garrison had always loved to learn, even before he had begun to walk. He loved to study and always wanted to know how things worked or were made. His mind was brilliant. He could remember and recall anything at any time.

After his studies, he often played the violin. Carolyn loved to listen to Garrison play, especially the slow works by Mozart, Vivaldi, Beethoven, and Haydn. Those were the only composers that Garrison liked. His favorite was Mozart. He loved Mozart's story. He saw himself in the child prodigy's tale. Garrison admired the greatness of Mozart compared to others of his time. He loved the way the musical notes flowed from one to the other. One moment he experienced sadness, the next he experienced happiness, and then down the road, moments later, another emotion hit him. No other composer had created music that Garrison could relate to. Garrison saw a lot of himself in Mozart, and many others agreed with him.

Garrison knew there had been many great men and women in the past. Iconic figures that had and would always stand the test of time. Garrison also knew that many great men and women would be formed, discovered, or created in the future. He had read many books and studied many people's lives. He had studied great military leaders, inventors, business people, scientists, and many others, but for Garrison, Mozart was the only one who had seen the secret of what awaited people in the afterlife. This one individual captivated his heart, his mind, and his soul. Garrison believed that music was the instrument that could open a person's soul. He believed that many discoveries could be made if people would allow all their senses to work together and let nature, the very nature that god granted humans, take control of their essence. In that rare moment, if the human body allowed itself this pleasure, the listener or the performer could create a portal into the afterlife. It had taken Mozart over thirty years to describe the idea of heaven while he was alive on this planet. Through Mozart's music, people experienced only a taste of something truly magnificent. Garrison could feel it in his music. Mozart's music made him sense what he might experience in heaven when it became his turn to enter paradise.

Mozart reached a level that no other composer before or after his time had ever been allowed to reach. No one composer had ever created so many musical masterpieces in so many different genres in such a short period of time. No one ever had, or would ever have, his innate sense of counterpoint and melody or his ability to change the mood of his music at the drop of a hat. Mozart could make listeners cry one minute and then turn that tearful world into instant and insane happiness. One could never fully explain Mozart's music, only experience it in its true brilliance. The power of Mozart's music was beyond any description or understanding, even god's.

Garrison thought this had to be the only reason that god had taken Mozart's life at such a young age. Any other reason was unthinkable. Could god have been jealous of his own creation? Maybe he didn't want one of his own creations to give away the secret of paradise.

Maybe Mozart was too close to revealing the secret, and god stopped him before it was too late. Garrison often thought of himself as the next Mozart. Almost everyone he met called him the next Mozart. He and his deceased mentor had lots in common with each other and with their biggest critic, the one entity that had created both of them. Garrison always thought boldly and was always brash in his thinking and sometimes in his actions. He survived mostly on instinct and intellect combined. That was a very powerful combination if used wisely. Garrison wondered, *If there is a god, does he approve of me? Does god approve of the perfection I demonstrate every day of my life?* Yes, Garrison often wondered if he was the next Mozart, not necessarily in the avenue of music but in some other nonrelated path.

The next morning, Garrison was sitting at the breakfast table when Loren told everyone that Lewis was coming home the following day. Garrison was glad and excited. Loren asked Garrison how Adam was doing.

"He is fine. Do not worry; I have everything under control. I am taking excellent care of my brother," he said.

When Garrison finished his breakfast, he excused himself and made his way out of the house. He went into the garage and looked for an axe. He found what he was looking for on the garage wall. To make sure no one would see him take the tool, he walked around the back of the house and stopped at the basement walk-out door. Garrison used the key to let himself inside. He knew that neither Loren nor Carolyn would want to be near the basement, much less in the basement, as long as Adam was down there. He had been very lucky that neither of the ladies had made her way downstairs, but he couldn't control what they would do. Hopefully they wouldn't see Garrison torturing Adam, but he knew that eventually the truth would have to come out.

Garrison walked to Adam's room and opened the door. Adam was now awake and still in pain. Garrison closed and locked the door behind him. He walked over to Adam with the tool in his hand. Adam's bloodshot and insanely panicked eyes got as big as Garrison had ever seen. Garrison was holding the axe. His dad had bought it years ago but had never used the tool. It still had the price tag on the iron head. The axe had not even been sharpened. Garrison looked at Adam and smiled sweetly. Without saying a word, he positioned himself next to the bed, brought the axe back over his head, and swung the blunt side down on Adam's right upper arm. Adam's whole body jumped in pain, with only the restraints holding him in place. Garrison pulled the axe over his head one more time, and with a little more force, he sent the axe down with authority on the same spot. Crack! Garrison heard and saw it; Adam heard and felt it. The humerus broke in two. Garrison calmly walked over to the other side of the bed. He positioned his feet to provide stability. He brought the blunt side of the axe back over his head and with great effort came down on Adam's left arm, smashing the bone inside the well-sculpted muscles of his victim.

Adam's torso and legs couldn't stay still. He was in so much pain. Garrison walked over to the foot of the bed and positioned his body against Adam's lower left leg. He drew back the axe, and with the blunt side, he came down hard on the tibia, breaking the bone in two. After repositioning himself once more, he took the axe and struck Adam's fibula. After several blows the bone finally broke. Garrison moved over to the other side of the bed and did the same thing to the other leg. Garrison placed the axe on the desk. He went over and released Adam's arm and ankle restraints. Adam couldn't move his arms or legs very well, considering the bones were completely broken. Garrison released the straps so Adam was free from all the restraints except the chain around his neck. Garrison quickly ran over to the pulley and began to pull on it. At first, the chain moved and became tighter as it lifted off the ground and rubbed on the corner of the cell entrance. The pulley was made to pull the chain with relative ease to the operator. Garrison did find it to be a little hard when the chain was to the point where it was basically in a semi straight line from the wall to the entrance of the iron cell, and from there to Adam's neck resting on the bed. Garrison pulled and tugged harder, and soon the chain drew closer to the wall, causing the chain around Adam's neck to pull toward the cell entrance. Each full turn pulled Adam. The chain choked Adam while little by little pulling him across and off the bed. Adam was moving around, but with his arms and legs completely broken in two, it was hard for him to keep from being strangled. He would have put his hands on the chain around his neck to prevent it, but the current state of his arms wouldn't allow him to do so. Obviously, his legs were no help to him either.

When Garrison continued to pull the chain, Adam suddenly fell off the bed. His face hit the floor first, then his limp arms, followed by his torso and his limp and lifeless legs. Garrison watched the whole thing and actually laughed when Adam's face hit the floor. His arms and legs looked like a pretzel. They were twisted and flopping in every direction. Garrison continued to pull on the pulley, and as he did, he noticed Adam's nose was bleeding from the fall. Adam was trying to move but couldn't do it very well. When Adam's neck chain got to the corner of the entrance to the cell, Garrison stopped and went over to Adam's body. He pushed Adam's torso with his right foot to move him more inside the cell. Garrison got in the cell and grabbed the chain. He pulled hard with his hand and moved Adam's grunting body about six or so feet into the cell. Garrison returned and tightened the chain a little. Adam lay on the floor crying, snorting, and moaning loudly. Just his torso, head, and hips were moving. His face was bloody from his broken and smashed nose. Garrison noticed three teeth on the floor. Apparently, Adam's teeth had broken from the fall.

Garrison's attention turned to Adam's moans. Adam was very upset, scared, and a little angry, but most of all he was in total, unbelievably agonizing pain. He wanted the pain to stop. He was exhausted physically and emotionally. Garrison walked out of the cell. He went over to the plate that he had brought downstairs a couple of days before. The silverware was lying on the plate. He picked up a spoon and walked into the cell again. He stood there and looked at Adam bleeding on the floor.

Garrison said, "Adam! Adam! Stop crying! I hope that you have learned your lesson. You really hurt me, you hurt my parents, and you have been a cancer to all of us. I hate you with all my being. I despise you, and I wish you were dead. But that would be too good for you, you fucking, disgusting monster. God must be ashamed to have allowed such a creation to develop in his animal lineage."

Garrison walked over to Adam and bent down on his knees beside his brother. "You know, Adam, the one image that I cannot get out of my mind is the way you mutilated my father. I will never get that imagine out of my head for as long as I live... and that seems to be forever. I cannot stop dreaming or thinking about how you tortured my poor father to death. Not to get too religious on you, dear brother, but I will quote the Bible for you in hopes that you will live a better life. The Bible said, 'And thine eye shall not pity; but life shall go for life, eye for eye, tooth for tooth, hand for hand, foot for foot.'" Garrison grabbed Adam's hair and gripped it tightly. He pushed the hair down to the floor as he placed his knee on Adam's chest. With his other hand, Garrison grabbed the spoon and guided it to the outside corner of Adam's left eye. Garrison quickly dug the spoon in the corner of the eye socket, went deep, and scooped Adam's eye out. The eyeball was still attached to the optic nerve. Adam fought as hard as he could, but both of his arms were bent at a ninety-degree angle because of the breaks. He had no control over his forearms or his hands. Garrison got off Adam's body and watched as Adam moved around on the floor like a fish out of water. Garrison left Adam flopping around. He walked out of the cell and locked the door behind him. He calmly placed the spoon down on the plate, turned the light out, and closed the bedroom door.

Garrison noticed he had some blood on his clothes, so he ran quickly to the bathroom upstairs, making sure no one saw him. When he got to his bedroom, he closed the door and took off his clothes. He got his shower and put on some clean clothes. Garrison took the bloodied clothes downstairs. He quickly got a garbage bag and placed the clothes in it. Then he threw the bag in the large garbage can in the garage.

Garrison was tired. He went to the family room where his violin was resting in its case on the couch. He opened the case and pulled out his violin and bow. He started to play a solo piece by Mozart he had memorized a couple of weeks before. He could see the notes in his head as if god were typing them out for the young boy as he played. Garrison played beautifully and flawlessly. He played as he had never played before. He felt all his senses working together as one. They were all in overdrive. He couldn't miss a note even if he tried. The feeling was exhilarating to him. Rarely had he felt this way in his young life.

As he continued to play, he was keenly aware of every sound the instrument was making, as well as the other sounds around him. He had only felt this feeling a few times in his life. Each time was better than the last. He felt as if he owned the world and could control and command anything. He loved feeling this way, and he didn't care how he had gotten this feeling, although down deep in his brain he knew the reason. He knew that he had let himself lose control. He had released the animal inside him. He had only allowed that to happen a handful of times in his life, and usually it was when things, animals, or people irritated him, but at that particular time, he allowed himself to be free.

Meanwhile, a part of Garrison's mind was on his brother in the basement, picturing how he was suffering, how he was moving around on the cold floor, and how much pain he must be feeling. It gave Garrison's heart that warm-and-fuzzy feeling inside. He needed some release and playing with Adam and seeing him in pain made him feel good. Garrison was a good boy, and he knew the difference between right and wrong, unlike his lesser brother. Garrison knew that he could not unleash his true feelings because he didn't want to ever turn into his brother.

As he played, he wondered if he could bottle this pure feeling of freedom, if somehow he could call upon all his senses and channel his feelings through his mind instead of having to act out his thoughts to awaken all the senses at once. Only a few times in Garrison's life had he felt that all his senses were working together as one. The first time had been when he first attacked the dog. The next time had been when he attacked his father. The other time was when he had shared his first meal of a captured animal with his father. Now, the experience with Adam had to be added to the list of those special moments. These were the only times when all his senses were so keen that he felt perfect. He heard and saw everything in his environment during these times. It was as if nothing bothered him and nothing could bother him. He felt whole, complete, and absolute with himself, with nature, and with life in general. Garrison started to make the connection to certain events in his life that would cause stress, strain, or anything that would get his emotions lathered up. Over time, the feeling subsided and eventually went away. He believed that these events helped awaken all his senses, as they seemed to work overtime and at a very high level. Garrison swore that he could hear more sounds, could see better, could even taste more flavors during these instances. He got that way on several occasions when he hunted with his father, as well as the other times when he killed or hurt an animal. Garrison knew there was somehow a connection. The higher his emotional state of being, the better his senses worked. Garrison thought at times that he could achieve perfection. If only he could harness this power, he could live a much better life in the future and quite possibly duplicate this feeling so that others could somehow feel the same way. Limitless wealth would fall upon him, wealth beyond his or his father's wildest dreams.

CHAPTER 17

Necrosis

The next morning, Garrison and the ladies were happy and looking forward to Lewis coming home. His recuperation had been going well, and he had gotten around fine the day before at the hospital. Lewis had been looking forward to coming home, but he had enjoyed his time away from his responsibilities in the basement. Lewis was also looking forward to some degree to speaking with Garrison about the Adam situation. He was feeling more like a member of an Italian Mafia, like the person who always cleans up the mess. Lewis didn't like this role, and he hated being controlled by not only Adam but also by what he was dealing with regarding Formula L. He wanted to have more time for his research into the creation of the formula, not to have to take care of and worry about some half animal, half human locked up in a cell in the basement.

The morning of Lewis's arrival, Garrison returned to the door on the right of the landing after his breakfast. He entered and made his way to Adam's room. Adam was still awake. The blood had dried on the floor, or so it seemed from Garrison's vantage point. Adam was barely moving. He was still in so much pain, unbelievable discomfort. His eye was still hanging by the optic nerve. It looked as if Adam hadn't attempted to touch it or move it much during the night. His arms and legs were black and blue now, and there was a lot of swelling. He looked a mess.

Garrison spoke to him. "Adam, can you hear me? Lewis is coming home today, and I want him to see you. He might be a little upset, but he has told me how wonderful it has been for him not to have to take care of you since he has been in the hospital. I assured him that I have been taking good care of you and keeping you company so you would not be bored in his absence. I hope you have not been bored with me. Have you, Adam?" Garrison laughed and went upstairs.

Garrison waited for Loren and Carolyn, and then they all went to the hospital to pick up Lewis and take him home. They drove to the hospital and entered his room. Lewis was packing his clothes and walking around the room to limber up per the doctor's instructions. He had been doing very well, and he could have gone home a couple of days ago, but the doctors had wanted to monitor him because he had experienced such a trauma. After a couple of hours passed, the nurse came in with the wheelchair, and everyone was ready to go home. Loren ended up driving after everything was placed in the car, and they all left the hospital. After thirty minutes or so, they reached the estate.

Lewis got out of the car and went inside while the other three helped with his suitcase and other personal belongings. Lewis wanted to see Adam, and Garrison was very excited to show him what he had done to his brother. Loren thought it would be best for Lewis to lie down, but Lewis was tired of lying down. He thought the steps might be a bit of a challenge, but he could make it. He felt that he had to, in all honesty. Loren asked him if he needed her help, but Garrison said he would take care of Lewis. Lewis agreed because he was afraid of what Garrison had done to his brother. He didn't want the ladies to see what damage, if any, might have been done while he was in the hospital.

Lewis and Garrison walked gingerly to the basement steps. Lewis took one step at a time so he wouldn't hurt himself. He was still very sore, and sometimes sudden movements would pull the stitches. Each step seemed to take longer than the last one. After what seemed to be many minutes, they finally got to the landing, and Garrison unlocked the door on the right. They went inside, and Garrison quickly closed the door. Immediately, Lewis heard Adam moaning.

Lewis said, "What is wrong with Adam?" He picked up the pace of his walk, but Garrison ran in front and stopped him before they got to the bedroom door.

Garrison said, "Now, Lewis, what you are going to see might come as a bit of a shock. I want you to be prepared and not to worry. I will clean up any mess that he made."

With that information, Lewis didn't know what to expect, but he knew it was going to be bad. He let Garrison go into the room first, then Lewis slowly and reluctantly followed. As he turned the corner and stepped inside, Garrison was blocking his view of Adam. Lewis looked around, but Garrison was uncomfortably close to him, and he noticed that Garrison had a large smile on his face and was giggling somewhat. Garrison quickly moved to his left and stepped back.

With his right hand, Garrison pointed to Adam, who was lying on the floor. "Tada!"

Lewis looked at Adam as he lay on the floor of his cell. His arms and legs were bent in odd shapes. His eyeball was hanging out of his head, and blood covered the floor.

"What in the hell happened to Adam?"

Garrison started to laugh. "Lewis, everything is going to be fine. I will take care of the situation."

Lewis said sharply, "Take care of the situation? There should have been no situation to take care of. I asked you to feed him until I came back. What happened in here?"

Adam was attempting to move to see Lewis, and he was trying to say something, but the duct tape prevented him from saying anything understandable. Lewis moved toward the caged cell, but Garrison stepped toward him and touched his right arm.

"Lewis, he is dangerous. You are still weak and sore. Do not go in there. He is very dangerous. Look, I know what I did was wrong, but he made my life, our life, miserable. You yourself said that your life would be better off without Adam in it, right? That is what you said. He is evil. He laughed at me and said some very bad things to me about my parents. I know. I know I cannot lash out like this again. I understand,

Lewis. I am not stupid. I know what you are thinking. I know I have acted like a monster here."

Lewis said, "You did."

Garrison continued. "But he had to pay for his sins, Lewis. He had to pay for the mistakes that he has made in his life. Just think. We can eliminate him, and all of our problems are gone."

Lewis was very tired and he had to sit down. Garrison pulled up a chair while Adam moaned more as he attempted to reach out to Lewis for help. Lewis sat down in the chair, and both Garrison and Adam were surprised that he didn't immediately go to Adam's aid. Garrison sensed that he might be winning here.

Garrison said, "Imagine no Adam. You know, Lewis, he will live forever, right? That is what you told me. He is going to live forever, and that means he will outlive you. You will be trapped down here in this basement with him until you die. You can leave, but if you do, you know I will eventually terminate his life. He will not ruin my life. The way I look at it, we can help each other here. I had my fun with him, Lewis, and now I need your help with the rest. I did this for the family, for myself, for the business, and for you. We do not need Adam. He is a liability." Garrison bent down on his knees beside Lewis. He said, "Please, forgive me. I know what I did was wrong, and it will never happen again. I was weak, and I messed up. That I agree with, and I accept that responsibility, but the reality of the situation is that he cannot be allowed to live. If he ever escaped and started biting people, this disease that he and I carry within us would get out of control. I know you are worried about that, and so am I. Heck, I am even worried about myself. I know you look at me as a monster right now, and I know that I disappointed you at the highest level, but this is for the best."

This was too much information for Lewis to process. He didn't know what to say. He looked around the room and said, "I... I just don't know, Garrison. I hear you, and I agree with many of your points. Maybe this is for the best. I cannot go on for the rest of my life living the way I have over the past couple years or so, and I certainly cannot leave you and the women upstairs. This is the only family I have." Lewis started to cry.

Garrison placed his hand on Lewis's leg and smiled. "I have and will always think of you as part of my family. I am in the same situation as you. He killed the only two people that I loved in this world. I wanted to be accepted as a normal little boy, but my father never really accepted me until the last few months of his life. I still think the only reason he showed me some attention was to get information out of me. He knew that I had gone through a similar kind of transformation process when I was young and that it had continued throughout my life. He was experiencing something that was odd and strange. He was scared, and I was the only one at that time that could help him through his lot in life. It was my fault that Dad was the way he was. I was the one that bit him. I need your help, Lewis, in controlling my anger because I feel like an animal at times. Just like that." Garrison pointed to Adam, who was still lying on the floor moaning even louder. "I don't want to be like that, so I need your help."

Lewis got control of his feelings, wiped his eyes, and quickly thought about what he was going to do. His options were limited because of his soreness. He wished that Garrison had waited until he got back on his feet. Although Lewis knew that Garrison was wrong in the way he had handled the situation, he recognized that Garrison was right in what he was saying about the circumstances. He also knew that Garrison was eventually going to kill Adam, or vice versa. Garrison was the lesser of two evils from Lewis's point of view. Lewis thought he had at least a fighting chance to control Garrison, but there was no way he could control Adam. Maybe this was all for the best, but in the back of his mind he didn't know what he was going to do with Adam's body. He couldn't call the police, obviously. They didn't even know that he existed, and if they ever found out what had happened, he and Garrison would be in a lot of trouble. He didn't want to call his friend from the funeral home; he would be suspicious about getting called to the estate again. The only thing left was to bury the body, but with this option there was always the fear that the body would be discovered. He couldn't dump the body because that would create a mess if it was ever discovered. Lewis didn't know what he was going to do. To make matters even worse, he was still hurting from the gunshot wound, so he couldn't even help Garrison lift the body, much less bury it somewhere. Lewis also didn't want to keep Adam alive; he knew he was in so much pain that it was unbelievable. But if they killed Adam, what would they do with his body? This was a major problem for Lewis to attempt to solve.

Lewis looked at Garrison and said, "Garrison, he is in pain. He must be suffering in a god-awful way. We have to do something."

Garrison replied, "I have given him some tranquilizer shots from time to time, but you're right. We have to end this."

Lewis said, "I didn't say end it, but we have to do something."

"I think it's about time to end this little game," Garrison said.

"Now wait a minute," Lewis said. "If you end his life, what are we going to do with the body?"

"Well, you said yourself a minute ago that we have to do something. What do you suggest?" Garrison asked.

Lewis sat there dumbfounded. Finally, he said, "I don't know, Garrison. I wish you would've waited. I hate talking about him like he is some kind of animal about to be put down."

Garrison said quickly and angrily, "Lewis! He is an animal."

"Okay, I understand why you feel that way. What do you think we should do?"

Garrison liked to be in control, and to have an adult ask him his thoughts was very special to him. He smiled and said, "My suggestion is to put the thing out of its misery and bury him in the woods. He is too big to bury at once, so I would cut the body up in pieces and bury them in different places in the woods. Deep in the woods."

Lewis wasn't sure about that idea. He thought it was sloppy. What if someone discovered the remains? Garrison thought the only sensible solution would be to have one of the local landscaping companies come out and help dig a few holes for some trees they wanted to plant.

Lewis thought for a while and came up with a similar idea: to have someone come out to the estate and dig a large hole for a koi pond or whatever. Then they could place the body parts in the hole and throw some dirt over the remains, then have the contracting company come back the next day and fill in the holes. They could have either Loren or Carolyn tell the workers that the owners had changed their minds about the trees or the koi pond or whatever project they decided on. Lewis thought this was the only way to dispose of the body. He couldn't think of a better idea at the time.

After much consideration, Lewis told Garrison about his plan to see what he thought. "Okay, Garrison, somehow we have to dispose of the body, the entire body. If we dig up some ground on the property, maybe we could place the body in the hole, cover it up somehow, and place a koi pond or a tree over the remains."

Garrison said, "I am concerned with the koi-pond thing. What if someone buys this house, doesn't like the pond, tears it up, and discovers the bones?"

Lewis said, "That's a good point. Maybe your idea of a tree or two would do the trick. I can get someone out here to dig the hole. I can tell them to come back the next day and, in the meantime, we could place the body in the hole, cover it up with dirt, and then have the tree planted in the hole. End of story… maybe. Or do we even need a tree? We could just throw the dirt back in the hole."

Garrison thought for a moment and said, "I think we need more than one hole. He is rather tall. I think we need to cut the body up in small pieces, place the remains in a bag, a sack, or something, and spread it out to four or five holes. The holes will not be that large, so we must make the bags no longer than three feet wide, right?"

Lewis thought for a moment and said, "Why do we need so many holes? Just one would do, I think. We can get Loren and Carolyn to help us. Oh, God, I forgot about them. You know we are going to have to tell them about Adam. I think they would understand… maybe." Lewis wasn't feeling well. He was in so deep; the whole family was in deep.

Garrison quickly said, "Yes, they have to be told. They will understand because they have as much to lose from this as we do."

Lewis agreed. "You're right. Do you want me to tell them?"

Garrison said, "Why don't we do it together?"

Lewis agreed, and both decided that they had to tell them that day.

Garrison looked over at Adam, who had heard every word. He moaned and tried to speak. He wanted to plead his case for his own survival, but they were not interested in his point of view. Adam was close to passing out from exhaustion, pain, and stress. Lewis got a tranquilizer shot, handed it to Garrison, and told him to give Adam the shot. Garrison reluctantly did it, and in a few seconds, Adam was out cold.

Garrison went upstairs with Lewis, and they called for the ladies to meet them in the great room. Loren walked in first and then Carolyn entered. Lewis sat down and started the story. He told them almost everything, from start to finish. He was careful not to tell the ladies how Garrison had tortured Adam. He explained the consequences of keeping Adam alive, saying that everyone's lives would be on permanent hold. He didn't tell them about Adam living forever if allowed to live a normal life. He didn't think the ladies were ready for that kind of information. It was obvious that both Loren and Carolyn didn't care for Adam, and yes, it would be easier for all of them if Adam were out of the picture. Lewis told the ladies that Adam was very sick and asked them not to go in the basement. He told them that Adam was dying and he didn't know why. Obviously, no other doctor could be consulted, but in his professional opinion, Adam was going to die. Lewis continued his sales pitch by saying that he didn't know what to do with the body. He couldn't call his friend from the funeral home again; that would be too risky. He thought the best way to handle this would be to dig one large hole and place the body inside. With help from all four of them, they could cover the body or parts of the body over with dirt.

Garrison began to speak up. He wanted to dig several holes, cut the body up, and plant small trees in those holes. This might help make sure no one would discover the body, at least not for a long time. Over time, the body parts would decay. Garrison privately didn't want Adam's entire body intact. He wanted the body to be cut up in many pieces and placed in several holes because he thought it would guarantee Adam could never... come back from the dead. Garrison didn't necessarily believe Adam would rise again, but he would feel better about the situation knowing Adam had been dismembered. In addition, Garrison had other plans for Adam's body.

Carolyn was upset, but she agreed with Lewis's plan. She had been with the family for a long time, and she loved Garrison as if he were her own. She reconfirmed her love to Garrison and said that she would do anything to make his life easier. She was concerned that Adam would somehow get loose. She was afraid he would kill one of them in the house. Therefore, she believed that his death would be a good thing for everyone, but she would also miss him because she had taken care of him almost as much as Lewis had over the past few months.

Loren agreed with Garrison and thought his idea was better, but it was obviously the messiest. Aside from that difference, she agreed with everything else being discussed. Loren was always the level-headed one of the household. She was unemotional, and this had served her well in the family business.

Garrison and Lewis were pleased with the truthful responses from the two ladies. Both knew that they could trust the women and that they would never say anything to anyone about Adam, Trevor, or Adelle. They would all be in major trouble with the police. It wouldn't benefit anyone to let the true story out.

After some intense discussions from all four, they finally decided that several holes would be the direction to go. It would be hard to explain one large hole and easier to explain a few smaller holes. Also, they respected Garrison's wishes since Adam was his brother. They decided on three holes about three feet in diameter and one large hole that would be about five feet long. They would plant small trees with the body parts under but not around the roots. Loren took over and said that she would get someone to dig the holes. Lewis said that he wanted the holes dug in front of the forest area immediately. He wanted them to bury the body parts first. They would order the small trees afterward and have them delivered, placed, and planted with Loren's supervision. Loren understood, and she left the room to make some calls. Meanwhile, Lewis called one of his friends who had an oscillating saw that could easily cut through any bone in the human body. By the end of the call, Lewis was very tired, and his wounds were starting to hurt so he went to lie down for a while. After his short nap, he asked Carolyn to drive him to his friend's house to pick up the saw.

Garrison stayed in the room with the women. He spoke to them in a serious tone, saying, "Loren... Carolyn... I wanted to say thank you. Thank you for always being there for me. Loren, I know that you have given up a lot of your life taking over the business, and I want to say I appreciate your hard work and your dedication. Carolyn, I want to thank you for being there for me like Loren has since day one. I can sense there is tension between you two, and I don't want that to be the case. Both of you are part of this family, and I never want either one of you to be jealous of the other. I love you both. I need for all of this to be the utmost secret. What we are about to do can never be told to anyone. Do you guys understand?" Both ladies nodded in agreement, and Garrison continued. "Because Adam was a secret when he was living, he has to be a secret when he is dead. What I am about to do will be very upsetting to you, so please do not freak out on me. Just trust me, even if whatever I do or what Lewis does totally disgusts you. We all have been through so much. All I ask is for you to be there for me this one last time."

With that, Garrison got up, and Loren said, "Garrison, I love you, and our secret will stay with me forever."

Carolyn said, "Like Loren said, our secret is secure with me as well. We were all family years ago. We are even closer now."

Garrison said, "You honor me and the memory of my parents with your devotion." He walked out of the room. Loren went into her office to call some workers to come over early the next day and start digging. Later, Loren, Carolyn, and Garrison went to the edge of the forest and marked off the places where they wanted the holes to be dug.

Early the next morning, two workers showed up at the estate. Loren and Garrison met with them and showed them where to dig. They instructed them to dig three holes about three feet in diameter and four feet deep. As Loren had anticipated, the workers wondered why the holes needed to be so deep just for trees. She told them she was following instructions and she expected them to do the same. She said their pay would be doubled if the instructions were carried out. The workers never said another word about the depth of the holes. The next hole, the fourth hole, needed to be about five feet in length and again about four feet deep.

Loren and Garrison went inside the house. They saw that Lewis and Carolyn were back with the saw. Lewis told Garrison he was going to see how Adam was doing. Obviously, Garrison wanted to join him, but the doctor told Garrison to stay upstairs and see if Loren needed any help with the workers. After several hours, the workers finished their jobs. Loren and Garrison went outside to inspect the holes. For the most part, the holes were exactly as ordered. Garrison studied each one carefully and looked at every inch. He was pleased so the workers got their money and left. Loren went inside and ordered four small trees for delivery two days later.

Garrison went inside and walked down the basement stairs. He knocked on the door to the right of the landing. Lewis let him in and told him that Adam was awake and in serious pain. His condition was not good. The pain and the stress had been too much for Adam, according to Lewis. Lewis noticed the pins in Adam's forearms, but he didn't want to remove them out of fear of hurting Adam further. Because of the Formula L in his system, he could stand more pain and suffering than anyone could imagine. It would take a lot of work for someone to kill off Adam with torture alone, no matter how severe the torture. Lewis wanted to let Garrison have it for the way he had treated his brother, but he knew Garrison had been upset, and he let it pass for now.

From the corner of his eye, Garrison saw the oscillating saw lying on the table. He thought it looked easy to use. Lewis was busy in the other room, at his lab. He was taking an inventory of what he had and didn't have in his lab. Garrison quickly took the key and opened the cell door. He went over to Adam and took the duct tape off his mouth. Adam moaned and cried. Garrison carefully bent down and looked at him. Adam returned the gaze with his only good eye.

In a very tired, pained voice, Adam said, "I hope you had your fun, you crazy fuck. Please leave me alone. Don't hurt me anymore. I am in so much pain."

Garrison said, "Are you sorry for what you did to this family?"

Adam asked in a serious manner, "Sorry for what?"

Garrison's heart raced and he couldn't control himself any longer. "Sorry for what? Is that what you said? Sorry for what? You mean to tell me that after all the shit you put me and my family through, you have the audacity to say to me, 'Sorry for what?' You really are a pathetic, putrid, stupid animal, you fucking subhuman, vile piece of crap."

Garrison stormed out of the cell, closed the door, and locked it. Adam was worried. He started to plead for Garrison's forgiveness, but his voice was barely above the soft tone used before the beginning of a classical music concert.

Garrison went over to Lewis. He controlled himself as best as he could and said, "So, Lewis, how long are you going to be down here?"

Lewis said, "Oh, not that long. I was checking on my supplies. You really went through the tranquilizers, didn't you, Garrison?"

Garrison smiled. He looked around the lab and waited for Lewis to finish what he was doing. He noticed the key to the cell door was on the table where he had placed it seconds ago. He quietly went over and picked up the keys without making a sound loud enough for Lewis to hear. Garrison also noticed the oscillating saw on the table. Lewis was standing near it, but he suddenly walked over to the far left of the long lab table. He was trying to find the notes that he had taken a couple of weeks ago, but Garrison didn't care what he was looking for, he was just happy that Lewis had moved away from the saw. Garrison picked up the saw and walked as quietly as he could to Adam's room. Lewis was still occupied with looking through his notes.

Garrison walked into the cell room and closed the door. He locked it from the inside. Adam had his eye on Garrison the whole time, but he was especially watching the oscillating saw. As Garrison was locking the cell door, Adam tried to move, but he couldn't. He growled, but it was a pitiful growl to say the least. He was tired, hurt, and in an extreme amount of pain. Garrison put the key in his pocket, looked over at Adam, and smiled.

"Now, Adam, are you ready to say that you are sorry for what you did to my family?" Garrison moved the saw up to his face and wiggled it around.

Adam stared at him with his one eye, showed his teeth—three of which were broken—and said, "Whatever you have in mind, brother, remember that I was the one that killed them all. I was the cause of their deaths, and I hope that haunts you for the rest of your miserable, fucking life." Then he relaxed as best he could. It had taken everything he had to speak those words.

Garrison was still standing there smiling as he listened to every word. "Well, that was disappointing to hear." He walked over and knelt next to Adam's left leg.

Adam was moving as best he could to get away from him, saying, "No... no... Get away from me, you sick fuck."

Garrison reached down and placed his hand on Adam's lower left leg. Adam yelled, but his voice was faint. Garrison turned the oscillating saw on and looked at Adam.

Adam yelled as loudly as he could, "No... no... no!" Garrison lowered the saw down slowly. Adam was already in great pain from moving around on the basement floor. In the lab, Lewis heard the sounds in Adam's room and walked as fast as he could, but he was still hurting from his gunshot wounds. As he made it to the doorway, he saw Garrison and Adam behind the closed door of the cell.

Lewis yelled, "Garrison, turn the saw off. What are you doing? Get the fuck out of there, boy! No... Garrison... *No!*"

Garrison didn't even look up; he never took his eyes off Adam. He gripped harder on the leg and continued the saw's slow descent. He brought the saw down just above the kneecap, and suddenly the skin broke. Adam screamed as loud as he could. The saw went back and forth so fast that it was hard to see it move. Garrison was having fun with his new toy as the blade dug deeper into the skin and through the muscles. He could feel and hear the saw as it hit the femur.

Adam was beyond himself. He curled his hands into fists, and the needles dug deeper into the meat of his forearms. His broken arms and legs felt as if they were on fire. All of Adam's pain sensors had lit up like a Christmas tree. Garrison continued to apply a lot of pressure to get through the bone.

Meanwhile, Lewis was pulling on the cell bars, trying to get in and yelling for Garrison to stop. Then he halfway gave up because he knew he wasn't getting anywhere and he was hurting from his wounds. There was no way he could get inside or stop this from continuing. He looked at Adam. He had never seen this much pain on anyone's face in his life.

Garrison moved the saw back and forth with more force. Sometimes Adam would move, and Garrison's hand, and thus the saw, moved as well, so the cut was not totally clean. Garrison decided to go down the outside portion of the leg first. He finally got through then started on the inside of the leg. He pushed through to the bone, and after a few moments, he finally broke all the way through. Garrison continued to cut through the muscles, tendons, and skin on the back part of the leg. Adam's body was as tight and tense as it had ever been. As the saw finally completed its job, Adam's lower leg was completely severed from the upper leg. Garrison turned the saw off and moved the detached leg away from the body that was inching away from Garrison.

Lewis watched the whole thing and said in a calm voice, "Garrison. Listen to me. There is a civil way of doing this, Garrison."

Garrison, without looking up, rose to his feet and said, "I know. But this son of a bitch didn't care about being civil when he tortured my father, now did he, Lewis? Stay out of it. This matter is between the animal and me."

The blood was gushing out of Adam's leg and spilling out onto the floor. Garrison bent down on the floor again and positioned himself by Adam's right leg. He proceeded to lower the saw again. He started above the kneecap as before. Garrison turned the saw on, and this time he held Adam's upper leg down with his left hand.

Adam was shaking hard. He was hardly making a sound, as he was having problems catching his breath. He would hold his breath for a long time, then exhale in a painful sigh. Adam wanted to die; he couldn't stand the pain any longer, but his body was made to live forever so it would take a lot for him to die. Formula L has many secrets.

Garrison wanted to see how much abuse the body could take before expiring. He hurried because he didn't want Adam to bleed out before his painful experience was complete.

Adams legs felt as if they were in an inferno, and the nonstop pulsating pain was like a wave of constant sharp knives jamming into his severed leg. This combined with the pain from the needles in his forearm and with his total exhaustion was something very few animals had ever felt.

Garrison started the saw on the top of the leg and cut through the muscles until he hit the bone, then he dropped down to the outside part of the leg. He changed directions and started on the inside and cut until he hit the bone. He pulled the saw out, moved back to the front of the leg, and pressed down hard so the blade would cut into the bone faster. He wanted to get this leg off as quick as he could because of the amount of blood Adam was losing. Garrison wanted Adam to experience as much pain and discomfort as possible before he died. He didn't know how much Adam could take before he died.

Garrison pushed on the saw, and finally it went through the bone completely. He cut the remaining tissue from the upper thigh on the back of the leg. Garrison slid the leg away from the rest of the body. He stood up and went over to Adam's right arm. He placed his left foot on the broken upper portion. He looked into Adam's tearful eyes and, without hesitating for one moment, turned the saw back on, placed it on top of Adam's right shoulder, and pressed down toward the armpit. Once Garrison got the saw through the collarbone, the rest was easy. It took repeated attempts, but finally he got through and disassociated the arm from the body. Adam stared straight ahead, hardly moving. Garrison repeated the procedure on Adam's left arm, placing his right foot on it but this time starting under the armpit. He brought the saw up toward the top of the shoulder and pressed hard to break through the skin and then through collarbone. After many repeated attempts, Garrison separated Adam's left arm from his torso. Adam was almost white. Blood covered the floor, but the flow was not as intense as it had been a few minutes ago. Adam was bleeding out. This final act made Garrison's revenge complete.

Garrison turned off the saw and stepped over Adam's torso. He walked over to the cell door, pulled out the key, and unlocked the door. Garrison's eyes met Lewis's. One set of eyes showed a sense of completion mixed with angered passion, while the other set held shock, fear, and disgust. Lewis was afraid that Garrison would go after him next. He didn't know what Garrison was capable of after what he had just witnessed. Garrison walked past Lewis and laid the saw, covered in deep-red blood, down on the desk.

He turned to Lewis and said, "I will get the trash bags, and we'll place the parts in them. Lewis, I know what I did was wrong, but now I feel complete. I am sorry you had to witness that. And don't worry. This is the last time you will ever see me do anything like this again. I hope you can find it in your heart to forgive me, but if you cannot find the compassion to forgive, I will totally understand."

Lewis opened his mouth, on the verge of being physically ill. Then he said, "I don't think he is dead yet, Garrison."

Garrison looked at the body and saw a slight chest movement. Garrison laughed a little and said, "He'll bleed out and will eventually

die." After Garrison said those words, Adam made a soft sigh and his
chest stopped moving. Moments later, he died. He had held onto his life
longer than Garrison had thought possible. If not for Formula L, he
guessed most animals would have died much sooner.

Garrison left the room and returned a few minutes later with a
box of heavy plastic garbage bags. He walked into the cell and took one
large bag out of the box. Lewis walked over to help Garrison. He held
the bag open for him as Garrison placed the detached right leg in the
bag. Lewis told Garrison to wash his hands to get all the blood off them
and then help him get the leg over to the lab table. Garrison did as
instructed. He helped Lewis wrap the leg up tightly and seal it with duct
tape. They were careful not to puncture the bag in any way, so no blood
would seep out. Garrison proceeded to do the same with the other leg,
repeating the same procedure and making sure no blood was on the
outside of the garbage bag. Again, Lewis wrapped up the bag with duct
tape, assisted by Garrison. Then they placed both arms in bags, and
Lewis taped them up.

Garrison was getting very tired, but Lewis needed the mess
cleaned up. Lewis didn't want the ladies to come down to the basement
and see the terror that had been unleashed in the cell. The torso was a
problem because it was bigger than the bags they had. Lewis instructed
Garrison to separate more of the body, so it could fit in the bag.
Garrison was more than happy to comply. He got out the saw again, and
this time he went over to Adam's head. He started the saw and placed it
on the lowest part of Adam's neck, where it met the shoulder. He
pressed hard, and the saw blade went in deep. He cut the neck as far as
it would go until he hit bone; then he moved the saw around to the front
of the neck and down the other side. Garrison placed the saw on the cut
portion of the neck and began to cut through the bone. As he did, the
head moved down toward the body and then over to the right side of the
torso. Garrison continued to cut the muscles and tendons that were still
attached to the back of the neck. Finally, the head was free from the
body.

Garrison picked the head up by the hair. He was going to place it in a bag held by Lewis. The bottom part of the bag was lying on the floor so Garrison released his grip, and Adam's head fell free and hit the hard basement floor through the thin plastic bag. As the head bounced, it made a weird sound. Lewis yelled at Garrison to stop playing around when the boy laughed at the funny sound.

Garrison wanted Lewis to wait because he thought he could get more body parts in the bag. Lewis swallowed hard and said he would wrap the head up separately. It was difficult for him to lift the head, so against his better judgment, he slid the bag across the floor with the head inside. After he got the head on the lab table, which was very difficult for him to do, he wrapped it up with duct tape like the others.

Garrison started up the saw again and this time went to work on the upper part of Adam's legs. He started on the right side and placed the saw as high as he could get on the thigh. He made his cut and went in deep. As he did, he went around to the front part of the leg. He moved the leg over and out, and continued to cut around the inside part of the leg. Garrison let the leg fall on the hard floor and then dug the saw in as deep as he could get so he could get to the bone. He worked very hard to cut through the femur. Garrison was aiming for the hip socket, but his cut was too low. With a lot of effort, he finally cut through the bone, and as he did, the leg fell off the torso and rolled over to its side.

Garrison knew where to cut the next time, and he went to work on the other leg. This time he started a little higher up. He used the same method as before, cutting through the skin, muscles, and tendons until he hit bone. He worked his way around the bone, going from the outside to the top, then to the inner thigh and the back of the leg. With great effort, he applied pressure on the saw and cut through some of the bone. He had to dig around the hip socket for a while in order to release the leg. With some effort, he finally got the leg separated from the torso. He called for Lewis to bring the bag over to him. He placed both upper legs in the bag, and Lewis and he wrapped the bag up, again using the duct tape.

After all this work, only the torso was left. Lewis said lifting the torso would hurt his wound. Garrison said that he could lift it if Lewis would put the bag down on the floor. Lewis just wanted the body covered. The sight was dreadful, this torso lying on the floor with no arms, legs, or head. After some work, they finally got the torso in the bag, but blood had covered the bag. Garrison placed another bag over the opening and wrapped the body up as best he could, sealing all loose ends with the duct tape.

It was getting late, and Garrison was very tired. Lewis couldn't be of much help, and he didn't want to ask Loren or Carolyn to carry the body parts to the holes in the forest. He thought that might disturb them too much. However, he had to tell them the status of the Adam problem. Lewis told Garrison to go upstairs and get cleaned up. Garrison had blood everywhere on his clothes. The blood was splattered on his face, arms, and legs. It was all over his body.

Garrison and Lewis went upstairs, and before they saw anyone, Lewis called Loren and Carolyn on the intercom and told them that Garrison looked a mess and that they shouldn't be shocked. Even so, when Loren and Carolyn got together, they were shocked by what they saw. Lewis assured them that he was fine.

He said, "I know this is very upsetting, but Adam died a calm death." Garrison looked at Lewis and smiled, knowing that the doctor was going to cover for him; it did his heart good. Lewis continued, "I can't do much because of my injuries, so I had Garrison help me put some body parts in a few bags. What he needs is some help hauling the parts to the holes in the forest. Then we have to shovel dirt over the bags. A lot of dirt, especially in the hole where Adam's torso will be laid. I suggest everyone get a good night's sleep, and tomorrow we'll get to work."

Everyone agreed on the plan of action for the next day. Carolyn helped Garrison get cleaned up and ready for bed. Before Lewis retired for the night, he poured himself a drink in the great room and sat down. He reflected for a moment on what had happened. He knew this eventually would all be for the best. He began to second guess himself over whether he could have or should have stopped the torture of Adam, but there was little he could have done, when it was all said and done.

Early the next morning, Garrison was the first one down to the kitchen. Loren was the second, followed by Lewis. Carolyn was the last one down. When Lewis asked her how she was doing, she said, "I didn't sleep well at all last night. I can't get over cutting up a body, putting the parts in bags, and then burying them. How awful is that? Do you know what I mean?"

Everyone agreed except Garrison, who calmly ate his breakfast. When everyone was finished eating, Lewis informed the ladies that there was a lot of blood on the floor in Adam's room and that they should be prepared for a terrible sight. He said it was like Trevor's situation. Loren asked how Lewis could cut up the body in his condition, and he had to speak the truth. He said that Garrison had helped him.

Garrison said, "I helped Lewis as best I could. Do not worry, it did not bother me. I am okay, and I know that sounds odd to you, but I am doing fine. To be honest with you, and you know that I am speaking the truth, I never really cared for Adam. When he died, I knew that you or Carolyn could not or would not go through the dismantling of his body. I knew Lewis could not in his condition, so it was up to me. The essential point is that what is done is done, and we must take care of business. You know that we cannot call the police, nor can we ask for any outside help. There is no one that is going to help us, so I took it upon myself to finish the job."

Everyone went downstairs and entered the door on the right of the landing. The ladies were taken aback by what they saw. All the coaching and talking couldn't prepare them for the grotesque sight that appeared before their eyes. Carolyn noticed the smell right off. Death hovered in the air like a thick blanket of horror. Even Loren, who was always the strong and controlled one, had problems with the blood everywhere, knowing the plastic bags were filled with pieces of Adam.

This was the same little animal, boy, or thing that all of them had witnessed coming out of Adelle.

Garrison broke the silence. "It is amazing how, in just a few years, everyone's lives have changed because a monster was allowed to enter this world. Remember, everyone, how much of a monster he was. He killed my father, and he was the direct cause of my mother killing herself… in front of all of us. I hope you will never forget that. I know I never will. So, let's get to work, shall we?"

Carolyn was not exactly up for all of this. She felt sick to her stomach. Loren was dealing with the situation at hand, but she would rather have been doing almost anything else. Lewis told Carolyn to get a wheelbarrow from the detached, all-brick storage garage. After a few minutes, she hauled the wheelbarrow to the door of the walk-out on the side of the mansion. Loren reluctantly picked up one of the bags with one of Adam's arms inside. She quickly placed it down and shook all over.

Garrison laughed. "Do not worry, Loren. I will carry them to the wheelbarrow. If you can help me with the larger bag and help with the dirt, I can get the rest."

Loren was very thankful. Garrison carried the bags out to the wheelbarrow and, after four bags, asked Carolyn to take them to the holes near the edge of the forest. It took a long time to reach the holes, even with Garrison helping. The wheelbarrow itself was heavy enough, but the added weight of the body parts made it even heavier. With great effort, they finally got to the holes. With Garrison's help, they emptied the wheelbarrow on the ground near them.

Lewis stayed out near the holes while Garrison and the ladies went back to the basement. This time Garrison picked up the remaining bags and, with Loren's help, they got the torso in the wheelbarrow. This wasn't easy because Loren didn't like picking up the bags with pieces of Adam inside them. Garrison helped Loren wheel the remains to the holes. Lewis instructed Garrison to place the bags in the holes. Garrison placed the bags with the forearm, the upper arm, and one of the upper parts of the leg in the first hole. He filled the second hole with the same body parts, one complete arm and one upper part of the leg. The third hole was filled with the lower parts of both legs. The fourth hole was the most difficult one to fill. Loren had to compose herself and help Garrison with the torso. Garrison took what seemed to be the bottom half of the torso while Loren took the upper half, and they flopped the body down in the dirt as Loren made a slight sound of disgust. Garrison picked up Adam's head and shot it as if it were a basketball.

As Garrison released the head from his hand, he yelled, "Three." The head, wrapped in plastic, hit the torso, and rolled to the edge of the dirt wall.

Lewis said, "Damn it, Garrison, stop playing around. This is serious work we are doing here."

Garrison laughed and said, "Yes, sir, I am sorry." Loren and Carolyn were visibly upset about Garrison's action.

Lewis told the ladies and Garrison to get three shovels from the garage. They did as instructed. When they came back to the holes, they immediately started to cover the bags over with dirt. It took a long time because Loren was older and couldn't dig a long time without taking many breaks. Carolyn wasn't as strong as Loren, and she was a more delicate type of woman. Garrison was the strongest of the three, but he couldn't take large shovelfuls of dirt at one time. After an hour, the bags were all covered.

Lewis called the local nursery and confirmed they were going to deliver the trees later in the day. Carolyn went inside and cleaned herself up. The four waited at the pool for the delivery truck to make its way to the house. Around midafternoon, it arrived. Lewis told them they could drive the truck over the grass back to the holes. The workers did as instructed. They moved the truck back as far as it could go, to the edge of the forest line. The trees were not that large, but it took everything both workers had to move the trees from the truck to the holes. Lewis instructed them to place the trees as carefully as they could. The first tree went in the hole, then the second tree, then the third. Lewis barked out instructions to be careful with the trees, and the workers tried to place them carefully in the holes. Lewis didn't want the men to let the trees fall hard in the dirt with the body parts underneath, but the body parts were well covered, and the workers were none the wiser.

The fourth tree went in the large hole. The torso was on the left side and the head was on the right. Lewis instructed the workers as to where to step. The last thing he wanted was for one of them to step on a covered body part. Lewis played the part of a particular old man who didn't want the dirt matted down around the trees. They placed the tree down in the middle of the hole, and the nursery workers' job was complete.

Lewis gave them a handsome tip for their work, and they got into their truck and went on to the next job. The ladies and Garrison got right back to work and started to fill in the remaining holes as fast as they could. Carolyn was the first to lose most of her energy. She ended up helping by holding the trees in place as Loren and Garrison filled in the remaining holes. This process took a long time and lasted well into dinnertime. Everyone was mentally and physically exhausted from the exercise.

Finally, after what seemed to be hours on end, the job was complete. When the last shovelful of dirt was spread, everyone looked at the completed work. Lewis was very tired, and he felt bad because all he had done was look around making sure no one was watching what they were doing. The four holes were at the front of the forest line, and if the trees grew, they would be visible from the house. Lewis told everyone they had done a great job and apologized to them again for not being able to help with the carrying and the digging. Everyone went inside and cleaned up.

That night, Loren gathered everyone in the car, and they all went out to eat at Vinnie's, a local restaurant that made good food and provided a quiet getaway for the locals. The four sat there looking at each other. The only one smiling was Garrison.

The ladies sat there in silence, but inside their souls, they were in a panic. They couldn't believe their ears. Part of them wanted to believe they had heard Garrison incorrectly, but the other part of them knew he was telling the truth. All the little clues were taking shape: the blood on the clothes, hands, and countertops, in the yard, or wherever. You can't hide blood very well because it smears, it stains, and it soaks in to give up the identity of its original host to willing and accepting eyes. Loren and Carolyn sat there staring quietly, occasionally trading glances back and forth. Garrison knew what they were thinking, and he hoped they meant what they said. This was his family now, and he wanted to keep his new family together for a long time to come.

Garrison broke a long silence by saying, "I want to thank everyone for their understanding and their devotion to the cause. Our lives are now free to live the way we want without having someone holding us back. I hope we never forget my parents. I also hope that we do not forget what they have done for all of us. Loren, I know you loved our family, and for that I say thank you. I know bringing Carolyn into the family might have hurt you at the time, but you are no less important to me or to this family."

"Carolyn, like Loren, you have been there every step of the way with me. You have taught me and loved me as one of your own, as has Loren. I love you just as I love Loren. Thank you for the time that you spent playing with me and teaching me. I know it has not been easy.

"Lewis, I know this has been very difficult for you, especially with all of my problems, beginning with the dog I ate. I am sorry for that. I truly am. I know you have been through a lot with me but especially with the birth of that awful animal. You saw me, my father and my mother go through some tough times and through some odd situations. I want to thank you for being there for all of us."

"The only way I could repay you, all of you, was to eliminate all of our problems. That problem was getting rid of the animal. I did this for all of you and, probably, mostly for myself, I guess. Loren… Carolyn… I took care of the situation with that animal. It was all me. The time I spent with him was not pleasant. I had to end the situation. I did not want to tell you about what really happened, and Lewis covered for me, as he does for everyone in this family. But I want an honest relationship with all of you. I do not want any secrets, and I do not want to lie to you or mislead you in any way."

Garrison leaned forward and lowered his voice. "I am much like my father was just before his death. I like to eat live animals. I truly enjoy eating them alive. I recognize this is abnormal. I understand this is disturbing to you. I know that I scare all of you. But understand that I have never hurt anyone that I loved, outside of biting my father that one time. That was a mistake, and I regretted it from the start. It is a personal demon, one that I have to live with for the rest of my life. I am sorry for that, and I beg your forgiveness. I want all of you to be a part of my life forever, but if you want to leave… it would sadden my heart, but I would understand if you wanted out. So, here is your chance. I hope you stay with me." Garrison leaned back and looked at the doctor. "Lewis, are you in or out?"

While looking down at his drink, Lewis said, "I'm in, Garrison… always have been… always will be."

Garrison looked at Loren as she straightened up and said, "Of course I'm in. You need me, and I need you. I have no one else in my life, and you are a part of my life and always were, so I can't leave."

Garrison turned his head and looked at Carolyn. She cleared her throat and said, "I think… no… I know I am in, but, Garrison, I can't go through any more stress like the kind of stress I have seen over the past couple years. Please promise me this is the end of the killings, the stress, and the other horrid things I have witnessed over the past years."

Garrison said, "I promise they will stop, but I cannot promise that my diet will change. Still, outside of that, I promise your stress level will be lower tomorrow, the next day, and the next day after that, and so on. In the future, your stress levels will be lower compared to what you have experienced over the past few years. That I can promise you." With those words said, they all relaxed and stared out from their private little world, savoring the newfound sense of freedom, even if it was mixed with horror.

About the Author

Kevin C. Popp was born and raised in Louisville, Kentucky, graduating in the early 1990's from Bellarmine University with degrees in Business Administration and Accounting. After working a couple of jobs after college, in 1997 he found a great company in the Financial Securities market, working in the finance department.

Kevin grew up as an only child, living modestly. His parents saved every dime they made, but when it came to Kevin's basic needs, he wanted for very little. His parents were much older than most of his friends' parents, thus his grandparents were older as well. His mom and dad spent the majority of his youth taking care of their parents, so his entire youth was surrounded by grandparents' illnesses, hospitals, nursing homes and eventual pending deaths.

One of Kevin's childhood memories was a struggle to find time to be alone. He felt strongly that he needed that time to himself, even for short time spans. He would regularly take long bike rides through the neighborhood, ultimately taking him through a park that his neighborhood bordered on. At times he would think to himself about money, politics or the concept of God.

Kevin took up golf at an early age and played the game well, but not to the level that he desired. He always admired people that were great at something, venerating intelligent, athletic, wealthy and attractive people, both young and old.

Kevin had many obsessions growing up, including golf, stamp collecting, money, stock market and numbers. He grew up thinking he was poor, but actually the opposite was true. He always saved more than others. At the impressionable age of twelve, he invested in the stock market and quickly enjoyed making money.

Although very intelligent, Kevin never liked school, and constantly daydreamed, thinking about things that never occurred to others. His mind, even to this day, continuously ponders and worries about everything, planning out numerous courses of action for every situation that he attempts or is forced into doing.

As an adolescent, Kevin was starved for attention so he attempted to be the class clown, only to find himself a colossal failure in that role. One area of his mind that was not a failure was his imagination. His mind worked continuously, exploring many subject matters. The one motif that kept his attention was horror. He loved watching 'monster' movies, and found that he could stomach the most ghastly scenes that included demonic possession, dismemberment, and torture at a young age. His mind was fascinated with the macabre, both real and imaginary, trying to understand the complicated relationship between life and death and how God played His part between the two.

As the years passed, Kevin could no longer find any outlet to whet his appetite for this strange, dark world resting in the innermost parts of his brain. One day at work, he decided to write a book, and began creating an outline. Before he knew it, he had over five typed pages of notes. Creation, he loved that word! So he began creating a story, not about anyone in particular, but a story that he created from his imagination alone. He quickly found that he could create something by writing down what was in his mind.

Although certainly not the twisted, heartless monster that you see in his books, Kevin says he sometimes has a dual personality, especially when he writes. While busy typing away, he loses himself in an imaginary world of a multitude of sadistic renderings, and his hope is that he is talented enough to bring his imaginary world into focus for all to see and enjoy. It is his goal, as the writer of this series, to disrupt not only your cognizant state of mind, but also your unconscious realm simultaneously. Like any great composer of music, artistry or writing, as you read his books, he wants you to experience what is in his mind and soul. He wants you to understand his repulsion and loathing for a portion of the human race, as well as the pursuit of perfection that is inside his being. He doesn't want to just scare you, he wants to firmly implant horrific torture scenes in your memories that will haunt you daily. He wants you to question the human race and the many gods they pray to. He wants to dominate your thoughts and force you to feel others' pain.

www.ingramcontent.com/pod-product-compliance
Lightning Source LLC
Chambersburg PA
CBHW030604180626
46816CB00005B/1674